RANDOM HOUSE

LARGE PRINT

Odd
Apocalypse

Dean Koontz

RANDOM HOUSE
LARGE PRINT

Odd Apocalypse

An Odd Thomas Novel

Copyright © 2012 by Dean Koontz

All rights reserved.
Published in the United States of America by
Random House Large Print in association with
Bantam Books, New York.
Distributed by Random House, Inc., New York.

A signed, limited edition has been privately
printed by Charnel House.
Charnelhouse.com

Cover design: Scott Biel
Cover image (man's face): Florene Caplain

Title page art from an original photograph by Thomas Csizik

The Library of Congress has established a
cataloging-in-publication record for this title.

ISBN: 978-0-307-99067-9

www.randomhouse.com/largeprint

FIRST LARGE PRINT EDITION

Printed in the United States of America

10 9 8 7 6 5 4 3 2 1

This Large Print Edition published in
accord with the standards of the N.A.V.H.

To Jeff Zaleski,
with gratitude for
his insight and integrity.

From childhood's hour I have not been
As others were—I have not seen
As others saw.
  —EDGAR ALLAN POE, "Alone"

Odd
Apocalypse

One

NEAR SUNSET OF MY SECOND FULL DAY
as a guest in Roseland, crossing the immense lawn
between the main house and the eucalyptus grove,
I halted and pivoted, warned by instinct. Racing
toward me, the great black stallion was as mighty a
horse as I had ever seen. Earlier, in a book of breeds,
I had identified it as a Friesian. The blonde who rode
him wore a white nightgown.

As silent as any spirit, the woman urged the horse
forward, faster. On hooves that made no sound, the
steed ran **through** me with no effect.

I have certain talents. In addition to being a pretty
good short-order cook, I have an occasional prophetic dream. And in the waking world, I sometimes
see the spirits of the lingering dead who, for various
reasons, are reluctant to move on to the Other Side.

This long-dead horse and rider, now only spirits in
our world, knew that no one but I could see them.
After appearing to me twice the previous day and

once this morning, but at a distance, the woman seemed to have decided to get my attention in an aggressive fashion.

Mount and mistress raced around me in a wide arc. I turned to follow them, and they cantered toward me once more but then halted. The stallion reared over me, silently slashing the air with the hooves of its forelegs, nostrils flared, eyes rolling, a creature of such immense power that I stumbled backward even though I knew that it was as immaterial as a dream.

Spirits are solid and warm to my touch, as real to me in that way as is anyone alive. But I am not solid to them, and they can neither ruffle my hair nor strike a death blow at me.

Because my sixth sense complicates my existence, I try otherwise to keep my life simple. I have fewer possessions than a monk. I have no time or peace to build a career as a fry cook or as anything else. I never plan for the future, but wander into it with a smile on my face, hope in my heart, and the hair up on the nape of my neck.

Bareback on the Friesian, the barefoot beauty wore white silk and white lace and wild red ribbons of blood both on her gown and in her long blond hair, though I could see no wound. Her nightgown was rucked up to her thighs, and her knees pressed against the stallion's heaving sides. In her left hand, she twined a fistful of the horse's mane, as if even in death she must hold fast to her mount to keep their spirits joined.

If spurning a gift weren't ungrateful, I would at once return my supernatural sight. I would be content to spend my days whipping up omelets that make you groan with pleasure and pancakes so fluffy that the slightest breeze might float them off your plate.

Every talent is unearned, however, and with it comes a solemn obligation to use it as fully and as wisely as possible. If I didn't believe in the miraculous nature of talent and in the sacred duty of the recipient, by now I would have gone so insane that I'd qualify for numerous high government positions.

As the stallion danced on its hind legs, the woman reached out with her right arm and pointed down at me, as if to say that she knew I saw her and that she had a message to convey to me. Her lovely face was grim with determination, and those cornflower-blue eyes that were not bright with life were nonetheless bright with anguish.

When she dismounted, she didn't drop to the ground but instead floated off the horse and almost seemed to glide across the grass to me. The blood faded from her hair and nightgown, and she manifested as she had looked in life before her fatal wounds, as if she might be concerned that the gore would repel me. I felt her touch when she put one hand to my face, as though she, a ghost, had more difficulty believing in me than I had believing in her.

Behind the woman, the sun melted into the distant sea, and several distinctively shaped clouds glowed like a fleet of ancient warships with their masts and sails ablaze.

As I saw her anguish relent to a tentative hope, I said, "Yes, I can see you. And if you'll let me, I can help you cross over."

She shook her head violently and took a step backward, as if she feared that with some touch or spoken spell I might release her from this world. But I have no such power.

I thought I understood the reason for her reaction. "You were murdered, and before you go from this world, you want to be sure that justice will be done."

She nodded but then shook her head, as if to say, **Yes, but not only that.**

Being more familiar with the deceased than I might wish to be, I can tell you from considerable personal experience that the spirits of the lingering dead don't talk. I don't know why. Even when they have been brutally murdered and are desperate to see their assailants brought to justice, they are unable to convey essential information to me either by phone or face-to-face. Neither do they send text messages. Maybe that's because, given the opportunity, they would reveal something about death and the world beyond that we the living are not meant to know.

Anyway, the dead can be even more frustrating to deal with than are many of the living, which is astonishing when you consider that it's the living who run the Department of Motor Vehicles.

Shadowless in the last direct light of the drowning sun, the Friesian stood with head high, as proud as any patriot before the sight of a beloved flag. But his only flag was the golden hair of his mistress. He grazed no more in this place but reserved his appetite for Elysian fields.

Approaching me again, the blonde stared at me so intensely that I could feel her desperation. She formed a cradle with her arms and rocked it back and forth.

I said, "A baby?"

Yes.

"Your baby?"

She nodded but then shook her head.

Brow furrowed, biting her lower lip, the woman hesitated before holding out one hand, palm down, perhaps four and a half feet above the ground.

Practiced as I am at spirit charades, I figured that she must be indicating the current height of the baby whom she'd once borne, not an infant now but perhaps nine or ten years old. "Not your baby any longer. Your **child**."

She nodded vigorously.

"Your child still lives?"

Yes.

"Here in Roseland?"

Yes, yes, yes.

Ablaze in the western sky, those ancient warships built of clouds were burning down from fiery orange to bloody red as the heavens slowly darkened toward purple.

When I asked if her child was a girl or a boy, she indicated the latter.

Although I knew of no children on this estate, I considered the anguish that carved her face, and I asked the most obvious question: "And your son is . . . what? In trouble here?"

Yes, yes, yes.

Far to the east of the main house in Roseland, out of sight beyond a hurst of live oaks, was a riding ring bristling with weeds. A half-collapsed ranch fence encircled it.

The stables, however, looked as if they had been built last week. Curiously, all the stalls were spotless; not one piece of straw or a single cobweb could be found, no dust, as though the place was thoroughly scrubbed on a regular basis. Judging by that tidiness, and by a smell as crisp and pure as that of a winter day after a snowfall, no horses had been kept there in decades; evidently, the woman in white had been dead a long time.

How, then, could her child be only nine or ten?

Some spirits are exhausted or at least taxed by lengthy contact, and they fade away for hours or days before they renew their power to manifest. This woman seemed to have a strong will that would maintain her apparition. But suddenly, as the air shimmered and a strange sour-yellow light flooded across the land, she and the stallion—which perhaps had been killed in the same event that claimed the life of his mistress—were gone. They didn't fade or wither from the edges toward the center, as some other displaced souls occasionally did, but vanished in the instant that the light changed.

Precisely when the red dusk became yellow, a wind sprang out of the west, lashing the eucalyptus grove far behind me, rustling through the California live oaks to the south, and blustering my hair into my eyes.

I looked into a sky where the sun had not quite yet gone down, as if some celestial timekeeper had wound the cosmic clock backward a few minutes.

That impossibility was exceeded by another. Yellow from horizon to horizon, without the grace of a single cloud, the heavens were ribboned with what appeared to be high-altitude rivers of smoke or soot. Gray currents streaked through with black. Moving at tremendous velocity. They widened, narrowed, serpentined, sometimes merged, but came apart again.

I had no way of knowing what those rivers were, but the sight strummed a dark chord of intuition. I suspected that high above me raced torrents of ashes, soot, and fine debris that had once been cities, metropolises pulverized by explosions unprecedented in power and number, then vomited high into the atmosphere, caught and held in orbit by the jet stream, by the **many** jet streams of a war-transformed troposphere.

My waking visions are even rarer than my prophetic dreams. When one afflicts me, I am aware that it's an internal event, occurring only in my mind. But this spectacle of wind and baleful light and horrific patterns in the sky was no vision. It was as real as a kick in the groin.

Clenched like a fist, my heart pounded, pounded, as across the yellow vault came a flock of creatures like nothing I had seen in flight before. Their true nature was not easily discerned. They were larger than eagles but seemed more like bats, many hundreds of them, incoming from the northwest, descending as they approached. As my heart pounded harder, it seemed that my reason must be knocking to be let out so that the madness of this scene could fully invade me.

Be assured that I am **not** insane, neither as a serial killer is insane nor in the sense that a man is insane who wears a colander as a hat to prevent the CIA from controlling his mind. I dislike hats of any kind, though I have nothing against colanders properly used.

I **have** killed more than once, but always in self-defense or to protect the innocent. Such killing cannot be called murder. If you think that it is murder, you've led a sheltered life, and I envy you.

Unarmed and greatly outnumbered by the incoming swarm, not sure if they were intent upon destroying me or oblivious of my existence, I had no illusions that self-defense might be possible. I turned and ran down the long slope toward the eucalyptus grove that sheltered the guesthouse where I was staying.

The impossibility of my predicament didn't inspire the briefest hesitation. Now within two months of my twenty-second birthday, I had been marinated for most of my life in the impossible, and I knew that the true nature of the world was weirder than any bizarre fabric that **anyone's** mind might weave from the warp and weft of imagination's loom.

As I raced eastward, breaking into a sweat as much from fear as from exertion, behind and above me arose the shrill cries of the flock and then the leathery flapping of their wings. Daring to glance back, I saw them rocking through the turbulent wind, their eyes as yellow as the hideous sky. They funneled toward me as though some master to which they answered had promised to work a dark version of the miracle of loaves and fishes, making of me an adequate meal for these multitudes.

When the air shimmered and the yellow light was replaced by red, I stumbled, fell, and rolled onto my back. Raising my hands to ward off the ravenous horde, I found the sky familiar and nothing winging through it except a pair of shore birds in the distance.

I was back in the Roseland where the sun had set, where the sky was largely purple, and where the once-blazing galleons in the air had burned down to sullen red.

Gasping for breath, I got to my feet and watched for a moment as the celestial sea turned black and the last embers of the cloud ships sank into the rising stars.

Although I was not afraid of the night, prudence argued that I would not be wise to linger in it. I continued toward the eucalyptus grove.

The transformed sky and the winged menace, as well as the spirits of the woman and her horse, had given me something to think about. Considering the unusual nature of my life, I need not worry that, when it comes to food for thought, I will ever experience famine.

Two

AFTER THE WOMAN, THE HORSE, AND the yellow sky, I didn't think I would sleep that night. Lying awake in low lamplight, I found my thoughts following morbid paths.

We are buried when we're born. The world is a place of graves, occupied and graves potential. Life is what happens while we wait for our appointment with the mortician.

Although it is demonstrably true, you are no more likely to see that sentiment on a Starbucks cup than you are the words COFFEE KILLS.

Even before coming to Roseland, I had been in a **mood.** I was sure I'd cheer up soon. I always do. Regardless of what horror transpires, given a little time, I am as reliably buoyant as a helium balloon.

I don't know the reason for that buoyancy. Understanding it might be a key part of my life assignment. Perhaps when I realize why I can find humor in the darkest of darknesses, the mortician will call my number and the time will have come to choose my casket.

Actually, I don't expect to have a casket. The Celestial Office of Life Themes—or whatever it might be called—seems to have decided that my journey through this world will be especially complicated by absurdity and violence of the kind in which the human species takes such pride. Consequently, I'll probably be torn limb from limb by an angry mob of antiwar protesters and thrown on a bonfire. Or I'll be struck down by a Rolls-Royce driven by an advocate for the poor.

Certain that I wouldn't sleep, I slept.

At four o'clock that February morning, I was deep in disturbing dreams of Auschwitz.

My characteristic buoyancy would not occur just yet.

I woke to a familiar cry from beyond the half-open window of my suite in Roseland's guesthouse. As silvery as the pipes in a Celtic song, the wail sewed threads of sorrow and longing through the night and the woods. It came again, nearer, and then a third time from a distance.

These lamentations were brief, but the previous two days, when they woke me too near dawn, I could not sleep anymore. The cry was like a wire in the blood, conducting a current through every artery and vein. I'd never heard a lonelier sound, and it electrified me with a dread that I could not explain.

In this instance, I awakened from the Nazi death

camp. I am not a Jew, but in the nightmare I was Jewish and terrified of dying twice. Dying twice made perfect sense in sleep, but not in the waking world, and the eerie call in the night at once pricked the air out of the vivid dream, which shriveled away from me.

According to the current master of Roseland and everyone who worked for him, the source of the disturbing cry was a loon. They were either ignorant or lying.

I didn't mean to insult my host and his staff. After all, I am ignorant of many things because I am required to maintain a narrow focus. An ever-increasing number of people seem determined to kill me, so that I need to concentrate on staying alive.

But even in the desert, where I was born and raised, there are ponds and lakes, man-made yet adequate for loons. Their cries were melancholy but never desolate like this, curiously hopeful whereas these were despairing.

Roseland, a private estate, was a mile from the California coast. But loons are loons wherever they nest; they don't alter their voices to conform to the landscape. They're birds, not politicians.

Besides, loons aren't roosters with a timely duty. Yet this wailing came between midnight and dawn, not thus far in sunlight. And it seemed to me that the earlier it came in the new day, the more often it was repeated during the remaining hours of darkness.

I threw back the covers, sat on the edge of the

bed, and said, "Spare me that I may serve," which is a morning prayer that my Granny Sugars taught me to say when I was a little boy.

Pearl Sugars was a professional poker player who frequently sat in private games against card sharks twice her size, guys who didn't lose with a smile. They didn't even smile when they won. My grandma was a hard drinker. She ate a boatload of pork fat in various forms. Only when sober, Granny Sugars drove so fast that police in several Southwestern states knew her as Pedal-to-the-Metal Pearl. Yet she lived long and died in her sleep.

I hoped her prayer worked as well for me as it did for her; but recently I had taken to following that first request with another. This morning, it was: "Please don't let anyone kill me by shoving an angry lizard down my throat."

That might seem like a snarky request to make of God, but a psychotic and enormous man once threatened to force-feed me an exotic sharp-toothed lizard that was in a frenzy after being dosed with methamphetamine. He would have succeeded, too, if we hadn't been on a construction site and if I hadn't found a way to use an insulation-foam sprayer as a weapon. He promised to track me down when released from prison and finish the job with a different lizard.

On other days recently, I had asked God to spare me from death by a car-crushing machine in a salvage yard, from death by a nail gun, from death by being chained to dead men and dropped in a lake. . . . These were ordeals that I should not have survived in days past, and I figured that if I ever faced one of those threats again, I wouldn't be lucky enough to escape the same fate twice.

My name isn't Lucky Thomas. It's Odd Thomas. It really is. Odd.

My beautiful but psychotic mother claims the birth certificate was supposed to read **Todd.** My father, who lusts after teenage girls and peddles property on the moon—though from a comfortable office here on Earth—sometimes says they **meant** to name me Odd.

I tend to believe my father in this matter. Although if he isn't lying, this might be the only entirely truthful thing he's ever said to me.

Having showered before retiring the previous evening, I now dressed without delay, to be ready for . . . whatever.

Day by day, Roseland felt more like a trap. I sensed hidden deadfalls that might be triggered with a misstep, bringing down a crushing weight upon me.

Although I wanted to leave, I had an obligation to remain, a duty to the Lady of the Bell. She had come with me from Magic Beach, which lay farther north along the coast, where I'd almost been killed in a variety of ways.

Duty doesn't need to call; it only needs to whisper. And if you heed the call, no matter what happens, you have no need for regret.

Stormy Llewellyn, whom I loved and lost, believed that this strife-torn world is boot camp, preparation for the great adventure that comes between our first life and our eternal life. She said that we go wrong only when we are deaf to duty.

We are all the walking wounded in a world that is a war zone. Everything we love will be taken from us, everything, last of all life itself.

Yet everywhere I look, I find great beauty in this battlefield, and grace and the promise of joy.

The stone tower in the eucalyptus grove, where I currently lived, was a thing of rough beauty, in part because of the contrast between its solemn mass and the delicacy of the silvery-green leaves that cascaded across the limbs of the surrounding trees.

Square rather than columnar, thirty feet on a side, the tower stood sixty feet high if you counted the bronze dome but not the unusual finial that looked like the much-enlarged stem, crown, and case bow of an old pocket watch.

They called the tower a guesthouse, but surely it had not always been used for that purpose. The narrow casement windows opened inward to admit fresh air, because vertical iron bars prevented them from opening outward.

Barred windows suggested a prison or a fortress. In either case, an enemy was implied.

The door was ironbound timber that looked as though it had been crafted to withstand a battering ram if not even cannonballs. Beyond lay a stone-walled vestibule.

In the vestibule, to the left, stairs led to a higher apartment. Annamaria, the Lady of the Bell, was staying there.

The inner vestibule door, directly opposite the outer, opened to the ground-floor unit, where the current owner of Roseland, Noah Wolflaw, had invited me to stay.

My quarters consisted of a comfortable sitting room, a smaller bedroom, both paneled in mahogany, and a richly tiled bathroom that dated to the 1920s. The style was Craftsman: heavy wood-and-cushion armchairs, trestle tables with mortise joints and peg decoration.

I don't know if the stained-glass lamps were genuine Tiffany, but they might have been. Perhaps they were bought back in the day when they weren't yet museum pieces of fantastic value, and they remained in this out-of-the-way tower simply because they had always been here. One quality of Roseland was a casual indifference to the wealth that it represented.

Each guest suite featured a kitchenette in which the pantry and the refrigerator had been stocked with the essentials. I could cook simple meals or have any reasonable request filled by the estate's chef, Mr. Shilshom, who would send over a tray from the main house.

Breakfast more than an hour before dawn didn't appeal to me. I would feel like a condemned man trying to squeeze in as many meals as possible on his last day, before submitting to a lethal injection.

Our host had warned me to remain indoors between dusk and dawn. He claimed that one or more mountain lions had recently been marauding through other estates in the area, killing two dogs, a horse, and peacocks kept as pets. The beast might be bold enough to chow down on a wandering guest of Roseland if given a chance.

I was sufficiently informed about mountain lions to know that they were as likely to hunt in daylight as in the dark. I suspected that Noah Wolflaw's warning was intended to ensure that I would hesitate to investigate the so-called loon and other peculiarities of Roseland by night.

Before dawn on that Monday in February, I left the guest tower and locked the ironbound door behind me.

Both Annamaria and I had been given keys and had been sternly instructed to keep the tower locked at all times. When I noted that mountain lions could not turn a knob and open a door, whether it was locked or not, Mr. Wolflaw declared that we were living in the early days of a new dark age, that walled estates and the guarded redoubts of the wealthy were not secure anymore, that "bold thieves, rapists, journalists, murderous revolutionaries, and far worse" might turn up anywhere.

His eyes didn't spin like pinwheels, neither did smoke curl from his ears when he issued this warning, though his dour expression and ominous tone struck me as cartoonish. I still thought that he must be kidding, until I met his eyes long enough to discern that he was as paranoid as a three-legged cat encircled by wolves.

Whether his paranoia was justified or not, I suspected that neither thieves nor rapists, nor journalists, nor revolutionaries were what worried him. His terror was reserved for the undefined "far worse."

Leaving the guest tower, I followed a flagstone footpath through the fragrant eucalyptus grove to the brink of the gentle slope that led up to the main house. The vast manicured lawn before me was as smooth as carpet underfoot.

In the wild fields around the periphery of the estate, through which I had rambled on other days, snowy woodrush and ribbon grass and feathertop thrived among the majestic California live oaks that seemed to have been planted in cryptic but harmonious patterns.

No place of my experience had ever been more beautiful than Roseland, and no place had ever felt more evil.

Some people will say that a place is just a place, that it can't be good or evil. Others will say that evil as a real power or entity is a hopelessly old-fashioned idea, that the wicked acts of men and women can be explained by one psychological theory or another.

Those are people to whom I never listen. If I listened to them, I would already be dead.

Regardless of the weather, even under an ordinary sky, daylight in Roseland seemed to be the product of a sun different from the one that brightened the rest of the world. Here, the familiar appeared strange, and even the most solid, brightly illuminated object had the quality of a mirage.

Afoot at night, as now, I had no sense of privacy. I felt that I was followed, watched.

On other occasions, I had heard a rustle that the still air could not explain, a muttered word or two not quite comprehensible, hurried footsteps. My stalker, if I had one, was always screened by shrubbery or by moonshadows, or he monitored me from around a corner.

A suspicion of homicide motivated me to prowl Roseland by night. The woman on horseback was a victim of someone, haunting Roseland in search of justice for her and her son.

Roseland encompassed fifty-two acres in Montecito, a wealthy community adjacent to Santa Barbara, which itself was as far from being a shantytown as any Ritz-Carlton was far from being mistaken for the Bates Motel in **Psycho.**

The original house and other buildings were constructed in 1922 and '23 by a newspaper mogul, Constantine Cloyce, who was also the cofounder of one of the film industry's legendary studios. He had a mansion in Malibu, but Roseland was his special retreat, an elaborate man cave where he could engage in such masculine pursuits as horses, skeet shooting, small-game hunting, all-night poker sessions, and perhaps drunken head-butting contests.

Cloyce had also been an enthusiast of unusual— even bizarre—theories ranging from those of the famous medium and psychic Madame Helena Petrovna Blavatsky to those of the world-renowned physicist and inventor Nikola Tesla.

Some believed that Cloyce, here at Roseland, had once secretly financed research and development into such things as death rays, contemporary approaches to alchemy, and telephones that would allow you to talk to the dead. But then some people also believe that Social Security is solvent.

From the edge of the eucalyptus grove, I gazed up the long easy slope toward the main house, where Constantine Cloyce had died in his sleep in 1948, at the age of seventy. On the barrel-tile roof, patches of phosphorescent lichen glowed in the moonlight.

Also in 1948, the sole heir to an immense South American mining fortune bought Roseland completely furnished when he was just thirty and sold it, furnished, forty years later. He was reclusive, and no one seems to have known much about him.

At the moment, only a few second-floor windows were warmed by light. They marked the bedroom suite of Noah Wolflaw, who had made his considerable fortune as the founder and manager of a hedge fund, whatever that might be. I'm reasonably sure that it had something to do with Wall Street and nothing whatsoever to do with boxwood garden hedges.

Now retired at the age of fifty, Mr. Wolflaw claimed to have sustained an injury to the sleep center in his brain. He said that he hadn't slept a wink in the previous nine years.

I didn't know whether this extreme insomnia was the truth or a lie, or proof of some delusional condition.

He had bought the residence from the reclusive mining heir. He restored and expanded the house, which was of the Addison Mizner school of architecture, an eclectic mix of Spanish, Moorish, Gothic, Greek, Roman, and Renaissance influences. Broad, balustraded terraces of limestone stepped down to lawns and gardens.

In this hour before dawn, as I crossed the manicured grass toward the main house, the coyotes high in the hills no longer howled, because they had gorged themselves on wild rabbits and slunk away to sleep. After hours of singing, the frogs had exhausted their voices, and the crickets had been devoured by the frogs. A peaceful though temporary hush shrouded this fallen world.

My intention was to relax on a lounge chair on the south terrace until lights appeared in the kitchen. Chef Shilshom always began his workday before dawn.

I had started each of the past two mornings with

the chef not solely because he made fabulous breakfast pastries, but also because I suspected that he might let slip some clue to the hidden truth of Roseland. He fended off my curiosity by pretending to be the culinary world's equivalent of an absentminded professor, but the effort of maintaining that pretense was likely to trip him up sooner or later.

As a guest, I was welcome throughout the ground floor of the house: the kitchen, the dayroom, the library, the billiards room, and elsewhere. Mr. Wolflaw and his live-in staff were intent upon presenting themselves as ordinary people with nothing to hide and Roseland as a charming haven with no secrets.

I knew otherwise because of my special talent, my intuition, and my excellent crap detector—and now also because the previous twilight had for a minute shown me a destination that must be a hundred stops beyond Oz on the Tornado Line Express.

When I say that Roseland was an evil place, that doesn't mean I assumed everyone there—or even just one of them—was also evil. They were an entertainingly eccentric crew; but eccentricity most often equates with virtue or at least with an absence of profoundly evil intention.

The devil and all his demons are dull and predictable because of their single-minded rebellion against truth. Crime itself—as opposed to the solving of it—is boring to the complex mind, though endlessly fascinating to the simpleminded. One film about

Hannibal Lecter is riveting, but a second is inevitably stupefying. We love a series hero, but a series villain quickly becomes silly as he strives so obviously to shock us. Virtue is imaginative, evil repetitive.

They were keeping secrets at Roseland. The reasons for keeping secrets are many, however, and only a fraction are malevolent.

As I settled on the patio lounge chair to wait for Chef Shilshom to switch on the kitchen lights, the night took an intriguing turn. I do not say an **unexpected** turn, because I've learned to expect just about anything.

South from this terrace, a wide arc of stairs rose to a circular fountain flanked by six-foot Italian Renaissance urns. Beyond the fountain, another arc of stairs led to a slope of grass bracketed by hedges that were flanked by gently stepped cascades of water, which were bordered by tall cypresses. Everything led up a hundred yards to another terrace at the top of the hill, on which stood a highly ornamented, windowless limestone mausoleum forty feet on a side.

The mausoleum dated to 1922, a time when the law did not yet forbid burial on residential property. No moldering corpses inhabited this grandiose tomb. Urns filled with ashes were kept in wall niches. Interred there were Constantine Cloyce, his wife, Madra, and their only child, who died young.

Suddenly the mausoleum began to glow, as if the structure were entirely glass, an immense oil lamp throbbing with golden light. The Phoenix palms backdropping the building reflected this radiance, their fronds pluming like the feathery tails of certain fireworks.

A volley of crows exploded out of the palm trees, too startled to shriek, the beaten air cracking off their wings. They burrowed into the dark sky.

Alarmed, I got to my feet, as I always do when a building begins to glow inexplicably.

I didn't recall ascending the first arc of stairs or circling the fountain, or climbing the second sweep of stairs. As if I'd been briefly spellbound, I found myself on the long slope of grass, halfway to the mausoleum.

I had previously visited that tomb. I knew it to be as solid as a munitions bunker.

Now it looked like a blown-glass aviary in which lived flocks of luminous fairies.

Although no noise accompanied that eerie light, what seemed to be pressure waves broke across me, through me, as if I were having an attack of synesthesia, **feeling** the sound of silence.

These concussions were the bewitching agent that had spelled me off the lounge chair, up the stairs, onto the grass. They seemed to swirl through me, a pulsing vortex pulling me into a kind of trance. As I discovered that I was on the move once more, walking uphill, I resisted the compulsion to approach the mausoleum—and was able to deny the power that drew me forward. I halted and held my ground.

Yet as the pressure waves washed through me,

they flooded me with a yearning for something that I could not name, for some great prize that would be mine if only I went to the mausoleum while the strange light shone through its translucent walls. As I continued to resist, the attracting force diminished and the luminosity began gradually to fade.

Close at my back, a man spoke in a deep voice, with an accent that I could not identify: "I have seen you—"

Startled, I turned toward him—but no one stood on the grassy slope between me and the burbling fountain.

Behind me, somewhat softer than before, as intimate as if the mouth that formed the words were inches from my left ear, the man continued: "—where you have not yet been."

Turning again, I saw that I was still alone.

As the glow faded from the mausoleum at the crest of the hill, the voice subsided to a whisper: "I depend on you."

Each word was softer than the one before it. Silence returned when the golden light retreated into the limestone walls of the tomb.

I have seen you where you have not yet been. I depend on you.

Whoever had spoken was not a ghost. I **see** the lingering dead, but this man remained invisible. Besides, the dead don't talk.

Occasionally, the deceased attempt to communicate not merely by nodding and gestures but through the art of mime, which can be frustrating. Like any mentally healthy citizen, I am overcome by the urge to strangle a mime when I happen upon one in full performance, but a mime who's already dead is unmoved by that threat.

Turning in a full circle, in seeming solitude, I nevertheless said, "Hello?"

The lone voice that answered was a cricket that had escaped the predatory frogs.

Three

THE KITCHEN IN THE MAIN HOUSE was not so enormous that you could play tennis there, but either of the two center islands was large enough for a game of Ping-Pong.

Some countertops were black granite, others stainless steel. Mahogany cabinets. White tile floor.

Not a single corner was brightened by teddy-bear cookie jars or ceramic fruit, or colorful tea towels.

The warm air was redolent of breakfast croissants and our daily bread, while the face and form of Chef Shilshom suggested that all of his trespasses involved food. In clean white sneakers, his small feet were those of a ballerina grafted onto the massive legs of a sumo wrestler. From the monumental foundation of his torso, a flight of double chins led up to a merry face with a mouth like a bow, a nose like a bell, and eyes as blue as Santa's.

As I sat on a stool at one of the islands, the chef double dead-bolted the door by which he had admitted me. During the day, doors were unlocked, but from dusk until dawn, Wolflaw and his staff lived behind locks, as he had insisted Annamaria and I should.

With evident pride, Chef Shilshom put before me a small plate holding the first plump croissant out of the oven. The aromas of buttery pastry and warm marzipan rose like an offering to the god of culinary excess.

Savoring the smell, indulging in a bit of delayed gratification, I said, "I'm just a grill-and-griddle jockey. I'm in awe of **this**."

"I've tasted your pancakes, your hash browns. You could bake as well as you fry."

"Not me, sir. If a spatula isn't essential to the task, then it's not a dish within the range of my talent."

In spite of his size, Chef Shilshom moved with the grace of a dancer, his hands as nimble as those of a surgeon. In that regard, he reminded me of my four-hundred-pound friend and mentor, the mystery writer Ozzie Boone, who lived a few hundred miles from this place, in my hometown, Pico Mundo.

Otherwise, the rotund chef had little in common with Ozzie. The singular Mr. Boone was loquacious, informed on most subjects, and interested in everything. To writing fiction, to eating, and to every conversation, Ozzie brought as much energy as David Beckham brought to soccer, although he didn't sweat as much as Beckham.

Chef Shilshom, on the other hand, seemed to

have a passion only for baking and cooking. When at work, he maintained his side of our dialogue in a state of such distraction—real or feigned—that often his replies didn't seem related to my comments and questions.

I came to the kitchen with the hope that he would spit out a pearl of information, a valuable clue to the truth of Roseland, without even realizing that I had pried open his shell.

First, I ate half of the delicious croissant, but only half. By this restraint, I proved to myself that in spite of the pressures and the turmoils to which I am uniquely subjected, I remain reliably disciplined. Then I ate the other half.

With an uncommonly sharp knife, the chef was chopping dried apricots into morsels when at last I finished licking my lips and said, "The windows here aren't barred like they are at the guest tower."

"The main house has been remodeled."

"So there once were bars here, too?"

"Maybe. Before my time."

"When was the house remodeled?"

"Back when."

"When back when?"

"Mmmmm."

"How long have you worked here?"

"Oh, ages."

"You have quite a memory."

"Mmmmm."

That was as much as I was going to learn about the history of barred windows at Roseland. The chef concentrated on chopping the apricots as if he were disarming a bomb.

I said, "Mr. Wolflaw doesn't keep horses, does he?"

Apricot obsessed, the chef said, "No horses."

"The riding ring and the exercise yard are full of weeds."

"Weeds," the chef agreed.

"But, sir, the stables are immaculate."

"Immaculate."

"They're almost as clean as a surgery."

"Clean, very clean."

"Yes, but who cleans the stables?"

"Someone."

"Everything seems freshly painted and polished."

"Polished."

"But why—if there are no horses?"

"Why indeed?" the chef said.

"Maybe he intends to get some horses."

"There you go."

"Does he intend to get some horses?"

"Mmmmm."

He scooped up the chopped apricots, put them in a mixing bowl.

From a bag, he poured pecan halves onto the cutting board.

I asked, "How long since there were last horses at Roseland?"

"Long, very long."

"I guess perhaps the horse I sometimes see roaming the grounds must belong to a neighbor."

"Perhaps," he said as he began to halve the pecan halves.

I asked, "Sir, have you seen the horse?"

"Long, very long."

"It's a great black stallion over sixteen hands high."

"Mmmmm."

"There are a lot of books about horses in the library here."

"Yes, the library."

"I looked up this horse. I think it's a Friesian."

"There you go."

His knife was so sharp that the pecan halves didn't crumble at all when he split them.

I said, "Sir, did you notice a strange light outside a short while ago?"

"Notice?"

"Up at the mausoleum."

"Mmmmm."

"A golden light."

"Mmmmm."

I said, "Mmmmm?"

He said, "Mmmmm."

To be fair, the light that I had seen might be visible only to someone with my sixth sense. My suspicion, however, was that Chef Shilshom was a lying pile of suet.

The chef hunched over the cutting board, peering

so intently and closely at the pecans that he might have been Mr. Magoo trying to read the fine print on a pill bottle.

To test him, I said, "Is that a mouse by the refrigerator?"

"There you go."

"No. Sorry. It's a big old rat."

"Mmmmm."

If he wasn't totally immersed in his work, he was a good actor.

Getting off the stool, I said, "Well, I don't know why, but I think I'll go set my hair on fire."

"Why indeed?"

With my back to the chef, moving toward the door to the terrace, I said, "Maybe it grows back thicker if you burn it off once in a while."

"Mmmmm."

The crisp sound of the knife splitting pecans had fallen silent.

In one of the four glass panes in the upper half of the kitchen door, I could see Chef Shilshom's reflection. He was watching me, his moon face as pale as his white uniform.

Opening the door, I said, "Not dawn yet. Might still be some mountain lion out there, trying doors."

"Mmmmm," the chef said, pretending to be so distracted by his work that he was paying little attention to me.

I stepped outside, pulled the door shut behind me, and crossed the terrace to the foot of the first arc of stairs. I stood there, gazing up at the mausoleum, until I heard the chef engage both of the deadbolts.

With dawn only minutes below the mountains to the east, the not-loon cried out again, one last time, from a far corner of the sprawling estate.

The mournful sound brought back to me an image that had been part of the dream of Auschwitz, from which the first cry of the night had earlier awakened me: **I am starving, frail, performing forced labor with a shovel, terrified of dying twice, whatever that means. I am not digging fast enough to please the guard, who kicks the shovel out of my grip. The steel toe of his boot cuts my right hand, from which flows not blood but, to my terror, powdery gray ashes, not one ember, only cold gray ashes pouring out of me, out and out. . . .**

As I walked back to the eucalyptus grove, the stars grew dim in the east, and the sky blushed with the first faint light of morning.

Annamaria, the Lady of the Bell, and I had been guests of Roseland for three nights and two days, and I suspected that our time here was soon drawing to a close, that our third day would end in violence.

Four

BETWEEN BIRTH AND BURIAL, WE FIND ourselves in a comedy of mysteries.

If you don't think life is mysterious, if you believe you have it all mapped out, you aren't paying attention or you've anesthetized yourself with booze or drugs, or with a comforting ideology.

And if you don't think life's a comedy—well, friend, you might as well hurry along to that burial. The rest of us need people with whom we can laugh.

In the guest tower once more, as dawn bloomed, I climbed the circular stone stairs to the second floor, where Annamaria waited.

The Lady of the Bell has a dry wit, but she's more mystery than comedy.

At her suite, when I knocked on the door, it swung open as though the light rap of knuckles on wood was sufficient to disengage the latch and set the hinges in motion.

The two narrow, deeply set windows were as medieval as that through which Rapunzel might have let down her long hair, and they admitted little of the early-morning sun.

With her delicate hands clasped around a mug, Annamaria was sitting at a small dining table, in the light of a bronze floor lamp that had a stained-glass shade in an intricate yellow-rose motif.

Indicating a second mug from which steam curled, she said, "I poured some tea for you, Oddie," as though she had known precisely when I would arrive, although I had come on a whim.

Noah Wolflaw claimed not to have slept in nine years, which was most likely a fabrication. In the four days that I'd known Annamaria, however, she was always awake when I needed to talk with her.

On the sofa were two dogs, including a golden retriever, whom I had named Raphael. He was a good boy who attached himself to me in Magic Beach.

The white German-shepherd mix, Boo, was a ghost dog, the only lingering canine spirit that I had ever seen. He had been with me since my time at St. Bartholomew's Abbey, where I had for a while stayed as a guest before moving on to Magic Beach.

For a boy who loved his hometown as much as I loved Pico Mundo, who valued simplicity and stability and tradition, who treasured the friends with whom he'd grown up there, I had become too much a gypsy.

The choice wasn't mine. Events made the choice for me.

I am learning my way toward something that will make sense of my life, and I learn by going where I have to go, with whatever companions I am graced.

At least that is what I tell myself. I'm reasonably sure that it's not just an excuse to avoid college.

I am not certain of much in this uncertain world, but I know that Boo remains here not because he fears what comes after this life—as some human spirits do—but because, at a critical point in my journey, I will need him. I won't go so far as to say that he is my guardian, angelic or otherwise, but I'm comforted by his presence.

Both dogs wagged their tails at the sight of me. Only Raphael's thumped audibly against the sofa.

In the past, Boo often accompanied me. But at Roseland, both dogs stayed close to this woman, as if they worried for her safety.

Raphael was aware of Boo, and Boo sometimes saw things that I did not, which suggested that dogs, because of their innocence, see the full reality of existence to which we have blinded ourselves.

I sat across the table from Annamaria and tasted the tea, which was sweetened with peach nectar. "Chef Shilshom is a sham."

"He's a fine chef," she said.

"He's a great chef, but he's not as innocent as he pretends."

"No one is," she said, her smile so subtle and nuanced that Mona Lisa, by comparison, would appear to be guffawing.

From the moment I encountered Annamaria on a pier in Magic Beach, I had known that she needed a friend and that she was somehow different from other people, not as I am different with my prophetic dreams and spirit-seeing, but different in her own way.

I knew little about this woman. When I had asked where she was from, she had answered "Far away." Her tone and her sweetly amused expression suggested that those two words were an understatement.

On the other hand, she knew a great deal about me. She had known my name before I told it to her. She knew that I see the spirits of the lingering dead, though I have revealed that talent only to a few of my closest friends.

By now I understood that she was more than merely different. She was an enigma so complex that I would never know her secrets unless she chose to give me the key with which to unlock the truth of her.

She was eighteen and appeared to be seven months pregnant. Until we joined forces, she had been for a while alone in the world, but she had none of the doubts or worries of other girls in her position.

Although she had no possessions, she was never in need. She said that people gave her what she required—money, a place to live—though she never asked for anything. I had been witness to the truth of this claim.

We had come from Magic Beach in a Mercedes on loan from Lawrence Hutchison, who had been a famous film actor fifty years earlier, and who was now a children's book author at the age of eighty-eight. For a while, I worked for Hutch as cook and companion, before things in Magic Beach got too hot. I had arranged with Hutch to leave the car with his great-nephew, Grover, who was an attorney in Santa Barbara.

At Grover's office, in the reception lounge, we encountered Noah Wolflaw, a client of the attorney, as he was departing. Wolflaw was at once drawn to Annamaria, and after a brief chat as perplexing as conversations with her often were, he invited us to Roseland.

Her powerful appeal was not sexual. She was neither beautiful nor ugly, but neither was she merely plain. Petite but not fragile, with a perfect but pale complexion, she was a compelling presence for reasons that I had been struggling to understand but that continued to elude me.

Whatever there might be between us, romance was not part of it. The effect she had upon me—and upon others—was more profound than desire, and curiously humbling.

A century earlier, the word **charismatic** might have applied to her. But in an age when shallow movie stars and the latest crop of reality-TV specimens were said to have charisma, the word meant nothing anymore.

Anyway, Annamaria did not ask anyone to follow her as might some cult leader. Instead she inspired in people a desire to protect her.

She said that she had no last name, and although I didn't know how she could escape having one, I did not doubt her. She was often inscrutable; however, as one believes in anything that requires hard faith rather than easy proof, I believed that Annamaria never lied.

"I think we should leave Roseland at once," I declared.

"May I not even finish my tea? Must I spring up this instant and race to the front gate?"

"I'm serious. There's something very wrong here."

"There will be something very wrong with any place we go."

"But not as wrong as this."

"And where would we go?" she asked.

"Anywhere."

Her gentle voice never acquired a pedantic tone, although I felt that I was usually on the receiving end of Annamaria's patient and affectionate instruction. "Anywhere includes everywhere. If it does not matter where we go, then surely there can be no point in going."

Her eyes were so dark that I could see no difference between the irises and the pupils.

She said, "You can only be in one place at a time, odd one. So it's imperative that you be in the right place for the right reason."

Only Stormy Llewellyn had called me "odd one," until Annamaria.

"Most of the time," I said, "it seems you're speaking to me in riddles."

Her gaze was as steady as her eyes were dark. "My mission and your sixth sense brought us here. Roseland was a magnet to us. We could have gone nowhere else."

"Your mission. What is your mission?"

"In time you will know."

"In a day? A week? Twenty years?"

"As it will be."

I inhaled the peachy fragrance of the tea, exhaled with a sigh, and said, "The day we met in Magic Beach, you said countless people want to kill you."

"They have been counted, but they are so many that you don't need to know the figure any more than you need to know the number of hairs on your head in order to comb them."

She wore sneakers, khaki pants, and a baggy beige sweater with sleeves too long for her. The bulk of the sweater's rolled cuffs emphasized the delicacy of her slender wrists.

Having left Magic Beach with nothing but the clothes she wore, Annamaria was at Roseland just one day when the head housekeeper, Mrs. Tameed, purchased a suitcase, filled it with a few changes of clothes, and left it in the guesthouse, though she had not been asked to provide a wardrobe.

I, too, had come with no clothes other than those

I was wearing. No one bought me as much as a pair of socks. I'd had to leave the estate for a couple of hours, go into town, and purchase jeans, sweaters, underwear.

I said, "Four days ago, you asked me if I would keep you alive. You're making the job harder for me than it has to be."

"No one at Roseland wants to murder me."

"How can you be sure?"

"They don't realize what I am. If I am killed, my murderers will be those who know what I am."

"And what are you?" I asked.

"In your heart, you know."

"When will my **brain** figure it out?"

"You have always known since you first saw me on that pier."

"Maybe I'm not as smart as you think."

"You're better than smart, Oddie. You're wise. But also afraid of me."

Surprised, I said, "I'm afraid of a lot of things, but not of you."

Her amusement was tender, without condescension. "In time, young man, you'll acknowledge your fear, and then you'll know what I am."

Occasionally she called me "young man," though she was eighteen and I was nearly twenty-two. It should have sounded strange, but it didn't.

She said, "I'm safe in Roseland for now, but there's someone here who's in great danger and desperately needs you."

"Who?"

"Trust in your talent to lead you."

"You remember the woman on the horse that I told you about. Last evening, I had a close encounter of the spooky kind with her. She was able to tell me that her son is here. Nine or ten years old. And in danger, though I don't know what or how, or why. Is it him that I'm meant to help?"

She shrugged. "I don't know all things."

I finished my tea. "I don't believe you ever lie, but somehow you never answer me directly, either."

"Staring at the sun too long can blind you."

"Another riddle."

"It's not a riddle. It's a metaphor. I speak truth to you by indirection, because to speak it directly would pierce you as the brightness of the sun can burn the retina."

I pushed my chair back from the table. "I sure hope you don't turn out to be some New Age bubblehead."

She laughed softly, as musical a sound as I had ever heard.

Because the beauty of her laughter made my comment seem rude by comparison, I said, "No offense intended."

"None taken. You always speak from your heart, and there's nothing wrong with that."

As I rose from my chair, the dogs began to thump their tails again, but neither moved to accompany me.

Annamaria said, "And by the way, there is no need for you to be afraid of dying twice."

If she wasn't referring to my nightmare of being in Auschwitz, the coincidence of her statement was uncanny.

I said, "How can you know my dreams?"

"Is dying twice a fear that haunts your dreams?" she asked, managing once more to avoid a direct answer. "If so, it shouldn't."

"What does it even mean—dying twice?"

"You'll understand in time. But of all the people in Roseland, in this city, in this state and nation, you are perhaps the last who needs to be concerned about dying twice. You will die once and only once, and it will be the death that doesn't matter."

"All death matters."

"Only to the living."

You see why I strive to keep my life simple? If I were, say, an accountant, my mind full of the details of my clients' finances, and if I saw the spirits of the lingering dead, and had to try to make sense of Annamaria's conversation, my head would probably explode.

The pattern of the yellow-rose lamp petaled her face.

"Only to the living," she repeated.

Sometimes, when I met her eyes, something made me look away, my heart quickening with fear. Not fear of her. Fear of . . . something that I couldn't name. I felt a helpless sinking of the heart.

My gaze shifted now from Annamaria to the dogs lounging on the sofa.

"I'm safe for now," she said, "but you are not. If you should doubt the justice of your actions, you could die in Roseland, die your one and only death."

Unconsciously, I had raised my right hand to my chest to feel the shape of the pendant bell beneath my sweater.

When I had first met her on the pier in Magic Beach, Annamaria had worn an exquisitely crafted silver bell, the size of a thimble, on a silver chain around her neck. It had been the only bright thing in a sunless gray day.

In a moment stranger than any other with this woman, four days before we came to Roseland, she had taken the bell from around her neck, had held it out to me, and had asked, "Will you die for me?"

Stranger still, though I hardly knew her, I had said yes and had accepted the pendant.

More than eighteen months before, in Pico Mundo, I would have given my life to save my girl, Stormy Llewellyn. Without hesitation I would have taken the bullets that she took, but Fate didn't grant me the chance to make that sacrifice.

Since then, I have often wished that I had died with her.

I love life, love the beauty of the world, but without Stormy to share it, the world in all its wonder will for me be always incomplete.

I will never commit suicide, however, or wittingly

put myself in a position to be killed, because self-destruction would be the ultimate rejection of the gift of life, an unforgivable ingratitude.

Because of the years that Stormy and I so enjoyed together, I cherish life. And it is my abiding hope that if I lead the rest of my days in such a way as to honor her, we eventually will be together again.

Perhaps that is why I so readily agreed to protect Annamaria from enemies **still** unknown to me. With each life I save, I might be sparing a person who is, to someone else, as precious as Stormy was to me.

The dogs rolled their eyes at each other and then looked at me as if embarrassed that I was unable to withstand Annamaria's stare.

I found the nerve to meet her eyes again as she said, "The hours ahead may test your will and break your heart."

Although this woman inspired in me—and others—the desire to protect her, I sometimes thought that she might be the one offering protection. Petite and waiflike in spite of her third-trimester tummy, perhaps she had crafted an image of vulnerability to evoke sympathy and to bring me to her that she might keep me safely under her wing.

She said, "Do you feel it rushing toward you, young man, an apocalypse, the apocalypse of Roseland?"

Pressing the bell hard against my chest, I said, "Yes."

Five

IF SOMEONE IN ROSELAND WAS IN great danger and desperately needed me, as Annamaria had said, perhaps it might be the son of the long-dead woman on the horse, though surely he could not be as young as the spirit imagined that he still was. But if it wasn't her child, I nevertheless suspected that the endangered person must be somehow related to her. Intuition told me that her murder was the mystery that, if solved, would be the slip string with which I could loosen the knots of all the mysteries in Roseland. If her murderer still lived all these years later, the person who needed me might be his next intended victim.

The two stables were not as vast or as ornate as the stables at the palace at Versailles, not so fabulously ostentatious as to inspire revolutionary multitudes to cease watching reruns of **Dancing with the Stars** and enthusiastically dismember all the occupants of Roseland, but they weren't typical board-and-shingle structures, either. The two buff-brick buildings with dark slate roofs featured leaded-glass windows with carved-limestone surrounds, implying that only a better class of horse had been wanted here.

No stalls opened directly to the outside. At each end of each building was a large bronze door that rolled on recessed tracks into a pocket in the wall. The doors must have weighed two tons each, but they were so expertly balanced, their wheels so well lubricated, that little effort was required to open or to close them.

Embossed on each door, three stylized Art Deco horses sprinted left to right. Under the horses was the word ROSELAND.

The waist-high weeds grew shorter as I drew closer to the first stable. They withered away altogether ten feet from the building.

I might not have perceived the **wrongness** in the scene if I'd been among the weeds instead of on bare earth. But something seemed incongruous, and I halted six feet short of the bronze door.

Before the call of the not-loon had pierced my first night on this estate, before I'd seen the ghost horse and his comely rider, long before I'd seen the creatures of the yellow sky, Roseland struck me as a place that was and was not what it seemed to be. Grand, yes, but not noble. Luxurious but not comfortable. Elegant but, in its excess, not chaste.

Every beautiful facade seemed to conceal rot and ruin that I could **almost** see. The estate and its people asserted the normality of Roseland, but in every corner and every encounter, I sensed deception, deformity, and deep strangeness waiting to be revealed.

On that patch of bare earth before the stable door, additional evidence of Roseland's profoundly unnatural character abruptly appeared before me. The sun was but half an hour into the eastern sky to my left, and therefore my morning shadow was a long lean silhouette to my right, reaching westward. But the stable cast **two** shadows. The first fell to the west; however, it was not as dark as mine, gray instead of black. The structure's second shadow was shorter but black like mine, and it tilted to the east, as if the sun were several degrees beyond its apex, perhaps an hour past noon.

On the dusty ground, a rock and a crumpled Coke can cast their images only westward, as I did.

Between the two stables lay an exercise yard about forty feet wide, bristling with weeds and wild grass seared brown during the autumn. I crossed to the second stable and saw that this building also cast two shadows: a longer, paler one to the west, a shorter black one to the east, just like the first structure.

I could imagine only one reason that a building might throw two opposing shadows like these, one paler than the other: Two suns would have to occupy the sky, a weaker one recently risen and a brighter one working its way down the heavens toward the western horizon.

Overhead, of course, shone a single sun.

In the center of the exercise yard stood a sixty-foot-tall Wakehurst magnolia, leafless at this time of year. The tree limbs flung a net of inky shadows westward, across the wall and the roof of the first stable, as should have been the case this early in the day.

Only the two buildings were under the influence of both the sun that I saw above me **and** a phantom sun.

Twice before, during my rambles, I had come here. I was certain that I had not simply overlooked this phenomenon on previous visits. The two opposing shadows were unique to this moment.

If the exterior of the structure could stand before me in this impossible condition, I wondered what surprises might await inside. In my unusual life, few surprises are of the lottery-winning kind, but instead involve sharp teeth either literal or figurative.

Nevertheless, I rolled the door aside far enough to slip inside. I stepped to my left, bronze behind me, to avoid being backlighted by the sun.

Five roomy stalls lay along the east wall, five along the west, with half doors of mahogany or teak. The center aisle was twelve feet wide and, like the floors of the stalls, paved in tightly set stones.

At the farther end, on the left, was a tack room, and opposite it a storage locker for food, both long empty.

The previous stables of my experience had earthen

floors, but the flat stone pavers were not the only curious detail here.

At the back of each stall was a three-by-four-foot window. Most of the leaded-glass pieces were three-inch squares except for those shaped to surround an oval pane in the center. Embedded within the oval of glass, a cord of braided copper wires formed a figure eight laid on its side.

The glass itself had a coppery cast and imparted a ruddy color to the incoming daylight. Some might have felt that the Victorian quality of the windows gave the stable the cozy glow of a hearthside, although my imagination conjured up Captain Nemo, as if the stable were the submarine **Nautilus** making way through a sea of blood and fire. But, hey, that's just me.

I didn't immediately switch on the stable lamps, which were primarily brass sconces on the posts that flanked the stall doors. Instead, I remained very still in the coppery light and the iron-dark shadows, waiting and listening for I knew not what.

After a minute, I decided that in spite of the double shadows outside, the building was the same inside as ever. Now, as always, the temperature was a comfortable sixty-five degrees, which I felt sure the big thermometer on the tack-room door would confirm. The air had that odorless, just-after-a-blizzard purity. The hush was almost uncanny: no settling noises, no rustle of a scurrying mouse, and no sound from without, as if beyond these walls waited a barren and weatherless world.

I flicked the wall switch, and the sconces brightened. The stable appeared as pristine as the odorless air promised.

Although it was difficult to believe that horses were ever kept here, photos and paintings of Constantine Cloyce's favorites could still be found in the halls of the main house. Mr. Wolflaw felt they were an important part of Roseland's history.

Thus far I hadn't seen displayed a photo or a painting of the blood-soaked woman in the white nightgown. She seemed to me to be at least as important a part of Roseland's history as were the horses, but not everyone thinks murder is as big a deal as I do.

Of course I might soon encounter a hallway lined with portraits of blood-soaked young women in all manner of dress, displaying mortal wounds. Considering that I'd yet to find a single rosebush anywhere in Roseland, perhaps that part of the estate's name referred to the flowers of womanhood who were chopped up and buried here.

Those hairs on the nape of my neck were quivering again.

As I had done on previous visits, I walked the length of the stable, studying the inch-diameter copper discs inset between many of the quartzite pavers. They formed gleaming, sinuous lines the length of the building. Depending on the angle from which you viewed it, in each shiny disc was engraved either the number eight or a lazy eight lying on its side, as was embedded in every window.

I couldn't imagine the purpose of those copper discs, but it seemed unlikely that even a press baron and movie mogul with money to burn, like the late Constantine Cloyce, would have had them installed in a stable simply for decoration.

"Who the hell are you?"

Startled, I turned, only to be startled again by a giant with a shaved head, a livid scar from his right ear to the corner of his mouth, another livid scar cleaving his forehead from the top of his brow to the bridge of his nose, teeth so crooked and yellow that he would never be asked to anchor the evening news on any major TV network, a cold sore on his upper lip, a holstered revolver on one hip, a holstered pistol on the other, and a compact fully automatic carbine, perhaps an Uzi, in both hands.

He stood six feet five, weighed maybe two hundred fifty pounds, and looked like a spokesman for the consumption of massive quantities of steroids. White letters on his black T-shirt announced DEATH HEALS. The behemoth's biceps and forearms bore tattoos of what seemed to be screaming hyenas, and his wrists might have been as thick as my neck.

His khaki pants featured many zippered pockets and were tucked into red-and-black carved-leather cowboy boots, but those fashion statements failed to give him a jaunty look. He had a gun belt of the kind police officers wore, with dump pouches full of speedloaders for the revolver and spare magazines for the pistol. Some of the zippered pockets bulged, perhaps with more ammo or with hunting trophies like human ears and noses.

I said, "Nice weather for February."

In **Othello,** jealousy is referred to as the green-eyed monster. Shakespeare was at least a thousand times smarter than I am. I would never question the brilliance of his figures of speech. But **this** green-eyed monster looked like he had no patience for petty emotions like jealousy and kindness, being preoccupied with hatred, rage, and bloodlust. He was too nasty a piece of work even for a role in **Macbeth.**

He took another step into the stable, thrusting the Uzi at me. " 'Nice weather for February.' What's that supposed to mean?" Before I could reply, he said, "What the"—imagine an ugly word for copulation— "is that supposed to mean, butthead?"

"It doesn't mean anything, sir. It's just an icebreaker, you know, a conversation starter."

His scowl deepened to such an extent that his eyebrows met over the bridge of his nose, closing the quarter-inch gap between them. "What're you— stupid or something?"

Sometimes, in a tight situation, I have found it wise to pretend to be intellectually disadvantaged. For one thing, it can be a useful technique for buying time. Besides, it comes naturally to me.

I was willing to play dumb for this brute if that was what he wanted, but before I could give him a performance of Lennie from **Of Mice and Men,** he said, "The problem with the world is it's full of stupid"—imagine an ugly word for the very end of the colon—"who screw it up for everyone else. Kill all the stupid people, the world would be a better place."

To suggest that I was too smart for the world to do without me, I said, "In Shakespeare's **King Henry VI, Part 2,** the rebel Dick says, 'The first thing we do, let's kill all the lawyers.'"

The eyebrows knitted further together, and the green eyes looked as hot as methane fires. "What are you, some kind of smart-ass?"

I just couldn't win with this guy.

Closing the space between us, poking my chest with the muzzle of the Uzi, he said, "Give me one reason I shouldn't blow you away right now, you smart-ass trespasser."

Six

WHEN SOME GUY HAS A GUN AND I don't, and he asks me for one good reason why he shouldn't kill me, I assume that he has no intention of blowing my head off because otherwise he would just do it. He either wants a reason to stand down or he's so sadly unimaginative that he's playing the scene the way he's watched it unfold on TV and in movies.

Old Green Eyes, however, seemed like a different caliber of thug to me. His demeanor suggested that he didn't need a reason to kill someone, only a strong desire, and his appearance argued that he was imaginative enough to think of a score of bloody ways to end this.

I was acutely aware of how far away the stables were from any inhabited buildings in Roseland.

Hoping there was nothing he would find incendiary in these nine words, I said, "Well, sir, I'm an invited guest, not a trespasser."

His expression was not that of a man convinced. "Invited guest? Since when do they let candy-ass punk boys through the gate?"

I decided not to be offended by his unkind characterization of me. "I'm staying in the tower in the eucalyptus grove. Been there three nights, two days."

He pressed the muzzle of the Uzi into my chest. "Three days and nobody told me? You think I'm dumb enough to eat crap on toast?"

"No, sir. Not on toast."

His nostrils flared so wide that I feared his brain might fall out through one nostril or the other. "What's that mean, candy-ass?"

"It means you're way smarter than me, or otherwise I wouldn't be on this end of the gun. But it's true. I've been here almost three days. Of course, it wasn't my charm that got us invited, it was the girl I'm with. Nobody can say no to her."

I believed that I saw a sudden sympathy in his expression at the mention of a girl. Maybe he thought that I meant a child. Even some of the most hard-case violence junkies can have a soft spot for children.

"Now **that** makes sense," he said. "You bring in some super-hot piece of tail, and nobody wants Kenny to know about her."

Instead of appealing to Kenny's compassion gland, I had inflamed other glands best left unconsidered and undisturbed. "Well, sir, no. No, that's not exactly the situation."

"What isn't?"

"She's very sweet, kind of spiritual, not hot at all, kind of dowdy, seven months pregnant, not that much to look at, but everybody likes her, you know, because it's such a sad case, a girl alone with nothing and a baby on the way, it tugs at your heart."

Kenny stared at me as if I had suddenly begun speaking in a foreign language. A foreign language, the sound of which offended him so much that he might shoot me just to shut me up.

To change the subject, I put one finger to my upper lip, at the same spot at which a cold sore blazed on Kenny's lip. "That's got to hurt."

I didn't think he could bristle any further, but he seemed to swell with umbrage. "You saying I'm diseased?"

"No. Not at all. You look as healthy as a bull. Any bull should be happy to be as healthy as you. I'm just saying that one little thing you've got there, it must hurt."

His quills relaxed a little. "Hurts like a sonofabitch."

"What're you doing for it?"

"Nothing you can do for a sonofabitch canker. Sonofabitch has to heal itself."

"That's not a canker. It's a cold sore."

"Everybody says it's a canker."

"Cankers are inside the mouth. They look different. How long have you had it?"

"Been six days. Sonofabitch makes me want to scream sometimes."

I winced to express sympathy. "Before you got it, was there a tingling in your lip, just where it eventually showed up?"

"That's exactly right," Kenny said, his eyes widening as if I had proven to be clairvoyant. "A tingle."

Casually pushing the barrel of the Uzi away from me, I said, "Within twenty-four hours before the tingle, were you out in very hot sun or cold wind?"

"Wind. Week before last, we had a cold snap. Blew in from the northwest like a sonofabitch."

"You got a little windburn. Too much hot sun or a cold wind can trigger a sore like that. Now that you've got it, dab just a little Vaseline on it and stay out of the sun, out of the wind. If you stop irritating the thing, it'll close up fast enough."

Kenny touched his tongue to the sore, saw that I disapproved, and said, "You some kind of doctor?"

"No, but I've known a couple doctors pretty well. You're on the security team, I guess."

"Do I look like I'm the entertainment director?"

I took a chance that we had bonded enough for me to laugh warmly and say, "I suspect you'd be entertaining as hell over a few beers."

Full of crooked dark-yellow teeth, his cold-sore grin was as appealing as a possum run down by an eighteen-wheeler. "Everybody says old Kenny's a hoot when you pour some beers in him. Only problem is, after about ten of 'em, I stop feeling hilarious and start tearing things up."

"Me too," I claimed, though I'd never had more

than two beers in the same day. "But I have to say, with some regret, I doubt that I can do such a handsome amount of damage to a place as you can."

I had plucked a perfect note from his pride.

"I have committed some memorable ruination, for sure," he said, and his fearsome facial scars grew a brighter red, as if the memory of past rampages raised the temperature of his self-esteem.

Gradually I had become aware that the quality of light in the stable was changing. Now I glanced to my right and saw that the eastern windows were still aglow with sunlight made ruddy by the coppery tint of the glass, but were not as bright as they had been.

Pointing the Uzi at the floor or perhaps at my feet, Kenny said, "So, kid, what's your name?"

I tensed a little and returned my attention fully to the giant, whom I had by no means yet won over.

"Listen," I said, "don't think I'm shining you on or anything, this really is my name, strange as it might sound. My name is Odd. Odd Thomas."

"Nothing wrong with the Thomas part."

"Thank you, sir."

"And, you know, Odd isn't as bad as some things parents do to kids. Parents can wreck you, man. My parents were the nastiest—"

To complete Kenny's observation of his parents as he made it, conjure in your mind several words, never spoken in polite company, that suggest incest, self-gratification, gross violations of laws protecting animals from the perverse desires of human beings, erotic obsession with the product of a major cereal company, and the most bizarre use of the tongue that you can imagine. . . .

On second thought, forget it. Kenny's characterization of his parents was unique in the colorful history of gutter speech. No matter how long you pondered the puzzle I've set before you, your solution would be the palest approximation of what he said.

Then he continued: "My born last name is Keister. You know what **Keister** means?"

Although we seemed to be laying the foundations of a friendship, I suspected that I could go from Kenny's A-list to his death list from one second to the next. I was concerned that acknowledging my awareness of the meaning of the word **Keister** might light his fuse.

But he **had** asked. So I said, "Well, sir, it's slang, and some people use it to mean a person's bottom, you know, like what you sit on, you know, like the seat of your pants, or even sometimes, well, buttocks."

"Ass," he declared, managing to hiss and growl the word at the same time, while thundering it out loud enough to rattle the stable windows. "**Keister** means **ass.**"

I dared to glance to my left, and I saw that the western windows admitted more and much ruddier light than had shone through them only a few minutes earlier.

"You know what my first name was, my born

name?" Kenny asked, though in such a way as to make the question a demand.

Meeting his gaze again and finding it no less disturbing, I said, "I guess it wasn't Kenny."

He closed his eyes and took a deep breath, his face squinched as if he must be preparing himself for a difficult revelation.

For an instant I considered bolting for the nearer door, but I was afraid that by trying to flee I would put the lie to my pretense of friendship, motivating the forsaken Kenny to shoot me in the back.

Although they were to one degree or another eccentric, everyone else at Roseland tried to maintain an air of normalcy. This colorful giant, this walking armory with screaming-hyena tattoos snarling on his massive arms, made no such effort. I found it all but impossible to see him working with the other members of the estate-security team whom I had met. The safest assumption was that he was not a Roseland guard and not to be trusted for a second.

He took another deep breath, blew it out, opened his eyes, and said, "My born first name was Jack. They named me Jack Keister."

"That's just cruel, sir."

"Sonofabitch bastards," he said, which I inferred to be a less infuriated reference to his parents. "I got teased from day one in **preschool,** the little sons-ofbitches couldn't even wait till first grade. Minute I turned eighteen, I went to court to change my name."

I almost said **To Kenny Keister?** but fortunately held my tongue.

"Kenneth Randolph Fitzgerald Mountbatten," he said, rolling the names across his tongue with all the authority of the finest British stage actor.

"Impressive," I declared, "and may I say, exactly fitting."

He almost blushed with pleasure. "They're names I always liked, so I strung 'em together."

Unfortunately, I couldn't think of anything more to say to him. Unless Kenny Mountbatten proved to be a more gifted raconteur than all the evidence thus far indicated, we had reached the conclusion of our conversation.

I would not have been surprised if he punctuated his final line of dialogue by shooting me in the gut.

Instead, he glanced left and then right, suddenly aware of the rapid change in the quality of light at the windows. An expression of such alarm came over him that in spite of his grievous scars, hideous teeth, and crocodilian eyes, I could see in his face a bit of the tormented little boy he had once been.

"I'm late," he said, a tremor of distress in his voice, "late, late, late."

He turned away from me and ran to the door through which we had both entered. Still repeating that word, he fled the building less like the Terminator that he had seemed to be and more like the White Rabbit frightened of what discipline might be imposed if he were late for tea with the Mad Hatter.

On the east side of the stable, the windows allowed in far less light than seemed possible for a morning that had so recently dawned nearly cloudless. Every pane of the western windows, however, glowed like a bright ruby.

A rapidly incoming overcast might have explained the declining light at the east windows, but not the fiery glow at those to the west. The possibility of a wildfire occurred to me, masses of dark smoke to the east, flames roaring to the west, but I didn't smell smoke, and surely no fire could have gone from an arsonist's match to a roaring inferno in mere minutes.

Not wanting to tread on Kenny's heels, much preferring that he forget all about me, I hesitated before going to the door by which he had departed. It now stood open about three feet.

At the threshold, I hesitated, for the world outside wasn't as it ought to have been.

Ten feet of bare earth lay past the door, as before, although not the rock and not the crumpled Coke can, each of which had earlier cast a single shadow, just as I did. The weeds rose beyond the barren zone, and at some distance a familiar copse of live oaks spread black limbs.

But it was all bathed in the ominous light out of which had flown the hellish bats bigger than eagles. Directly overhead and to the west, high-altitude rivers of ash and soot serpentined through a yellow sky. The eastern heavens were dark mustard fading to black. The night brimmed the mountains and the foothills, on the verge of spilling toward me, a night in which no starlight could pierce the apocalyptic mantle encircling the world.

Minutes ago, the morning was fresh, and now the day was creeping toward its bed in the far Pacific. The mystery of the building's two shadows still played out, but I was not a good enough detective to deduce the meaning of them or to predict the resolution that seemed to be rushing toward me.

Intuition warned me, however, that to venture into this sudden yellow twilight would be dangerous if not suicidal. Beyond lay a Roseland somehow terribly different from the estate that I knew. And whatever the nature of that difference, it would not be anything as benign as that **this** Roseland would have roses.

I rolled the bronze door shut and could find no way to lock it. For fear of fire, perhaps no one locked in horses. And from the time when Roseland had been built, in the 1920s, there had been no gangs of horse thieves in California who needed to be locked out.

As I retreated along the stone- and copper-decorated aisle to the center of the building, the sconces on the stall posts began to dim. And then the lights went out.

Seven

NIGHT APPROACHED THE EASTERN WIN-dows, and every leaded pane of coppery glass to the west seemed to offer a view into a furnace. The interior of the stable was char-black except where grids of faux fire smouldered red-orange on posts and stall doors.

In the gloom, I couldn't discern if Nature's rule of a single shadow for each object still held within the building or whether instead extra, inexplicable shadows fell to all sides of everything.

Curiously devoid of any scent to this point, the stable now smelled of ozone, the bleachlike odor that lightning often flenses from the air and that lingers sometimes hours after the thunder has rolled away and the storm has wrung itself dry. But there was no rain in this day nor any threat of rain.

I didn't know for what I was waiting, but I knew it wouldn't be the Welcome Wagon lady with free gifts from local merchants. In retrospect, Kenny's abrupt departure—"Late, late, late!"—seemed less that of someone tardy for an appointment than that of a man terrified of being caught here after nightfall. A massive, tough, heavily armed man. Spooked like a little boy.

The unscheduled twilight, so soon after dawn, had such cosmic implications that my heart seemed to shrivel. It raced like that of a rabbit when the peaceable bunny sees the eye shine of the night-prowling wolf.

Terror can inebriate quicker than whiskey. Evidently I was about to receive a double-shot chaser, and I needed to get a grip, stay sober, steady.

To the east, the leaded windows were now full of night—except for the lazy eight embedded in the center of each. Those copper figures glowed without transmitting their luminescence through the dark glass, and I didn't think their brightness was just a reflection of the red—and increasingly sullen—light that burned through the western windows opposite them.

Following Kenny's hasty exit, a hush at first lay over the stable, but suddenly I heard something bumping softly outside, against the western wall. More than one thing. Several. At various points along that flank of the building.

A figure rose at a reddened window, but it was without detail, silhouetted against the drowning sun. I had an impression of a head, a flailing arm, a grasping hand.

At first I assumed that it was a man. Although head and arm and hand were misshapen, the extreme angle of the sun and imperfections in the thick glass might have been the cause of the distortions.

As the scarlet sunset purpled, shadows loomed at other windows, less distinct, more deformed, perhaps half a dozen individuals. By the second, I was less inclined to believe that those knocking and scraping their way along the wall of the stable were human.

For one thing, they seemed not to care about the noise they made, yet no voices were raised. Even with the intention to be quiet, human beings seldom can restrain from comment or at least grumbled cursing; we are the chattering species, as much as we are anything else.

Furthermore, those at the wall were not testing its sturdiness or announcing their arrival. They were fumbling their way along it, no doubt seeking a door, but not as ordinary men would seek it. The descending night did not fully reign. The land was light enough for a man to find his way. Their halting, thumping progress suggested that, if people, they were blind or lame, or both.

I couldn't believe that a legion of the disabled had crossed the fields of Roseland to explore the stable or to confront me—for what reason?—as I huddled in it.

Whatever creatures threw their twisted shadows on the windows and knocked their limbs against the walls, I preferred not to meet them. And whatever they might want from me, I was not prepared to give it.

The first of them turned the corner and found the north door, by which Kenny had recently fled. It beat upon the bronze, not as if knocking politely for admission but as if determining the nature of the barrier. In addition to the pounding, there were questing sounds in the area of the door handle.

Wondering for the first time how Kenny had gotten those facial scars, I hurried from the middle of the stable toward the south door.

I didn't want to risk making my way through this goblin night to the stone tower in the eucalyptus grove. I was even less charmed, however, by the prospect of remaining here for whatever hoedown these visitors had planned.

As I approached the south door, that great bronze panel rang with the blows of something seeking entrance. Being a mere fry cook and seer of ghosts, lacking the talent to teleport, I now had no way out.

To my left, the tack room couldn't be locked. It contained no furniture these days, and therefore the door couldn't be barricaded.

The ten empty stalls behind me offered no hope of concealment.

Beyond a door to my right lay the feed room, which was about twelve feet on a side. Because it had no windows, it was now as black as any dungeon.

I had seen the feed room on a previous visit. I

knew that along the right-hand wall were empty shelves, and opposite them stood two five-foot-long bins, each about four and a half feet deep and four feet back to front.

The bin nearest the door had three lids on top, hinged at the back, and was divided into three compartments. Unless I dismembered and distributed myself, I wouldn't fit.

The second had two lids but was one big compartment. Strongly constructed of heavy and well-joined wood, it was lined inside with tight-fitted stainless steel. Each lid featured a drop lip that set in a groove on the bin edge, making a rubberless seal, perhaps to keep the mice out of the grain.

Given any other reasonable choice, I wouldn't have climbed into that empty bin, which as I recalled bore an uncomfortable resemblance to a casket. But if the insistent visitors currently pounding on the doors at both ends of the stable were hostile, the alternatives to the bin were to die in the tack room or die in the aisle, or die in one of the horse stalls, and I didn't consider any of those options to be reasonable.

Whether or not my unknown adversaries had the benefit of eyes, I was as good as blind when I pulled shut the feed-room door behind me—no lock, of course—and felt my way to the second bin. I lifted one lid and pushed it back until the automatic hinge latch held it open at full extension.

I didn't need to be quiet getting into the bin, because those who wanted to come into the stable to have a powwow or a chow-down were making those bronze doors ring like bells.

On the underside of the lid was a six-inch-long pull handle with a knob on the end. If you were standing before the bin, you could lean across it and reach that peg to jiggle the hinge latch loose and then to draw the lid back toward yourself.

As I heard the wheels of the north door rumble in their tracks, I swung up and into this most inadequate of hidey-holes and lowered the lid, closing myself in the feed bin with the hope that its name wouldn't prove to be as apt now as it had been in the past.

Sitting on the floor of that box, facing forward, I held tight to both pull handles, which were welded to the lids, hoping that if anyone came into the room and tried to open the bin, it would seem to be warped and corroded and wedged shut with age.

The south door, too, rolled aside, especially loud because the pocket that received it lay behind the back wall of the feed room.

After the doors were opened wide enough to suit the visitors, all was silent, as if once they had filed into the aisle between the rows of stalls, they just stood there. Doing what?

They were probably listening for any sounds I might make, just as I was listening intently to them. But as I was one and they were many, they ought to search more confidently, aggressively.

Another minute passed. I began to wonder if

they had actually entered the stable after opening the doors or if instead they were still outside, at the threshold.

I might have thought the isolation of the feed bin prevented me from hearing them, but along the front of that long box were two rows of five holes, one a foot above the other. Four inches in diameter, each hole was covered with a fine-mesh screen, perhaps to allow air inside to prevent mold from forming on the grain that had been kept there back in the day. I should have been able to hear anything other than the most stealthy of movements.

The chlorine-like smell of ozone intensified to such an extent that I worried it might tease a sneeze from me.

Without faith to act as a governor, the human mind is a runaway worry generator, a dynamo of negative expectations. And because your life is yours to shape as you wish with free will, if you entertain too much anxiety about too many things, if you place no trust in providence, what you fear will more often come to pass. We make so many of our own troubles, from mere mishaps to disasters, by dwelling on the possibility of them until the possible becomes inevitable.

Therefore I told myself to stop worrying about sneezing, to place myself in the care of providence. Quick now, here, now, always, if we are in a condition of complete simplicity (as the poet said), hope and trust will more reliably keep a man afloat, while fear is more likely to sink him.

Silence upon silence . . . Just when I began to think the visitors had gone, the feed-room door opened.

Whoever it was didn't have a flashlight. Evidently night had swallowed the day entirely, because through the screened holes, I could detect not even the faintest glow of sunset seeping in from the windows in the main part of the stable.

At least one of the pack shuffled across the threshold. The searcher seemed big, heavy if not tall, for there was a cumbersome quality to the movements.

The first lid on the feed box nearest the door swung up with a soft rattle and a faint creak of hinges. And then banged shut. The second lid. The third.

In a lightless room, the seeker had peered into the three pitch-black compartments of the bin and had judged them empty. Unless this individual was equipped with the latest generation of the highest of high-tech night-vision goggles, he could by his very nature see as well in the dark as any cat.

Firmly gripping each lid of my hideaway by its pull handle, I strained to keep both of them down in anticipation of an imminent attempt to throw them open.

The searcher shuffled to the second bin, did not at once try to open it, but instead strummed the screens of a couple of the ventilation holes in front of my face.

If the darkness didn't fully blind the hunter as it blinded me, the fineness of the wire mesh should prevent me from being seen clearly if at all. I was unnerved, however, to think that we might be eye to eye.

Distraction was dangerous. I needed to concentrate on pulling down with all my might on the lids, so that if my adversary abruptly yanked on them, they wouldn't budge and would seem to be corroded shut.

Another strumming of the screens appeared to be a taunt, as if the hunter knew where I was and wanted to twist my nerves a little, perhaps to salt my flesh with fear sweat and thereby make me tastier.

Now sniffing. Sniffing at the screened holes, like a bloodhound seeking a scent.

I was grateful that the air was so redolent of ozone, for surely that would make me harder to detect.

The sniffing swelled into a vibrant snort, an incredibly noisy fluttering of nares and septum, not the snort of either a man or a dog, but of some predatory creature.

Bleachy ozone tingled in my sinuses, but I trusted providence to prevent a sneeze, refused to worry, declined to dwell on negative possibilities, and I did not sneeze, did not sneeze, still did not sneeze, but then I farted.

Eight

IN THE HOLLOW STEEL-LINED BIN, MY unfortunate eruption resonated such that it would have humiliated me if my first concern had been social acceptance. My first concern, however, was survival. At the moment, I didn't have the capacity for embarrassment because terror filled me.

Narcissists are everywhere in this ripe age of self-love, which amazes me because so much in life would seem to foster humility. Each of us is a potential source of foolishness, each of us must endure the consequences of the foolishness of others, and in addition to all of that, Nature frequently works to impress upon us our absurdity and thereby remind us that we are not the masters of the universe that we like to suppose we are.

Even before I revealed myself by that indelicate sound—and just for the record, it was **only** sound—I knew that I wasn't a master of the universe. I merely hoped that I might be the master of the feed bin, and in fact its **secret** master.

That modest ambition was now unfulfilled as the searcher in the dark scrabbled at the lid, tried to tear open one and then the other, and then both at the same time.

With desperate tenacity, I held fast to the pull handles, which were easier to grip than the edge of the lid with which my adversary was struggling.

As it strove to get at me, it not only snorted but also snarled and grunted and growled and even squealed, leading me to conclude that my suspicions were correct, that it wasn't human, for it didn't once say "sonofabitch."

Others of its kind crowded into the dark room. An evil chorus of bestial sounds, their voices were nothing like those of monkeys, but the cacophony was equal to that of a monkey house in a lightning storm.

The first through the door continued to pry furiously at the lids as others began to pound on them and on the sides of the bin. They rocked my haven back and forth, as well, although it was too cumbersome and there was too little room for maneuvering to allow them to tumble it on its side.

I felt like a mouse sealed in a can and subjected to the sport of cruel little boys.

Because my years have been filled with fighting and chasing and being chased, more on foot than in cars, and because I have eaten far less fried food than I have prepared for others, I'm in pretty good physical shape. But already my arms had begun to ache from the strain of holding down the lids.

Remaining a positive thinker was going to get more difficult minute by minute.

One or more of this hungry crowd—if it was in fact a hope of dinner that drove them and not something even more unthinkable—scratched fiercely at the screens in the ventilation holes and then did more than scratch. The fine wire mesh slit with a sound like a pull-tab slider parting the teeth of a tiny zipper, which suggested that they either had knives or exceedingly sharp claws.

They could not seize me by reaching through holes as small as four inches in diameter, but they could poke at me with blades or sticks, which I expected them to do at any moment. If they could see to any extent in darkness, which seemed to be the case, and if the ventilation screens no longer inhibited their view of me, they would know exactly where to jab for maximum effect.

I searched the blackness in front of me for any hint of animal eye shine, but I could detect none. If not for their expressions of anger and need, I might have thought they were robot assassins whose stares were dead black because their eyes were cameras that took in the entire spectrum of light but gave back nothing.

Hands slick with sweat, my grip on one of the pull handles slipped slightly. My primary adversary reacted instantly to that minor fumble, wrenching at the lid with greater fervor.

My heart knocked so hard that its frantic rhythm was a tom-tom pulse in my ears, and even in the chaos of the assault upon the feed bin, I could hear my ragged breathing.

Since I lost Stormy, I have no need of my life. If I should be taken young by some divine act of mercy, perhaps sudden death by accident or a cerebral embolism, I would not care. But like most people who have glimpsed a scene from the latest remake of **The Texas Chainsaw Massacre** while channel surfing, or have dipped into a Stieg Larsson novel on an unfortunate page, I fear dying in a prolonged and messy fashion that involves either torture or being devoured alive.

Now that I didn't have to worry about revealing myself with a sneeze, the astringent scent of ozone of course faded a bit, so that suddenly I could smell the horde of zombies or rabid black bears or whatever they were. To call their stench body odor would be like describing the reek of a rotting cabbage as less fragrant than a rose.

I began to gag, and their stink was so intense that I could also **taste** it. If I started to retch, I might be convulsed with nausea and wouldn't be able to pull hard enough on the lids to keep the beasts out. The very thought of retching caused me to retch. A bitter mass rose in my throat, I choked it down, but I knew that I wouldn't be able to swallow it again.

Suddenly the pack in the feed room fell silent and halted their assault. Their smell swiftly ebbed, receded entirely, as did the tang of ozone.

Beyond the torn screens in the ventilation holes, the light of the stable sconces—if not also daylight—seemed to plume into the dark room through the open doorway, as if it were not real light at all but instead a phosphorescent exhalation of cold breath, which then lay as a pale and uneven gray condensation on the rough board walls.

I was accustomed to being the target of violence. But I wasn't familiar with bad guys who, at the height of their assault and having victory within their grasp, abruptly turned peaceable and went away to meditate.

Whatever they were, the motivation for their retreat was not likely to be an attack of conscience and a tender desire to dispense a little mercy.

Some people misunderstand evil and believe it will relent, and because their misplaced hope inspires dark hearts to dream darker dreams, they are the fathers and mothers of all wars. Evil does not relent; it must be defeated. And even when defeated, uprooted, and purified by fire, evil leaves behind a seed that will one day germinate and, in blooming, again be misunderstood.

I had defeated nothing. I knew better than to believe that my mysterious attackers would not return. The question was—**when**?

Holding fast to the pulls on the underside of the

feed-bin lids, I listened but heard nothing except my less frantic breathing and an occasional twang as my weight shifting ever so slightly upon the stainless-steel liner caused it to flex.

After a minute or so, the pale light, the absence of ozone, and the silence drew me to the conclusion that the grunting pack had not left of their own will but had been somehow swept away when the too-early nightfall was magically undone and the day restored to morning.

I didn't know how night could have come so quickly after dawn or how it could have been rolled back, as if time were not a river with a fixed course but instead a changeable wind gusting now toward but now away.

My curious life has been filled with supernatural events, but never before one like this.

An argument could be made that the many strange things I see and experience are in fact as natural as the sun and moon, and that the five senses of other human beings have not yet adapted to the full reality of the world.

That theory would seem to suggest that I am special, better than others, but I know that isn't true. In spite of my talent, I am not any better than any other soul seeking redemption, no more than a good musician is a better person than those with no musical talent, and I am worse than some.

Willing to entertain the possibility that I would not be torn asunder and eaten if I ventured forth,

I let go of one of the lids, pushed up the other, and clambered out of the feed bin.

I believed that I now knew what a lobster felt as it languished in a tank beside the maître d' station in a restaurant, while hungry patrons, waiting to be seated, tapped the glass and remarked upon its size and succulence.

Stepping out of the feed room, I saw that the south door was closed and the north one stood open precisely as far as it had when I first entered the stable. The sconces, which had failed earlier, now glowed. At the windows, the day was as it should be: plenty of light, brighter to the east than to the west.

Warily, I proceeded through the stable to the open door, but no threat manifested.

When I switched off the lights and stepped outside, the morning was fair and mild and right. The bright brush of a single sun painted the trees and grass and sloping land, leaving the distant ocean still half dark like gray slate through which were smeared some of the softer colors of the clay from which it had been formed. The stable cast a single black shadow, to the west, as did I. The rock and the crumpled Coke can had reappeared; they, like all things around me, spilled their silhouettes only westward in ordinary daylight.

For a moment some power had imposed chaos on the day, followed by this reprieve. This is the world of men and women in their flesh, and more often than not they rebel against order, preferring the perceived freedom of a measured chaos. But chaos half-loosed cannot be long controlled; it is all or nothing. This reprieve would be brief.

Whatever might be happening at Roseland, it was misconceived by men in the quest for power, because it was a lust for power of one kind or another that quivered at the root of every base human desire. I sensed that not only the land sloped from east to west; within the grounds of this walled estate, reality also was tilted from the norm and was being steadily levered to an ever more severe angle, until Roseland would abruptly slide to ruin, reason would slither down to madness, and everyone here would cascade into death.

The sun was hardly risen, but already time was running out.

Nine

IF THE ONSET OF NIGHT SO SOON AFTER dawn and then its equally astonishing repeal had been observed by others in Roseland, they were remarkably unmoved by it. As I crossed the estate, I expected to see at least a couple of people on terraces or lawns, regarding the sky with wonder if not terror, but no one was out and about. Although I couldn't understand how such a stunning cosmological event could be confined to the stable, apparently only I had experienced it.

I see the lingering dead, but I don't have hallucinations. And I didn't believe that Chef Shilshom spiked my almond croissant with peyote. If the guard at the front gate, where I was headed, did not remark on an eclipse of the sun, then the change from day to night, to day again, had been weirdly localized.

Nine feet high and three thick, the wall surrounding Roseland's fifty-two acres had been built of concrete faced with stones gathered from the property. In the only gap, the impressive gates at the driveway entrance were not formed from pickets and rails through which the curious might peer, but were solid panels of bronze decorated with copper discs like those in the floor of the stable.

The gatehouse was of the same stone. Like the guesthouse tower in the eucalyptus grove, its windows were narrow and barred, and its ironbound-oak door stood like a challenge to barbarians.

About fourteen feet on a side, the building was large for its purpose, containing an office, a kitchenette, and a bathroom. I'd had only a glimpse inside, through the open door, on our second day here. But I could not have failed to notice the gun rack on the farther wall: two shotguns—one with a pistol grip—and two assault rifles.

Apparently, they intended to leave no doubt in the minds of door-to-door salesmen that when they said no, they were serious.

On the north side of the structure, adjacent to the driveway, an extension of the sloped roof, supported by four posts, provided a six-foot-deep shelter where a guard might stand in bad weather to speak with arriving guests. In that shade, to the right of the door, Henry Lolam sat in a captain's chair with a padded seat.

He was perhaps thirty, and handsome in such a boyish way that on first encounter he seemed callow. Unlined face, mouth as innocent as that of a child who had not yet spoken one curse, cheeks the pink that sometimes blushes peach skins, he looked as if nothing hard in the world had touched him, as if he'd drifted through it like dandelion fluff on the softest warmest breeze that ever blew.

His green eyes were alien in that boyish face, full of loss and anguish and, at times, bewilderment.

As on the two other occasions when I had sought him out, Henry was reading a book of poetry. On a small table beside his chair were other haphazardly stacked volumes by such poets as Emerson, Whitman, and Wallace Stevens, a dangerous crew to let into your head.

Some will be skeptical of the contention that a security guard—a "rent-a-cop," in the mocking Hollywood argot of our times—might be immersed in poetry. The uniqueness of every soul is not a theme that our current culture, obsessed with group identities, cares to assert. But Henry was himself and no one else, and judging by the intensity with which he focused on those verses, he sought from them something profound.

While he lingered over the last stanza of a poem, I leaned against a porch post and waited. He was not rude, merely preoccupied.

I had come here to ask him about Kenny Randolph Fitzgerald Mountbatten, who claimed to be a Roseland security guard even though he hadn't worn the uniform—gray slacks, white shirt, blue blazer—that the other guards wore and though he was in so many ways more flamboyant than Henry and his colleagues.

Waiting, I watched what appeared to be a peregrine, judging by its immense wingspan and the universal pattern of its underwings. These falcons generally hunted smaller birds, rather than rodents, making spectacular swoops and seizing their prey in midair.

When Henry closed the book and looked up, a lost expression marked his eyes, as if he knew neither me nor where he was.

I said, "I'm sorry to interrupt, sir."

His confusion, or whatever it might be, ebbed, and in ebbing washed a smile onto his beach-smooth face. He appeared as boyish as any preadolescent in a Norman Rockwell painting—as long as you did not care to see more in his eyes than the green of them.

"No, no," Henry said. "I enjoy our chats. Sit down, sit down."

To the left of the door, he had earlier put out a second chair, apparently in anticipation of my visit. I settled in it, deciding there was no point in asking about an eclipse.

"I've been brushing up on my UFO history," Henry said.

He was intrigued by reports of abductions by extraterrestrials and alien bases on the far side of the moon. Although I could not say why I felt so, I suspected that he sought the same thing in UFO lore that he pursued in poetry.

Aware of the irony of a spirit-seer debunking the possibility of visitors from outer space, I nevertheless said, "I'm sorry, sir, but I just can't buy into flying saucers and all that."

"Several of those who've been abducted have passed lie-detector tests. There's a lot of documentation."

"See, it doesn't make sense to me that a superintelligent race would come all the way across the galaxy just to abduct people and put probes up their rectums."

"Well, that's not the **only** thing they do in their examinations."

"But it always seems to be the first and most important thing."

"Don't you think a colonoscopy is advisable now and then?"

"I can get one from a doctor."

"Not as thorough as the one the aliens give you."

"But, sir, why would aliens be interested in whether I have colon cancer?"

"Maybe because they **care**," Henry said.

I had learned that to get to a subject that I wished to discuss, I had to indulge Henry's bizarre fascination with proctologists from other worlds. Indulging him, however, didn't mean taking a craziness pill and tripping with him, and I remained a skeptic.

"I suspect they're just very caring," Henry persisted.

"Coming fifty light-years to give me a colonoscopy is so caring it's downright creepy."

"No, Odd, you see, fifty light-years to them might be like fifty miles to us."

"Coming even fifty miles to force a probe up my butt without my permission is a pretty good definition of a pervert."

Henry's face was alight with wonder at the idea of aliens, and dimpled with the amusement that any mischievous boy feels when he gets a seemingly legitimate chance to talk about butts and such.

"They're probably taking DNA samples, too."

I shrugged. "So I'll give them a lock of my hair."

Smiling dreamily, but turning the book of poetry over and over in his hands as if agitated, he said, "Some UFO experts think the aliens have conquered death and just want to give us immortality."

"Give it to everyone?"

"They're so compassionate."

"Lady Gaga's cool," I said. "But a thousand years from now, I don't want to have to listen to Lady Gaga's seven hundredth album."

"It wouldn't be boring like that. Immortal, you could change careers again and again. Be a singer like Lady Gaga, and she can be a fry cook."

I grimaced. "I can't sing, and I have a hunch she can't cook."

He thumbed repeatedly, insistently through the pages of the book without looking at it, making a sound like shuffled cards. "Enhanced by alien technology, we'll all be able to do **everything** perfectly."

"Then why do anything at all?"

"What do you mean?"

"If there's nothing to learn because we know it all, what's the challenge, why would the effort matter, what would be the point?"

For a moment he continued riffling the pages of poetry, but then his hands grew still and the smile flatlined.

I waited for his reply, but he didn't make one. After a while, he said, "I'm supposed to be on vacation. Eight weeks in Hawaii."

Noah Wolflaw didn't seem like a guy who would play Santa Claus to his employees, but I didn't remark on the generosity of a two-month vacation.

Henry gazed now at the falcon as it circled lazily, patient in its quest for prey. Subtle but unmistakable, his look of desolation was so unsuited to his boyish face, I suspected that he was in some emotional distress and that, into my silence, he might say something revealing and useful to me.

"I spent two weeks in Hawaii and just couldn't stand it anymore. Flew to San Francisco for a week, and that was no better."

The peregrine glided silently, and I as well felt falconish, in my mind circling above the guard, waiting patiently for him to speak words that might be meat to me.

"It wasn't those particular places," Henry continued. "Wherever you go these days, it's all wrong, isn't it? I don't know why, but it is."

I didn't believe that he wanted any comment from me. He seemed to be thinking out loud.

"People are so different from how they used to be. So fast. There's an endless opening of possibilities."

Fearing that he might wax as cryptic as Anna-maria, I sought a little clarification: "You mean the Internet, technology, and all that?"

"Technology changes nothing. People were people before and after the steam engine, before and after the airplane. But . . . not quite now. Walls. That's what it is. The problem is walls."

I waited, but he said nothing more, and at last, with some exasperation of which I'm not proud, I said, "Walls. Yes. How true. We have to have walls, don't we? Or maybe we don't? You start with walls, and then you need a ceiling. And floors. And doors. It just never stops. Tents. That might be the answer."

If he heard my words, he didn't detect my sarcasm. "Five weeks of vacation left, but I just couldn't stand being out there anymore. I hate the wall around Roseland, but the gate in it is a gate to nowhere."

When after a while he didn't continue, I prodded him by saying, "Well, as I see it, that gate is a gate to **everywhere.** The whole world's beyond it."

I figured he was ruminating on my sage comment, but he wasn't. He flew off on what seemed to be an-other line of thought.

" 'Things fall apart; the center cannot hold.' "

Although I recognized those words, I didn't at once know from what source he was quoting.

Before I could ask, Henry recited the famous lines of poetry about the falcon and the falconer, a metaphor for man and God, the former flying ever farther from the latter, the pagan cruelty of the human heart breaking loose from civilizing tradition.

"Yeats," I said, naming the poet, and might have been pleased with myself if I had understood what the hell he was talking about.

"I hate it here, this Roseland without roses, but at least there's a wall, and with a wall the center might still hold."

He wasn't hysterical, just enigmatic, but I really wanted to slap him until he made sense, the way the hero sometimes slaps the raving hysteric in the movies. But no matter how frustrated I may be, I never slap a man who is carrying a pistol in a shoulder holster under a blazer tailored to allow a quick draw.

Henry shifted his attention from the falcon to me. In his Huck Finn face, his eyes were as bleak as those of Hamlet.

His vulnerability could not have been more obvious. I sensed that the ease with which he opened himself to me was an indication that he was friendless, sought friendship, and could be cultivated to such an extent as to reveal secrets of Roseland that would help me understand why I was here and what I must do.

True friendship, however, is a sacred relationship even if it doesn't involve formal vows. The friends I've made in Pico Mundo and everywhere I've gone since leaving home have kept me from despair, have nurtured hope. When I considered how I might **cultivate** Henry, I meant **manipulate.** There's nothing wrong with manipulating bad men in pursuit of truth, but I didn't think Henry Lolam was bad or deserved the contempt that manipulation represented. To pretend friendship here would be to devalue all the real friendships in my life.

While I hesitated, the moment of opportunity passed, and Henry said, "Guests in Roseland are rare."

"The lady I'm traveling with seems to have . . . charmed Mr. Wolflaw."

"She's not his type. She's not low or flashy, or cheap."

By insulting his employer, Henry raised my hopes that he might treat me as a confidant without requiring that I fake friendship.

Silence seemed to serve me best, and after a moment, Henry said, "You're not her lover."

"No."

"What are you to her?"

"A friend. She's alone. She needs protection."

He held my stare as if he meant for the intensity of his gaze to drive his next words deep: "He doesn't want her. It may be the baby."

"Mr. Wolflaw? What would he want with the baby?"

Having raised the issue, he retreated from exploring it. "Who can say? Maybe he needs . . . something new."

I could tell that he didn't mean anything as innocent as that the baby was a new experience, a novelty, so I said, "New? New what?"

"Sensation," he said, looking away from me to the hunter gliding in the high blue day. "Thrills."

Those two words evoked such an array of horrifying possibilities that I meant to press him for an explanation.

Before I could speak, he held up one hand to stop me. "I've said far too much and not enough. If you want to protect her, you should leave now. This is . . . an unhealthy place."

I couldn't tell him that my supernatural gift and Annamaria's mission—whatever that might be— had brought us here. To reveal my sixth sense to anyone but a friend of long acquaintance might cause considerable trouble.

According to Annamaria, someone in Roseland was in great danger, perhaps the boy about whom the dead blonde worried. I didn't feel the endangered person was Henry. I still had to find who needed my help.

"We can't leave today," I said. "But soon, I hope."

"If it's money, I can give you some."

"That's very kind of you, sir. But it's not money."

"I tell you it's an unhealthy place, and you aren't surprised."

"A little surprised."

"Not at all. What are you, I wonder?"

"Just a fry cook."

"But you have no job."

I shrugged. "This rotten economy."

He looked away from me and shook his head.

Like an angel suddenly thrown down and remembering its wings only at the penultimate moment, the peregrine plunged, with its fearsome talons seized a smaller bird in flight, and swooped up, away, toward a tree where it could perch in feathered splendor to feed upon its terrified, feathered catch.

Henry gave me a meaningful look that seemed to ask if I dared recognize that the falcon had been a sign that portended my fate if I remained long in Roseland. "I know you're not stupid, Odd Thomas. But are you a fool?"

"Less than some folks, sir, but more than others."

"Surely you fear death."

"Not really. Not death. Just how it might happen. Like being locked in a garage with a hungry crocodile and being eaten alive. Or being chained to dead men and dropped in a lake. Or having a hole drilled in my skull, and then the guy who drilled it drops a bunch of fire ants through the hole, into my brain."

I don't know whether Henry punctuated every conversation with reflective silences or if only I inspired that response.

He shifted restlessly in his chair and searched the

sky, as if hoping for another sign that might con-vince me to leave Roseland.

Finally I got around to the reason I had come. "Sir, is there a guy named Kenny on the security team?"

"We don't have a Kenny, no."

"Tall, muscular guy with bad scars on the face, wears a T-shirt that says 'Death heals.'"

The slow turning of Henry's head, the long look before he spoke, told me that Kenny was known here even if not by name.

"You've been warned to stay inside, behind locked doors, between dusk and dawn."

"Yes, sir, but I was warned about mountain lions, nothing else. Anyway, I didn't run into him at night. It was this morning."

"Not after sunrise."

"More than half an hour after. Up at the stables. Who is he if he's not a guard?"

Henry rose from his chair, went to the gatehouse door, opened it, and glanced back at me. "Take her and leave. You don't know what kind of place this is."

Getting to my feet, I said, "So tell me."

He went inside and closed the door behind him.

Through a window, I saw him picking up the tele-phone.

If I had come to Roseland alone, perhaps I would have left, as Henry advised. But Annamaria, on her mysterious mission, would not leave, and I could not abandon her to the mercy of . . . Of who knew what?

Ten

ACCOMPANIED BY THE BUZZ OF BUM-
blebees, by darting wrens that sang complex songs
in high tinkling trills, by bright butterflies that
seemed out of season, and for a while by a pair of
scampering squirrels, I felt like a character in a Disney movie, and I half expected the squirrels to start
talking as I followed the property line south from
the gatehouse.

That gave me no comfort. Bad things happen to
good animals in some Walt Disney movies. Think
of Bambi's mother and Old Yeller, the former shot
down in front of her child, the latter foaming at the
mouth with rabies and killed by the boy who loved
him. People don't always fare better. Even the sweet-
est of princesses get poisoned by witches. There was
a touch of Quentin Tarantino in Uncle Walt.

Henry Lolam had said that he hated Roseland but
nonetheless returned to it because, with its encircling masonry, "the center might still hold." I knew

what the poet, Yeats, had intended by his lines, but I didn't know what the security guard meant.

The high, wide structure was reminiscent of a fortification, but it wasn't, after all, the Great Wall of China. It wouldn't hold back the Mongol hordes or their equivalent. A determined man could easily climb over it, either to enter or to leave.

Even in the early 1920s, such a massive construction project would have been costly. The income tax had been new and low in those days, and Constantine Cloyce had been an incredibly wealthy man. But if his purpose was to define his fifty-two acres, building the wall two-thirds this height and half this width would have done the job as well at a fraction of the cost.

Until now, I hadn't given any thought to this rampart. But the conversation with Henry pricked my curiosity.

Although I followed the property line, I gave no indication that the wall intrigued me. Always at Roseland, I felt watched, but now more than usual. Certainly, Henry must be keeping an eye on me from the gatehouse. He had seemed to wish me well; perhaps he still did. But his attitude changed when I mentioned the giant with the scars.

After a hundred yards, the manicured lawn and flower gardens gave way to wild grass, and two hundred yards after that, I ascended a gentle slope and passed through a stand of California live oaks ranging in size from sixty to ninety feet in height. The wildlife had abandoned me except for nuthatches whistling in the majestic branches of the black-trunked trees.

Screened from the gatehouse and the main house, I went to the wall. The stones provided toeholds, handholds, and I scaled those nine feet with alacrity.

Atop the palisade, on hands and knees, I discovered what I might have unconsciously expected. Set in the grout lines among the dark stones were serpentine patterns of the bright copper coins on each of which was engraved the slightly elongated figure eight that I had seen elsewhere.

Dappled with sunshine and oak-branch shadows, the cap was of the same material as the wall, sawn into flags and set in an irregular but fitted pattern. With my palms flat on the cool stone, I could feel the faintest vibrations, as though buried within this massive rampart must be machinery of some kind.

Leaning forward, I put my left ear to the stone, but I could hear no noise arising from inside the wall.

If those rapid, small-arc oscillations produced a sound, it would not be a heavy throb or thrum, but instead a high-pitched hum or even a whine.

The longer I considered those vibrations, the less they seemed to be the product of laboring machinery and the more the source struck me as electronic.

I got to my knees, fished in a pocket of my jeans, and extracted a penknife that I had purchased when I'd gone into town to buy some clothes. I had gotten the small knife specifically to pry one of the copper discs from its mortar bed, though I hadn't taken one from the stable or from the mausoleum—where they also decorated the floor—because I assumed that if the vandalism was noticed, I would be the first suspect to whom they turned.

More important, they might realize the missing copper disc was not a case of vandalism but a consequence of investigation. If they suspected that I was more than a mere guest enjoying the pleasures of Roseland, I might learn the secrets of this place suddenly and violently.

A full nine feet above the ground, atop the wall, a missing bit of copper would not readily be noticed. When I set to work with the penknife, digging out the mortar, I soon discovered that the copper would not readily be **removed**, either. By the time I burrowed down an inch, when the blade of the penknife snapped, I realized that the discs were not as thin as coins but were instead the blunt ends of inch-diameter copper rods. For all I knew, they extended the entire depth of the wall and into its concrete footing.

Copper was far too soft a metal and too expensive to serve as structural reinforcement. Steel rebar would have been used for that purpose. The copper had some other function. Considering the expense of embedding so many rods in a long work of masonry, I could only assume they must be no less essential to the true purpose of the wall than was the web of rebar that maintained the structural integrity.

I threw the pieces of the broken knife into the tall wild grass beyond the estate and crawled forward on hands and knees until I came out from under the overhanging branches of the oaks. I got to my feet and walked the yard-wide wall, as if I were again—or still—a boy adventuring.

The rise in the land hid the distant main house and all other structures from me—and me from them.

Within fifty feet, I came to what appeared to be a foot-wide, shallow black bowl turned upside down in the center of the wall cap. When I knelt again, I saw that this object was supported on four-inch-long steel pins, and that it was a rain deflector set over a six-inch-square ventilation grill.

I thrust one hand under the bowl and felt a faint, warm draft barely fluttering against my fingers. When I bent my head to the deflector, I smelled something that reminded me of new-sprouting spring grass and ripe summer grass and wild straw-berries, although the fragrance was not in fact like any of those things, but unique. Abruptly the draft turned cold, and though the scent that came with the change of temperature was also unique, it reminded me of things that it smelled nothing like: dry leaves but also dead leaves wet with a not-unpleasant mold and also the so-faint but stirring scent released by cracking ice.

Cool changed to warm and warm to cool every twenty seconds, for what reason and to what purpose I couldn't guess. I had no idea why a wall would need to be ventilated or why the flow of air and odor would not be consistent.

I rose and continued perhaps four hundred feet until I came to another rain deflector and vent. Here, I found the same conditions.

Immediately ahead, another hurst of oaks spread branches over the wall, and a few hung low. I considered jumping off the rampart, but I didn't know what ankle-fracturing hole or rock the long grass might hide, and so I slid backward off the top, hung by my hands, and dropped a little more than three feet.

I backed away from the wall, trying to spot the rain deflector curved over the vent grill. But it was far above my head, had a low profile, and was a nonreflective black that made it difficult to see. When I had backed off far enough to detect the thing, it was a hardly noticeable shape that didn't seem out of place or intriguing.

Puzzled by my discoveries, I turned away from the wall and found the muzzle of a pistol aligned with my left eye.

Eleven

THE HAND HOLDING THE PISTOL HAD long, blunt fingers and bristles of wiry black hair between the knuckles, and the guy to whom the hand belonged had a face to match his fist: hard, clenched features and a beard shadow that would not be shaved away even with a wood-chipper.

Paulie Sempiterno was chief of the Roseland security team, and in neatly pressed gray slacks, white polo shirt, and handsome blue blazer, he still looked as if he spent most of his time in alleyways breaking people's knees with a baseball bat and decorating their faces with chain patterns.

He said, "I don't like you, pretty boy," and his rough voice chilled the whistling nuthatches to silence in the trees behind him.

Although I had met him only once before and had done nothing to offend him, I believed that he was sincere, that he disliked me in fact intensely. Even if he hadn't said a word, I could read his contempt in the way that his thick purple lips sneered back from teeth that looked formidable enough to crunch up a pork chop, bones and all. The gun in my face was another clue.

He said, "Wolflaw's a flaming idiot, he's always been an idiot, but I didn't expect **this,** not even from him. Houseguests! And not just overnight. What the hell is he thinking? Why stop there? Why not have a wedding for you and your knocked-up sweetie? Invite a hundred of your inbred moron relatives, hire an orchestra, ask the governor to stop taking bribes long enough to come down from Sacramento and officiate."

Stocky, barrel-chested, thick-necked, antisocial, Sempiterno would have been a classic strong-and-silent type if he could have shut up for a minute. But he had a mad-on, and he wanted me to know he had a mad-on, and he evidently thought I was so slow-witted that I wouldn't understand his position until he had used a thousand words to paint a picture of it.

He said, "Anyway, you're not just some houseguest, pretty boy. Looking here, looking there, snooping around, up to the stables, talking to Shilshom about a horse when there isn't any horse, haven't been horses here for a long time, now walking on the wall. Who the hell walks on top of a nine-foot wall? Nobody, that's who. Except you. Why the hell were you walking on the wall?"

When he paused for longer than one quick inhalation, I figured I was being invited to reply. "Well, sir, the view's nice from up there. You can see so much farther."

Thrusting the pistol closer to my left eye, just in case I had forgotten about it, he said, "How's **this** view. You like **this** view? More dramatic than the Grand Canyon. I don't know what you're up to, wall-walker, but you're up to something. I don't like people who are up to something. You know how much tolerance I have for people who are up to something?"

"None?" I guessed, pretty sure that my answer had won a prize, if there was a prize to be won.

"Less than none. What're you up to?"

"I'm not up to anything, sir. To be frank, I'm just freeloading off Mr. Wolflaw. He's charmed by the girl I'm with, and I'm along for the ride. Could you put the gun away? I'm harmless. I really am."

He glared at me. His glare could melt a polar bear's testicles.

If he'd had a cold sore on his lip, we would have been friends by now.

"I know you're going to be major trouble," he said. "I'd really like to put a bullet in your face."

"Yes, sir, I know you would. I appreciate that. But you really don't have a reason to put a bullet in my face."

"The reason is I don't like it."

"Besides, if you kill me, the girl I'm with will be upset, and Mr. Wolflaw is so charmed by her that he'll be upset, too, and there goes your job. Not to mention prison, gang rape, and the loss of your right to vote."

Even the prospect of being turned away from the ballot box didn't seem to faze him. "The girl's not his type. She's nobody's type. The bitch creeps me out."

"Ah, sir, that's just mean. She's not a Victoria's Secret model, but she's pretty in her way."

"I'm not talking about how she looks. With this face, I'm gonna make fun of how other people look?"

"Good point."

At last lowering the pistol, he said, "It's how she stared at me the very first time I saw her. Like she's a speed-reader and my whole story's no longer than the list of ingredients on a cereal box."

I nodded. "She seems to look straight into your heart."

"Wasn't any damn romance-novel moment," Sempiterno said. "It was like I went through airport security and in ten seconds flat came out scoped, poked, and naked."

If you're open to it, a smile can find you at the most unlikely times. "I like the way you say things, sir."

Again he favored me with that bruin-emasculating glare. "What the hell's that supposed to mean?"

"Nothing. Just that you have a way of putting things."

"I say what I say. I don't care what you think." He holstered his pistol. "If Noah Wolflaw, the idiot, wants you here, I can't make you leave. But you better understand, pretty boy, he doesn't love the girl and he doesn't like you, he's all about himself. And whatever he wants from you two—when he takes it, you're going to wish to hell you'd listened to me and been long gone."

As he turned away from me, I said, "I'm thinking we'll probably leave in the morning."

Having taken only two steps, he halted, facing me again. "Leave today. Don't stay the night. Leave now."

"Maybe after lunch."

He stared at me as if, with his willpower alone, he could cause me to spontaneously combust. After a silence, he said, "Maybe I know after all why Wolflaw wants you here."

"Why?"

Instead of answering me, he said, "Whatever you're looking for in Roseland, you'll find its opposite. If you want to live, look for death."

He turned away again and strode toward the conclave of massive oaks. At his approach, the whistling nuthatches in the aviary of branches all fell silent again. When he stepped into the shadows of the trees, the flock flew, wings rattling through the veils of oval leaves, and flung themselves into the sky, at risk of falcons.

Among the trees I saw a battery-powered mini truck, a vehicle often used by landscapers, which was longer than a golf cart, smaller than a pickup, roofless, with two seats and an open cargo area. This one was jacked up on fat tires that, with other alterations, made it pretty much an all-terrain vehicle.

Paulie Sempiterno got behind the wheel. Purring softly, the trucklet seemed almost to float among the trees, out into the golden meadow, and toward the rise beyond which stood the main house.

I don't take offense at any rude names that I am called. I did find **pretty boy** sad, however, because I'm as ordinary looking as any actor who has ever played Tom Cruise's pal in a movie and whose primary job is, by his very ordinariness, to make the star look even more extraordinary than he does in real life.

When he sneered those two words, Mr. Sempiterno wasn't mocking me; successful mockery must be based on at least a grain of truth. You can't mock a dog for being a dog, but in trying to do so, you make yourself a person worthy of mockery. The security chief thought me a pretty boy only by comparison to himself, suggesting that his assessment of his somewhat unfortunate appearance was far too harsh, and that was where the sadness lay.

In this case, the term **pretty boy** might also mean other than what it seemed to mean. People sometimes speak in code, often without realizing they are doing so, as much a mystery to themselves as to others. Considering my average-guy looks, perhaps I enjoyed some other blessing that Mr. Sempiterno recognized but lacked—and that he envied. If I could puzzle out what that might be, maybe I would have a valuable clue to the truth of Roseland.

As the security chief receded across the meadow, I decided to continue following the property line but also to surrender myself to the third and final aspect of my extrasensory perception.

In addition to an occasional prophetic dream and my ability to see the spirits of the lingering dead, I have what Stormy Llewellyn called psychic magnetism. If I need to locate someone whose current whereabouts I don't know, I concentrate on his name or face, give myself to impulse and intuition, wandering as whim takes me—on foot, on skateboard, in a car, whatever—until I find him. More often than not, I am brought to my quarry within half an hour.

The search is usually but not always successful, and I can't either control or foresee where or when the encounter will occur. If my paranormal abilities had been purchased from a store, the vendor more likely would have been Dollar Mart than Tiffany.

In this case, I didn't have either a name or a face on which to focus. I could only allow Annamaria's words to run over and over through my mind in a memory loop—**there's someone here who's in great danger and desperately needs you**—and hope that I would be drawn sooner than later to that individual.

With everyone warning me to leave and giving me

such curious advice as to look for death if I wanted to live, I suspected that what time I might have to save the nameless someone was pouring away like sand out of a fractured hourglass. I have in the past failed some people, including she whom I loved more than life itself. Every failure hollows out my heart a little further, and no success is able to refill any of that emptiness. I seem to be less likely to die at the hands of some villain than to fall dead when the walls of my heart collapse into the emptiness that they enclose. I couldn't bear another failure; therefore, if time was running out, I would have to be faster than time.

. . . **there's someone here who's in great danger and desperately needs you. . . .**

I returned to the property line, moving toward the place where the oaks overhung the stone wall.

Out of those tree shadows, the great black stallion suddenly rushed, reared over me, and carved the air with its hooves.

Astride the horse, the barefoot blonde pointed down at me as she had done the previous night. Instead of anguish, her face was now contorted with fear.

However afraid she might be to cross over to the Other Side, she had nothing to fear anymore in this world. I knew, therefore, that her terror must be for me, and that she had come to warn me of some threat more imminent than the vague danger of which Henry Lolam and Paulie Sempiterno had spoken.

As the jet-black stallion settled to all fours and whipped its long tail soundlessly from side to side, the woman shifted her attention from me to something behind me. Her face now seemed to be wrenched more with revulsion than with fear, and her mouth opened in a silent cry of horror.

I looked behind me, but I saw nothing more than the knee-high wild dry grass fired by morning sun and as golden as the woman's hair, the land sloping down to the north, and the first grove of oaks, this side of which I had earlier climbed the estate wall.

But the creepiest feeling possessed me, similar to the sensation that shivers through any of us upon discovering a letter from the IRS in the mail. I was overcome by the conviction that if only I tilted my head at a certain angle or possessed eyeglasses of precisely the right prescription, or could peer through the current sunlight to glimpse the dusk that was still many hours away, I would see what the ghost saw.

When I turned to the horse and its rider again, they no longer loomed over me. They were twenty feet away, at the edge of the woods. The woman gazed back at me, waving me toward her with her right arm, her gesture and her posture urgent.

No one knows better than I that reality is more complex than the five senses can discern. Our world with all its mysteries is a moon to another bigger and more mysterious world unseen, orbiting so close to the larger sphere that perhaps sometimes the curve of one passes through the curve of the other with no damage to either, but with strange effects.

Not daring to take the time to look back again, I ran toward the horse and rider.

Twelve

THE VAULTED CEILING OF THE CATHE-
dral of oaks was reminiscent of church windows, although there was more leading than stained glass,
more darkness than light, in the sun-gold and leaf-
green patterns that might have been an abstract de-
piction of Eden.

Trotting among the huge trees, the black horse almost vanished, revealed only by the sheen of its coat
as drizzles of light quivered across it. As I chased
after her, the woman remained easy to see, the white
silk gown blooming brightly when touched by sun,
still softly radiant even where gloom prevailed.

I don't know why shadow and light should play
across spirits, alternately obscuring and revealing
them, in the same way that they affect living people
and all things of this world. Ghosts have no sub-
stance either to reflect light or to provide a surface
onto which shadows could fall.

A psychiatrist might say that this quality of the apparitions proves that they are not otherworldly. He might suggest instead that they must be psychotic delusions and that I merely lack the wit to imagine them unaffected by light and shadows, which real spirits—supposing they existed—would surely be.

I wonder sometimes why those who theorize about the human mind can so easily believe in the existence of things they cannot see or measure, or in any meaningful way confirm as real—such as the id, the ego, the unconscious I—but nevertheless dismiss as superstitious those who believe the body has a soul.

The woman brought the horse to a halt beside a tree. When I caught up with her, she pointed straight up into the great oak's laddered limbs, clearly suggesting that I climb.

The fear in her face—fear for me—was no less visible in this sun-and-shadow-dappled realm.

Although in the past I had encountered malevolent spirits that sometimes went poltergeist on me, hurling everything from furniture to frozen turkeys, I could not recall one of the lingering dead attempting to deceive me. Deception seems to be a capacity they shed with their bodies.

Convinced that this woman knew of something horrendous that was bearing down on me, I scrambled to the tree and climbed. Trunk to limb, that limb to another, bark rough beneath my hands, I ascended to the first crotch, about fourteen feet above the ground.

When I peered down through the screening

branches, I could see part of the spot at which the horse and rider had been. They were not there now.

Of course, as spirits, they were free to be or not to be, and as neither the horse nor the woman could speak, they didn't have to ponder that choice in a soliloquy.

Wedged in the first crotch of the tree, I soon began to feel foolish. As a card-carrying member of the human species, I have within me a bottomless well of foolishness and a kind of perverse thirst for it. Just because I'd never met a spirit with the capacity to deceive didn't mean that all of them would, for the rest of my life, prove to be incapable of steering me wrong.

The lingering dead are generally a bummed-out bunch, more often than not tethered to the place where they died. They aren't able to zip off to the multiplex to catch the latest Hollywood comedy of ill manners and to enjoy a thirty-dollar bag of free-range popcorn cooked in government-approved fish oil. After years of constant worrying about what waits for them on the Other Side, after clinging for so long to this world in the hope of seeing their mur-derers brought to justice, they really need some fun.

I could picture those two spirits, the woman and the horse, racing across Roseland, laughing heart-ily—if silently—at how easily they conned gullible Odd Thomas into scampering up a tree, sheltering there, and shivering in anticipation of a nonexistent boogeyman, when in fact the worst thing I really had to fear was being pooped upon by a bird on a higher branch.

Then the boogeyman arrived.

Boogeymen.

The first indication that I had not been duped by a ghost came when the faint bleachy smell sliced through the foliage, adding its sharp edge to the soft fragrances of the oak bark and the green leaves and the weather-split acorns that still hung like damaged ornaments in the tree.

Although the ozone odor was far less pungent here than in the stable, it was no less out of place. In the open air, it wasn't as likely to intensify to the degree that it did in a closed room. But I had little doubt that, just as before, this smell was a herald of something weirder and more dangerous than spirits of the dead.

A swift change in the quality of light solidified my expectation of another encounter with the stinky pack that could see in the dark. The golden morning sunshine twinkling in the gaps between the leaves became yellow-orange as its angle of origin shifted east to west.

I might not be able to understand the inscrutable stuff that half the people I meet say to me, but I am reliably dead-on when I anticipate mayhem. If I could find a national competition of confused and paranoid psychics, I would win the trophy and retire.

Carpeted with the small, oval, dry leaves of the

live oaks, the woods didn't allow any living thing to pass through quietly. Anyway, the pack that had hoped to extract me from the feed bin was not in the least concerned with stealth. They arrived in a blundering rush, so boisterously tramping across the sheddings of the trees that the crunching-crackling masked any snarling and snorting in which they might have been engaged.

I squinted this way and that, through the layered foliage, but what limited views I had of the ground revealed nothing useful about the recent arrivals. The oaks threw down more darkness than before, and the jack-o'-lantern light did not thrust through the limbs in crisp blades as had the morning sun, but fluttered through, fitful and sullen, as if a breeze that I could not feel fanned flames that I could not see, blowing reflections of fire through the woods.

Of the pack, nothing was visible except shadowy shapes, some of them swift but others lurching, all of them agitated and seeming to be urgently seeking something. Most likely they were not searching for maidens of good reputation to marry and to have children who would spend long evenings with them, hearthside, playing flutes and violins in family musicales.

Both the lithe and the clumsy among them followed the same erratic path through the oaks, as though they were crazed, weaving away to the east, to the north, then south. Their frantic progress was easy to track by the trampling of a million dry oak leaves.

Each time they drew near, I could again hear their grunting and growling as in the stable. But to me on my high perch, those guttural noises had a somewhat different character from what I thought that I had heard through the screened ventilation holes of the feed bin.

They were still like the sounds that animals made, but they were not only animal in nature. I thought that I heard a human quality in some of these exclamations: a wordless expression of desperation, a pathetic whine of anxiety that I might have unconsciously issued myself in a moment of great stress and danger, and a tortured snarl of anger that wasn't mere animal rage but expressed a bitter, brooding resentment suggestive of emotions that come only with intelligence.

The air was not cold. My light sweater and jeans were adequate to the day. A chill crept through me nonetheless.

This was as much a mob as it was a pack.

An animal pack is a group of individuals, all sharing much the same personality of their species, operating according to their best instincts and the habits of their kind.

On the other hand, a mob of people is disorderly and lawless. They are stirred to a peak of excitement not by the hunt, as is an animal, not by a worthy need for sustenance, but by an **idea** that might be true or a lie—and that is most often the latter. When it is an evil idea, which a lie always must be, those swept up by it are immeasurably more dangerous than any animal that ever lived upon the Earth in all its history. People in a lie-driven mob are savage, cruel, and capable of such violence that a mere lion would flee from them in terror, and a fierce crocodile would seek the safety of swamp waters.

Judging by the sound of them, there were many more here than had been in the stable, perhaps a score of them or even twice that.

A greater urgency informed their actions, too. By the moment, the sounds they made suggested that they were driving themselves into a frenzy of such intensity that nothing could appease them but blood and plenty of it.

Three times they had rushed past the tree in which I hid, and their sense of smell—or whatever other perception served them best—had thus far failed them. As they poured past a fourth time, I still could see nothing of the beasts except shadows that seemed to promise fantastic deformities as they jostled one another in their eagerness to find me.

Already the yellow-orange sunlight was beginning to turn deep orange. I wasn't likely to get a better look at these creatures unless they took their search vertical and came face-to-face with me in my oaken redoubt.

What we fear too much we often bring to pass.

They were almost gone away to the north of the woods when abruptly they turned back. These things of shadow, half-perceived sinister shapes, flowed around the tree, like a sea tide washing around a pinnacle of offshore rock.

The last of them lapped into place, and the crackle of leaves splitting underfoot ceased. They went mute, as well, as hushed as those monsters that hide under a child's bed and, by their perfect silence, tempt him to feel safe enough to lean out, lift the covers, and look under.

I was not tempted to feel safe. They had found me.

Thirteen

BEING TREED WAS NOT AS HOPELESS AS being boxed in a feed bin. Because I had escaped the latter, I thought I might survive this predicament in the oak.

Having been mostly jobless since I left Pico Mundo, having recently become rootless, I had no health insurance. Consequently, I was motivated not merely to live but also to avoid hideous disfigurement that the state was too bankrupt to have repaired for me and that would require me to live in the subcellar of an opera house. I've never much cared for opera, but jazz clubs don't have subcellars.

In the open air, the aggregate stench of the crowd around the oak didn't induce nausea as rapidly as in the stable, but I pinched my nose and breathed through my mouth. The smell wasn't as lovely as stale sweat and rotten breath; I thought they must also have stink glands, like skunks, except that skunks were considerate enough to limit their malodor to their spray, while these things seemed to ooze it continually from every pore.

Squint as I might, I could not see the true forms or the faces of those gathered below and, presumably, gazing up at me. Again, dusk had come too early, long before noon. The dwindling light grew red-orange. Where it lay like a radiant dust upon the figures at the base of the oak, it revealed nothing, as if I were studying them through a pair of infrared goggles in which the batteries were nearly dead.

And then as the darkness slowly deepened, their eyes began to glow. Pink at first and almost pretty, like little fairy lights, they rapidly became as red as I imagined the eyes of wolves might be at night, although these creatures were nothing as endearing as wolves.

In the past, I had found myself pitted against murderers, serial killers, drug dealers, crooked cops, a misguided former billionaire and monk, kidnappers, terrorists, and others who at some point in their lives had slipped or been dragged, or plunged gleefully, into the dark side. I don't do battle against vampires and werewolves for the simple reason that they don't exist.

Nevertheless, gazing down through the oak branches at the red-eyed mob, I was tempted to picture a few dozen escapees from a young-adult novel who were looking for blood and new girlfriends.

Whatever they were, however, I sensed that they wouldn't be sufficiently good-looking to get dates for the prom.

There was a reasonably good chance that these beasts were not climbers. Mountain lions can climb, but coyotes can't. Bears can climb, but wolves can't. Squirrels are great at it, rabbits embarrass themselves trying. I might merely have to wait out these creatures until this strange twilight relented, as it had done before.

One of them began to climb.

Abandoning the first crotch of the tree, I scampered up as quickly as a boy playing monkey.

Glancing down, I was heartened to see that my pursuer—no more than a shadowy form—was struggling to ascend. It seemed to be poorly equipped for climbing. Judging by its growls, its squeals of rage, and the furious thrashing of greenery, the thing regarded the tree as a conscious adversary that was willfully thwarting it, and it retaliated by smashing at the branches and shaking from them great sprays of leaves.

The higher I went, the less foliage between me and the sky, the better the light should have become. But this sun sought the sea as fast as a burning ship that had taken cannonballs through its hull.

In a couple of minutes, I would have no light at all. Feeling my way blindly through an oaken maze, high above the earth, seemed as sure a way to die as any.

Before I ran out of twilight, I began to run out of tree. These higher limbs were less formidable than lower ones, and they sagged treacherously. My feet slipped frequently, and my hands ached from gripping with such intensity.

I halted and eased down to sit with my back against the much-diminished main trunk. I straddled a limb that didn't offer much of a butt rest and that would restore to me a boys'-choir voice if my weight suddenly shifted.

Even over my rough breathing, I could hear thrashing far below, as the infuriated creature tried to ascend by beating the oak into submission. I took comfort that its IQ, while no doubt high enough to allow it to run for elective office, seemed to be only a fraction of mine.

The ozone odor remained with me, faint but persistent. At what must have been a height of sixty feet, however, I could smell nothing of the mob below.

A minute or two later, that stink began to rise to me once more, and I realized that the climber must be making progress, after all.

Darkness took the sky above, and for a moment I could only feel and imagine the black limbs of the oak, not see them.

The loss of light didn't bring the beast below to a halt. It continued to thrash vigorously through the resisting tree, snapping branchlets, raising such commotion in the leaves as a squall of wind might have done. Grunts of satisfaction seemed to indicate that safe footing had been found, while snarls and squeals of frustration no doubt marked those moments when the way upward was neither obvious nor easy. Twice, an ugly wet chortling, disturbing and protracted, seemed to suggest that the thing was delighted by the prospect of tearing off my face, putting it on a kaiser roll with mustard, and eating it.

As the odor of the creature grew stronger, I began to feel like Jean Valjean in **Les Misérables,** except that instead of the implacable Inspector Javert, my pursuer was a red-eyed demonic mutant something.

The absolute darkness was now relieved by what appeared to be the light of a rising yellowish moon. The oak around me reappeared, though like a less than fully imagined tree in a dream. I remained unable to see the climber below.

I could no longer afford to wait for this unscheduled night to recede and to take the mysterious creatures with it, as happened in the stable. This event had already lasted longer than the first, and I had no reason to expect that in another minute I would find myself freed from the current weirdness and returned to the daylight of that kinder, gentler Roseland.

As the stench grew, I rose gingerly, pressing my back to the trunk, and gripped a branch above me, first with one hand, then with both. I turned on the limb to peer down into the quadrant of the great oak through which the thing was making its way.

The action I intended might result in losing my footing, losing my overhead grip, and plunging through battering, skewering phalanxes of limbs and branches with a cry far less triumphant than the cry with which Tarzan conquered jungles. But I could see nothing else to do but wait for the beast to appear below me and, as it attempted to clamber up to my level, kick it repeatedly in the face until it lost its grip—or bit off my foot.

Sometimes I wish I liked guns.

I've had to resort to them at times, but always with reluctance. The terrifying games that my disturbed mother played with a pistol when I was a boy have left me with an abiding aversion to firearms and a preference for simpler weapons—in this case as simple as my foot—that might sooner or later get me killed.

The singular stink had become nearly thick enough to make my eyes water, but the climber had not yet appeared, although the noise of its ascent was greater and closer.

Only when something swung around from the farther side of the oak onto my limb, behind me and slightly to my left, did I realize there had been at least one other climber in addition to the freak that I'd been tracking. It seized my right shoulder in one brutish hand, and I knew next would come a bite, a slash.

Before claws or teeth could draw blood, I thrust backward with my entire body. My feet slipped off the curve of bark—and treaded empty air. I was hanging only from the limb above my head, but with that sudden move I also knocked my attacker off the tree. Clutching fast to my shoulder was its only hope, but its terrible weight was such that I felt as if, in its grasp, my muscle might be separating from the shoulder bone. Pain shot up my arm and into my right hand, which slipped off the branch.

I hung now only by my left hand, but the abrupt change in my position jolted the creature clinging to me, and its hand—which felt poorly articulated, of limited dexterity—slipped off my shoulder. With a howl, the thing fell away and quickly had the howl knocked out of it as it slammed through the unforgiving architecture of the oak. The beast, of which I hadn't a single glimpse, must have crashed into the mob at the base of the tree, because shrieks of pain and outrage rose from below.

As those cries began to subside, the crepitation of a thousand long, leathery wings reverberated through the blind-dark woods. The swarm, most likely the same that I had seen descending out of the northwest the previous evening, seethed among the oaks, attacking the beasts below, who squealed in terror.

As I restored my two-hand grip on the overhead limb and began to swing gently back and forth in the hope of regaining my footing, I steeled myself against the likelihood that one of the immense bats—if that's what they were—would soar up through the branches below me and tear off a piece of my face. At the taste of me, it would call up others of its kind, and an Odd feast would begin.

I regained my footing, not expecting to keep it long. But as I shivered, listening to the tumult and the screaming below, I dared to hope that the prey at ground level might be so plentiful that the flock, the colony, whatever it should be called, would be satiated by what it killed on the woodland floor.

From a TV documentary, I remembered a variety of bat that had curved incisors as sharp as razors and another variety that possessed claws so sharp and so precisely hooked that it could rip fish out of the water and fly away with them. Nature films can inspire as many nightmares as any blood-soaked monster movie ever made.

Abruptly the darkness ebbed as morning light once more flowed down over me and through the branches to the floor of the woods. The tide of sunshine washed away the creatures that the unnatural night had brought with it, as if they had never existed. As far as I could see, nothing dead or alive waited on the carpet of leaves below.

Fourteen

ALL IN WHITE AND IMMENSE, LIKE AN array of taut mainsails and topsails and staysails, Chef Shilshom seemed about to glide away wherever the wind might carry him. But the kitchen, of course, was windless, and the chef was intent upon adding to a pile of eyes on the cutting board beside the sink, where he was blinding several pounds of potatoes before peeling them.

My morning had been exhausting, especially as I'd eaten nothing but an almond croissant, and I needed to fill my fuel tank. "Sir, I don't want to bother you, but Roseland is taking a lot out of me today. I could use some protein."

"Mmmmm," he said, and pointed to a warm quiche on a cooling rack and to a fresh cheesecake to which the lemon glaze had recently been applied.

As a guest granted kitchen privileges, I could have made a ham sandwich or searched out a leftover chicken breast. Instead I cut and plated a wedge of the quiche **and** a slice of the cheesecake, and poured a glass of milk.

I don't worry about cholesterol. Considering my gift and the limited life expectancy it almost certainly ensures, my arteries will be as squeaky-clean as those of a newborn when I die, even if I eat nothing but ice cream at every meal.

Sitting on a stool at the island nearest to the chef, I watched him carve the faults out of the potatoes with an intensity that was a little disturbing. Tip of the tongue pinched between his teeth, plump cheeks rosier than usual, eyes slitted as if with contempt, and a fine dew of perspiration on his forehead all seemed to indicate that in his imagination he was cutting the eyes from something potentially more responsive than potatoes.

Since coming to Roseland, my attempts to get information out of Chef Shilshom had been relatively subtle, my approach for the most part oblique. That strategy hadn't gotten me anywhere. Earlier, over the croissant, I had been a bit bolder, and although I hadn't pushed him so hard as to make him spill a single secret, I had rattled him enough to expose his concealed hostility when his reflection in the window revealed him glaring at me behind my back.

Halfway through my wedge of quiche, I said, "Sir, do you recall earlier when I asked you about the horse I sometimes see?"

"Mmmmm."

"A black stallion, a Friesian."

"If you say so."

"Since Mr. Wolflaw keeps no horses, I thought it might belong to a neighbor, and you said perhaps it did."

"There you go."

"But I wonder, sir, how did the horse get through the front gate, with a guard there and everything?"

"How indeed?"

"Perhaps it climbed over the estate wall."

The chef could not easily pretend distraction when taunted with such absurdity. He glanced at me but then preferred to talk to the current potato that he was mutilating. "There haven't been horses here in many years."

"Then what did I see?"

"I wonder."

I finished the rest of my quiche and said, "Sir, did you notice an eclipse of the sun a short while ago?"

Now peeling the potatoes, he said, "Eclipse?"

"Day turning to night. Like a few thousand years ago people thought God was turning off the sun as punishment, so they went mad with fear and tore their hair out and sacrificed babies and lashed themselves with brambles and promised never to fornicate again, because they were ignorant, though that wasn't really their fault, considering that there wasn't either the History Channel or NatGeo back then, and maybe some of them tried to Google 'sun goes out' to learn what was happening, but they were way too far ahead of their time."

Peeling determinedly, Chef Shilshom said, "I don't understand you, Mr. Thomas."

"You aren't the first," I assured him.

I tried the cheesecake. It was delicious.

"Sir," I continued, "putting the mystery horse aside for a moment, do you know of an animal in these parts that is at least the size of a man, perhaps larger, with crimson eyes that glow in the dark and a really horrendous odor?"

The chef had been taking the skin off a potato in a single long ribbon, as if he collected spud peels the same way that some people collected string in giant balls that grew as big as automobiles. But partway through my question, his hand faltered, and a prematurely severed peel unraveled into the sink.

I doubt that Sherlock Holmes was my great-grandfather, but I deduced that the incident of the severed peel indicated Chef Shilshom knew the stinky animals to which I referred. He appeared alarmed by what I'd said, and intent on concealing his concern.

He at once continued peeling, but he took so long to decide on his response that his anxiety became more apparent. Finally he said, "Horrendous odor?"

"Very stinky, sir."

"As large as a man?"

"Yes, sir. Maybe larger."

"What did they look like?"

"I only ran into them in the dark."

"But still you must have seen something of them."

"No, sir. It was very dark."

He relaxed a little. "We have no animals that big in these parts."

"What about bears?"

"Well."

"California black bears?"

He said, "Mmmmm."

"Maybe the bears climbed the estate wall to kill and eat all the mountain lions."

The slippery potato popped out of his hand and thumped around the stainless-steel sink.

"Could it be bears?" I pressed, though I knew it hadn't been anything as cuddly as the killing machine that is a bear.

Having retrieved the potato, the chef began to peel again, but he lacked the composure with which he'd begun the chore. He hacked clumsily at that example of Idaho's finest, and I felt embarrassed for him.

"Maybe you should stay in at night, Mr. Thomas."

After skinning the rest of the potato in a most unfortunate manner, the chef dropped it in a large pot half filled with water.

I said, "The first time I ran into them was in the stable, this morning, about half an hour after dawn."

He picked up another spud and went at it as though he despised everything Idahoan and was particularly infuriated by potatoes.

"The second time," I said, "was just twenty minutes ago, in a grove of oak trees, where it got so dark I thought there must be an eclipse."

"That doesn't make sense, Mr. Thomas."

"It didn't make sense to me, either."

"There was no eclipse."

"No, sir, I guess not. But there was something."

Watching him, I finished the slice of cheesecake.

Dropping the second potato in the pot, putting down the peeler, Chef Shilshom said, "My medication."

"Sir?"

"I forgot to take it," he said, and he left the kitchen by the hallway door.

At the back sink, I rinsed my plate, fork, and glass. I put them in the dishwasher.

The food lay heavy in my stomach, and I felt as if I had eaten my last meal.

. . . there's someone here who's in great danger and desperately needs you. . . .

Mentally reciting Annamaria's words, hoping to engage my psychic magnetism as I had tried to do before I'd been warned into the tree by the mute rider on the spirit horse, I wandered across the kitchen and left it by one of the two swinging doors that served the butler's pantry.

I passed through the formal dining room, the cozy informal drawing room that was a fraction the size of the main drawing room, and along a paneled hallway, past closed doors that I had no impulse to open.

More than once in the past couple of days, the layout of the great house had confused me, not

merely because of its size but also because its architect seemed to have invented a new geometry with a
previously unknown dimension that frustrated my
memory. Rooms proved to be connected in ways
that repeatedly surprised me.

By the time I arrived at the library, by a route that
I would not have thought could bring me there, two
things puzzled me: the depth of the silence in the
great house, and the absence of staff. No vacuum
cleaner in a distant room. No voices. No one mop-
ping limestone floors or polishing mahogany floors,
or dusting furniture.

The previous day, I had for the first time availed
myself of the invitation to treat the ground level of
the house as my own home, and had spent some
time in both the card room and the fully equipped
gym. I had encountered only the head housekeeper,
Mrs. Tameed, and a maid named Victoria Mors.

Now, as I stood on the threshold of the library,
wondering at the stillness in the house, I realized
that neither the housekeeper nor the maid had been
engaged in any obvious labor when I had come upon
them. They had been standing in the card room, in
the middle of an intense conversation. Although I
apologized for interrupting them in their work and
intended to leave, they assured me that they had
finished the task at hand and had chores elsewhere.
They had left at once, but I hadn't considered, until
this moment, that neither had with her any cleaning
supplies or even as much as a dust rag.

A house as large as this one—with its ornate moldings, carved-marble fireplaces, richness of architectural details, and room after room of antique furnishings—should keep Mrs. Tameed and half a dozen maids bustling from morning till night. Yet although the house was immaculate, I had encountered only the two of them, and I had yet to see either woman working.

Crossing the threshold, I found the library deserted. The large, rectangular room was wrapped by laden bookshelves except for a few windows covered with heavy brocade draperies. I didn't pause to read the titles on any of the thousands of spines, didn't settle in an armchair. Guided by psychic magnetism, I went directly to the open staircase in the middle of the room.

Twenty feet overhead, the mahogany ceiling was deeply coffered. A five-foot-wide mezzanine encircled the room twelve feet above the floor.

The bronze spiral staircase featured a railing in which the balusters were wound through by beautifully wrought vines with gilded leaves. Perhaps it was meant to represent the tree of knowledge.

At the top of the stairs, a bridge connected the two longest sides of the mezzanine. Without hesitation, I went to the left. Upon reaching the end of the bridge, I turned right.

In the southwest corner of the mezzanine, set at an angle between the bookshelves, a heavy wooden door stood under a pediment surmounted by a bronze torch with a gilded flame. I passed through the door into a junction of second-floor hallways.

The invitation to enjoy the public rooms of the main house did not include the second floor. I was abusing the privilege granted to me. I didn't hesitate to do so. I don't think I'm really bad, but I'll admit to being naughty.

Considering that the head of security, Paulie Sempiterno, had so recently expressed the sincere desire to put a bullet in my face, my violation of Mr. Wolflaw's privacy might result in something worse than a stern lecture about good manners. Caution seemed essential.

As if the very thought of Sempiterno conjured him, his rough voice rose from behind one of the closed doors along the west wing, to my right.

Another voice, more worried and less angry than the security chief's, was unquestionably that of Chef Shilshom. He evidently had not gone to fetch a forgotten medication in his little apartment in the servants' wing on the ground floor.

A third voice, quieter than the other two, might have been that of Noah Wolflaw. His bedroom suite lay in the west wing.

I was able to hear only the louder words, but the tenor of the conversation was clearly argumentative. I imagined that Sempiterno wanted to grind me up in a wood-chipper, Shilshom wanted to roast me with onions and carrots before serving me as a peace offering to whatever red-eyed animals prowled Roseland, and Wolflaw couldn't bring himself to assent to my being either chipped or cooked because he was still enchanted by Annamaria for reasons that even he could not explain.

Although I was tempted to listen at the door, prudence and psychic magnetism turned me away from the voices. I proceeded along the south hallway, in the first half of which all the doors were on the right. Staying on the carpet runner, treading quietly, I was grateful that whatever power guided my feet had never required me to break into a lively dance.

Just before the south wing met the south end of the east wing, I was compelled to a door on the right. I hesitated with my hand on the knob, listening, but I heard no slightest sound beyond.

Entering, I discovered a parlor that was part of a bedroom suite. In a wingback chair sat a boy with wide, staring, all-white eyes that seemed blinded by thick cataracts.

Fifteen

WHEN THE CHILD DID NOT REACT TO me in any way, I quietly closed the door to the hall and stepped farther into the room.

His hands lay in his lap, palms upturned. His lips were slightly parted. Motionless, silent, he might have been dead or comatose.

The parlor and the connecting bedroom that I glimpsed through an open door were not furnished or decorated to the taste of a young boy of eight or nine. A white ceiling of ornate plaster medallions depicting clusters of bristling arrows, walls hung with tapestries featuring complexly patterned borders around scenes of stag hunts, English furniture of a period I couldn't identify, numerous bronzes of hunting dogs on tables and consoles, and a Persian rug in rich shades of gold and red and brown were decidedly masculine but better suited to a man with decades of sporting pursuits behind him than to a boy of tender years.

The draperies were closed over the windows, and the light came from a table lamp by the sofa and a floor lamp beside the armchair, both with pleated silk shades. Shadows gathered in the corners, but I was confident that the child was alone.

I approached him without eliciting a response and stood staring down at him, wondering about his condition.

The terrible blank eyes were so white that the cataracts allowed no slightest suggestion of the irises and pupils beneath. He appeared to be totally blind.

Although I couldn't hear him inhale or exhale, his chest rose and fell slightly. His breathing was slow and shallow.

Except for those eerie eyes, he was a good-looking boy with clear pale skin, refined features that suggested he would grow quite handsome in time, and thick dark hair. He might have been a bit small for his age; the armchair dwarfed him, and his feet didn't reach the floor.

I thought I saw in his features a suggestion of the horse-riding woman, but I could not be certain.

. . . there's someone here who's in great danger and desperately needs you. . . .

I believed that I had found the person of whom Annamaria had spoken—and the son of the ghost rider. I didn't know the nature of the danger, however, or what I could do for the boy.

His upturned left hand twitched and the heel of

his left shoe bumped twice against the front of the armchair as if a doctor had rapped his kneecap to test his reflexes.

I said, "Can you hear me?"

When he did not reply, I sat on the ottoman in front of his chair. After watching him for a while, I reached out and took hold of his right wrist to time his pulse.

Although he was at rest and breathing slowly, his heart raced: 110 beats per minute. But there was nothing irregular in the rhythm, and he seemed in no serious distress.

His skin was so cold that I pressed his right hand between both of mine to warm it.

He did not at first react, but suddenly his fingers clutched me and squeezed tight. A small gasp escaped him, and he shuddered.

Cataracts were not his problem, after all. His eyes had been rolled farther back in his head than I would have thought possible. The irises descended. They were ginger-brown and clear.

Initially he seemed to stare through me, at something far beyond this room. Gradually his focus changed, and he looked at me, though not with surprise, as though we knew each other or as if nothing could amaze or perplex him in spite of his youth and inexperience.

His fingers relaxed their grip on me, and he withdrew his hand from mine. His frost-pale skin gradually began to color as though with reflected flames, although the nearby fireplace was dark and cold.

"Are you all right?" I asked.

He blinked a few times and surveyed the room, as if reminding himself where he was.

"My name's Odd Thomas. I'm staying in the guesthouse."

His attention returned to me. His stare was unnervingly direct, especially for a child. "I know."

"What's your name?"

Instead of answering, he said, "They told me I've got to keep to my rooms as long as you're here."

"Who told you?"

"All of them."

"Why?"

He got up from the chair, and I rose from the ottoman. He went to the fireplace and stood there, staring through the fire screen at the logs stacked on the brass andirons.

After deciding that he might not say any more without being pressed, I asked again, "What's your name?"

"Their faces melt off their skulls. And their skulls turn black when the air touches them, and all their bones black. And then the black blows away like soot, there isn't anything left of them."

The pitch of his voice was that of a boy, but seldom if ever had I heard a child speak so solemnly. And more than solemnity, there was a quality to his speech that chilled me, a sadness that might be despondency, the incapacity for the present exercise of hope, perhaps not yet despair but just one stop up the line from that worse condition.

"Maybe twenty girls in uniforms and kneesocks," he continued, "walking to school. One second to the next, their clothes are on fire, and their hair, and when they try to scream, flames fly out of their mouths."

I moved to him and put one hand on his slender shoulder. "A nightmare, huh?"

Gazing into the cold firebox, as if seeing burning schoolgirls instead of logs or andirons, he shook his head. "No."

"A movie, a book," I said, trying to understand him.

He looked up at me. His eyes were lustrous and dark—and no less haunted by something than Roseland was haunted by the spirit rider and her horse.

"You better hide," he said.

"What do you mean?"

"It's almost nine o'clock. That's when she comes back."

"Who?"

"Mrs. Tameed. She comes back at nine o'clock to get my breakfast tray."

Glancing toward the door, I heard a noise in the hallway.

"You better hide," the boy repeated. "If they know you've seen me, they'll kill you."

Sixteen

PAULIE SEMPITERNO HAD SAID HE wanted to put a bullet in my face because he didn't like it. Having looked in a mirror often enough, I could understand that motive. But I could not imagine why I should have earned a death sentence merely because I'd seen the boy on the second floor. Although the child was strange, I at once believed his dire warning.

When I fled the parlor through the connecting door to the next room, I saw that the bed was made, which meant Mrs. Tameed might not need to go farther than the front room. But then I spotted the boy's breakfast tray on a small table, on which also was a stack of books.

Through another doorway, I glimpsed a bathroom. Windows in bathrooms were usually too small to serve as escape routes, which left the tub drain.

As I peered into a walk-in closet, I realized it was no safer than the bathroom. I heard Mrs. Tameed, in the other room, ask the boy if he had finished breakfast, and I stepped into this last possible refuge, leaving the door ajar an inch.

In **Rebecca,** both book and movie, the head housekeeper, Mrs. Danvers, was a walking hatchet in a long black dress, and you knew the first time she came on scene that eventually she was going to chop someone or set the house on fire.

Mrs. Tameed had not graduated from that school of dour and secretive servants. Six feet tall, blond, solid but not plump, with hands that looked strong enough to massage Kobe cattle after they'd been fed their grain and beer, she had a generous smile and one of those open Scandinavian faces that seemed incapable of expressions that were deceitful. Although you might not have thought her a woman who could keep terrible secrets, you would have seen in her, as I did, something of an Amazon who, handed a dagger and a broadsword, would have known how to use them to deadly effect.

When she entered the boy's bedroom, she didn't merely walk but **strode** to the table to collect the breakfast tray, shoulders back and head high, as if even this mundane chore was of great import.

Appearing behind her in the doorway, the boy said, "I want to talk to him about more privileges."

"He isn't of a mind to speak with you," Mrs. Tameed said, and her voice was cool, not dismissive but firm and without a trace of deference, as if the child must be far lower than she was in the social structure of Roseland.

The sweet choirboy voice was a generation younger than the words delivered in it: "He has an obligation, a responsibility. He thinks no rules apply to him, but no one is above everything."

Tray in hand, the housekeeper said, "Listen to yourself, and you'll hear why he won't speak with you."

"He brought me here. If he won't speak with me any longer, then he should at least take me back."

"You know what being taken back would mean. You don't want that."

"I might. Why wouldn't I?"

"If you hope to speak with him, you need to take another tack. He won't believe for a minute that you want to be taken back."

When she advanced on him, the boy retreated, and the two of them disappeared into the parlor.

Easing open the closet door, I heard her say to him, "Remember, keep the draperies shut and stay away from the windows."

"What would it matter if the visitor saw me?"

"It might not matter, but we can't take any chances," Mrs. Tameed said. "You talk about responsibilities. If we had to kill him and the woman, you would be responsible for their deaths."

"Why should I care?" the boy said, sounding petulant and more like a child than he had previously.

"You shouldn't care. You should be above caring about their kind, as we are. Maybe you're not. You're . . . different, after all."

"If it's such a risk to have them here, why did he invite them?" the boy asked, and I knew the man of whom he'd been speaking must be Noah Wolflaw.

"Damn if I know," Mrs. Tameed said. "None of us understands it. He says the woman intrigues him."

"What does he want to do to her?" the boy asked, and in his tone was a lascivious insinuation that was too knowing for his age.

"I don't know that he intends to do anything to her," said Mrs. Tameed. "But he can do anything he wants to the bitch, as I can, as any of us can, and that's no business of yours, you runt."

"Were you always such a snake," the child asked, "or did you grow into what you are?"

"You little shit. Talk to me too much that way, I'll stake you out in the fields some night and let the freaks do what they want with you."

This threat silenced the boy, and I figured that the freaks were the creatures who magically brought an enveloping darkness with them wherever they went.

Being called a snake inspired the housekeeper to spit out a bit more venom before she left: "Maybe the freaks will bugger you a few times before they chew your face off."

If there had been a Mr. Tameed and if he had been of a kind with his wife, I imagined that their marriage bed must have been as filled with love as any dog-fighting pit.

Mrs. Tameed got in one last shot, more enigmatic than her other insults: "You're just a dead boy. You aren't one of us and you never will be, **dead boy.**"

The door between the parlor and the hallway closed emphatically, but I didn't at once leave the closet. I waited for the boy to tell me that Mrs. Tameed was definitely gone.

After a couple of minutes, when he didn't appear, I cautiously returned to the parlor.

In defiance of the housekeeper's orders, he had drawn aside the draperies at one of the windows and stood gazing out at the southern vista, which included the gardens and the stepped cascades of water leading up to the mausoleum on the hilltop. He did not respond to my return. The color had gone out of his face, which was now as pale as it had been when I'd found him in some kind of trance with his eyes rolled back in his head.

"What did she mean—'dead boy'?"

He didn't answer.

"Is it a threat? Do they intend to kill you?"

"No. It's just the way she is. It doesn't mean anything."

"I think it does. And I think **you** know it does. I'm here to help you. What's your name?"

He shook his head.

"I can help you."

"No one can."

"You want out of here," I said.

He only stared at the distant mausoleum.

"I'll get you out of Roseland, to the authorities."

"Impossible."

"Over the wall. It's easy."

He turned his head to look at me. Sorrow didn't merely pool in his melancholy eyes, but radiated from them, so that in meeting his stare, I felt my heart grow heavier.

"They know where I am at all times," the boy said, and he drew back the left cuff of his sweater, revealing what looked too much like a manacle to be a wristwatch.

When I went to him and examined the item, I saw that it was locked on his wrist, the keyhole somewhat like that on a handcuff. The bulk was greater than a watch. Considering the slenderness of the wrist that it encircled, the stainless-steel restraint appeared cruel, although his skin was not chafed.

"It's a GPS monitor," he said. "If I leave this suite, they'll be warned immediately by a tone that sounds throughout the house. And at the gatehouse. And through the walkie-talkies the security men carry with them. If I leave the second floor, a different tone sounds, and a third tone if I leave the house."

"Why are they keeping you here?"

Instead of answering, he said, "They can track my movements on a map of the house and grounds that displays on their cell phones. As soon as I step off the second floor, someone shows up to stay at my side wherever I go."

More closely studying the tracking device, I said,

"Yeah, it looks kind of like a handcuff lock. I know something about them. I can probably pick it with a paper clip."

"If you try, an alarm goes out, just like when I leave this suite."

When I raised my eyes to meet his, he stared at me through unshed tears.

"I won't fail you," I said, but the promise sounded arrogant, like a challenge to Fate, and I thought I was more likely to fail him than to free him.

Seventeen

I WORRIED THAT RESCUING THIS BOY would be more difficult if he was discovered to have disobeyed his keepers' instructions. I drew shut the draperies.

"We don't have to get you out of Roseland. We just have to get the police in. They might think I'm a crank, but I have a good friend who's the chief of police in Pico Mundo. He'll believe me, and he'll get the attention of the authorities here."

"No. Not the cops. That would be . . . the end of everything. You don't understand who I am."

"So tell me."

He shook his head. "If you knew, the people here . . . they'd kill you deader than dead."

"I'm tougher than I look."

Maybe he wanted to laugh in my face, but instead he returned to the armchair in which he had been sitting when I first found him.

Once more I sat upon the ottoman. "You told Mrs. Tameed that he brought you here and should at least take you back. Who do you mean?"

"Him. Who else but him? It's all because of him."

"Noah Wolflaw?"

"**Wolflaw**," he said, and the contempt with which he spoke the name suggested a lifetime of distilled bitterness that a mere boy should not have accumulated.

"Brought you here. Do you mean kidnapped?"

"Worse than kidnapped."

He seemed to have taken inscrutability lessons from Annamaria.

Knowing too well the depths of evil to which some human beings can descend, I steeled myself for his answer when I asked, "Why does Wolflaw want you here? What does he . . . expect from you?"

"I'm his toy. Everyone's a toy to him." His voice quavered, and under the contempt that flowed through his words, there seemed to be another quite different river of emotion that was closer to sadness than to anger, a sense of tragic loss.

I remembered Henry Lolam at the gatehouse, suggesting that Noah Wolflaw wanted Annamaria's baby for "sensation" . . . for "thrills."

My chest tightened and my throat seemed thick with phlegm, but it was disgust that choked me, disgust and an aversion to hearing this boy speak of abominations.

"I know what Hell is," he said, and he seemed to shrink into the depths of the wingback chair. "Hell is Roseland."

After a hesitation, I asked, "He . . . touches you?"

"No. It's not that kind of thing he wants from me."

I was relieved in one regard but was forced now to consider what might be worse than my worst fear for him.

The boy said, "I'm here because he had one moment of remorse."

That was an unlikely thing for a child to say, and it was also enigmatic.

Based on our conversation thus far, I doubted that I could squeeze a clarification from him.

Before I could even try to press him for an explanation, he said, "Now he keeps me here to reassure himself that there aren't any limits to what he can do."

Frustrated by both the restrictions imposed upon him—and me—by the GPS transponder on his left wrist and by his unwillingness to be forthcoming, I said, "I only want to help you."

"I only wish you could."

"Then help me help you. Where did he take you from? How long has he kept you? What's your name? Do you remember your parents, their names, the address of your house?"

At that moment, his ginger-brown eyes seemed to have remarkable depth, unlike any they had possessed previously, unlike any eyes I'd ever seen, a plumbless lonely deepness into which it seemed dangerous to stare, as if I might see a despair so singular that, like the face of a Gorgon, it would turn me to stone.

"Your hair is dark, but your mother was a blonde."

He stared at me but said nothing.

"She had a great black Friesian that she adored. And she rode it well."

"Whoever you are, maybe you already know too much," the boy said, seeming to confirm what the spirit had conveyed to me. "You better not speak of her to any of them. Leave while he still might let you go. Which isn't much longer. If you think there's no danger to you . . . then go to the mausoleum. In the mosaic, press the shield that the guardian angel holds high."

His eyes rolled up into his head until his gaze was as blind as that of a white-marble statue. His hands slid off the arms of the chair and turned palms-up in his lap.

Perhaps he could fall away into this trance state by an act of will or perhaps this condition overcame him like a seizure comes upon an unmedicated epileptic. I suspected, however, that he had chosen to voyage inward—if that was where his attention went—and thereby to dismiss me.

For a while, I watched him. He was not going to return by his choice, and it seemed pointless to shake him out of his trance and try to force him to cooperate with me.

I had not imagined that when I found the person who desperately needed me, he would reject my help.

Before leaving, I inspected the bedroom more thoroughly than I had been able to do when rushing to hide from Mrs. Tameed. Like the parlor, this chamber seemed to be furnished and decorated for a grown man. The theme was hunting and hounds. No toys. No comic books. No movie posters. No video-game console. No television.

Hardcover books were stacked not only on the breakfast table from which the housekeeper had retrieved the tray, but also on one nightstand and on the dresser. The authors were not those in which a nine-year-old would immerse himself: Faulkner, Balzac, Dickens, Hemingway, Graham Greene, Somerset Maugham. . . .

My immediate suspicion was that these weren't the child's private quarters, that he lived here with someone. But the walk-in closet and the dresser contained clothing only for a young boy. In the bathroom, a single toothbrush, as well as the lack of an electric razor and other adult-grooming aids, supported what I had found in the bedroom.

In the parlor once more, I stood over him, as baffled as I was worried. He looked so vulnerable, and I knew that I must help him, but he seemed to be as jealous of his secrets as were all the others in Roseland.

To encourage me and Annamaria to leave the estate sooner than later, he had given me a clue to follow at the mausoleum.

Suddenly I recalled something that Paulie Sempiterno had said after he decided not to shoot me in the face: **Whatever you're looking for in Roseland, you'll find its opposite. If you want to live, look for death.**

I intended to go directly to the mausoleum, where the only dead were neatly packaged as ashes in urns. Or so I thought.

Eighteen

CAUTIOUSLY I MADE MY WAY DOWN through the great house to the kitchen again, but I might as well have gone singing and dancing, because no one seemed to be in residence. Chef Shilshom had not yet returned to his potatoes, and I wondered if the conference in Noah Wolflaw's quarters was still under way.

Outside, as I crossed the south terrace toward the arc of steps that led up to the fountain, I saw the groundskeeper, Mr. Jam Diu, farther up the slope, on the lawn between the stepped cascades. A stocky man with the smooth pleasant face of a Buddha, he might have been Vietnamese, but I didn't know for sure because we'd spoken only once and briefly, when I complimented him on the landscaping and he complimented me on having the taste to recognize his perfect work.

Mr. Diu possessed perhaps the only sense of humor among the residents of Roseland, and if the events of the day became steadily more grim—which was a good bet—I might seek him out in hope of a laugh or two.

At the moment, he had no wheelbarrow or gardening tools. He appeared to be studying the carpet-smooth lawn, perhaps looking for a tuft of crabgrass to annihilate.

I was free to visit the mausoleum, which I'd done before, but I did not at this point want Mr. Diu to engage me in conversation and possibly follow me inside. With him in tow, I wouldn't be free to press the angel's shield in the glass-tile mural, which the boy had suggested that I do.

Departing the terrace, I initially headed east, then changed course once I was out of view of the groundskeeper and the house. I intended to approach the mausoleum from the south.

No sooner had I put them both out of sight than I was halted by the realization that during the previous two days and so far in this one, I'd never seen Mr. Jam Diu performing any landscape maintenance. Neither had I seen a single member of what I assumed must be a full-time crew of six or seven landscape-maintenance personnel.

Not once had I heard a lawn mower. Or a leaf blower.

I recalled the immaculate interior of the house—where the only apparent housekeepers were Mrs. Tameed and Victoria Mors, who never seemed to be engaged in housework.

Those facts were connected. They meant something. For the moment, however, the meaning was no clearer to me than would have been a document written in braille.

Ahead of me, bordered on three sides by California live oaks, lay a long grassy fairway. At the midpoint stood a big lead sculpture of Enceladus, one of the Titans from classical mythology. He gazed into the sky and raised one fist in defiance.

The Titans had warred with the gods. They were crushed under the rocks that they piled high in an attempt to reach the heavens.

Ambition and stupidity are a dangerous combination.

Something about Enceladus struck me as wrong. When I drew close, I saw that he cast two opposing shadows, one darker and shorter than the other.

Not good. When this inexplicable condition had occurred before, at the stable, an impossible nightfall had brought forth a mob of the creatures that Mrs. Tameed called freaks.

Galleons of dark clouds were sailing in from the north, but most of the sky remained clear. The sun was well short of high noon.

I shaded my eyes with one hand and studied the shadows among the surrounding trees, expecting to see something of fantastic form and hostile intent. As usual, I felt watched. But any observers, if they existed, were well concealed.

As I watched, the east-leaning shadow shrank back

into the Titan, leaving only the darker and shorter shadow. Having begun to slip into disorder, Nature had now set itself right.

I can live with the lingering dead as long as they don't haunt and embarrass me while I'm in the bathroom. I'm more rattled by that occasional apparently supernatural event that is outside of my usual experiences, because I'm concerned that it will become a continuous part of my life. If I can't depend on sunrise and sunset to follow a reliable schedule, if everything at all times casts two opposed shadows, then perhaps tomorrow birds will bark and dogs will fly, and then certainly, a week from now, I will be one totally loco fry cook talking to pancakes on the griddle and expecting them to answer.

Leaving Enceladus, the Titan, who had been crushed like roadkill on the highway to Heaven, I continued to the end of that cul-de-sac of lawn.

Before entering the woods, I looked around, hoping that the ghost rider might appear and either assure me that the way was safe or warn me off. But my spirit guide lacked the reliability of Tonto as surely as I lacked the striking wardrobe and the sexy mask of the Lone Ranger.

I walked among the crowded oaks, where the shade was so deep that no underbrush or grass could grow. Gold coins of sunshine were scattered on the dark woodland floor, and on that bare and stoneless soil my footsteps were as nearly silent as those of a sneak thief.

The quiet halted me. The bare earth puzzled me. The doubloons of light made me realize there should also have been a wealth of dead leaves all around me.

I recalled the crunch-and-crackle of the mob of freaks rushing this way and that in the other hurst of oaks.

Live oaks are perpetually green, but they drop their small oval leaves all year, and in profusion. Even if Mr. Jam Diu and a crew of industrious elves had that very morning raked up, bagged, and carried away all that the trees had shed, a few score of recently cast-off dead leaves would already have littered the ground, but not one snapped underfoot. And there were no elves. And speculating from all available evidence, I didn't think that Jam Diu, in his position as groundskeeper, ever broke a sweat.

This grove of trees was associated with the formal landscaping of Roseland, which accounted for less than twenty of the fifty-two acres, and the other grove was in the wild fields of the estate. I could see no other difference between them that might explain this neatly swept earth.

The most important issue at hand, however, was not how the groundskeeper maintained the grove in such pristine condition or even why he felt it necessary to do so. I had to keep uppermost in mind the imprisoned boy.

Beyond the oaks, I climbed a meadow where the wild grass was in places waist-high. It had been bleached white-gold by the heat of the past summer. The rainy season had thus far been so dry that no storms had either beaten down the stiff parched grass or brought forth fresh green shoots.

At the top of the hill, I paused, looking southwest toward the mausoleum, which lay a few hundred yards away. After a moment to rest, I would have headed toward that building if movement at the periphery of vision hadn't drawn my attention.

From the crest of the hill, the land in general descended. But the ground fell and rose and fell again in a series of waves, like a golden sea frozen in one moment of motion after a storm, when the worst turbulence had passed but the swells remained formidable and the troughs were still deep.

Half concealed by the waist-high grass and foreshortened by the angle at which I viewed them, further camouflaged by virtue of being grub-white in the white-gold pasture, they came along a crest two waves of land below me. They numbered no fewer than twenty, no more than thirty, and they passed in a peculiar gait, swift yet shambling.

Some of them were hunchbacked, their heads thrust forward and seemingly deformed, though at that distance it was difficult to tell if the asymmetric appearance of their skulls was real or a trick of light and shadow. Their arms seemed improperly jointed, flailing almost spasmodically at the tall grass, like the long limbs of agitated orangutans.

The majority were erect, without humps between their shoulders, heads held high, skulls sleeker than those of their awkward brethren. These specimens appeared to move with greater grace and might have proceeded even more rapidly if not for the malformed individuals scattered among them, who by their very presence were a hindrance.

Most might have been about six feet, some taller, some shorter. From a distance they seemed to be muscular, brutish, and I had no doubt that they would be deadly adversaries.

This time they brought no twilight with them, but they seemed to see as well in sunshine as in the pitch dark. I was certain that these were the same creatures from which I'd hidden in the feed bin and high in the oak. At this remove, I couldn't hear them, but they looked as their growling and grunting and squealing had suggested that they might.

They disappeared off the crest, into a swale, moving away, and I let out a pent-up breath, relieved that it was my good fortune to have escaped their notice. I should have backed off the highest hill, on which I stood, but I was transfixed, waiting for another glimpse of them.

Fear slipped down my spine along vertebrae of ice. My mind seemed frozen with astonishment at what I'd seen, and my thoughts wouldn't thaw, wouldn't flow forward from the memory of that pack.

They appeared on another rise, heading toward a

farther crest. They were now at sufficient distance that they had the quality of a mirage, and so they might not really have faded away as they seemed to, but might only have disappeared into yet taller grass.

Although I had not seen them close enough to be sure of their appearance, I had certain impressions on which I felt that I could rely. The impression of long flat heads and blunt fleshy snouts. The impression of arms, and therefore of hands unseen. They were walking upright, in fact running, but they were not animals that should be able to run on fewer than four legs. Only primates could stand that erect— men, apes, gibbons, monkeys. . . . These creatures belonged to none of those species. I also thought I had seen short, pointed tusks that were dark against their pale faces, sharp tusks with which to wound and eviscerate, which made me think of wild boars. Boars, hogs, swine of some kind, their bodies recast in rough primate molds, their faces tortured and sick with violence. The malformed and crookbacked individuals were no doubt accepted because every member of their tribe, malformed or not, was to one degree or another an abomination.

They didn't reappear on the far slope, as if they dematerialized the way that ghosts sometimes do. But they were neither spirits nor figments of my imagination. Whether they were native to Roseland or were visitors who arrived and departed through some veil between this place and another realm beyond my understanding, they were surely to be avoided at all costs. They seemed to be perpetually on the move, like sharks, continually feeding, perhaps able to smell blood even when it was still safely circulating in the veins of their prey.

Nineteen

I DECIDED THAT A VISIT TO THE MAU-
soleum must be delayed. I backtracked down the
sloped meadow, through the oaks where no leaf had
yet been shed, and across the long yard, past Enceladus not yet crushed.

If I might die here this day, which seemed ever
more likely, there was something in my bedroom
that I needed to carry with me into death.

At the eucalyptus grove, I hurried along the flagstone path and arrived at the tower just as Noah
Wolflaw was leaving. I can't say which of us looked
the most alarmed, but he was the only one of us carrying a shotgun.

In ordinary times, if there ever were any in Roseland, Wolflaw was Mount Vesuvius in a quiet phase,
a solid figure of such calm demeanor that he seemed
as enduring as any lofty cloud-capped peak of granite. But you sensed his power, volcanic and always

pending, the energy that had made him such a successful and wealthy man.

Tall, large-boned, with flesh forged to his frame as if by a maker of armor, he was imposing even when he wasn't carrying a short-barreled, pistol-grip 12-gauge. The planes of his face were bold geometry, gray eyes set deep in perfectly elliptical sockets, nose a great isosceles wedge, chin a jutting plinth from which his jawbones rose like buttresses. His thick dark hair was a mane that any stallion or lion might have coveted. Only his mouth, full-lipped and yet seeming smaller than it should have been, encouraged you to imagine that inside this strong man might be a weak one.

"Thomas!" he declared upon seeing me.

He addressed me that way not with an imperious refusal to grant me a **mister,** but because he found my first name so peculiar that he felt uncomfortable using it. On the day we met, he informed me that he would treat my surname as my first because " 'Odd' makes me feel as if I'm spitting on you." He didn't seem to be a man of such delicate sensibilities that my name should trouble him, but perhaps he found himself uncharacteristically chivalrous and courtly in the company of Annamaria, who enchanted everyone she met.

Wolflaw's shotgun alarmed me nearly as much as had the recent encounter with the primate swine, but he didn't threaten me with it, as I half expected that he would.

Instead, he said, "How does she do what she does? And what is it that she does? I always talk to her with clear intent, and she answers in the most gracious way, yet I wind up bewildered, having either forgotten or abandoned my intentions."

He was speaking of Annamaria, of course, and I could only say, "Yes, sir, I sympathize. But I always have the feeling there's truth in everything she says and that I'll understand it in time. Maybe not tomorrow, maybe not next month, maybe not next year, but eventually."

"She's got that regal graciousness Grace Kelly used to have, though Grace Kelly was a real looker. You're probably so young you never heard of Grace Kelly."

"She was an actress. **Dial M for Murder, Rear Window, To Catch a Thief.** She married the prince of Monaco."

"You're not the clueless pup that some might take you for."

This was how he talked to me—and pretty much to everyone—when Annamaria wasn't present. "Thank you, sir."

As he spoke, he warily surveyed the eucalyptus grove around us, which was ribboned with shadows and sunshine that fashioned a kind of camouflage in which something might lurk and be difficult to see. "I came here to tell her the two of you have to leave. Today. Within the hour. Now. Do you know what she said to me?"

"I'm sure it was memorable."

His gray eyes were made for glaring, like stainless-steel blades going for the bone. "She told me that what I wish to see come to pass would not happen if the two of you left now, that you would leave in the morning at the earliest, when my purpose in bringing you here was fulfilled."

"Yes, that sounds like her."

"I've never before had a guest refuse to leave when told to." Anger creased his beetled brow, and when he leaned toward me, a beam of sunlight piercing the eucalyptuses seemed to lay a sharper edge on his steely stare. His voice was buttered with menace, and the threat slipped from him without hesitation: "If you presume to tell your host when you'll leave, maybe you'll **never** leave when all is said and done."

I didn't take his meaning to be that he feared we would stay forever. I took his meaning to be a promise of an urn and a niche in the mausoleum.

That was an extraordinary and revealing thing for him to have said. Pressure was building in Vesuvius.

"Who the hell does she think she is?"

"Did you ask her that, sir?" I wondered, because her answer was of interest to me, as well.

The steel went out of his eyes, the menace out of his voice, and he looked around the fragrant woods again, not as if worried that a pack of mutant swine was closing in this time, but as if he couldn't quite recall how he had wound up here.

"No. She did this trick with a flower, like an illusionist's act in Vegas or something." He seemed rattled by the memory of her bit of magic. "Have you ever seen her do the trick with the flower?"

Before I could reply, he rolled on.

"Suddenly, I hear myself telling her that of course she could stay, the two of you, stay as long as necessary, if that's what she wanted. I said I was just concerned about your welfare, you know, with the mountain lion on the prowl. And I apologized for being so thoughtless. I think I might even have kissed her hand. I never in my life kissed a woman's hand. Why would I kiss a woman's hand?"

He inhaled deeply, blew out a long exhalation of frustration, and shook his head as if astonished by his behavior.

He continued: "So she says you'll both leave when what I wish to see come to pass has happened, when my purpose for bringing you here is fulfilled—but what the hell purpose is she talking about?"

"**Your** purpose, sir."

"Don't be a smart-ass, Thomas."

"No, sir."

"I don't **know** why I brought her here. It was a crazy thing to do. Reckless. I don't want her. I told Paulie that I might want her, just as an excuse, because I didn't know how to explain myself, but he knew she wasn't my type."

"Mr. Sempiterno is very insightful."

"Shut up."

"Yes, sir. We'll be gone tomorrow," I promised.

Now he seemed to be talking more to himself than

to me: "I don't want her. She's disgusting, repellent, knocked up and bloated like a cow. Nothing to get a man's sap rising. I don't want anything to do with her, and I never will."

"We'll be gone tomorrow," I repeated.

His attention returned to me, and his too-small mouth puckered with distaste, as if I were something he would never want to find stuck to the sole of his shoe, let alone talking to him face-to-face. "You told Henry Lolam you met the one who calls himself Kenny. No one's seen him in years. You told Chef Shilshom you saw bears with red eyes."

"Maybe not bears, sir. Just something."

He swept the woods with his gaze again. Even with his hard but handsome face and steely eyes, he didn't look as strong as before, because a tremor worked his mouth.

"You see any of them in broad daylight?"

"No, sir," I lied.

"Night's one thing, daylight's a whole different ball game." He focused on me once more. "You're always picking at people, Thomas, always trying to get information out of them, picking and picking."

"I'm just a curious guy, sir. I always have been."

"Shut up."

"Yes, sir."

"Nothing here is any of your damn business. Do you hear me, Thomas?"

"Yes, sir. I'm sorry. I've abused your hospitality."

His scowl was even more impressive than his glare. "Are you being funny?"

"No, sir. If I say so myself, when I'm actually being funny, you'd find it hard not to laugh."

"When I say shut up, I mean shut up. Shut up."

"Yes, sir."

"Until you leave tomorrow, stay in the guest tower."

In consideration of the shotgun, I nodded.

"Stay in the tower, lock the doors, lock the windows, draw the draperies, and wait until morning."

I nodded.

Seeing my attention on the shotgun, he realized belatedly that he needed to explain it. "Thought I might do some skeet shooting."

He pushed past me on the flagstone path, and I started toward the tower door.

He said, "One other thing."

Turning to him, I was happy to see that the shotgun cradled in his arm was still pointed at the ground.

"There aren't phones in your rooms, but you've probably got a cell phone. I want you to understand, there's nothing here that the police would be interested in. You understand?"

I nodded. I didn't have a cell phone because I never needed to play video games or surf the Net, or exchange nude photos with a congressman.

"I'm well connected with the local authorities," Wolflaw said. "Better connected than you are with your own pecker. A couple of them were former security guards here. I've done a lot for them. I've done more for them than you could ever guess, and I can assure you that they won't take kindly to some worthless drifter bad-mouthing me. Is that clear?"

I nodded.

"You suddenly a dumb mute or something?"

"I understand, sir. About the cops. Stay in the tower, lock the doors, lock the windows, draw the draperies, don't call the cops or even the fire department if the place is burning down, but just wait until morning and then, come sunrise, keep on keepin' on right out the front gate."

He glared at me, his girly mouth puckered in contempt, and I figured that he might soon feel comfortable calling me Odd instead of Thomas, because he said, "You really are a shithead."

"Yes, sir. I'll tell Annamaria you said so."

We stared at each other, plenty of animosity on his end, mere curiosity on my end, until at last he said, "Listen . . . I'd rather you didn't."

"Didn't what?"

"I'd rather you didn't tell her. I don't know what's wrong with me. This is crazy. Does she have me hypnotized or something? Why the hell should I care if you tell her or don't tell her that I called you a shithead?"

"Then I'll tell her."

"Don't," he said at once. "I don't care what she thinks of me, she's nothing to me, she's as plain as a powdered doughnut without the powder. I don't want to do anything with a woman like her, but I'd rather you didn't tell her about my outburst."

"Strange, the way she affects people," I said.

"Extremely strange."

"I won't tell her."

"Thank you."

"You're welcome."

I watched him walk away through the eucalyptuses and up the vast sunlit lawn toward the main house. Even in the open, where nothing could sneak up on him, Wolflaw nervously looked left and right, and glanced back repeatedly. He was probably on guard for the mountain lion, listening for the cry of the loon, alert to the possibility that he might suddenly be confronted by the Jabberwock with eyes of flame and the frumious Bandersnatch.

Twenty

WHEN STORMY LLEWELLYN AND I were sixteen, we spent an evening at a carnival. In an arcade tent, we came across a fortune-telling machine the size of a phone booth, about seven feet tall. The lower three feet were enclosed, and in the glass case atop that base sat what a plaque claimed to be the mummified remains of a Gypsy woman, a dwarf who had been famous for her prognostications.

The withered, spooky figure—possibly a construct of plaster, paper, wax, and latex rather than a preserved corpse—was all tricked up in Gypsy gear. For a quarter she dispensed a small printed card in answer to your question. A quarter doesn't seem like much to charge for a life-changing prediction, but the dead can work cheap because they don't have to buy food or subscribe to cable TV.

A young couple who visited the machine ahead of us had asked if they would have a long and happy marriage. Although they gave Gypsy Mummy eight quarters, they never received an answer that seemed clear to them. Stormy and I heard the potential groom, Johnny, read all the answers to his girl, and although the fortune-teller's responses were oblique, they were perfectly clear to us. One of them was this: **The orchard of blighted trees produces poisonous fruit.** The others were no more encouraging.

After Johnny and his bride-to-be left in a snit, we asked Gypsy Mummy the question that the other couple had posed. Into the brass tray slid a card that read YOU ARE DESTINED TO BE TOGETHER FOREVER.

Stormy framed it behind glass and hung it above her bed, where it remained for a few years. Now it was in a smaller frame on the nightstand in my guest-tower bedroom.

When I lost Stormy, I never considered destroying the card in anger. I have no anger. I have never raged at man or God about what happened. Sorrow is my legacy from that terrible day, and as well a humbling awareness of my inadequacies, which are beyond counting.

To keep the sorrow from overwhelming me, I remain focused on the beauty of this world, which is everywhere to be seen in rich variety, from the smallest wildflowers and the iridescent hummingbird that feeds on them to the night sky diamonded with fiery stars.

And because I am able to see the lingering dead, I know that something lies outside of time, a place to which they belong and to which one day I will go. The prediction of Gypsy Mummy, therefore, has not proved finally wrong; it may yet be fulfilled, and I keep sorrow in check by anticipating the fulfillment of that much-desired destiny.

Since leaving Pico Mundo, I had taken the fortune-teller's card with me when I traveled where my intuition propelled me. But for fear of losing it in some moment of desperate action, I didn't carry it on my person all day, every day.

Recent events had led me to believe that the evil in Roseland was of an unprecedented nature. Annamaria was a help to me but not a shield, and my chances of surviving until morning didn't seem to be good. I had no silly notion that as long as Gypsy Mummy's seven words were in my possession, I would be invulnerable. But I felt, perhaps foolishly, that were I to die and step out of time, the powers that be on the Other Side would feel more obliged to lead me directly to Stormy if I carried with me evidence of the promised destiny.

I don't mind being considered foolish. I'm as much a fool as anyone, more so than some, and keeping that truth always in mind prevents me from becoming cocky. Cockiness gets you killed.

I pried up the fasteners on the back of the frame, removed the rectangle of chipboard, and retrieved the card. I put it in one of the plastic windows in my wallet.

Otherwise, those windows were empty. I carried

no photo of Stormy because I had no need of it. Her face, her smile, her form, the beauty of her graceful hands, her voice were all vivid in my mind, indelible. In memory, she lived and moved and laughed, but all that a photograph could offer was one frozen moment of a life.

Over my sweater, I put on a sports jacket that I had bought during my shopping trip to town. I wasn't trying to spiff up my image. A sports jacket provided pockets and concealment.

As Noah Wolflaw had instructed, I locked the narrow, barred windows and drew shut the draperies. I turned on all the lamps so that much later, when nightfall came, the light leaking around the draperies would suggest that I was in residence.

After locking my suite of rooms, I climbed the winding stone stairs from the vestibule to the second floor. The knuckles of my right hand chased the door as it swung open before they could quite rap the wood.

Raphael, the golden retriever we'd rescued in Magic Beach, was lying on the floor, holding a Nylabone in his forepaws, gnawing it with gusto. He thumped his tail in greeting, but the Nylabone was at the moment of greater interest to him than any chest scratch or tummy rub he might get from me.

Boo was either elsewhere in the suite or had gone out to explore Roseland. As a spirit dog, he could walk through walls if he wished and do any of the usual ghosty things. But I had previously observed that, like any living dog, he had considerable curiosity and enjoyed exploring new places.

As before, the draperies were closed, and the only light came from two stained-glass lamps. Annamaria sat at the same small dining table. No mugs of tea stood steaming for either her or me.

Instead, on the table rested a shallow blue bowl eighteen inches in diameter, filled with water, in which floated three enormous white flowers. They were somewhat like magnolia blooms but larger, as big as cantaloupes, lusher, the petals so thick they seemed artificial, as if made of wax.

I had seen these flowers before, on an immense tree that grew outside the place where she had lived for a while in Magic Beach. We had eaten a meal together at a table where three blooms floated in a large shallow bowl like this one.

Knowing the names of things is a way of paying respect to the beauty of the world that sustains me and keeps my sorrow in check. I know the names of many trees, but not the name of the one from which these flowers came.

Approaching the table, I said, "Where did you get these?"

The lamp glow fell upon the flowers, the waxy petals bounced it softly to Annamaria, and this indirection played a trick on the eye, so that it seemed the light on her face shone from within her.

She smiled and said, "I took them from the tree."

"The tree is back in Magic Beach."

"The tree is here, Oddie."

I had only ever seen one tree with these blooms, the nameless one in Magic Beach, with its great spreading black branches and its eight-lobed leaves.

"Here in Roseland? I've been all over the estate. I haven't seen anything with these flowers."

"Well, it's here as surely as you are."

Less than a week earlier, she had performed a trick with one of these white flowers. A friend of mine, a woman named Blossom, her only audience, had been wonderstruck by it. Now it seemed that she likewise impressed Noah Wolflaw, although the illusion apparently disturbed him in a way it didn't disturb Blossom.

"In Magic Beach, you promised to show me something with a flower like this."

"And indeed I will. Something that you will remember always."

I pulled out the chair in which I had been sitting earlier.

Before I could settle, she raised a hand to stop me. "Not now."

"When?"

"All things in their time, odd one."

"That's what you said before."

"And it's what I say again. You have a pressing matter to attend to, I believe."

"Yeah. I found the one who needs me. A boy who won't tell me his name. I think he really might be her son . . . if that makes any sense."

Reflections of the blooms in the bowl flowered in her big dark eyes. "You have no time for an explanation, and I don't need one. Do what you must."

Something nuzzled my hand, and I looked down to see that Boo had materialized. He felt as solid to me as any real dog, as all spirits felt to me. His tongue was warm as he licked my fingers, but my hand did not become wet.

Annamaria said, "And remember what I told you earlier. If you should doubt the justice of your actions, you could die in Roseland. Do not doubt the beauty of your heart."

I understood why she counseled me with those words. Mere days earlier, in Magic Beach, I had been caught up in a series of events that required me to kill five people involved in a terrorist plot, one of them a lovely young woman with large pellucid blue eyes. They would have murdered hundreds of thousands, perhaps millions, if I had not killed them, and they would have murdered me. But the killing, especially of the woman, even though in self-defense, had left me dark inside and sick of myself.

That is why I told you at the start that I had recently been in a **mood,** not as buoyant and quick to find the humor in any moment as I have usually been. That was surely why I dreamed of Auschwitz, too, and worried about dying twice.

"The boy needs you," she said.

After looking one last time at the flowers in the bowl, I went to the door.

"Young man." When I glanced at her, she said, "Trust the justice of your actions and come back to me. You are my one protector."

The retriever and the white shepherd were staring at me. Neither wagged his tail. Henry Ward Beecher once said, "The dog was created especially for children. He is the god of frolic." I agree with that sentiment. But dogs can sometimes give you the most solemn look you will ever see on a human or an animal face, as if occasionally they are able to foretell, as if they see something in your future that they dread on your behalf.

I stepped out of Annamaria's suite, pulled the door shut, fished the key from my pocket, and locked her safely inside.

Twenty-one

LEAVING THE GUEST TOWER, I REAL-
ized that among the eucalyptuses, as in the oak
grove around the Enceladus lawn, no leaves lay on
the ground either where the earth was bare or where
a sparse grass grew, or on the flagstone path.

Brooding on that and a great deal more, I made
my way to the groundskeeper's building by a round-
about route that prevented me from being seen by
anyone who might be at a window in the main
house. By lawns, by wild fields, by the cover of trees,
I circled to the north end of the huge estate, always
watchful for the mysterious pigs, if pigs they were, as
well as for the stallion and his rider.

The swine scared me, but at least the only horse
in Roseland was a spirit. I find horses beautiful and
noble and all that, but . . . One night years earlier,
three women on horseback hunted me through the
desert around Pico Mundo. They wanted to carve

open my skull and take my brain. And their steeds were no less scary than the women.

I had chanced upon them in the middle of a ceremony that no man was ever meant to see. I thought they were Wiccans, but they despised Wiccans almost as much as they despised reason. According to those three, mere witches were wimps.

Their ceremony was for the most part so dull that it wasn't worth a ticket at any price, especially not at the cost of my life. The event was rather like a university women's society meeting, with a reading of the minutes and a report from the treasurer, except that these three met in the nude, brewed magic-mushroom tea, and structured their get-together around the sacrifice of three plump doves. The poor birds never did anything to anyone but had the misfortune to be symbols of peace, and nothing infuriated those particular women more than the concept of peace.

They were a nasty trio. And their horses seemed to track me by scent, as if they were half Appaloosa, half bloodhound. The flaring nostrils, the black lips skinned back from big square teeth, the flashing eyes . . . Consequently, I find movies like **Seabiscuit** and even **Black Beauty** to be as disturbing as **The Silence of the Lambs.**

The groundskeeper's building was a sizable two-story stone structure in a shallow, picturesque glen that was sunny in the center and ringed by lacy California pepper trees. The small leaves of the peppers shimmered in a soft breeze of hardly greater force than an infant's breathing.

The ground-floor windows were larger than those at the guest tower, but they were barred. The man-size door was locked. Behind three garage doors were evidently vehicles used by the landscapers, wherever they might be. From Henry Lolam during one of my visits to the gatehouse, I had ascertained that Jam Diu occupied an apartment on the second floor, and that there were also rooms on that level for other live-in members of the landscaping staff, though Henry had never quite confirmed that said staff existed.

Although it might be dangerous to assume that Jam Diu would still be pottering around up near the house, searching for that one hateful dandelion that could destroy the perfection of Roseland, I made the assumption anyway. I boldly tried the front door, but it was locked. The garage bays had power roll-ups and offered no exterior handles for manual operation.

At the back of the building, I found two doors and a series of barred windows. Kicking in a door might be difficult if a deadbolt was engaged.

Besides, I was wearing rubber-soled Rockports. If you're going to go around kicking down doors, you need to wear jackboots or the equivalent, so you don't wind up lying on the ground with a fracture of the heel bone, sobbing like a baby.

Matt Damon and Tom Cruise and Liam Neeson and Bruce Willis and other men of their stature have kicked down numerous doors without sustaining the slightest injury to the calcaneus, which is the heel bone. Sometimes they have even done it barefoot. But I do not claim to be as tough as those gentlemen are, nor do I have access to the superlative health-care plan of the Screen Actors Guild.

On my way across the estate, I had thought hard about Wolflaw's bewilderment as to why he had asked Annamaria to be his guest—and remembered Henry Lolam and Paulie Sempiterno being equally mystified. If these people harbored secrets that might destroy them, inviting strangers to stay in Roseland was self-destructive.

Annamaria might have charisma, in the truest sense of the word, and she might inspire in people a desire to assist her, but she was not a voodoo priestess casting spells that could bring her into any inner sanctum where she wished to go. She had told Wolflaw that he had a purpose in bringing her and me to Roseland, and she seemed to have at least some general idea of what that purpose might be, even if it was her curious nature not to share her insight, to be as enigmatic with me as with everyone else.

Having quietly worked on murder investigations in Pico Mundo with Chief Wyatt Porter, who was like a father to me, I knew that some habitual criminals, especially those who commit violent acts with a perverse edge, want to be caught. Not all of them.

Perhaps not even most of them. But some of them. They don't necessarily know they want to be caught, but they unconsciously follow signature behaviors that link their crimes, taunt the police, and take ever-bigger risks that sooner or later must inevitably bring them down.

Whatever bizarre business Wolflaw was up to, he might on some profound level be weary of it, feel trapped by it, and want to bring it to an end. But as with any deeply bad habit, stopping the madness could be difficult.

As I stood there considering whether I should try to break down one of the rear doors to the ground-skeeper's building, I suddenly wondered if Wolflaw, in his unconscious desire to be exposed and stopped, might have literally given me the key to get the job done.

I tried the guest-tower key, and it turned the deadbolt. The locks in both buildings were keyed alike.

On the bottom floor were the garages. Of the three bays, two contained vehicles. They were scaled-down, open-bed trucks of the kind landscap-ers used, but they appeared to be antiques, so old that they had polished-brass fittings, bug-eyed head-lights, and fancy wire wheels that no company these days would include on such a utility vehicle. They were in mint condition.

Open to the garage portion of the structure, a tool-storage area offered shovels and rakes and pick-axes and sickles hung on the wall. They seemed to be as clean as surgical tools.

In the middle of this space were racks of open shelving around which I walked. All were empty and dust-free.

Inlaid in the concrete floor were many of the copper rods with the elongated figure eight inscribed in the exposed end.

Nowhere could I find bags of fertilizer, cans of insecticide, bottles of fungicide, or other gardening supplies.

I went through the drawers of a storage cabinet, which mostly contained hand tools. I found a hacksaw, which I took, and a packet of spare blades, which I slipped into an inner jacket pocket.

I also took a screwdriver. It wasn't as good as a knife, but it could do damage. The handle was wood instead of plastic.

Although the better Odd Thomas in me rebelled at the very thought of stabbing someone with a screwdriver or any other weapon, I knew from grim experience that, cornered and desperate, I could do to bad men what they wanted to do to me. And bad women. There is in me a darkness that, by darkness challenged, will rise up and have its way. I act in the defense of the innocent, but I sometimes must wonder if I will be innocent in my own heart, or even redeemable, at the end of my strange road.

The ground floor also contained Mr. Jam Diu's office. The desk drawers were empty, as was the filing cabinet. In the concrete floor were more of the copper rods.

Because of the lack of an interior staircase, I used exterior stairs at the east end of the building to climb to the second floor. A hallway served five rooms and one bath in the first two-thirds of the building; although they might have been intended as quarters for live-in gardeners back in the day, they were unfurnished.

At the end of the hall, a door opened into Jam Diu's efficiency apartment. These immaculate quarters were furnished and decorated almost as sparely as a Zen monk's cell.

He had no television but a first-class music system. Although the world might prefer streaming music off the Internet, Jam Diu hung with his CDs. His collection seemed to consist entirely of classics, piano and orchestral, though I spotted one Slim Whitman album that must have been a gift from some misguided soul.

In the bedroom, as you would expect of any true music lover, a Beretta shotgun and an assault rifle were fixed to the wall with quick-release spring clips. They were loaded. On a set of open shelves were perhaps a hundred boxes of ammunition for the two visible firearms, but also for handguns.

Apparently Mr. Jam Diu worried about something more aggressive than aphids and bark beetles.

The pistols and revolvers were in the bottom two drawers of a highboy. So much for the screwdriver.

I put it in the back of the lowest drawer and, from the selection of six handguns, I chose a Beretta Px4 Storm. Double-action 9 mm with a four-inch barrel. Seventeen-round magazine.

He had a spare magazine. I loaded both with copper-jacketed, low-recoil rounds. Through my mind's eye ran the primate swine in the tall grass, and I dropped a box of twenty rounds in one sports-jacket pocket.

In the drawers were simple, premium-leather, double-thick, concealed-carry, belt-slider holsters custom to each of the handguns, with a built-in spare magazine carrier. My belt threaded easily through the eyelets, and in two minutes, the loaded 9 mm was on my hip, under my jacket.

And so it would soon begin. I hoped that I wouldn't have to shoot anything but swine—and that the definition of **swine** would remain strictly biological.

Spare linens were kept in the bedroom closet. I took a bath towel and a pillowcase. I wrapped the hacksaw in the towel and put the towel in the pillowcase, which made a good sack.

I intended to do my best not to be seen as I went about the business at hand. But if I encountered someone, I could justify the sack somehow—perhaps by saying that I was going on a picnic in the meadow and that the sack contained my lunch—whereas explaining a hacksaw would be more difficult.

With luck, I wouldn't run into anyone until I had thought of a better story than the stupid picnic.

In the living room, before leaving, I paused to scan the fifty or so volumes in a bookcase. They were mostly tomes of ponderous philosophy, though there were four thick books of photography too tall for the shelves and laid flat.

Every volume in that quartet was about Hong Kong. The photos presented the city as it had been in the late nineteenth century and on through every decade until the current day.

Jam Diu sounded Vietnamese to me. But I'm just an ignorant psychic fry cook who knows nothing more about Asian cultures than he knows about molecular biology.

Hong Kong had once been a British colony. Now it was a Chinese province. The groundskeeper spoke English without either an Asian or a British accent.

Jam Diu might not be his real name. In fact, if Roseland was as much a nexus of deceptions and conspiracies as it appeared to be, his name was more likely to be Mickey Mouse than Jam Diu. Whatever his name, I thought perhaps he was sometimes homesick for Hong Kong.

I left the building, locking everything behind me, and returned to the cover of the trees and wild fields.

The temptation was to feel safer now that I was well-armed, but I didn't allow myself to be tempted. Experience had taught me that overconfidence is an invitation to the Fates to bring onstage two or three muscle-bound guys in porkpie hats, who want to lock me in a walk-in freezer until I fully solidify or intend to toss me into the giant revolving drum of a concrete-mixer truck and pour me into the footing of a new sewage-treatment plant.

Guys who wear porkpie hats are always, in my experience, up to no good—and pleased about it. Whether that style of headwear turns previously benign men into sociopaths or whether men who are already sociopaths are drawn to that style is one of those mysteries that will never be solved, though the Department of Justice has probably funded a score of scientific studies of the issue.

As I headed east-southeast, the clouds coming in from the north loomed at my back. But the sky ahead was so blue and the land so sun-drenched that, under other circumstances, I might have wandered happily through the meadow while singing "The Sound of Music."

Of course, one must always remember that although **The Sound of Music** is the most feel-good movie musical of all time, it is crammed full of Nazis.

Twenty-two

CARRYING THE HACKSAW DISGUISED
as a picnic lunch in a pillowcase sack, I approached
the mausoleum from the south, first through weedy
fields and then across forty or fifty feet of lawn as
flawless and lush as that in an erotic dream about a
golf course.

The forty-foot-square, windowless limestone mega-
tomb boasted an elaborate cornice and carved panels
depicting stylized sunrises and Edenesque landscapes.
The entrance, a ribbed bronze door flanked by immense columns, wasn't on the north side of the building, where it would have faced the house, but here on
the south side.

According to Mrs. Tameed, superstition dictated
the location of the entrance. The original owner had
thought it would be bad luck to be able to look out
of any window in the main house and see the door
to this house of the dead.

The slab of bronze swung smoothly, soundlessly on ball-bearing hinges. As I eased the door shut behind me, I switched on the lights: three gold-leafed chandeliers and a series of wall sconces.

This enormous empty chamber would have been an ideal ballroom for a really cool Halloween party. Then I flashed on a mental image of people in harlequin masks waltzing with red-eyed primate swine, and I decided that I'd rather spend that holiday evening alone, with the doors locked and the shades drawn, biting my fingernails to the quick.

Inlaid in the walls were glass-tile murals that re-created famous paintings with spiritual themes. In the spaces between those works of art were niches waiting to receive urns of ashes.

Only three niches were filled. After the founder of Roseland, Constantine Cloyce, and his family died, subsequent owners felt no eternal attachment to the property and chose to have their mortal remains interred elsewhere.

The nameless boy had told me to come here. Before returning to the main house to free him, I thought it wise to heed his advice.

He had urged me to "press the shield that the guardian angel holds high" in one of the mausoleum mosaics. I hadn't realized until now that all fourteen of those reproductions were of works that included a guardian angel.

No titles of the paintings were given, but inlaid at

the bottom of each mosaic was the surname of the artist: Domenichino, Franchi, Bonomi, Berrettini, Zucchi. . . .

Fortunately, not all of the angels had shields. And only the one in the Franchi piece was held high, to protect a child not from demons but from divine reproach.

The shield was reddish-brown and contained a lot of tiny pieces of colored glass. With a little trepidation, I swept my hand back and forth across the entire shield. Exactly nothing happened.

I rapped my knuckles here and there on the shield, listening for a hollow spot. I didn't hear one.

As I began to think I had chosen the wrong mosaic, I noticed that one of the larger glass tiles, about an inch square, was not grouted to those that surrounded it. I pressed only that tile, felt it give a little, pressed harder, harder still, and with a click it abruptly sank an inch into the wall.

Something hissed. And then with a low rumble, an entire section of limestone, seven feet high and four wide, containing the mural, rolled away from me. It retreated about three and a half feet before coming to a halt.

The main wall from which that section detached was eighteen inches thick, leaving a two-foot gap on each side, in which lights had come on automatically. A narrow flight of stairs led down both to the left and to the right.

I should have known that if I survived the challenges of my adventurous life long enough, one day I would have my Indiana Jones moment.

Supposing that these stairs led down to the same space, I chose those on the right. They were steep. I clung to the handrail, acutely aware of how ironic it would be if, after surviving endless assaults by numerous homicidal sociopaths, I stumbled and broke my neck.

Indeed, both sets of stairs descended to a nine-foot-high vault as large as the mausoleum above, which contained the most astonishing mechanical apparatus I had ever seen.

Along the center of the chamber were arrayed seven spheres, each maybe six feet in diameter, connected to the floor and the ceiling by a three-inch pole or pipe. The pipes were fixed, but the huge spheres rotated so fast that their surfaces were golden blurs, and though I knew that, even if hollow, they were solid forms, they almost looked like shining bubbles that might float away.

Along the north wall, except where the stairs terminated, and along the entire south wall, score upon score of bright flywheels in several sizes—some as small as CDs, others as large as ash-can lids—were arrayed atop a series of bell-shaped machine housings, to which they were linked with gleaming pitmans, sliding blocks, and piston rods. The glimmering crank wrists at the end of the glossy connecting rods turned cranks in shafts, and the wheels spun, spun, spun, this one fast, that one faster, some clockwise, others counterclockwise, yet giving the impression of an intricate synchronization.

Now and then, from this flywheel or that, arising off its outer rim, series of golden sparks flew toward the ceiling. They were not really sparks but something for which I had no name, pulses of golden light shaped like raindrops, and they didn't shoot out at high speed, like sparks, but glided to the ceiling, where they were absorbed into a mesh of copper wire more intricate in its abstract patterns than the most complex of Persian carpets.

But for the copper ceiling and the concrete walls, everything in the vault, all the visible parts of the strange machines, appeared to have been plated with precious metals, some with gold and others with silver. The vault reminded me of a jewel box, glittering and twinkling and shimmering all around.

The purpose of it all was beyond my comprehension, but perhaps the most amazing thing was that all those moving parts produced no sound, no hum or buzz, not one tick or creak. The only noise that rose from this busy assemblage was the faint whispery whoosh of displaced air as flywheels scooped up a draft and flung it forward, as the big spheres drew in atmospheres to rotate with them.

No parts could be engineered and machined to such perfection that friction was entirely eliminated, nor was any lubricant equal to the job. But no spot of grease or drip of oil could be seen; I detected no scent of them, either, no indication that lubrication was required, and yet no friction heat arose from those mechanisms.

The eeriness of such frantic motion occurring in utter silence can't be overstated. I felt as though I had stepped into a realm of cosmic machinery between our dimension and another, where the engine that maintained order in the universe raced on eternally in exquisite balance.

Nevertheless, the vault did not have a futuristic feeling. Some aspects of it struck me as Victorian, and other features had a Deco flavor. Rather than suggest a construct from the next millennium, it seemed antique, or not so much antique as timeless, as though it had existed forever.

The feeling of being watched, which never quite left me as long as I had been in Roseland, now grew more intense.

From the gleaming rims of racing flywheels, like tiny helium balloons, greater showers of honey-colored drops of light rose to the copper tapestry overhead. Their ascent was in contrast to all the rotational motion, and a sudden sense of buoyancy overcame me, not a positive feeling but a queasy expectation that I might drift off my feet and . . . away.

The deep, accented, disembodied voice that I had heard before dawn, when I approached this mausoleum as it glowed like a lamp, spoke now behind me: "I have seen you—"

I turned, but found no one.

"—where you have not yet been," he whispered.

When I turned again, I saw a man with a mustache standing at the farther end of this service aisle that led between spheres and flywheels. Tall and gaunt, he wore a dark suit that hung loosely on his bony frame. By his appearance and solemn attitude, he reminded me of an undertaker.

Louder than before, he said, "I depend on you," and he crossed the end of the room from this aisle to the next, disappearing behind the spheres.

I hurried after him, turned right, and peered into the next aisle. He was gone. I circled through the vault, but he had vanished as if he could walk through walls.

Spirits do not speak. But living men do not dematerialize like ghosts.

As for ghosts, when I turned once more, I came face-to-face with the woman in white, her long blond hair ribboned with fresh blood and tangled as it might have been by wind on the night when she took her last horseback ride.

Blood streaked her nightgown, too, and for the first time she manifested with three entrance wounds in her chest. The one directly over the heart and the one just below it had evidently been fired from close quarters because the fabric of the gown looked scorched around the wounds. The round that shattered her sternum had been fired from a greater distance than the other two; it had probably been the first shot and had most likely killed her instantly. That her murderer fired twice again at point-blank range, into her corpse, suggested rage of a singular intensity.

The weapon had surely been a powerful rifle. The large-caliber, high-velocity ammunition appeared to have caved in her chest.

As if she saw that the violence committed against her distressed me, the wounds and the blood faded, and she appeared as she looked before the trigger had been squeezed. Lovely. The hint of a strong will in her posture and expression. Her gaze direct and, it seemed to me, honest.

She turned, walked away, and paused after three steps to glance over her shoulder.

Realizing that she wished to lead me to something, I followed this beauty to the end of the vault. In one corner, a tight spiral staircase led to a yet-lower level of the mausoleum.

She wanted me to go with her into that deeper place.

Twenty-three

SPIRALING IRON TWISTED DEEPER INTO a darkness that was not the absence of light but the absence of hope, for the light below was as golden as that in the vault of spheres and flywheels above.

I had dreamed of Auschwitz and in the dream had been afraid of dying twice. Annamaria had assured me that I would die once and only once, and that it would be "the death that doesn't matter."

In all our lives, however, there are many days when we die a little, when we are wounded by loss or failure, or by fear, or by seeing the suffering of others for whom we are able to offer only pity, for whom we are powerless to offer aid, who are beyond mercy.

The spiral stairs were like an auger bit boring sharply down through the layers of Roseland. When a well-driller cores earth and rock in search of water, he occasionally pulls to the surface fossils or fragments thereof. Some are bizarre creatures with eyes on stalks and whip tails and many-jointed legs, things that crawled the floors of ancient seas long gone. The sight of them impressed in stone can make Earth seem less known than unknown, and the nip that twitches through your blood is the chill of the sudden suspicion that you are a stranger in a strange land. The sole sound in the subcellar of the mausoleum was my footsteps on iron treads, and in the silence at the bottom of the stairs, I came upon a scene so outré, so bleak that I could have found nothing more horrifying on an alien planet orbiting a distant star.

This space was higher than the first cellar, maybe eleven feet. Later, I would take in the parallel arrays of gold-plated gears in the three feet immediately under the ceiling, embraced above and below by shallow silver-plated tracks. They were not fixed in the tracks, were not merely receiving and transmitting force and motion, but were themselves moving across the chamber, out of a hole in one wall and into a hole in the opposite wall. The first, third, and fifth arrays were churning east to west; the second, fourth, and sixth moved west to east. Teeth meshed with teeth, and by the biting of one another, the gleaming wheels turned as relentlessly and as silently as the flywheels in the upper cellar. I couldn't understand what they were meant to achieve, what they might be driving, if they were driving anything more than themselves.

But the mystery of the gears mattered not at all in light of the dead women who sat on the floor with their backs against the walls.

As I have said in at least one other volume of this continuing memoir, I will not tell everything that I saw. The tableau in the subcellar was as grossly indecent as it was horrific. The innocent dead deserve their dignity.

Numbers do not define the degree of this villainy, for each of these women was a special soul, as is each person ever born. What had been done to each was an injustice and an iniquity so monstrous that the mind rebelled and the heart sank at the wickedness of it, and any one victim was sufficient to require the execution, with extreme prejudice, of whoever had done this to her. Later, when I counted them, I found there were thirty-four.

Yet the room was as odorless as it was hushed . . . and that was not the most puzzling thing about the scene.

They were all naked, seated side by side on the floor, their backs against the concrete wall. Although each of their souls had been unique, they were physically of a type. All were blondes of one shade or another, a few with shorter hair, most with hair that fell shoulder-length or longer. Some might have been as young as sixteen; none appeared to be older than her late twenties. They had once been lovely, with refined features. Their eyes were blue or blue-gray, or blue-green, and they stared wide-eyed, some because death had caught them that way and others because pins had been used to keep their eyelids from closing.

As the quiet spirit of the nightgowned rider led me through the subcellar, with the silently meshing-churning golden gears two feet overhead, the resemblance between her and the dead women became ever more marked.

My first assumption was that she had been the first victim, and that her murderer wasn't satisfied to kill her once. He found surrogates who resembled her, and he killed them as if to kill her again.

Evidently, none of these dead women clung stubbornly to this world, because I had seen no lingering spirits in Roseland except that of the rider and her faithful horse. I was grateful for their haste in crossing over, because if the subcellar had been crowded with their anguished and beseeching ghosts, I might have been incapable of coping.

Although most of them had been tortured in one way or another, I will not say with what techniques or what instruments. With some the brute had worked on their hands, with others their feet, their breasts. But except for the straight pins in the eyelids, which the lack of blood suggested were inserted postmortem, their faces were untouched.

The murderer wanted always to be able to see the stallion rider's face in each of theirs. Maybe he came here to review his collection, to feel their stares upon him, to lord over them the fact that he lived and even flourished in spite of what he'd done to them.

That this subcellar full of corpses remained free of any whiff of decomposition perplexed me less than did the condition of the thirty-four dead women. They looked as if every one of them had been killed that very morning.

Twenty-four

SUCH FLAWLESS PRESERVATION WAS impossible. These women were not embalmed, not mummified. Besides, mummies don't have the smooth skin of maidens, silken hair, clear eyes. And even embalmed bodies deteriorate.

I assumed that Noah Wolflaw must have murdered them. He'd bought Roseland from the second owner, the reclusive South American mining heir, in 1988, twenty-four years earlier. If this macabre collection had come with the property, Wolflaw would have called the police and would have been eager to have the cadavers removed.

Considering that the riding ring and the exercise yard for horses had been weed-choked for many years, considering that the strangely spotless stables offered no speck of evidence that animals had been kept there in several decades, I believed the bareback rider and her stallion must have been murdered many years before Wolflaw purchased the place. Chef Shilshom had seemed to confirm the long absence of horses from Roseland.

But when the rider's spirit led me around this crypt to the last of the thirty-four bodies—more likely the first in order of death—it proved to be hers. The condition of the cadaver argued that her spirit must have departed it less than an hour previously. If this was Wolflaw's work, then there had been at least one stallion stabled in Roseland after he purchased the estate.

Hers was the only body that wasn't naked, and it wore the long white silk-and-lace nightgown in which her spirit manifested. Of the thirty-four, she alone had not been tortured, which seemed to confirm that she indeed had been the first to be murdered and that her killer had acted on that one occasion in the heat of passion; thereafter, he chose his victims with patient calculation, abusing them sexually and physically in an almost ritual fashion before finally taking their lives.

The shock of this discovery diminished slowly, but the horror grew moment by moment. In my short life, I have seen many detestable things, and I have been called upon to do repugnant things that have for a while broken me. But nothing in my experience had weighed upon me with greater power than the grievous scene in that subcellar of the mausoleum.

For a while, I had to close my eyes to such abundant evidence of evil, as if to look upon it too long would invite infection.

My legs felt weak. I swayed in my self-imposed darkness. Locked my knees. Steadied myself.

A comforting hand on my shoulder had to be that of the spirit rider. I am able to feel the touch of the lingering dead, though usually they don't attempt to reassure me.

A life of supernatural encounters has put a keener edge on my imagination, which has been sharp since birth. The rider's hand had been on my shoulder mere seconds when I became convinced that it wasn't she who touched me but instead someone or something with less sympathetic intentions.

Opening my eyes, I discovered that the hand belonged, after all, to my spirit companion. I held her gaze for a moment and then met the stare of her seated corpse.

I am amazed that there are still nights when I sleep well.

The bullet wounds in the cadaver's chest were hideous. I didn't want to dwell on them.

Nevertheless, after a hesitation, I knelt beside the body and touched the gore-stained nightgown to confirm what I suspected. Yes. The blood that had soaked into the fabric was still tacky—and it looked wet and liquid in the wounds, which made no sense.

The murderer had staged the victims in his obscene collection as if they were dolls with which he'd played and which he discarded when he grew bored with them. They sat with their legs splayed, their slender arms limp at their sides, palms turned up as if in supplication.

Except for the woman in the nightgown—which was rucked up past her knees—his other dolls were accessorized with nothing more than the instruments of their destruction. Some had been strangled with neckties, which were still cinched so deeply in the flesh of their throats that the murderer must have been not merely enraged but in the ferocious grip of a sour and festered malignity, implacable rancor. Some had been stabbed two or three times, others much more often, and in each case the knife remained in the last wound administered.

In the case of the thirty-three who were naked, on the floor between their spread legs were hand-printed index cards, evidently to assist the killer's memory. As a little girl will name her dolls, so each victim in this sick man's collection was named, although I assumed these were the names with which they had lived.

Reluctantly, I went to one knee before the second corpse, trying not to look at her, to focus only on the index card. The killer had printed TAMMY VA-NALETTI and beside the name had drawn four neat little stars, which perhaps suggested how much he had enjoyed his time with her.

My revulsion didn't abate, nor my sadness. But now a dark fog of anger, which doesn't come easily to me, rose as if from the marrow in my bones and spread through my inner landscape.

Each of these women was someone's daughter, someone's sister, someone's friend, perhaps someone's mother. They weren't toys. What he'd done to them was not a sport that could be scored with a system of stars. Precious in and of themselves, every one of them might also have been as precious to someone as Stormy had been to me.

Anger is a violent emotion, vindictive, and as dangerous to he who is driven by it as to anyone on whom it is turned. If anger is personal and selfish— and it usually is—it clouds your thinking and therefore puts you at risk. I had to remain clearheaded to deal with what would come next. I needed to keep Stormy Llewellyn out of this, to take this cruelty less personally, to trade anger for righteous indignation, which despises evil acts solely because they are evil. Anger is a red mist through which you see the world, but wrath is clarity. The angry man shoots too often from the hip and misses his target or hits the wrong one, while a wrathful man proceeds without malice but with a thirst for justice.

A date was printed under Tammy Vanaletti's name. It couldn't be her birthday because it was only eight years earlier, and she looked to be in her early twenties. The most logical conclusion was that he had murdered her on that date.

Tammy had been stabbed. The blood on the lips of her wounds appeared fresh.

I had no idea how this could be the case more than eight years after her murder. But I sensed that the part of my mind that never slept or rested was, like a loom, weaving all the seemingly disparate threads of Roseland into a fabric.

I went corpse to corpse, reading each card but not touching it. The date of each death was nearer the present than the one before it. Ginger Harkin, the most recent victim, had been killed less than a month earlier.

Of the thirty-three whose death dates were provided, all had been killed in the past eight years. The periodicity of the killer's murderous urge seemed to be less than three months. Four victims per annum, year after year, with now and then an extra.

This much murder couldn't be called a homicidal impulse or even a psychotic compulsion. This was the man's work, his occupation, his **calling**.

When I turned again to the nameless spirit, I said, "Was it Noah Wolflaw who killed you?"

After a hesitation, she nodded: **Yes.**

"Were you his lover?"

Another hesitation. **Yes.**

Before I could ask a third question, she raised one hand to display an engagement ring and wedding band, which of course were not real but only the **idea** of the nuptial jewelry that she'd once worn in this world.

"His wife?"

Yes.

"You want him brought to justice."

She nodded vigorously and placed both hands over her heart, as if to say that justice was her fondest desire.

"I'll bring him down. I'll see him in jail."

She shook her head and drew one index finger across her throat in the universal gesture that meant **Kill him.**

"I'll probably have to," I said. "He won't go easily."

Twenty-five

THE LINGERING DEAD DON'T ALWAYS provide helpful information, and even those who want to assist me are hampered by their psychology in death as in life. In fact, because they are lost between this world and the next, their reason is often bent by fear, by confusion, and perhaps by other emotions too complex for me to imagine. As a result, they're likely at times to behave irrationally, hindering me when they mean only to help, turning away from me when they should turn toward.

Eager to get as much from Wolflaw's murdered wife as I could before she might become less cooperative, I said, "There's a boy in the house. Just as you suggested."

She nodded vigorously. Her eyes welled with tears, because even spirits can weep, although their tears do not water anything in this world.

Because the boy had said that he'd been taken from someplace and that he wanted to be taken back,

I had assumed he was no relation to Noah Wolflaw and didn't belong in Roseland. But the woman's tears forced me to reconsider my assumption.

"Your son."

Yes.

"Is Noah Wolflaw his father?"

After another hesitation and a look of frustration, she replied in the affirmative. **Yes.**

"I assume you don't know much more about me, just that I can see you and others who haven't crossed over. But I want you to know that I've been drawn here because of your son. I'm meant to help him, and I will try my best."

She appeared hopeful but also uncertain. Her maternal anxiety, carried with her even into death, made her a pitiable figure.

"He says he wants to be taken back, but I don't know where he was brought from. Was he living somewhere else for a while, maybe with his grand-parents?"

No.

"With an aunt or uncle?"

No.

"I promise you, I'll take him back."

To my surprise, she reacted with alarm, adamantly shaking her head. **No, no, no.**

"But he wants to go back, he wants it more than anything, and he'll have to go somewhere when this is over."

Obviously distressed, the late Mrs. Wolflaw

pressed her hands to her head as though she was mentally tortured by the thought of her boy being taken anywhere.

"Serial killing isn't the entire story of Roseland. Something damn strange is going on here, and it won't end well. There's not going to be a Roseland anymore, or if there is, then it'll surely be notorious, a magnet for the morally confused, the mentally unhinged, cultists, freaks of all kinds. The boy will have to go back wherever it is that he wants to go."

Fear twisted her lovely face, but anger caused her to swing a fist at me.

The lingering dead can touch me—and be felt—when the intention is benign. But when they mean to harm, their blows pass through me with no effect, confirming their immaterial nature.

Why this should be, I don't have a clue. I didn't make the rules, and if I were allowed to rewrite them, I would impose a number of changes.

I don't even know why I should be, just that I am.

Again Mrs. Wolflaw swung at me, and a third time. Her failure to connect dismayed her so that desperation wrenched her face, and she let out a plaintive howl to which I was deaf and the world unheeding.

She was frightened and frustrated more than angry. I didn't think that she could work up the white-hot fury that alone can transform a harmless ghost into a dangerous, furniture-slinging poltergeist.

She proved me right by turning away from me,

rushing past the dead women, and vanishing as she reached her own bullet-riddled body.

Sometimes it seems that I am dreaming when I am in fact awake, my reality as unreal as the lands I walk in sleep.

Alone except for the convocation of the dead, I looked up at the six arrays of golden gears. Shining teeth meshed, bit without rending, chewed without consuming, revolved without a sound, moving across the room from wall to wall, as if they were the clockworks in Hell by which the devil measured progress toward eternity.

Twenty-six

IN THE CLOCKWORK CRYPT, THE TIME-less dead gave silent testimony to the human potential for evil. To meet their sightless eyes would be to weep. This was no more a time for weeping than it was a time for laughter, and I moved back toward the spiral stairs, rich in wrath but without anger.

Ozzie Boone, the best-selling mystery writer who lives in Pico Mundo, is my four-hundred-pound mentor, friend, and surrogate father. He has appeared in some volumes of these memoirs, and his advice on writing shapes them all.

He told me that I must keep the tone light because the material is often so dark. Without the leavening of humor, Ozzie says, I will be writing for a small audience of bitter nihilists and dedicated depressives, and I will fail to reach those readers who might be lifted by the hope that lies at the heart of my story.

My writing can't be published while I'm alive, if only because I would be besieged by people who would mistakenly conclude that I can **control** my sixth sense. They would expect me to serve as a medium between them and their loved ones on the Other Side. Others would even more completely misunderstand my gift and come to me to be healed of everything from cancer to bunions.

And here, beyond the limits of Pico Mundo, I must consider the police and the courts, where I would not likely find a sympathetic ear for my story of another world within the world they know, of a more complex reality within the reality of all things material. I would be called guilty, and the guilty on whom I turned my wrath in defense of the innocent would be declared innocent victims. My best hope would be prison, my likely destination a madhouse, and during the years that I waited for that decision, I would not be able to use my gift to help anyone because I would be woven immobile in a web of lawyers.

At the stairs, I registered something that I had seen before but not considered: a door in the farther wall. From here the stairs went up to rooms I'd already visited, but the door led to something new.

New isn't always better. iPhones are better than rotary-dial models, but not so many years ago, some maniacs had a big new idea that they should announce their grievances by flying airliners into skyscrapers.

Nevertheless, carrying the pillowcase containing the hacksaw, I crossed to the door, hesitated, and opened it. Beyond lay a down-sloping tunnel approximately six feet wide and seven high.

As I was at the north side of the mausoleum and as the main house stood north of this building, I assumed the tunnel led under the stepped cascades, under the lawn, under the terrace, terminating in the basement of the residence.

My ultimate intention since leaving the guest tower was to sneak into the house unnoticed and then do what must be done to unravel the mysteries of Roseland and free the boy. The tunnel offered a sneakier route than I could have hoped to find—as long as I didn't encounter Wolflaw or Sempiterno, or a swine presuming to walk like a man.

This was more than a passageway. It apparently served some other purpose, as part of the baroque mechanism that I'd discovered in the cellar and subcellar of the mausoleum.

The floor, walls, and ceiling were sheathed in copper plates, and overhead rectangular lamps striped the length of the tunnel with shadow and light. Inlaid in each wall was a single clear-glass tube through which pulsed slow-moving golden flares reminiscent of the raindrop-like luminous bursts thrown off by the flywheels.

One moment the pulses seemed to be moving toward the house, the next moment away from it. Staring directly at them for longer than a few seconds made me queasy and gave me the curious, confusing thought that I was here but not here, real but not real, both approaching the house but at the same time retreating from it.

I took care not to look directly at the tubes anymore. I kept my eyes on the path ahead and proceeded a few hundred feet.

At the end of the passageway, I opened a copper-clad door and fumbled for the light switch. Beyond lay a wine cellar with stone walls, a concrete floor decorated with the exposed ends of copper rods, and a couple of thousand bottles in redwood racks.

Something as normal as a wine cellar seemed abnormal here. You torture and kill women, you imprison your own son, you and your staff are armed for Armageddon, your house—maybe your entire estate—seems to be a machine of some kind, you have a pack of swine things chasing around the property, and you sit down of an evening with a good Cabernet Sauvignon and a bit of nice cheese to—what?—listen to Broadway show tunes?

Nothing in Roseland was as normal as show tunes or cheese, or wine. Maybe this had once been an ordinary mansion for a typical billionaire with the usual perversions, but not any longer.

I was tempted to open one of the bottles to see if it contained blood instead of Napa's finest.

Behind one of two distressed-oak doors lay narrow enclosed stairs. I assumed they went up to the kitchen.

I had learned all I was ever likely to learn from Chef Shilshom, unless I attached wires to his private parts and teased information out of him with electric shocks. That wasn't my style. Besides, the thought of getting a glimpse of the chef's private parts made me want to scream like a little girl who finds a tarantula on her shoulder.

With much to do and perhaps too little time in which to do it, I went to the second door and gingerly opened it. A long basement corridor waited beyond, closed doors on both sides and a door at the farther end.

I listened at the first door on the left before opening it. The large room was full of hulking iron furnaces and massive boilers that appeared to date from the 1920s. They looked as if they had just come out of the factory, but I couldn't tell if they were actually still in service, for they were quiet.

On the right, the first door opened to a storeroom in which nothing was stored, and when I opened the second door on the left, I found Victoria Mors, the maid who worked at the direction of Mrs. Tameed, doing laundry.

The washers and dryers were newer than the furnaces and boilers, but like the wine cellar, their very ordinariness made them seem out of place in this weird and increasingly grotesque world within the walls of Roseland.

Victoria Mors was sorting clothes and bedding, transferring them from a laundry cart to the washers. None of the machines was yet in operation, which was why I hadn't heard motor or agitator noise that would have warned me that the room was occupied.

She seemed as startled to see me as I was discomfited to see her. We stood unmoving, staring at each other, our mouths open, as if we were a couple of figures from an animated Swiss clock that had suddenly stopped with the opening of the door.

Like Henry Lolam and Paulie Sempiterno, surely Victoria thought that Noah Wolflaw's invitation to Annamaria and me was reckless and inexplicable. While I was searching for words, I knew that she was deciding whether to cry out in alarm, because I was welcome only on the ground floor of the house.

Before she could scream, I stepped into the laundry room, smiled my dumb-as-a-spatula fry-cook smile, and raised the pillowcase sack in which I carried the towel-wrapped hacksaw. "I have some delicate laundry, and they told me to bring it down to you."

Twenty-seven

SLENDER, FIVE FEET TWO, VICTORIA Mors wore the black slacks and simple white blouse that served as a uniform for her and Mrs. Tameed. Although she was probably in her late twenties, I thought of her as a girl, not a woman. She was pretty in an elfin sort of way, with large faded-denim eyes. Barrettes held her strawberry-blond hair back; but now—as every time I'd seen her—a couple of strands had escaped the clasps and curled down the sides of her face, which with her rosy cheeks gave her the look of a child fresh from a session of jump rope or hopscotch. Although her body would have suited a ballerina, she sometimes moved with a charming, coltish awkwardness. She tended to look at me sideways or else with her head lowered and from under her lashes, which seemed like girlish shyness but was more likely sour suspicion.

There in the laundry room, she stared at me directly, and her large, pale-blue eyes were open wide with solicitude, as if hovering over my head were a vampire bat of which I was unaware.

She said, "Oh, you didn't have to bring the laundry yourself, Mr. Odd. I would have come to the guest tower for it."

"Yes, ma'am, I know, but I hoped to save you the effort. It must be exhausting for you and Mrs. Tameed to take care of this big house. All the dusting and sweeping and polishing and the endless picking up after. Although of course I suppose there must be several other maids I haven't met."

"Haven't you?" she said, by her tone and expression managing to present herself as a dim but winning girl who couldn't quite follow conversations in which exchanges were longer than six words.

"Have you worked at Roseland for long?"

"I'm ever so glad for the job."

"Well, who wouldn't be?"

"We're like a family here."

"I feel the warmth."

"And it's such a lovely place."

"It's magical," I agreed.

"The beautiful gardens, the wonderful old oaks."

"I climbed one, spent an entire though very short night in it."

She blinked. "You did what?"

"I climbed one of the wonderful old oaks. All the way to the wonderful top, where the limbs were almost too small to support me."

Perhaps because I'd gone well past six words, she was confused. "Why would you do that?"

"Oh," I said, "I just had to."

"Climbing trees is dangerous."

"**Not** climbing them can be just as dangerous."

"I never do anything dangerous."

"Some days, just getting out of bed is dangerous."

She decided not to look directly at me anymore. Returning to the task of sorting laundry from the cart into the two washing machines, she said, "You can just leave your things, and I'll deal with them, Mr. Odd."

"My things?" I asked, because I can pretend to be as obtuse as anyone.

"Your delicate laundry items."

I couldn't yet decide whether or not I wanted her to starch the hacksaw, so I held on to the pillowcase sack and said, "Mr. Wolflaw must have very high standards. The house is immaculate."

"It's a beautiful house. It deserves to be perfectly kept."

"Is Mr. Wolflaw a tyrant?"

Glancing sideways at me as she continued to feed the washing machines, Victoria seemed to be genuinely hurt on behalf of her boss. "Whyever would you think such a thing?"

"Well, people as rich as he is can sometimes be demanding."

"He's a wonderful employer," she declared, with a

note of disapproval aimed at me for doubting the exemplary nature of the master of Roseland. "I never want another." With the tenderness of an infatuated schoolgirl, she added, "Never ever."

"That's what I thought. He seems like a saint."

She frowned. "Then why did you say 'tyrant'?"

"Due diligence. I'm going to apply for a job."

She met my eyes directly again, and said dismissively, "There aren't any openings."

"Seems like there aren't enough security guards."

"Two of them are on vacation."

"Ah. Henry Lolam says he gets eight weeks off. That's a generous vacation."

"But there aren't any openings."

"Henry only took three of his eight weeks. He says the world is changing too much out there. He only feels safe here."

"Of course he feels safe here. Who wouldn't feel safe here?"

I suspected that the thirty-four dead women in the subcellar of the mausoleum had at some point not felt safe in Roseland; however, I didn't bring up the subject because I didn't want to be boorish.

If I had ever fantasized about being a CIA interrogator, I'd lost interest in the job when the law limited them to extracting information from terrorists only with the offer of candy. But I was pleased with myself for getting some interesting responses from the maid even without a Three Musketeers bar.

Now that I'd switched techniques and had begun to needle her a little, our chat might turn hostile, in which case I would have to solve the problem she presented before she could report my presence in the house to anyone.

Unfortunately, I hadn't yet figured out how to deal with her, because I was not inclined to shoot her as a first option.

She was nearly finished sorting the laundry.

I said, "Henry Lolam told me Roseland is an unhealthy place, but I think he must have been joking, considering that he can't bear to be away from it."

"Henry reads too damn much poetry, he thinks too damn much, and he talks too damn much," Victoria Mors said, sounding not at all like a schoolgirl.

"Wow," I said, "you really are like a family."

For just an instant, the hatred in her eyes told me that she wanted to bite off my nose and turn me over to Paulie Sempiterno so that he could put a bullet in my face.

But Victoria Mors was a quick-change artist. As I set down the pillowcase sack, she retracted her fangs, blinked the venom out of her eyes, washed the vinegar out of her voice with honey, and spoke with the quivering emotion of a winsome child defending the honor of her beloved father.

"I'm sorry, Mr. Odd."

"De nada."

"Please forgive me."

"Forgiven."

"It's just, well, I can't stand it when someone's unfair to Mr. Wolflaw, because he's really so . . . he's so incredible."

"I understand. It really steams me when people say bad things about Vladimir Putin."

"Who?"

"Never mind."

Victoria had finished with the laundry, so she wrung her hands as if she'd spent a lot of time recently learning dramatic skills from silent-movie melodramas.

"It's just that poor Henry, he's a nice man, he is rather like a brother to me, but he's one of those people—you could give him the world, and he would be unhappy because you didn't give him the moon, too."

"He wishes aliens would come and make him immortal."

"What's wrong with him? Why can't he be happy with everything he has?"

As if Henry exasperated me, too, I said, "Why indeed?"

"Noah is a brilliant man, one of the greatest men who ever lived."

"I thought he ran a hedge fund."

As I finished speaking, the laundry-room door opened, and the tall, gaunt, mustachioed man in the dark suit entered the room, the one who had told me that he had seen me where I had not yet been and that he depended on me. His deep-set eyes were dark, too, and bright with fevered emotion, arguably the most intense eyes I'd ever seen, his stare so penetrating that I might not have been too surprised if it had actually boiled my brain in my skull.

He came toward me, reaching out imploringly with one bony hand. "I intended none of this."

Instead of grasping the hand that I reflexively held out toward him, the man passed **through** me, as if he were a ghost. For the brief moment that we occupied the same space, an electrical current seemed to surge from the core of my body to every extremity, neither painful nor thrilling, but making me acutely aware of the neural pathways by which I felt pain and pleasure, hot and cold, smooth and rough, sound and sight and smell and taste. The routes taken by every nerve in my flesh were as clear in my mind's eye as were the highways on any map I'd ever read. No ghost could ever have such an effect.

Once through me, he kept going, fading away two steps farther into the laundry room. Although he vanished, four words rang out in his accented voice after he was gone: "Throw the master switch."

Victoria Mors turned her head to watch the apparition vanish. Then she met my eyes.

Neither of us spoke, but she didn't have to say anything for me to know that she had encountered the tall gaunt man before, and I didn't have to say anything for her to realize that I knew enough about

Roseland to be unfazed by this bizarre event, enough to be a mortal danger to them all.

I caught her under the chin with a right uppercut and followed with a left that nailed her above and slightly to the side of the right eye, and she dropped like a sack of laundry down a chute.

Twenty-eight

I WASN'T PROUD OF MYSELF. I WASN'T exactly ashamed of myself, either, but I admit to being grateful that the laundry room didn't have a mirror.

Never before had I punched a woman. Not only was she a woman, but she was also smaller than I was. Not only was she a woman and smaller than I was, but she was also pretty in a cute, elfin way, and I felt as if I'd just beaten up Tinker Bell. Yes, I know, Tink was a fairy, not an elf, but I can't help how I felt.

I took solace in the belief that she knew the darkest secrets of Roseland and therefore must be a bad girl. She couldn't work here and be unaware of the grim collection of dead women in the mausoleum subcellar, which was easily accessible from the basement of the main house.

Worse, she seemed to be in love with Noah Wolflaw or at least admiring of him. What kind of person, laundress or not, could have tender feelings for a torturer and murderer of women?

I opened her mouth to be sure she hadn't severely bitten her tongue when I delivered the uppercut, but there wasn't any blood in there. She was going to have nasty bruising and a mean headache. I felt sorry about that, although probably not as sorry as I should have been.

In one corner of the laundry room was a seamstress station. I found a pair of scissors in a drawer.

Fishing among the clothes in one of the washing machines, which as yet contained no water, I found some garments—none of them unmentionables—that I could cut and rip to use as binding material.

Working quickly, worried that she would regain consciousness and berate me in a most unpleasant fashion, I securely tied her wrists in front of her and then bound her ankles. I connected those bindings with a hobble, which would prevent her from getting to her feet.

After opening the door and scoping the hallway, I cradled the maid in my arms and hurried with her to the furnace room next door. She was slender but she weighed substantially more than Tinker Bell.

I put her down in a corner, where she could not be seen from the door because of an intervening boiler as big as a space-shuttle booster rocket. She began to mutter like a sleeper in the midst of a disturbing dream as I hurried out of the room.

Once more in the laundry, I put away the scissors.

Snatched up a few lengths of cut fabric that I still needed. Threw the mutilated garments in the trash. Retrieved the pillowcase sack with hacksaw.

When I returned to Victoria Mors, she was moaning but not yet conscious. I sat her up with her back against the wall, positioning her approximately as the thirty-four women were arranged in the mausoleum subcellar, though of course she was still clothed, hadn't been tortured, was alive, and remained an admirer of Noah Wolflaw.

Using a yellow sash from a pair of cotton slacks in the laundry, I tied a noose around her neck. I secured the free end of the sash to an inch-diameter water line that came out of the wall and ran to the boiler. The pipe was securely anchored, and jerking on it with all my strength caused little noise; no one in the hallway could have heard it. Now she wouldn't be able to scooch along the floor and reach the door after I left.

As I knelt beside her, Victoria's eyelids fluttered. She opened her eyes and for a moment did not seem to know me. Then she must have recognized me, because she spit in my face.

"Nice," I said, and wiped off the spittle with a piece of a T-shirt that I had earlier scissored apart.

The act of spitting evidently caused some discomfort, because she winced and worked her jaws to assess the damage from the punch.

I said, "I'm sorry I had to hit you, ma'am."

In spite of the pain, she spit in my face again.

After wiping off the spittle, I said, "Do you know about the dead women in the mausoleum?"

She advised me to have an erotic experience with myself.

"Obviously you **do** know about the dead women."

She suggested that I had fornicated with a close relative.

In this light, her faded-denim eyes appeared to be the pale blue-purple of highly poisonous belladonna flowers. They were still large and limpid, but there was no mistaking them any longer for the eyes of a shy and winsome girl.

"What is this place, what is the purpose of all the strange machinery?"

Now in a mood to dispense culinary advice, she recommended that I make a dinner of the end product of her digestive tract.

Drawing the pistol from my belt holster and pointing it at her face, I said, "Who was the man who came into the laundry room?"

Refusing to be intimidated, she continued to favor me with her belladonna stare and told me in no uncertain terms to shove the pistol up a part of my anatomy that wasn't designed to serve as a holster.

"Don't underestimate me," I warned. "I'm more dangerous than I look."

After informing me that I had a face reminiscent of a monkey's posterior, she said, "You'll never get out of Roseland alive."

"Maybe none of us will." I pressed the muzzle of

the Beretta against her forehead. "I've killed a num-ber of people, ma'am, and I expect I'll have to kill some here."

"I'm not afraid of you."

"Maybe not," I said, "but **I'm** afraid of me."

That was too true. With the excuse that I am a defender of the innocent, I have done things that curl in my memory like worms in an infected apple. When I sleep, they squirm and wriggle forth to crawl the dreams from which I wake in a sweat.

Earlier she had told me that she never did any-thing dangerous, not even anything as relatively unchallenging as climbing an oak tree. As her fun-damental aversion to risk returned, she closed her eyes and shuddered.

Deciding to appeal to whatever shred of decency might still hang tattered in her heart, I took the gun away from her face, and in a tone of voice marked both by distaste and by a sympathetic desire to un-derstand, I said, "Is this some kind of cult, you've been caught up in it and you can't see a way out? Is Noah Wolflaw your Jim Jones or something?"

"Cultists are deranged," she said. "Ignorant and deranged. Cultists? No. We're the sanest people who ever lived."

"Ever, huh?"

"You and your kind are the deranged ones, and you don't even know it."

"Enlighten me."

Every feature of her face contorted to form a sneer

of maximum power and hauteur. "You bear the whips and scorns, but we don't and never will. You bear them, and they drive you mad."

"Well, that clears up everything," I said, and wondered if some voodoo priest I didn't remember meeting had placed a curse upon me that would condemn me to a life of association with people who spoke always in riddles.

Her face grew red and dark with hatred, and the contempt in her voice was so thick that her words seemed in danger of clotting on her tongue unspoken. "**Your** thoughts are enslaved to a fool, but ours will never be."

In spite of her denial, this seemed like cult talk, words passed down from the supreme leader and repeated by followers who only half understood them but resorted to them as mantras, whether they were appropriate to the moment or not.

Now that she was talking, I tried to bring her back to the issue of the dead women in the mausoleum. "You called Wolflaw one of the greatest men who ever lived. How can you follow him so submissively when he's treated those women like dolls to be played with, broken, and discarded?"

Shared gender with the victims was not enough to squeeze a drop of pity from Victoria Mors. "They're not women like me. They weren't like us. They were like **you**. Animals, not gods. Walking shadows, poor players. Their lives signified nothing."

The more she said, the madder she seemed, the

pretense of sanity now too far behind her to be retrieved.

Yet something in her words seemed familiar to me, as if in some other place and time I had heard certain of these phrases used in a rational context, for a nobler purpose.

I felt contaminated by this Victoria, who seemed like the evil twin of the laundress, but I pressed her further. "Where did those women come from? How did Wolflaw persuade them to let him bring them here?"

She smirked like a child with a dirty secret that she relished revealing. "Noah never leaves Roseland to go farther than to town. Paulie cruises far and wide for them. Henry goes fishing, too, all over the state and into Nevada, elsewhere."

"They . . . participate with Noah?"

She shook her head. "No. They don't care what he does, though they have no taste for it themselves. But you interrupted me before I could tell you the best part."

"So tell me."

"I'm better than all of them, better than Paulie or Henry, at setting the hook and reeling in the pretties. Once I've identified one who has the look Noah wants, I scheme to meet her. I chat her up. They always like me. We delight in each other's company. I'm so good at making them like and trust me. I'm petite, almost a waif. I've got this pixie face. Who can distrust a pixie?"

"Like an elf, I thought, a pretty elf."

Victoria fired up a warm and saucy smile and winked at me. For a moment, the mask of pixie innocence and charm was so well crafted that I could see nothing of the demon behind the elfin beauty even though I knew it festered there.

"Sooner than later," she continued, "we meet for lunch. I pick her up where she works or at her home. We never reach the restaurant. I've got a little hypodermic gun. Tranquilizer puts her out almost instantly. When she wakes, sometimes hours later, sometimes days, depending on how far we have to drive, she's tethered to a post of Noah's bed, and she learns what she is and what we are."

Pixie or elf, the sight of her sickened me. "And what **are** you?"

"Outsiders," she said, and I thought she capitalized the word. "We're Outsiders, with no limits, no rules, no fears."

If what they had was not a cult by name, it was a cult in every way that mattered.

"He's not your Jim Jones," I said. "He's your Charles Manson, Ted Bundy with apostles."

"Sometimes he lets me watch." She saw that she revolted me, and she grinned wickedly. "Poor boy, you can never understand. You're a walking shadow, a poor player. You don't signify."

Those words, which she had spoken before, again rang familiar to me.

A part of me still wanted to understand, to find

a reason why she had no choice but to submit to Wolflaw. "He must have some hold on you."

"Love," she said. "Love for eternity."

Apparently love of their kind meant never having to say you're sorry **about anything**.

As though talking about watching Wolflaw with the women made Victoria's mouth water, she spat an unusual volume with special force in my face. "The foot will be on your neck within the hour."

Cleaning off with the now-damp piece of T-shirt, I said, "What foot would that be?"

"The inaudible and noiseless foot."

"Oh, right, that one." I wasn't going to get anything more useful out of her. I balled up the cloth and said, "Be a good girl. Open wide."

She pressed her lips together. I pinched her pert nose, and she held her breath until she had to gasp for it, and I shoved the wad of cloth in her mouth.

Although her words weren't clear, I thought she called me a stupid cocker, although I wasn't sure why being compared to that lovely breed of spaniel should be considered an insult.

She tried to tongue the cloth back at me, but I held her mouth shut. With some pleasure.

I snatched up the last length of cloth and tied it around the lower part of her face as she tried and failed to bite me, knotting it at the back of her head, to prevent her from expelling the wad in her mouth.

Holstering the pistol, I was relieved I hadn't needed to shoot her. Shooting one woman, even a murderous one, had been traumatic enough to last me a lifetime.

Once, in a burned-out Indian casino, I had watched a 150-pound mountain lion creep up behind a woman who worked really, really hard at being bad; she had been holding me at gunpoint, and rather than take a bullet in the gut and another one in the head, I hadn't warned her and had allowed the big cat to go at her like a famished pothead chowing down on a triple-patty cheeseburger. I didn't like myself much—in fact not at all—for doing that, but somehow it was easier to live with than pulling a trigger.

Bound foot and hand, hobbled, gagged, tightly leashed to a water pipe, Victoria Mors glared poisoned darts at me from her belladonna eyes.

I crossed the room, switched off the lights, cracked open the door, saw that the way was clear, and stepped into the basement hall.

I wished that I were Harry Potter with his invisibility cloak and all the other fabulous gear that a young wizard carried with him. But I had a 9-mm pistol, plenty of spare ammunition, and a high-quality hacksaw, which was more armament than I'd possessed on other perilous occasions. Besides, if all you had to do was throw on such a cloak, there would be little fun sneaking into the dragon's lair, either for you or the dragon.

For a moment, I stood at the closed door to the furnace room, listening. I had no doubt that Victoria was shrieking behind the stifling gag. Even at risk of strangulation, she would be trying to rattle the water pipe. But I could hear nothing.

In the laundry room one last time, I went to the sink and washed my face with liquid soap and hot water.

The really bad woman whom I allowed to be killed by a mountain lion once spat a mouthful of red wine in my face.

Women don't find me as appealing as they do, say, that singer Justin Bieber. But I take comfort from the fact that Justin Bieber wouldn't know how to escape from a walk-in freezer after being chained there by a couple of huge guys in porkpie hats. He couldn't sing his way out of a spot like that; inevitably, he would be a Biebersicle.

Hoping that the tall gaunt man would appear again to explain who he was and what master switch he wanted me to throw, I continued along the hallway, checking rooms. I didn't find anything interesting until the door at the end.

Twenty-nine

STEPPING THROUGH THAT END DOOR, I seemed to be in a different building from Noah Wolflaw's elegant mansion. The large rectangular room had a plasterboard ceiling and beadboard walls, all painted white. Set in two pairs in the farther wall, the four windows were covered by oilcloth shades hung on old-fashioned roller bars.

In one corner stood a wooden cabinet with a metal sink on top. On one side of the sink was a lever-action, cast-iron hand pump to draw water from a well.

A large oak desk backed up to each set of the windows, and on each desk was a work lamp with a green-glass shade. The office chairs were entirely of oak, with hard-rubber wheels on steel-shank castors. They were in fine condition but looked a hundred years old.

On each desk stood also a candlestick phone of

brass painted matte black, with the mouthpiece at the top, the earpiece on a cord and hanging from a cradle, and an early rotary dial on the base.

Along the shorter walls were oak filing cabinets and what seemed to be a map chest with wide, shallow drawers. In the open part of the room, two drafts-man tables stood back-to-back, with oak stools, and to the right of them was a large oak table high enough that you would have to stand at it to work.

On the tall table lay a four-inch-thick set of blue-prints bound on the left. The cover page presented a pen-and-ink rendering of the main house as it would appear when viewed from the west. Under that su-perb drawing, the name ROSELAND was handsomely hand-lettered. And in the title block at the bottom, to the left, were the words CONSTANTINE CLOYCE RESIDENCE.

This appeared to be the room in which the orig-inal contractor and perhaps an on-site architect worked back in the day when Roseland was being built. It must have been the first thing constructed, and the meticulous preservation of the space sug-gested that Constantine Cloyce, the press baron and silent-movie mogul, intended to create an estate that would have the historic importance of someplace like the Hearst Castle.

The only things this space had in common with the rest of the house were the concrete floor, in which were embedded copper circles etched with elongated eights, and the dustless, ageless quality of a hermetically sealed exhibit in a museum.

As I toured the room, I was suddenly drawn to reconsider the oilcloth-covered windows because I realized there should be none in a basement room. Putting down the pillowcase containing the hacksaw, leaning across one of the desks, I pinched the ring pull and put up the shade.

The view beyond the window stunned me, and I stood paralyzed by disbelief. When I could think to move, I went to the other desk, reached across it, and put up the shade at the second window, as if I hoped to find a different scene or the blank basement wall that should have been there. The same vista greeted me.

In addition to the door by which I'd entered, another waited in what would be the west wall, flanked by the desks. I went to it, hesitated, opened it, and stepped outside.

The long driveway that sloped down from the main house to the county road was gravel instead of cobblestones as it had been before. At the farther end of that long lane, neither a gatehouse nor gates existed to guard admittance to Roseland.

No stone wall encircled the huge property. The land, which had not yet been excavated and shaped to the needs of the construction team, rolled away to neighboring parcels with nothing between but property-line-marker stakes painted white.

The parklike landscaping did not exist. Instead, fields with waist-high grass and weeds were shaded by many fewer oak trees than those that I had walked among in the past few days.

Distracted by this impossible vista, I walked perhaps thirty feet along the graveled drive before I quite realized that I had moved away from the door.

Turning, I looked back and saw that no palatial residence rose behind me, as if Wolflaw's great house had vaporized.

Two structures were there instead, the first being a clapboard building with a tar-paper roof and four front windows flanking an open door. This must be the construction shack from which I had stepped a moment earlier.

The second, perhaps a hundred feet to the left of the larger building, was obviously an outhouse.

For most people, reality is as simple as a painting, hanging before them in their frame of reference, understood and unquestioned. I live with the awareness that under the apparent painting are countless layers, previous scenes that have been painted over. Any physicist well-schooled in quantum mechanics or chaos theory knows that reality is a beast of mysterious dimensions and potentials and that the more we learn, the more we realize how much we don't know.

Because that understanding of reality has shaped my life, I am seldom knocked flat by astonishment.

In the absence of Roseland, I was still on my feet, but I felt like Wile E. Coyote after he'd been run down by a bulldozer.

The sense that the architect had structured this place by the application of a new geometry with a mysterious dimension, which I mentioned before, was nothing compared to the shock of this latest discovery. Finding rooms connected in ways I didn't remember, the feeling that there was always more to any room or passage than the eye could see now seemed prescient.

Distant engine noise drew my attention to the west once more. On the paved but primitive two-lane county road, one coming from the south and one from the north, were what appeared to be two Ford Model T's, black with open passenger compartments.

As they passed each other about where the gates to Roseland would one day be, other traffic appeared in the north. Laden with bales of hay, a horse-drawn wagon clopped and rattled along.

I stood trembling, not in fear as much as in mystification. My heart knocked out hoofbeats, too, but they were faster than those of the draft horse.

Rowing lazily through rising thermals, three ducks sailed low across the land, as silent as the flywheels and rotating spheres under the mausoleum that did not yet exist here.

If man-made aircraft plied these skies, they would

be biplanes, not airliners. Here, no ocean had ever been flown across; and no boot prints marked the soil of the moon.

A breeze whispered in from the north. With it came a fear that if the construction-shack door blew shut, some connection would be broken and I would not be able to open it and return to Roseland in its twenty-first-century grandeur.

I might be stuck here in a world with no penicillin, no polio vaccine, no Teflon cookware, no John D. MacDonald novels, no music by Paul Simon or Connie Dover or Israel Kamakawiwo'ole, no comfortable athletic shoes, no Velcro.

On the other hand, here I would find no reality TV, no TV of any kind, no nuclear weapons, no road rage, no talking on a cell phone in the movie theater, no tofu turkey.

In the end, as much might be gained as lost— except that this far in the past, most of the friends I'd ever made and loved hadn't been born.

Hurrying inside, I pulled the door shut against a past in which neither I nor my parents had yet been conceived.

I went to the interior door and opened it. Beyond waited the basement hallway, yet when I turned to look at the windows, I saw Roseland still unrealized.

The construction shack was above ground, the basement below grade. One existed then, the other now. Yet somehow they were linked spatially and chronologically. As an air lock on a spaceship served

as a transition chamber between the atmosphere inside the vessel and the vacuum of outer space, this
room connected one moment perhaps ninety years
past with the present.

I closed the door to the basement, returned to one
of the desks, and sat in the antique office chair to
calm my nerves and to think.

Generally speaking, just as Sherlock Holmes reasoned his way to solutions with the help of his pipe
and violin, I am better able to mull over a complicated problem when I am frying. But I lacked a griddle, a spatula, and something to cook.

After a while, I searched through the desk drawers
but learned nothing except that whoever worked here
had been obsessed with order and neatness. I learned
the same from the drawers of the second desk.

When I returned to the blueprints on the table,
I saw more in the title block of the cover page than
had interested me previously. The impressed seal of
the architect. His name—James Lee Brock—and
his address in Los Angeles. Under the architect's
name were two words and a name—MECHANICAL
SYSTEMS: NIKOLA TESLA.

All I knew of Nikola Tesla was that he was called
the Genius Who Lit the World, and that as the
nineteenth century turned to the twentieth, he had
nearly as much to do with the electrification of civi-
lization and the associated industrial revolution as
did Thomas Edison.

And on my first day in Roseland, chatting with

Henry Lolam at the gatehouse, I learned that Constantine Cloyce had been interested in cutting-edge science and in the supernatural, having been friends with an unlikely spectrum of people that included the psychic and medium Madame Helena Petrovna Blavatsky, and at the extreme other end, the famous physicist and inventor Tesla.

Finding Madame Blavatsky's fabled name on the blueprints would have been strange, but it was nowhere to be seen. Whatever might be going on at Roseland, I suspected now that it might have nothing to do with the supernatural and everything to do with science. Weird science, but science nonetheless.

In the wide, shallow drawers of the map chest, I found many sets of mechanical-systems plans, all signed by Nikola Tesla. Among them were drawings of—and engineering specifics related to—the spheres, the flywheels standing on the bell-shaped machines, the intricate arrangements of gears I'd seen in the subcellars of the mausoleum, and much more.

I felt pretty sure that I knew the identity of the tall, gaunt, mustachioed man who had spoken to me on three occasions. Mr. Nikola Tesla. Considering that he died decades ago but wasn't a lingering spirit like any I'd previously encountered, I knew **who** he was but not **what** he was.

Thirty

NONE OF THE DRAWINGS OR ENGI-neering details enlightened me as to the purpose of all this exotic machinery. In high school, I was a member of the baseball team, not the science club.

With a renewed sense that time was running out, I retrieved the pillowcase sack with the hacksaw. I returned to the basement hallway, closing the door behind me.

To my right were narrow, enclosed service stairs. I assumed the stairs in the wine cellar went up to the kitchen, but I had no idea where these might lead.

Like every floor and stair tread in this house, these were as tight as if they had been built yesterday. Not one creak betrayed me as I ascended two flights to the main level with the intention of going to the second floor, where the boy was imprisoned.

As I reached the ground floor, however, I heard heavy footsteps above me, descending. Alarmed, I opened the landing door, slipped out of the staircase, and dashed across the immense foyer to another door that, for all I knew, led to a meadow in the Pleistocene epoch, where a herd of mastodons would stomp me into mush.

It was a coat closet.

From the size of the closet—hangers and rod space for maybe two hundred coats—I inferred that Constantine Cloyce intended Roseland to be **the** social locus along this part of the coast. In its early days, the estate might have been just that, but perhaps not for long.

Out in the foyer, a door was flung open with such force that it banged hard against its stop, and footsteps slapped across marble.

A second door opened almost as violently as the first, and other footsteps sounded as Mrs. Tameed said, "I smelled ozone on the second floor."

Paulie Sempiterno, who had apparently crashed into the foyer through the front door, said, "I started to smell it halfway back from the gatehouse."

"Then it's not localized."

"We don't know for sure yet."

"I know," Mrs. Tameed declared.

"It could be just a few eddies."

"No, it's finally full tide," Mrs. Tameed said, except that between the **full** and **tide,** she inserted a crude but alliterative word that I won't repeat.

"But we haven't had one in years," Sempiterno said.

Suddenly I smelled ozone.

They must have smelled it in the foyer, too, because they spat out four crude words, two each, alternating one word at a time, as if they were in a cussing contest.

Their footsteps raced off, seemingly in different directions, and I didn't hear any doors slamming.

I didn't know what was meant by full tide, since we were a mile or farther from the ocean. Whatever it meant, I thought that trying to hide from it in a coat closet would probably prove to be a mortal mistake.

After waiting half a minute for the way to clear, I ventured into the foyer. I moved quickly toward the front door to peer through one of the sidelights, to see if Sempiterno was hulking around out there. He wasn't.

As I tried to decide whether to dare the service stairs again, where the door stood open, I heard footsteps hurrying down, and Mrs. Tameed shouting— "Carlo! Carlo, quick!"—at the top of her voice and in evident panic.

A columned archway separated the foyer from the drawing room, and from that formidable space, out of sight for the moment but not for long, Sempiterno shouted back to her: "Here! Here! I'm coming!"

Carlo?

If this were a sex farce by a British playwright, hilarious antics would ensue when we all collided in the foyer. The terror in their voices, however, suggested that something big was about to happen, something that would reveal more about Roseland than I had yet learned, more than they would approve of me knowing.

Deciding not to stay for the rest of this act, I stepped outside and closed the front door behind me.

In the circular terminus of the driveway, under the portico, stood the electric all-terrain mini truck with balloon tires. Paulie Sempiterno had earlier been driving it overland.

I went to the vehicle, not with the intention of commandeering it, but to pretend to be admiring it if Sempiterno plunged out of the house. My hope was to distract him from considering that I might have recently been inside and overheard him talking with Mrs. Tameed.

The astringent scent of ozone was mild, not strong enough to burn the nostrils. But I remembered what it previously portended.

Although no early twilight descended, I scanned the grounds and spotted a pack of the piggish things that Mrs. Tameed called freaks. They were far away, acres of north lawn between us, but they were coming toward the portico with their characteristic determination, in their usual unpleasant mood.

As I started toward the house, steel panels dropped out of the limestone lintels in the window surrounds and snugged down to the sills. A larger sheet of steel whisked over the front door, meeting the threshold so tightly that I couldn't have slipped even a note of urgent appeal under it.

Now I knew what had taken the place of the

window bars when the house had been—per Chef Shilshom—remodeled. Mmmmm? Indeed. There you go.

Because the pack was somewhat slowed by its deformed members, I might be able to outrun them. For a while. Although upright, these things were reminiscent of wild boars, which are relentless predators. And though I don't mean this in a braggadocious way, I'm sure that I smelled singularly delicious to them.

I ran to the mini truck, which had a roll bar instead of a roof and no doors to close out either sunshine or a pack of freaks. The keys were in the ignition. I got behind the wheel.

The electric motor was so quiet that, as I put the vehicle in gear, I could hear the distant snarling and squealing of the primate swine even though they were still the better part of a football field away from me.

An electric vehicle doesn't serve for a high-speed chase as well as anything with an internal-combustion engine. Try to picture Steve McQueen in **Bullitt,** pursuing his quarry through the streets of San Francisco in a Chevy Volt. Right.

Instead of daring to lead the pack on a chase across the fields and hills of Roseland, I cruised out of the portico and west on the driveway, toward the gatehouse. The windows there were barred. Henry Lolam had a sidearm, a shotgun, and a rifle. We could hole up for the duration and read poetry to each other while the hogs threw themselves furiously at the ironbound oak door.

The balloon tires made a flabby **budda-budda-budda** sound on the cobblestone pavement. I could no longer hear the freaks.

When I glanced back, I discovered that they had come to a halt. They stood on the north lawn, heads held high—except for those that were humpbacked and otherwise twisted—looking at me, at the house, at me, as if making a choice might flummox them.

They were like creatures from an apocalyptic revelation, not only hideous in appearance but also an embodiment of the foul and pitiless forces that, since time immemorial, have haunted the world. Pale, brutish, powerful, they seemed to have come from some level of the inferno that Dante had overlooked. Several of them appeared to be wearing ragged garments, though I supposed that I must have been mistaking the shaggy coat of a boar for clothing.

Their indecision allowed me to open a considerable lead, and I grew confident of achieving the comparative safety of the gatehouse. I parked by the covered stoop and hopped out of the trucklet, leaving the motor running just in case.

Henry wasn't sitting on the stoop, reading poetry. He stood at a barred window, peering out at me.

I tried the door. Locked. I knocked. "Henry, let me in."

Still at the window to the left of the door, his voice

muffled and distorted by the glass, Henry said, "Go away."

His boyish face was eerily without expression, although his green eyes appeared as anguished as ever.

"Freaks, Henry. You know about the freaks. Open the door."

I thought he said, "You're not one of us."

Glancing east, I discovered the freaks had decided on a course of action. They hustled along the driveway, toward the gatehouse.

"Henry, I'm sorry I needled you about aliens and colonoscopies. I should be open-minded. Let me in. I promise I'll believe in them."

Through the closed window, I heard some of his words: "There . . . no aliens . . . wish . . . were."

"It's a big universe, Henry. Anything's possible."

"Aliens . . . can't free me . . . Roseland."

"Maybe they can free you, Henry. Let me in. We'll talk."

His face hardened into hatred that I'd never before seen in him. I thought he said, "You're . . . nothing . . . pathetic cocker."

I recalled Victoria Mors calling me a stupid cocker as I was trying to shove the gag in her mouth.

The pack was two hundred feet away, but shambling faster. Most did indeed wear ragged, filthy clothing, obviously not for modesty or even for warmth as much as for decoration. Here a head scarf, there a winding of fabric around an arm. This one with multiple necklaces of braided cloth. That one with a ropey arrangement of loops and tassels around its waist.

Ozone scented the day, and the air shimmered as it does on a hot summer afternoon when heat rises off scorching pavement in wriggling thermals. This was a California February, however, the weather mild, even slightly cool.

Although they looked fierce enough to kill with hands, with tusks and teeth, some of the advancing creatures carried weapons. They favored three-foot lengths of pipe secured to their wrists with lanyards, but I also saw a sickle. Pickax. Billhook. Hatchet.

Tall, bodies slabbed with muscle, bristling with ratty patches of wiry white and gray hair, heads thrust forward, they were grunting in unison now, suddenly more organized than before, coming along the driveway like the phalanxes of a nightmare army, like orcs out of Mordor, and there was no wizard to help me defend against them. Most had porcine faces fitted with wolfish grins. Others wore asymmetric faces, eyes at different levels, skulls badly misshapen by irregular growths of bone, and their limbs were ill-jointed, awkwardly long. Here were all the ideologies of violence distilled and given material form, animalistic but not merely animals, for they had an implacable aggressive intent that seemed disturbingly human.

The air between me and them, in fact all around me, writhed as if tortured with heat, and I thought the pack might shimmer away like a mirage. But the thermals—or whatever they were—raveled back into the earth, the air stabilized, and the freaks were so close that I could smell them.

I sprang into the mini truck, popped the brake, and fled.

Thirty-one

THE ELECTRIC MOTOR ACCELERATED a bit quicker than an arthritic grandfather getting up from his favorite armchair. I turned left between the gatehouse and the gate. Racing south across a wide lawn in the mini truck, I glanced back after fifty yards. They were still coming, but they weren't gaining ground. Fifty yards farther, when I looked, they were falling behind.

The flawless lawn gave way to Nature's plan. I trucked on, ascending a gentle slope for about two hundred yards, while various insects leaped and flew out of the tall grass in front of me, like terrified pedestrians throwing themselves out of the path of a drunk driver.

At the top, as I turned east to drive around rather than through a grove of oaks, I looked back and saw that the freaks had not chased after me into the meadow. They were heading toward the main house.

I didn't stop to leap out of the truck and do a vic-

tory lap around it, but instead angled east-southeast.
I intended to circle the developed part of the estate
and return to the guest tower, to see if Annamaria
might be under siege.

On that rolling land, the big tires and apparently
customized suspension provided a ride that was less
like bounding over rough territory than like being
on a boat as it slid up the face of a wave, down the
back, and wallowed through a trough toward the
next wall of water.

I weltered along a glen, searching for an easy way
up the next slope, which was thick with brush in
some places and rocky in others. Abruptly the landscape all around me rippled vertically, as if snakes
of heat were rising from it again, though the air remained cool.

Paulie Sempiterno and Mrs. Tameed had spoken
of eddies and a full tide. They hadn't been talking
about the sea, but about this phenomenon.

As I squinted at the way ahead, resisting a greasy
nausea, the quality of the light changed, although
not as dramatically as when morning had turned to
night in a minute. The pale grass became a darker
gold, the silver weeds tarnished. Racing shadows
swelled and withered and swelled and slithered
across the land.

I slowed, braked to a halt, and reluctantly looked up.

For a moment, I saw again the yellow sky that
frightened me more than did the primate swine.
These were not merely Earth's heavens in the throes

of Armageddon. An apocalypse is a revelation, and this was an **apocalyptic** sky, in the sense that it revealed what humankind, by its arrogance and reckless certitude, would bring down upon itself.

The quivering thermals that had brought the fearsome skyscape now shimmered it away. The heavens became mostly blue again, with an armada of ordinary storm clouds still threatening in the north, where they had been all morning, as if riding at anchor.

I hadn't imagined those hostile yellow heavens any more than I had dreamed that I'd stepped through a doorway into a time prior to Roseland's existence. Both moments had been as real as the warm saliva that Ms. Victoria Mors had spat in my face.

I sat in the landscaper's truck, in the glen between two hills, letting my heart quiet itself. Usually I can knit clues into a theory while on my feet and dodging anything thrown at me, but in this case I needed a moment of stillness to make sure that I didn't drop a stitch.

The massive wall around Roseland, perhaps housing fantastical machinery like that I had seen in the cellars of the mausoleum, not only physically isolated the estate but also set it apart in other ways. These acres were an island of the irrational in the sea of everyday reality.

Whatever the intention had been behind Roseland's creation, the dire events of the moment were side effects that no one had expected. After the fact, they had taken steps to defend against those side effects: the bars on windows, the steel shutters, all the guns and stores of ammunition.

The freaks might be only an infrequent threat. Nevertheless, to live in this bedlam, the people here must have believed that whatever benefit they received from the system they created was worth the cost of nightly wariness and occasional full assaults by creatures that seemed to belong here less than to some other time or place.

I thought that I knew what the benefit might be, why they didn't simply pull the master switch and eliminate the mortal threat of the freaks.

And I suspected that the benefit was simultaneously a curse. It led to their conviction that they were far superior to anyone not of Roseland. Not merely superior. They saw themselves as gods and the rest of us as animals.

Men and women who seek to become gods must first lose their humanity.

Noah Wolflaw's homicides and the complicity of the others in his crimes seemed neither insane nor criminal to them, any more than I would consider myself mad or criminal for hooking a fish, gutting it, and cooking it for dinner. I satisfied a hunger. Wolflaw would say that he merely satisfied a more exotic appetite. To him, my fish was as far below me on the ladder of species as the women he killed were below him.

Wolflaw had not merely lost his humanity. He had thrown it away with all the force that he could muster.

My next step, after checking on Annamaria, would be to find out who the people of Roseland really were. They were either not who they claimed to be or not **only** who they claimed to be.

I am one **mega**suspicious pretty-boy, pathetic, stupid cocker.

The time-out had served me well. I drove farther along the glen, looking for a place where the hillside was navigable.

Suddenly he was standing forty feet in front of me. I could have driven straight through him, but I braked to a halt.

There in the wild grass, he wore a three-piece suit and a necktie. From five feet in front of the trucklet, he regarded me with that deadpan look that had once been famous.

He was portly, with a round face and full cheeks and two chins, but not immense like Chef Shilshom. Unlike the chef, he had come by his physique not by indulgence but because of genetics, having been stout as a small child. His lower lip protruded far past the upper, as if he were pondering how best to deal with a problematic person whom he wished to be rid of but did not wish to insult.

"This is not a good time," I told him. "My plate is full. My cup runneth over. I'm sorry. I don't usually speak in clichés. And those weren't references to your weight. I'm just frazzled. I'm not able to deal with one more complication."

Among some of the lingering dead who have come

to me for help, a couple have been famous performers in their lifetimes. In spite of what you might think if you closely follow the entertainment-news programs on TV and the Internet, celebrities do have souls.

In the first three of my memoirs, I have written about my rather long relationship with Mr. Elvis Presley's spirit. He appeared to me when I was in high school, and we hung around together for quite a few years. For reasons he was slow to make clear to me, the King of Rock 'n' Roll was reluctant to move on to the Other Side, though he wanted to be there. The problem was not anything as simple as that he was worried there would be no deep-fried peanut-butter-and-banana sandwiches in the next life. Eventually I helped him cross over.

Then came Mr. Frank Sinatra. His spirit was my companion only for a few weeks. They were memorable days. As a poltergeist, as in life, Mr. Sinatra could throw a heck of a hard punch when you needed backup.

I don't know why I assumed that if the spirit of another famous person were to come to me, seeking assistance in moving on from this world, he or she would have been a renowned singer.

The gentleman in the suit walked around to the passenger side of the mini truck. He had an unusual aura of authority because it was in no way stern or superior and because it was twined with an air of congeniality.

"Sir, I am honored, I really am, that you would

come to me for assistance. I'm an admirer. If I survive this, I'll do what I can for you. But, see, there's so much going on in Roseland that my head will explode if I have to think about one more thing."

He put his hands to his head and then flung them away, fingers wide, as if depicting the consequences of a detonating skull.

"Yes, exactly. I'm sorry about this. Never say no to a spirit in need. That's my motto. Well, it's not my motto, but it's a principle of mine. I don't have a motto. Unless maybe 'If it's worth eating, it's worth frying.' I'm babbling, aren't I? That's because I'm such a fan. I really am. I guess you hear that all the time. Or did when you were alive. I guess you don't hear it as often since you're dead."

The dire situation in Roseland was not so much the reason for my nervous babbling. And I was not rattled by the fact that I really was an admirer of his work. Those were both causes, but I was also intimidated by that deadpan expression, which suggested that he had the patience to outwait me until my resistance wilted, and because it reminded me of the wit and intelligence that were behind it. Elvis? Piece of cake. Sinatra? Mostly easy. But I was out of my league with this one, who was probably smarter than me by a factor of ten.

"You've waited a long time to cross over," I said. "Must be thirty years. Give me another day. Then we'll talk. Or I'll talk, since you can't. But just now, you know, there's all these bad people. And dead bodies. The woman on the horse. The imprisoned boy. And a ticking clock. You know all about ticking clocks. Who knows more about ticking clocks than you? And I've got pigs to deal with! They're big, mean, walkin'-tall pigs, sir. You never had to deal with primate swine. I'd be no good for you right now."

He smiled and nodded. He waved me on.

As he turned away, before he dematerialized, I said, "Wait. Mr. Hitchcock."

He faced me once more.

"You weren't . . . you didn't . . . I mean, you didn't die here, did you?"

He grimaced and shook his head. **No.**

"Did you ever visit Roseland when you were alive?"

He shook his head again.

"Back in the day, did you ever do business with Constantine Cloyce's movie studio?"

He nodded, and his expression was uncharacteristically fierce.

"I guess you didn't like working with him."

Mr. Alfred Hitchcock put one finger in his mouth, as if to make himself gag.

"But you're not here because of him."

No.

"You're here just for me."

Yes.

"I'm flattered."

He shrugged.

"Just let me get the boy out of here. Then we'll

take a meeting. That was a Hollywood joke. Not a very good one."

His smile was grandfatherly. I thought I was going to like him, assuming that I would live long enough to know him better.

He waved me on again.

I drove a hundred feet along the glen until I found a navigable place in the hillside. When I looked back, Mr. Hitchcock was gone.

I cruised to the top, started down the farther slope—and braked sharply when I saw four freaks beyond the next vale, in single file, following the ridgeline of a lower hill.

Although the novelty of their appearance had worn off, they were no less strange than ever, creatures that might have stepped out of a delirium inspired by a tropical disease, conjured by a mind in the sweaty grip of malaria, more suited to a world with a yellow sky than to even this Roseland, which itself seemed at times to be a fever dream.

Because the electric vehicle was quiet and because the swine things were as usual intent upon making their way toward whatever mayhem they had in mind, I hoped they might not notice me. They noticed. They came to a halt and turned to stare directly at me.

I pulled the wheel to the right, intending to turn 180 degrees and retreat at full speed. The vehicle wouldn't move. The battery was dead.

Thirty-two

THE FREAKS SAW ME, BUT THAT DIDN'T mean they would find me important enough that they would deviate from their current mission just to rip my head off. There's nothing special about my head, except to me, of course, no tattoos or nose rings or gold teeth that would make it a worthy trophy.

This squad included none of the grotesquely deformed kind with ungainly limbs. They were all strapping specimens who conformed to the highest standards of their monstrous breed, any of them worthy of a best-in-show prize at the next competition on the Island of Dr. Moreau.

They seemed more organized and purposeful than previous groups. They hadn't been shambling along the crest of the hill, but instead trotting single file in what seemed to be a disciplined procession. Furthermore, each held the same weapon in its right hand—an axe with a head that included both a cutting edge and a hammer. This uniform weaponry and the fact that they all sported foot-long scraps of red cloth that dangled from their left ears suggested perhaps a smaller tribe within the larger one.

They were on a reconnaissance mission or had a particular target and a timetable for taking it out. Or perhaps this was lunchtime in Swineville and the slops were in the trough, in which case the burly young beasts would want to get there before the best stuff had been scarfed up by greedy pigs.

Sitting in the mini truck, I sought to inflate my optimism until it was bigger than the balloon tires. But the cold sweat on my brow and on the palms of my hands belied my confident smile.

I stared across the vale at the four, trying to show no fear. They stared at me, probably insulted because I wasn't showing any fear.

When you consider how difficult it often can be for two people of the same nationality, the same community, the same race, and the same religion to understand each other's point of view and to live in harmony, you can see why I had doubts that this encounter would end with hugs and professions of eternal friendship.

The four freaks moved at the same time, coming off the far crest and descending the hill toward the vale between their slope and mine. They didn't advance at a run, but slowly, and not in single file, but side by side.

Perhaps their measured reaction, so different from the frenzied pursuits and snarling fury I previously witnessed, meant that they were not as driven by hatred as others of their kind, that they did not love violence for violence's sake, that they were a more moderate sect open to dialogue and compromise.

I got out from behind the steering wheel and stood beside the mini truck.

When the four were halfway down the farther hill, they began to swing their axes at their sides, in unison: forward, back, forward, back, forward and around in a full circle; forward, back, forward, back, forward and around. . . .

Considerably less hopeful of finding common ground, I drew my pistol. Although I disliked firearms, I wished I had a handgun of a higher caliber than 9 mm.

The Beretta had seemed more than adequate until I found myself without wheels, in open land, challenged by four primate swine in circumstances that allowed a better look at them than I'd had before. Each towered over six feet and weighed perhaps three hundred pounds. The articulation of their knee joints, hips, and spines was nearly human, which ensured that any comic potential in their appearance was forfeited; in them I could see no slightest suggestion of Porky Pig. They had long-toed feet and hands with fingers, not cloven hooves, although it appeared that the nails on all of their limbs were of dark-brown hornlike material that tapered into talons designed to eviscerate.

I would have preferred to flee rather than to try to

stand them off, but I wasn't confident that I could outrun them. I was lighter and more limber than they were, and I should therefore be faster. Wild boars, however, have a top speed of thirty miles an hour. I didn't know whether there was enough swine in these creatures for them to run that fast, but I knew for sure that, if they could, there wasn't enough swine in me to escape them.

As they reached the bottom of the opposing hill and entered the grassy vale, I fired one round into the air. In retrospect, letting off a warning shot in that situation seems as foolish as shaking a finger in disapproval at a looming grizzly bear.

I hoped to chase them away rather than be forced to kill them, even if they might be looking forward to—as Mrs. Tameed vividly suggested to the nameless boy—buggering me a few times before chewing off my face.

When they kept coming across the narrow vale, I took a two-hand grip on the pistol, stepped into the isosceles stance, drew down on the brute at the right end of the line, and squeezed off five rounds.

I thought three of them hit their target. The beast staggered, dropped its axe, and swayed.

Copper-jacketed hollow points were killing ammo. They bloomed on penetration, and the damage to tissue could be grievous.

For a moment, the impact of the bullets knocked the beast's voice out of it, but then it began to shriek.

Surprised that it remained on its feet, I pumped

out two more shots. The second caused the wounded creature to clasp one hand to its throat. Then it toppled backward.

The three other swine things neither rushed toward nor away from me. They stood beside their fallen comrade, staring at it, as if not quite sure what had brought it down.

Still in a shooting stance, I sighted on another beast but waited, hoping that they would now see the wisdom of withdrawal.

The three turned and gazed up at me, at that moment not with rage and hatred, but with puzzlement. They looked back and forth from me to the dead creature, as though wondering how and why I had killed it. But then I thought that their expression might be less puzzlement than indecision. Among ordinary pigs, some have been known to eat their young; so perhaps these three were considering whether to pursue me or instead to settle down for a bit of cannibalism while the carcass was fresh.

I'd seen enough of their kind to have noted that instead of the sameness of faces within most other animal species, there were numerous differences in their features, one to another, not as many as among human beings, but enough to make them seem less like a pack and more like a gathering of individuals.

Now, as they looked from their dead companion to me, the unique quality of each grotesque face made them more terrifying than ever. If they didn't think as one, all on the same track of blind instinct, if each could scheme in its singular fashion about how best to pursue and trap and kill its quarry, the likelihood of escaping them in any extended chase would be hardly greater than the likelihood of foiling black-robed Death himself when he knocked on your door with his harvesting scythe in one bony hand and a termination notice in his other.

Sunshine winked off the blades of the axes and laid a sheen on the skull-crushing hammer heads.

The freaks turned their attention from me and the corpse to one another. Their wide jackal mouths cracked open, but if they made any sounds, I could not hear them.

Each snaky, hairless, white tail, with a tuft of gray at the tip, raised straight up—one, two, three.

Their pointed ears twitched. Pricked forward. And then flattened back along their skulls.

They spread out at the foot of the slope, putting more space between one another.

Again, they swung their axes forward, back, forward, back, and around in a complete circle. As if the blades were stropped sharper against the whetting air, flares of sun flew from the weapons.

I had needed seven rounds to bring down the first freak. At that rate, I'd need twenty-one shots to kill the remaining three.

Ten rounds remained in the Beretta's magazine. The spare in my holster contained another seventeen, but I doubted that I would have the time to swap it for the empty one as they stormed toward me.

Shakespeare has Falstaff say that discretion is the better part of valor, and on that slope I opted for discretion. I ran to the crown of the hill and down the other side.

I am aware that Falstaff was a fighter but also a coward, a thief but also a charmer. He serves as a role model only for those who believe that self-esteem is the highest of all values. The playwright meant for him to be a comic figure but not an admirable one, for he knew that when such men lose their capacity to amuse, they are dangerous in the extreme. They are the Charles Mansons and the Pol Pots of our time, no crime too terrible to dissuade them from committing it.

All of us are cowards at some time in our lives, but I took comfort in the fact that when I fled that hillside, I left no allies behind. With only my own butt at risk, I could justifiably claim that my action was caution rather than cowardice. Or so I told myself as I fled pell-mell into the glen where I had earlier parked for a moment in the mini truck, making thin quaverous sounds of childlike terror, repressing the urge to wet my pants, and turned north in the hope of making it on foot to the guest tower. By such self-deceptions do we survive—and also begin to put the most essential part of ourselves at risk.

Thirty-three

THE TOPOLOGY OF THAT PART OF ROSE-land was complicated, the hills and vales turning into one another in such a way that I was reminded of the folds and fissures on the surface of the brain. I was like a thought slipping through the fissures, and the thought was: **Move, move, live, live!**

I stayed entirely in the lower places, some of which were shaded by looming hillsides, others by banyan trees that grew on slopes and by California laurels that rooted in swales between the hills, where the soil was always a little moist. Weaving quickly between trees, ducking under low branches, racing across open areas, I relied on intuition to decide which way to go each time the rumpled land folded upon itself in such a way that the path branched.

Focused on moving fast and faster, I dared not look back and risk faltering. Besides, if the freaks were gaining on me, I would rather not know until one of those taloned hands snared my sports jacket and wrenched me off my feet or until an axe cleaved my skull and killed me in the instant, sparing me what horrors I might have to endure if I were taken alive.

Only a couple of hours earlier, I had been cozy in the main-house kitchen, eating quiche and cheesecake. My biggest problems had been how to penetrate the armored mysteries of Roseland and how to make sense of what people here told me when they pulled a cloak of inscrutability over themselves before every conversation.

At least the swine things weren't inscrutable. They didn't play word games with me or pretend to be distracted, or in any other way deceive. The freaks made their intentions clear: They wanted to club me, chop me, eat me, and sit around later reminiscing about the taste of me. They were as open about their intentions as were IRS agents.

I followed so many branching paths that I was not sure anymore whether I was moving toward or away from the guest tower. And I would not have been surprised to see on a hillside the abandoned vehicle with balloon tires and the three freaks playing cards while they waited for me to run in a circle and back into their arms.

A couple of times, the cool air shimmered with what seemed to be currents of rising heat, and I saw things in my peripheral vision that weren't there when I turned my head for a closer look. Some of them might have been nothing but shadows that appeared solid and menacing only from the corner of the eye. But others were far more specific: an impression of a great pile of human skulls, of coyotes feeding on several dead freaks, of a naked woman chained to a post as cowled figures touched torches to the kindling at her feet. . . .

One vision did not vanish when I looked directly at it. I came out of a grove of laurels, and twenty feet ahead, the path divided around a promontory of land. Marking the crossroads was a leafless black-limbed tree that someone had used as the framework for a mobile of sun-bleached bones. Hanging from the branches were the delicate skeletons of children, some of whom had been perhaps as young as three, none older than ten, when they were murdered and stripped of their clothing and arranged just so in this insane celebration of cruelty.

The sight was like a road sign announcing that ahead lay a town in the thrall of savage violence that knew no limits.

For the first time in my headlong flight, I faltered when the apparition didn't dissolve before me. But I regained my footing and hurried on, taking the path to the right.

I could imagine only that somehow I was running in two Roselands at once: the estate to which I'd come with Annamaria a couple of days before, and another that existed in some alternate reality parallel to ours.

The fork I'd taken at the black tree festooned with

white bones proved to be a short path. The hills crowded close, closer, and grew steeper as the way narrowed. I soon came to a dead end at a junction of three formidable slopes, weeds and thorny brambles to the left and right, a slide of raw earth and jumbled rocks ahead.

The brambles would snare and perhaps eventually tangle me to a halt. I clambered up the rocks, some of which shifted underfoot, and soon I was forced to holster my pistol and proceed at a sort of inclined crawl, desperately grabbing for handholds to prevent myself from crashing backward when stone that seemed firm abruptly proved treacherous and tumbled out from under my feet.

Gasping for breath, heart thundering, I could hear the freaks behind me—but I couldn't smell them. Although they sounded close, a fluke of landscape must have made their voices seem nearer than they really were, because their foul stench should have announced them as they bore down on me.

Halfway up the slope, they caught me. One of them snared the left leg of my jeans. Holding to my perch with my hands, I kicked frantically, connecting with something, maybe its head. But it would not let go, and in fact the beast pulled hard to dislodge me.

A rock came loose from the slide debris in which it was seated, slipped out from under my right hand, and rattled down the hillside. Still clinging to the slope with my left hand, I twisted onto my side and reached cross-body with my right hand to snatch the Beretta from my holster.

A freak loomed over me, and a second freak to my left, and a third to my right, all of them about to fall atop me. The whites of their eyes were pinked with blood, their irises as yellow as the strange sky that I had glimpsed earlier.

Their slash mouths, their bristling teeth, their long pink tongues spotted with black were not made for words of mercy but for the vicious rending and efficient consumption of prey that, as it fed them, might be still alive and screaming.

Three axes were raised, two with blades toward me, one with the hammer brandished. As I drew my pistol, I knew that I could at most kill one before the other two cracked my head and pried it open like a clamshell. I was ready for death if only because nothing on the Other Side could possibly smell as bad as these swine things did.

Before I could bring the Beretta to bear, the creature over me bore down with its disgusting body, pale skin slick and stubbled with irregular patches of prickly hair—but then reared away from me just as a hole appeared between its eyes. The back of its skull exploded. It fell out of sight, disappearing as suddenly as if a trapdoor had opened under it.

Although I didn't hear the initial shot, the second and third were loud and clear and close. The remaining pair of freaks appeared to fling themselves away from me. One axe clattered to the rocks beside my head and the other twirled out of sight, like a baton thrown too enthusiastically by the ugliest drum majorette in the history of parades.

The rock slide wanted to shift under me. I was determined not to ride a cascade of earth and stone onto the bodies of the freaks, which sprawled on the floor of the dead-end passage below.

Gasping, spitting because I had the notion that a drop of the freak's sweat had fallen into my open mouth, I turned onto my stomach again and sought firm purchase.

A pair of red-and-black, carved-leather cowboy boots appeared beside me. Beyond the big hand that reached down to assist me was a massive forearm and Herculean biceps crawling with screaming hyenas.

Thirty-four

I TOOK HOLD OF HIS HAND, WHICH seemed twice the size of mine, and the tattooed giant helped me to my feet. We staggered to the summit of the eroded slope.

In the west, the sun-dappled sea glittered like a pirate's chest of jewels. My last sight on Earth had almost been the teeth of the monstrous swine as they spread wide to bite.

My rescuer's facial scars were as livid as before, his teeth no less crooked and yellow, but now the cold sore on his upper lip glistened with protective ointment.

"Odd Thomas," he said. "You remember me?"

"Kenneth Randolph Fitzgerald Mountbatten."

He beamed, delighted that I remembered his name, as if he were so plain that people usually forgot him the moment he was out of sight.

Overhead, having wandered farther than usual from the ocean, a lone gull soared high and swooped down, making symphonic gestures as if conducting music only it could hear. Having so recently faced pig death, I felt some of the bird's joy in being alive.

"Thank you for saving my life."

Kenny shrugged and looked embarrassed. "I didn't really."

"No, sir, you really did."

Slinging the strap of the assault rifle over his shoulder and surveying the surrounding hills, Kenny said, "Well, I have a way with guns and fighting, that's all. Kill or be killed—there's only one option there, far as I'm concerned. Each of us has some gift. What's your gift, Odd Thomas?"

Holstering my pistol to prove that I wanted to believe in the idea of the concept of the possibility of the hope that we might be lasting friends, I said, "Fry cookery. I'm a wizard at the griddle."

His neck was nearly as thick as his head. Even his ears looked muscular, as if he did one-lobe push-ups every morning.

"Fry cook. That's a good gift," he said. "People need food more than anything."

"Well, maybe almost as much as anything but not more."

The air smelled fresh, with a trace of ozone that repeatedly almost faded away but always returned, though it was never strong enough to be unpleasant.

Kenny sounded apologetic when he said, "I checked the guesthouse tower. No one's been staying there."

"Am I already back to being a candy-ass punk boy who shouldn't have been let through the gates?"

He rolled his eyes and shook his head. "I didn't mean anything by that. It's just my way. It's kind of how I say hello."

"I usually say, 'Pleased to meet you.'"

"Anyway," he said, "I figured it out. You're an invited guest here, not there, which is none of my business, being as how my job is there, not here, and being as how I'm hardly ever here and don't know why I am even when I am."

I said, "I guess all of you must have gone to the same school."

"What school?"

"To learn how to talk that way."

"What way?"

"The way of confusion."

Kenny shrugged. "I was just saying."

"Sir, I need to find the mini truck."

"The electric sonofabitch you were driving around in, looking for trouble?"

"That's the one."

"I saw you and said, 'That crazy little sonofabitch is going to run into a bunch of sonofabitch porkers,' and you sure enough did."

"I thought they were called freaks."

"Maybe here they're freaks, but there we call 'em porkers, though I call 'em porkers here, there, it doesn't matter to me."

"Consistency is a good quality in a man."

"I don't know about that," Kenny said. "But I found the truck just as those three sonsofbitches were running after you over the hill. I can show you where it is."

"That would be great, sir. The battery's dead, but there's something on the front seat that I really need."

"Then I will," he said, and strode south along the crest of the hill.

I needed to take three steps for every two of his. Hurrying along, I felt like a Hobbit playing sidekick to the Terminator.

With warm sun on my face, listening to the songs of cicadas in the tall grass, I was profoundly grateful not to have been bubbling in the stomach acid of four porker freaks.

I said, "So my Roseland is here and yours is there."

"Seems that way."

"Here is here," I said. "But where is there?"

"Thinking about it makes my head hurt, so I don't."

"How can you **not** think about it?"

"I'm real good at not thinking."

"Well, I'm bad at it," I said.

"Anyway, being here doesn't happen to me every year and it never lasts long. None of it matters, because I always end up back there."

"Back there—**where**?"

"Back there in my Roseland."

"Which is **where**?"

"You need to loosen up, Odd."

"I'm as loose as I need to be."

Kenny favored me with a smile as yellow as a yield sign. "Now and then you need to take a night just to drink yourself brainless. Helps you cope."

"Where's your Roseland?" I persisted as we climbed out of a glen toward another hilltop.

He sighed. "Okay, now I have a big sonofabitch headache."

"So you might as well think."

"I saved you from the porkers. Isn't that enough?"

"Well, I told you what to do about your cold sore."

"It hasn't worked yet."

"It will if you keep your tongue away from the damn thing and don't keep licking off the ointment."

"You're kind of like a cold sore yourself," Kenny said.

"So tell me where your Roseland is, and I'll stop annoying you."

"Okay, okay, okay. All right. This woman I was with for a while, she never stopped nagging, just like you. I finally figured out how to put an end to that."

Dreading his answer, I said, "How did you put an end to it?"

"By just doing what the crazy bitch wanted. It was the only way to shut her up."

"So where is your Roseland?"

"Maybe it's way in the future from here."

"Maybe?"

"It's like a theory."

"So you **have** been thinking about it."

"But I don't care."

"Well, **I** care."

"What is is. It doesn't matter why."

"You're not only a thinker, you're a philosopher."

He growled with disgust. "I wish some sonofa-bitch porkers would show up so I could shoot 'em."

"Way in the future, huh? Sir, do you mean you have a time machine?"

He told me that he didn't need any fornicating time machine, except that he didn't use the term **fornicating.** Then he said, "It just happens. But only in Roseland. Never anywhere else. Sometimes I look up, sky's blue for a minute, other times for a few hours, and the world's not all crap like it has been most of my life. I'm here where the world's not crap yet, instead of there."

"Just look up and it happens?"

"Or turn around. Next thing, the blue goes away, the sky's as yellow as a cat's diarrhea, and everything's screwed up again. It's like something pulls me here, but then it pushes me back where I came from. It probably does the same with the porkers— pulls 'em here but then pushes 'em away."

"That can't be what Tesla built the machine to do."

"What machine?"

"The pulling and pushing must be a side effect. The porkers in your time—are they just in your Roseland?"

"Hell, no. They keep popping up everywhere. They're worse than cockroaches."

"Why is your sky yellow?" I asked.

"Why is yours blue?"

I said, "It's supposed to be blue."

"Not where I come from."

As we walked, he took the slung rifle off his shoulder and carried it at the ready.

Drawing my pistol, I said, "What's wrong?"

"Nothing yet. Relax."

After a while, I said, "If the sky's yellow and your future is crawling with porker freaks, it must be a pretty hostile place."

"You think?"

"Something must have happened between now and then."

"What happens happens."

"But what is the what that did?"

"Who knows? Maybe the war."

"Nuclear war?"

"A few of 'em were nukes."

"A **few** nuclear wars?"

"They were little ones."

"How can a nuclear war be little?"

"And bio. Maybe that was worse."

"Biological warfare?"

"And what they called the nano swarms."

"What are nano swarms?"

"I didn't go to any sonofabitch college, you know. And I don't hang out with a bunch of candy-ass techno geeks. Whatever the nano swarms were, the sonsofbitches ate themselves in the end."

"Ate themselves?"

"Well, after they ate a lot of other stuff."

I mulled that over.

He said, "And those professors."

"What professors?"

"The sonsofbitches doing experiments."

"What kind of experiments?"

"With pigs."

"Nukes, viruses, nano swarms, pigs," I said.

"Vampire bats. Nobody knows where **they** came from. Some say the Chinese made 'em as a weapon. Or maybe it was that weirdo billionaire in Nebraska. Then there was the big government solar-energy thing."

"What government solar-energy thing?"

"The project that blew up in space."

"Why would that matter if it was in space?"

"Because it was big."

"How big could it have been?"

"Really big."

After we walked a minute in silence, Kenny said, "You feel better knowing all that?"

"No," I admitted.

When he looked smug, one snaggle tooth over-hung his lower lip. "So now it's in your head, what're you going to do?"

"Drink myself brainless."

"It's the best thing," Kenny said.

We arrived at the mini truck with the depleted battery. In the vale below, maybe twenty carrion crows gathered on the dead porker.

As I took the pillowcase sack out of the vehicle, I said, "What do you do in your Roseland?"

"I work security for this honcho, he's one lunatic sonofabitch."

"Lunatic how?"

"He thinks in Roseland he'll live forever."

After a hesitation, I said, "Is his name Noah Wolflaw?"

"Wolflaw? No. Calls himself Constantine Cloyce."

Kenny's green eyes sparkled with sunlight, but there didn't seem to be any deception in his direct gaze.

Suddenly he said, "Yellow sky."

I glanced up, but the heavens were blue.

When I looked back to Kenny, he was gone, and in the place where he had been, the air shimmered for a moment.

Thirty-five

SO AS I STOOD BY THE DEFUNCT MINI truck, swapping the Beretta's half-depleted magazine for the fully loaded spare, as then I plucked seven bullets from the extra ammunition that I carried in a sports-coat pocket and replenished the first magazine, I brooded about the discovery that the secret of Roseland had something to do with time. If some kind of localized disorder in time was a side effect of what was going on here, my sense that I was running out of time might be true in ways I couldn't yet comprehend.

Before encountering the porkers, I'd been on my way to the guesthouse to make sure Annamaria remained safe. Now I recalled a thing that happened in Magic Beach a few days earlier, when we encountered a pack of coyotes that boldly stalked us and seemed about to attack. Annamaria had spoken to them as if they understood her—and with only words she got them to retreat. Whatever the nature of the gift that she possessed, she had nothing to fear from animals, probably not even from the porkers; if she was killed, her murderer would be a man driven not by an animal nature but by the worst of his very human impulses. With Roseland counting down to some kind of detonation, I had to trust in Annamaria to take care of herself for now.

Carrying the pillowcase sack in one hand and the pistol in the other, taking my bearings from hilltop after hilltop, alert for more of the bacon brigade, I made my way to the statue of Enceladus, the Titan. From there I ventured into the oak grove that surrounded that lawn. As before, not a single fallen leaf littered the earth under the trees.

I put down the pillowcase and, from one of the low branches, I selected a twig with three leaves. I snapped it off and threw it on the ground.

As if I were watching a time-lapse film of a few weeks' growth, the tree sprouted a new twig at the break point, leafed out exactly as it had been, and fully restored itself in less than a minute.

When I thought to look on the ground where I'd thrown the broken twig, it wasn't there.

Finally, almost twenty-two, I got my haunted house, for which I was singularly well prepared, and it was a country house, as was the one in **The Turn of the Screw**, and it had a history of perversity, like the place in **Hell House,** and in it might be people who should be dead but were not, as in **The Fall of** the House of Usher, and there was an imprisoned child in jeopardy, as in Poltergeist. The only ghost in Roseland, however, was the rider of the spirit stallion, and she was neither menacing nor truly at the center of the problem that I, as an unofficial exorcist, needed to resolve.

Instead of flailing poltergeists and phantoms from the grave, with which I might have easily contended, I faced a threat consisting of swine things, cosmic clockworks, a thoroughly insane movie mogul, and the conspirators that he had drawn around him with the power that he wielded, power given to him, perhaps unwittingly, by the late great Nikola Tesla, who, although long dead and although not a ghost, nevertheless ricocheted like an immaterial pinball in and out of the scene, who said that he had seen me where I'd not yet been, and who encouraged me to throw the master switch, wherever that might be.

Some days I just want to go back to bed and pull the covers over my head.

Instead, from the tree, I broke off the same twig that I'd broken before and held it in the open palm of my left hand. Within a minute, the tree repaired itself, and the twig vanished even though, at the last moment, I closed my fist around it.

Roseland didn't need a platoon of gardeners. In the landscaped portion of the grounds—as opposed to the wild fields—the trees and the shrubs and the flowers and the grass were in a kind of stasis, neither growing nor dying, somehow maintained in exactly the same condition in which they had been since . . . Perhaps since one day in the early 1920s.

The residents of Roseland were not outside of time. Clocks still ticked and hours passed. Sunrises and sunsets came and went. Weather changed, as did the seasons. Time did not stand still within these estate walls.

Evidently, by the transmission of a current of some exotic energy through root and trunk and limb and leaf, through every blade of grass and every flower petal, all remained as it had been. Wind might strip some leaves from the trees, but new growth appeared even as the torn leaves fell and, upon the ground, ceased to exist. Or perhaps the new leaves were in fact the old ones, and perhaps each damaged tree or plant—but nothing adjacent to it—slipped back in time to a moment just before the leaves had been plucked from it, and then rejoined the present.

If I dug down into the earth, I would most likely find some kind of metal mesh or those copper rods embedded in the foundations of the buildings. Suddenly I knew what the elongated 8 represented when you read it horizontally rather than vertically: It was the symbol for infinity.

I felt dizzy. I wished I were as good at not thinking as Kenny claimed to be.

I returned to that peninsula of flawless lawn in which Enceladus raised a fist to challenge the gods, and I followed it to the acres of grass surrounding the main residence. From a distance, I could see that

the windows and doors of the house were still covered with steel panels.

Around one corner of the mansion came a rag-
tag mob of freaks in a violent frenzy because they
had not been invited inside for lunch. They were
overturning patio furniture and pounding on the
shutters.

I retreated into the Enceladus lawn, screened from
the house by the time-frozen oaks. I stood by the
Titan, trying to get my mind around the ramifications of the theory that Roseland was not a time
machine—no, nothing that simple—but a machine
that could **manage** time, reverse or retard its effects,
and ensure against the otherwise inevitable decline
of all things, which is the way of Nature.

In the main house, as in the guest tower, everything appeared to be immaculate, pristine, as if
nothing ever wore out or broke down or produced
dust. Wooden floors and steps were as tight and
squeak-free as the day that they were installed. No
cracks in the marble or limestone.

The kitchen appliances were new; but most likely
they had been replaced not because those of the
1920s didn't still work but because newer ovens and
refrigerators offered features and conveniences that
the older models did not.

Out of nowhere, as if conjured, a hundred or more
bats with seven-foot wingspans appeared at the tree-
encircled end of the long lawn. They flew toward
me, in such tight formation that they appeared to

be a solid mass, a tidal flow two feet above the grass, abroad in daylight as bats should never be.

The urge to flee was countered by the recognition that I could move at only a fraction of their speed. Perhaps they didn't see well in daylight. Like most predators, they must track their prey by scent. But maybe their natural guidance system, echolocation, also played a role in identifying food, in which case absolute stillness might be wiser than movement. The enormous lead statue, in the shadow of which I stood, might mask me from detection.

Perhaps, maybe, might be, might: With such qualifications did I stand paralyzed in hope that I would not be devoured alive.

Their wings beat in unison so many times per second that the thrum of them became almost a buzz, and their orchestral timing was no less impressive than it was fearsome. Heads as big as grapefruits, they approached with chins dropped, mouths open, curved incisors bared, flat noses sifting from the air the scents of blood, sweat, minute particles of dander shed by skin or fur or feathers, and the pheromones of fear.

I could not breathe as they rushed past so low that I looked down on the soft brown fur that covered their bodies and on their membranous wings. In the passing, they vanished through a sudden shimmering in the air, as if through a curtain between my time and theirs.

Limp with relief, I climbed onto the granite

plinth on which the huge Titan stood. I sat with my back against his left calf, knees drawn up, shoes pressed against his right foot, not sure if the lead from which he was cast had afforded me some protection, but taking shelter there with my usual persistent optimism.

As my heartbeat returned to normal, I brooded again about Roseland. About time past, time present, and time future . . .

The stasis evident in the landscaped grounds, in the house, and in the furniture that stood in its rooms apparently did not extend to less place-fixed objects like bed linens and cake pans and cutlery. Linens and clothes didn't launder themselves as the oak repaired the broken-off twig, and dirty dishes didn't revert to a time when they were clean. The current that moved strongly through the structure— call it the Methuselah current—flowed secondarily through things that stood on the house's floors and hung on its walls; but it must not be able to invade and maintain items that were smaller and less stationary.

What of the people who lived here?

In Kenny's grim and tumultuous future, the owner of Roseland called himself Constantine Cloyce, perhaps because in the chaos of that time, he no longer needed to conceal his true identity behind false ones. Perhaps people in that coming age were so preoccupied with defending and feeding their families and themselves that they had no curiosity about the past. If there was no Internet or TV or radio possible under that turbulent yellow sky, and if what public records existed were moldering in the drawers of buildings gone to ruins, he did not have to periodically change his name and to some degree his appearance. He didn't have to pretend to be Noah Wolflaw or a South American heir to a mining fortune. He could be in name who he had always been in fact: Constantine Cloyce.

Logic insisted that the residents of Roseland were even less place-fixed than were tableware and clothes, and therefore weren't guaranteed immortality merely by living within those walls. They must age normally and, perhaps every few decades, have to undertake some regimen or undergo some process to revert to their youth.

Dropping thirty or forty years overnight, losing gray hair and wrinkles and weight and the effects of gravity on the face that came with age, they would appear to be new people, nearly unrecognizable as who they had been. They would need to do hardly more than change their names and hairstyles to pass for new residents of Roseland, especially as they were reclusive, having little contact with locals.

I remembered Victoria Mors saying that she never did anything dangerous, and now I understood why. Maybe they were able to undo the effects of aging and reverse the ravages of disease, but they were not invulnerable. They could be shot and killed or they could perish in an accident.

For the same reason, Henry Lolam took three of his eight weeks of vacation and then returned to Roseland. He felt safer within its walls. Immortality made him a prisoner of Roseland, and he was his own jailer.

Although I had scores of questions, I had fewer now than just an hour earlier. Those for which I most urgently wanted answers all involved the nameless boy.

If Noah Wolflaw was in fact Constantine Cloyce, then the spirit rider of the stallion was Madra Cloyce, his wife from the 1920s, which was when she must have been shot and killed, back when there had been horses on the estate.

I remembered how she had hesitated and seemed frustrated when, in the subcellar of the mausoleum, among the corpses, I asked her if she was Noah Wolflaw's wife. With her answers limited to a nod or a shake of the head, she could not tell me that Wolflaw was Cloyce, and that she was therefore the wife of both.

The nameless boy was no longer nameless. He was the son of Madra and Constantine, who was supposed to be dead. He had died young. His name—Timothy—was on a plaque beneath the burial niche in the mausoleum wall where his ashes were supposedly interred, but obviously he was alive.

From where had Noah Wolflaw—Cloyce—taken him, and why did the boy want more than anything to be taken back there? If he was nine-year-old Timothy, why was he **still** nine all these decades later? Why didn't they let him grow up and then maintain himself as did the rest of them? **Had they kept him a child for almost ninety years?**

The answers couldn't be found in the shadow of Enceladus. They waited to be discovered in the main house.

From the northwest, caissons of dark clouds rolled in on silent wheels, though I expected that they would raise some thunder before the day was done. The pending storm had conquered a third of the sky, and it was moving faster than before to secure the heavens from horizon to horizon.

For some reason, anticipating the storm, I thought of Victor Frankenstein at work high in the old mill that, in the movie though not the book, served as his laboratory, harnessing bolts of lightning to bring his creation to life, the shambling thing with a criminal's brain and a merciless graveyard heart.

The only route by which I could return to the barricaded house was through the mausoleum, by way of the mural based on Franchi's painting of a guardian angel and child.

Alert for the thrum of bat wings, motivated to move fast by the memory of those curved incisors, I sprinted across the lawn, hurried through the grove of oaks in stasis, and ran overland through fields and hills where plants still waxed and waned as Nature intended.

En route, I found that the vision of Frankenstein's old mill came repeatedly into my mind's eye. I didn't at first know why the image nagged at me.

As I approached the mausoleum from the south, that mind's eye blinked, and the old mill assaulted by lightning became the guest tower in the eucalyptus grove at Roseland. The bronze dome atop that stone structure featured an unusual finial resembling a giant version of the stem, crown, and case bow of an old pocket watch. And the secret of Roseland had to do with **time**. . . .

My apartment and Annamaria's occupied the lower twenty feet of that sixty-foot tower. The winding stairs leading from the ground floor to the second also led to a third and final level. The keys we'd been given did not unlock the door at the top of those stairs.

Being ever curious, I'd tried and failed to learn what occupied those upper forty feet. I'm not one of those snoops with an unhealthy inquisitiveness that Big Brother hires by the tens of thousands these days. But I have learned that when my gift draws me to a new place where I am needed, my chances of survival increase if, upon arrival, I scope the territory for trapdoors, deadfalls, and hidden snares.

Now I halted on the south lawn of the mausoleum, out of sight of the main house, considering whether I should return to the guest tower, after all. On the way, I could stop by Jam Diu's place and borrow an axe from the unused landscaping tools. The events of the day had put me in a mood to chop something, even if it had to be only a door.

After a hesitation, I felt drawn toward the main house more than to the guest tower. Time was surely out of joint in both places, but if the hands on the clock of apocalypse were spinning toward a catastrophe, I needed to get to the boy soon.

Thirty-six

IN THE MAUSOLEUM, THE MOSAIC OF the Franchi painting remained recessed from the rest of the north wall, exposing the two sets of stairs that led down to the first cellar.

I had assumed that after a delay, the entrance to the secret world below would close automatically behind me. Now, standing to one side, I put a finger to the tile in the angel's shield that I had pressed to unlock the door, but it remained countersunk, and the slab of stone did not move forward to plug the hole where it belonged.

After searching the wall at the head of one set of stairs and then at the head of the other, I found no switch. Intuition told me that I should waste no more time here. Events in Roseland were rapidly coming to a tipping point.

I went down into the first cellar where, along the center of the chamber, the seven golden spheres were spinning silently on the seven poles. The many flywheels flew without a sound, and from their outer rims, radiant drops of golden light glided to the tapestry of copper wires on the ceiling, where they were absorbed and transmitted along the elaborate patterns until they dimmed and vanished.

With my recent discovery of the primary purpose of the machinery—the management of time—I hoped to understand, if only dimly, how these various devices conspired to perform such an astonishing feat. But I was as mystified as ever.

Neither a gift for frying nor one of a psychic nature requires also that the recipient be a blazing genius. I knew other fry cooks, none of whom was likely to win a Nobel Prize in science. And when you can see the lingering dead and have occasional prophetic dreams, you tend to be too distracted either to become an international chess champion or to create the next Apple Inc.

At the spiral stairs in the corner, I went down again into the subcellar. In that lower space, six arrays of golden gears churned silently and ceaselessly in their silver tracks overhead, and the collection of dead women waited, their pinned-open eyes watchful unto eternity.

Perhaps here in the immediate presence of the machine—or a key part of the machine—the generated stasis was stronger even than it was elsewhere. Seated on the floor, leaning against the walls, the grisly trophies were as freshly dead as when the master of Roseland murdered them.

Corpses in stasis are still just corpses. But I wondered if in the quiet of the night their killer ever fell into a fever of guilt or a morbid despond, and if he then imagined that he might encounter these women on the move, their bloody wounds as compelling as stigmata, their accusing voices rough and half trapped in their necktie-throttled throats.

Anything I might do to him was so much less than he deserved.

Perhaps because the timeless cadavers were not bothered by creatures drawn to carrion, I realized that the house must have been free of insects and rodents when Tesla's machine was first switched on. I'd seen no immortal spiders weaving infinite webs, no houseflies with an antique look, no rats grown wise from living fifty ratty lifetimes.

If such rats resided behind the wainscoting, there would be no reason to expect them to be sages. Even a lot of human beings grow no wiser past a certain age—or ever.

Constantine Cloyce—now Noah Wolflaw—had been seventy when he apparently faked his death in 1948. Now at the age of 134, he seemed to have learned neither humility nor the wisdom of moral living. And repeatedly telling me to shut up was hardly the sophisticated and amusing banter you expected from a man of his age and experience.

I crossed the subcellar to the door beyond which lay the copper-sheathed passageway that led underground to the main house. Through the glass tubes embedded in the walls, flares of golden light seemed to be moving simultaneously toward and away from the main residence, and I avoided looking at them to spare myself the queasiness and the confusion that I'd felt the first time I had been here.

In the wine cellar under the house, I didn't proceed into the basement corridor as before. Instead, I took the narrow service stairs up to the ground floor.

I entered the kitchen with caution, in case Chef Shilshom might be preparing a banquet for a celebration worthy of Edgar Allan Poe's Prince Prospero. In an apocalyptic time threatened by a plague called the Red Death, the prince threw a great party to deny his mortal nature. That hadn't turned out well. I suspected that the several residents of Roseland would not fare any better than Prospero.

The only illumination came from two lights above the sinks. The windows were covered by steel shutters.

At the moment, no freaks hammered at those defenses, and the house was hushed. Maybe the pull and push of Tesla's machine had shoved them back to their time, but I doubted it. Something about the silence struck me as ominous.

Off the kitchen lay a room that served as the chef's office. I stepped inside and quietly closed the door.

Here Chef Shilshom planned menus, prepared shopping lists, and no doubt puzzled over the proper thing to serve the master of the house when next a young woman, resembling the late Mrs. Cloyce, was brought to Roseland to be tortured and murdered. Meals for special occasions are always tricky to plan.

Constantine Cloyce might be the only one whose sense of superiority, arising from his potential immortality, inspired him to murder mere mortal people as sport, but the others in this place were just as insane. Their madness was evidenced by the fact that they assisted him, either to continue to be allowed to live forever or because they saw no crime in killing mortals who would sooner or later die anyway.

None of them had lived so long that longevity itself could have driven them insane. I could imagine that, after a few hundred years, the repetitive character of human experience might lead to a tedium that would leave them chronically depressed or so desperate for new and more extreme sensations that torture and murder became a kind of Valium that relieved anxiety. But Cloyce was only 134, the others most likely younger. Something other than longevity accounted for their descent into one form of madness or another.

In Chef Shilshom's office, a massive chair had been custom built to accommodate his bulk, its seat as wide as two of me, its castors as big as baseballs. When I sat in it, I felt like Jack in the castle at the top of the beanstalk.

The computer on this desk was the only one I'd seen on the main floor, though there were probably others in the wing that contained the servants' suites. I switched it on, accessed the Internet, and went looking for Nikola Tesla.

Apparently Serbian, he was born on July 10, 1856, in Smiljan, which seemed to be either in Croatia or in the Austro-Hungarian Empire, or in a place called Lika, or in all three. It sounded sort of off-planet to me, but the problem was most likely just the semi-coherence common to biography sites on the Web.

He died on January 7, 1943, in a two-room suite in the New Yorker Hotel, which was in New York and nowhere else. Two thousand people attended his funeral at St. John the Divine cathedral. Tesla was cremated, and his ashes were thereafter kept in a golden sphere at the Nikola Tesla Museum in Belgrade.

More than one online source informed me that a golden sphere was Tesla's favorite shape.

Hmmmm. Interesting.

In 1882, Tesla solved the problem of the rotating magnetic field and built the first induction motor. Not that I have the slightest idea what that means. But the induction motor powered the industrial revolution at the turn of the century; it has been used both in heavy industry and for simple household appliances ever since.

Behind me, something outside scratched on the steel shutter that covered the window. Scratched, tapped, and scratched again.

The sounds were subdued, compared to the racket previously made by the pack of freaks, but I was pretty sure the creature inquiring at the window was not just a curious raccoon.

The freak was just trying to determine in what ground-floor rooms its lunch might be waiting. I focused on the computer again.

After coming to America, Tesla worked with Thomas Edison, but they fell out because Tesla believed that Edison's direct-current electricity transmission was inefficient. He said all energies were cyclic and that generators could be built to transmit electricity first in one direction and then in the other, in multiple waves according to the polyphase principle.

Given that primate swine were stalking Roseland and a murderous sociopath was in charge of the place, I decided that I didn't have time to look up and understand "polyphase principle."

Anyway, Tesla went into business with George Westinghouse. Alternating current, which changes direction about sixty times per second and allows long-distance transmission with a minimum of energy loss, soon became the world standard.

In 1895, at Niagara Falls, Nikola Tesla designed the world's first hydroelectric power plant.

Marconi is still cited as the inventor of radio, but Tesla patented the basic system of radio in 1900, years before Marconi. Marconi's patent was eventually declared invalid.

Again at the steel shutter behind me: **Tap, tap, tap . . . tap, tap, tap . . . tap, tap, tap.**

The tapping was eerily discreet. As if some secret lover had come to keep a previously arranged assignation.

I didn't answer with a tapping of my own, because I could too easily imagine a lady freak who wanted to be Juliet to my Romeo.

Reading further, I discovered that among Tesla's discoveries were fluorescent bulbs and laser beams. Wireless communications. Wireless transmission of electricity. Remote controls. He took the first X rays of human bodies, ahead of Roentgen.

This was a superbrainy guy.

In Colorado, in 1899, applying something that he referred to as "terrestrial stationary waves," he lighted two hundred lamps at a distance of twenty-five miles, without wires, by transmitting electricity through the air.

Here's a cool one that's related. He built a transmitting tower on Long Island, between 1901 and 1905, which rose almost to 190 feet, with a copper dome 68 feet in diameter, standing on hundred-foot-deep foundations. It was meant to turn Earth itself into a massive dynamo and, through a magnifying transmitter, send unlimited amounts of electricity anywhere in the world.

When J. P. Morgan, who was financing the project, realized there was no way to charge anyone for the electricity because there would be no way to know who was tapping the flow, he pulled all funding.

Albert Einstein was an admirer of Nikola Tesla.

Einstein's theory of relativity holds, among other things, that space and time are not absolute concepts, but relative.

Hmmmm.

Tesla was so brilliant that he could solve mathematical problems of the highest complexity entirely in his head, without resort to paper and pencil.

More astonishingly, he could visualize complex inventions like the induction motor in every detail and then diagram them as quickly as he could draw.

Scratching. Tapping.

"We don't need any magazine subscriptions," I muttered.

Reading on, I discovered that Tesla was a good friend of Mark Twain. In addition to **Adventures of Huckleberry Finn,** Twain wrote **A Connecticut Yankee in King Arthur's Court,** which is cast as a dream arising from a blow to the head but is for all intents and purposes a **time-travel** story.

Hmmmm.

In 1997, **Life** magazine placed Nikola Tesla among the one hundred most famous and world-changing people of the past thousand years.

Of course that was before reality TV, Twitter, Twaddle, and the like managed to reduce the average attention span of most of the world's population to two minutes, wither our long-term memory to fourteen months, and convince us that the most admirable of all individuals are not the likes of George Washington, Albert Einstein, Marie Curie, Jonas

Salk, Mother Teresa, and Nikola Tesla, but instead whatever celebrity just won **Dancing with the Stars** and whatever dancing cat just drew ten million hits for its YouTube video.

Tapping. Scratching. Knock-knock.

"Who's there?" I asked softly. "Juno," I replied in a quiet but authentic piggy voice. "Juno who?" I asked with sincere puzzlement. And I answered: "Juno how much I'd like to get in there and ham it up with you?"

I learned also that Tesla had his peculiar side. Sometime between 1899 and 1900, in his laboratory in Colorado Springs, he believed that he had received signals from another planet. Serious people examined his evidence and agreed. He once said that with the right application of an electric current, he could easily split the Earth in two. Fortunately, Tesla didn't leave notes as to how this might be done, for otherwise those guys in the **Jackass** movies would already have done it.

In short, he not only could think outside the box, but he could think outside the bigger box in which the first box had come. Such a man might be able to meet the challenge of harnessing time and using it as he wished.

Before I was tempted to surf over to YouTube to look at that dancing cat, I backed out of the Internet and shut down the computer.

As the tapping and scratching came again at the shutter, I heard Chef Shilshom in the kitchen, cursing profusely, as though he thought he might be Victoria Mors. He seemed to be coming this way.

I sprang off the Jabba the Hutt office chair, snatched up the pillowcase sack, and darted through the door between the chef's office and the walk-in pantry, which also had an entrance from the kitchen.

In the pantry, I left the door to the office a half-inch ajar and waited to see if the quiche king would appear.

The chef breached the room in great white billows, more than agitated but less than panicked, as though he had just seen Captain Ahab stumping toward him on one good leg and one of polished whalebone. He didn't appear to be in a mood either to bake or to broil.

From a cabinet that might have contained a trove of exotic spices or his personal collection of antique egg cups, he took what appeared to be a 12-gauge semiauto combat shotgun.

Thirty-seven

A FRIGHTENED, ANGRY, FOUR-HUNDRED-
pound, antisocial chef with a combat shotgun never
leads to anything good.

I slipped away from the door between Chef Ram-
bo's office and the pantry. Eased through the dark.
Found the other door by the thin line of light that
glowed at the bottom of it. Entered the kitchen. Left
the kitchen. I crept along a hallway where one door
or another might suddenly be flung open by a Rose-
lander, whereupon I'd be discovered and sternly rep-
rimanded for not remaining behind locked doors in
the guest tower—or shot.

When I reached a side hall and then a discreet
service door to the main drawing room, I ducked
into that vast space, which felt like a stately common room on some exceedingly formal luxury liner
from a distant era, which in the movies are peopled
by beautiful women in glamorous gowns and men
in tuxedos and platoons of waiters in white jackets

serving drinks on silver trays. Islands of Persian carpets offered several arrangements of furniture, armchairs and side chairs and sofas and chaises enough to seat a quarter of high society's top four hundred.

The windows were shuttered. None of the Tiffany lamps glowed. Of the five chandeliers, only the one in the center of the room provided light.

Directly under that glitteration of candle-shaped lamp bulbs and pendant crystals stood a circular banquette that surrounded a twice-life-size statue of the Greek god Pan. Pan had the head and chest and arms of a man, the ears and horns and legs of a goat, and he was badly in need of a fig leaf.

The periphery of the room was curtained with shadow. The corners folded away in the dark.

My intention was to slip around the darker part of the chamber, staying well away from horny Pan, until I came to another service door, hidden in the wall paneling, catercorner from the one through which I had entered. That would take me to a short hallway that also served the library, where I hoped to climb the circular bronze stairs to the second floor.

I was still about six acres away from my destination when I heard hurried footsteps on marble. Through the deep, columned archway that separated the drawing room from the better-lighted foyer, I saw Noah Wolflaw—alias Cloyce—and Paulie Sempiterno, both with shotguns, coming this way.

Allergic as I am to buckshot, I dropped to my hands and knees and hid behind a sofa.

Even as the madman and his chief lieutenant arrived in the drawing room, a door opened toward the farther end of the chamber, perhaps the one I had used. Others joined Cloyce and Sempiterno at the center of the big room, under the lit chandelier, beside the shameless Pan.

Peering warily around the end of the sofa and over a forest of furniture, I discovered that Jam Diu and Mrs. Tameed had arrived. The gardener carried a shotgun. Mrs. Tameed, almost a foot taller than Mr. Diu, wore a gun belt with a holster on each hip, and in her right hand she held one of a pair of door-buster handguns, aimed at the ceiling.

The pistol-packing Swede could have kicked a lion in the butt and made it mewl like a frightened kitten. Jam Diu looked like Buddha gone bad.

The room had excellent acoustics, and I could hear everything they said. Victoria Mors had gone missing. She wasn't in her private rooms, and she didn't answer when called on her Talkabout, which was evidently a walkie-talkie that they all carried to keep in touch in the immense house. They were certain she'd been in the main residence when the shutters went down.

Not in the least embarrassed to declare the obvious, Paulie Sempiterno said, "Something's wrong."

That something was me.

Mrs. Tameed said, "Where's that phony [expletive deleted] little [expletive deleted] bastard?"

Again, that would be me.

"Henry called from the gatehouse earlier," Cloyce said, "after the shutters fell here. Thomas was pounding on the door down there, trying to get in. The freaks were after him."

"Then he's dead," Jam Diu said.

Mrs. Tameed said, "Probably he's dead. But don't underestimate the [expletive deleted], [expletive deleted], [hyphenated expletive deleted] creep."

Considering that Mrs. Tameed was far older than she appeared, I wondered if, under another name, she had worked in the Nixon White House.

"If he was out of the house when the shutters went down," said Jam Diu, "then he can't have gotten in again. Let's not waste time worrying about him. He's just an ignorant clocker."

Clocker. Not **cocker.**

"Even a clocker can catch a lucky break now and then," Paulie Sempiterno said.

"I'm more concerned there might have been a shutter breach," Jam Diu said.

"There's no shutter breach," Cloyce assured him. "Whatever has happened to her, it's not a freak that's gotten her."

They agreed to search the house for Victoria Mors, working in teams of two, always staying on the same floor, starting at the top of the house.

"She's not in my suite," Cloyce said. "But there's a lot of other territory to search. Every damn closet, every corner. Let's move."

They all left the drawing room through the columned arch and, from the foyer, took the stairs to the second floor.

I settled from my hands and knees onto my side behind the sofa, and then rolled onto my back. Spears and daggers and darts of light, cast up from the pendant crystals of the chandelier, were frozen in bright violent patterns on the center of the plaster ceiling, but darkness bled away to the walls.

Clocker. I was a clocker because I was certain to age and die, at the mercy of the ticking clock. Being able somehow periodically to restore their youthful appearance and health, they were what Victoria had called "Outsiders, with no limits, no rules, no fears."

They were also delusional. Reality imposes limits whether we choose to recognize them or not. These so-called Outsiders might be as bright as the prismatic reflections that the faceted crystals threw on the ceiling, but they were no less surrounded by darkness than were those spear-point patterns of light.

Perhaps these people did live without rules, at least in the sense that they acknowledged no natural law, but I had seen how fear circumscribed their lives. Victoria Mors would do nothing risky, lest she die by accident. Henry Lolam could not bear to be long outside the walls of the estate, because proximity to Tesla's machinery and the Methuselah current was his best insurance of great longevity.

I could see now why Henry fantasized about having a close encounter of the third kind, during which aliens would grant him immortality. He wanted to live forever, but without the bonds that tied him so tightly to Roseland. They were all to one degree or another prisoners of this estate, psychologically if not physically.

The longer that they lived, the longer they **wanted** to live. And the longer they lived, the more their world shrank. Their spectrum of experience grew narrower year by year. Their sociopathic arrogance, their sense of godlike power, and their contempt for clockers were continuously distilled into an ever more poisonous brew.

I wondered who these people were with whom Constantine Cloyce formed the deranged community of Roseland. Did all of them date back to the 1920s, were they his servants then? What had been the original names that they had outlived?

If they were all from that time, I suspected that they must be far more insane than I yet knew. The gauntlet I must run to save the boy would be bristling with more and sharper spears than the arsenal of prismatic lights on the ceiling.

Thoughts of longevity brought me inevitably to memories of Stormy Llewellyn, who had died so young. Of necessity, I had come to be at peace with my loss, to live with a certain emptiness but not with a constant anguish. Now a melancholy ache weighed me to the floor longer than I intended to lie there.

It seemed to me that if Nikola Tesla could have defeated Death by inventing a fantastical machine, I should have defeated the Reaper by being smarter and quicker than I was on that desperate day in Pico Mundo when I became the eternal lover of a woman I could never again kiss in this world.

Having given the four searchers plenty of time to ascend to the second floor and to proceed away from Cloyce's suite of rooms, I got to my feet, drew the pistol from my holster, picked up the pillowcase sack, and slipped shadowlike along the dark perimeter of the drawing room.

Some there be that shadows kiss; / Such have but a shadow's bliss.

By those words is the prince of Arragon described in **The Merchant of Venice** when he fails to choose correctly and, by his wrong choice, loses all hope of wedding Portia.

My friend Ozzie Boone, writer of mysteries, used to mock me for having been an indifferent student in school and especially for knowing nothing of Shakespeare. Since leaving Pico Mundo, as time permits, I have immersed myself in the works of the Bard. Initially, I read the plays and the sonnets for the simple pleasure of seeing Ozzie's pride in me when one day I returned to my hometown. But soon I read them to glimpse a world that was so right in Shakespeare's time but that has gone so wrong in ours.

His words, written over four hundred years ago, often encourage me and keep my spirits high. But sometimes lines come to me that strum a darker chord, and they pierce as I would much prefer not to be pierced.

Some there be that shadows kiss; / Such have but a shadow's bliss.

Thirty-eight

THE MASTER OF ROSELAND'S SUITE was off the west wing. Had the windows not been protected by steel shutters, most rooms would have offered me a view of the land rolling down to the coast and to the sea a mile away.

Cloyce had left burning not just a lamp or two but all the lights, as though when he returned, he didn't want to have to spend even a moment on the threshold of darkness, fumbling for a switch.

He'd once claimed not to have slept in nine years, but I was sure his assertion was a great exaggeration if not outright nonsense. The truth might be that he'd not slept **well** in nine years or longer, perhaps because he left the lights on all night, unable to tolerate a room that was as midnight-black as his mind.

His quarters were as sumptuously furnished as any chamber in the house. The Tiffany lamps, the antique bronzes, and the paintings were likely to bring millions.

I found nothing particularly strange until I got to a spacious chamber that I imagine he thought of as his trophy room. On the walls were the mounted heads of a lion, a tiger, a gazelle with magnificent ringed horns, and other specimens he must have shot and shipped back from Africa.

On one wall numerous framed black-and-white eight-by-ten photographs included several taken on safari. A young Constantine Cloyce, surely no older than thirty, was recognizable in spite of his hairstyle, which was of that era, and his lush mustache. He posed with various kills, holding a rifle, solemn and proud in some pictures, grinning and proud in others.

To have had the time and resources to be an adventurer at such a young age, he must have **inherited** the newspaper fortune that had allowed him later to launch a movie studio. If he was thirty in the photos, the safari dated to 1908, fourteen years before he began to build Roseland.

In some of the photographs, another young man appeared with him. He must have been a pal of Cloyce's because in two photos, rifles having been set aside, they stood behind the animals they had shot, arms around each other's shoulders. Henry Lolam looked the same then as now, though back then he must have had another name.

Farther along the wall were photographs of Roseland during its construction. In some of them, Cloyce posed with others.

I saw Nikola Tesla first. He appeared in four pictures, always wearing a business suit and tie when the others dressed casually. In two, he was such a strikingly hawkish figure with such intensity of expression that, by comparison, the people with him seemed to be no more real than those life-size photo cutouts of famous folks that you once could pose with in carnivals and boardwalk arcades. In the other two, those with him looked real enough—although Tesla seemed to be uncomfortable, as if he thought he didn't belong with his current company.

Mrs. Tameed posed with Cloyce in one shot. She looked forty now, but appeared to be twenty-something in the photo. If there had been a greater age difference, I might not have recognized her except maybe by her height. Hair cut short, wearing a cloche hat, she was dressed in the flapper style of the period—sleeveless dress with a knee-length skirt, a V-neck bodice with cleavage revealed—that shocked the parents of that free-spirited generation.

I had difficulty imagining that Mrs. Tameed had ever been as frivolous and cheerful as she seemed to be in that picture. I would have thought that she insisted on wearing jackboots from the day she started to walk and that her greatest regret as a young woman had been her inability to grow a mustache to match Hitler's.

She was in another photo with Cloyce. This time she and Victoria Mors flanked him, both dressed as flappers, both hanging on him. They appeared to be a tipsy and dissolute trio.

In that picture, Victoria looked as young as she did now, tender and elfin and sprightly. I wondered if she maintained herself in a more constant state of youth than did the others. And if she did so—why?

In another shot of Cloyce with four men, dating perhaps before the 1920s, I knew only two of the others. Paulie Sempiterno stood slightly to one side, somewhat but not much younger-looking than he was now, glowering at the camera as if he distrusted the photographer and the very idea of cameras. Jam Diu looked ten years older then than now. He wore white shoes, a white suit, and a white Panama hat; and he boasted a Fu Manchu mustache that dangled two or three inches below his chin.

I had seen everyone currently of Roseland except Chef Shilshom. But if he had been of normal size in those days, I would not have recognized him.

The mounted heads of animals on two walls lent this place none of the men's-club atmosphere that might have been intended. Instead, at least for me, each head was Death in masquerade, his skeletal face concealed behind animal masks, as in Prince Prospero's abbey where he had partied in costume. Their presence oppressed me. I imagined that their glass eyes followed me as I toured the room.

I was eager to move on, but I wanted to investigate the contents of a highly polished mahogany cabinet with inlaid geometric patterns of ivory and ebony. Behind its doors were shelves filled with DVDs.

A man given to murder for pleasure might have a

collection of films, but I doubted there would be a single Muppet movie among them. No titles were printed on the narrow spines of the cases. Expecting either pornography or tales of extreme violence, I took one from the top shelf and saw taped to the front a photograph of one of the naked women in the subcellar of the mausoleum, in the very pose in which he had arranged her in that **other** trophy room.

I checked a few more on the top shelf. Like the first, they bore photos of the victims in death, each labeled with a name and date. But there were a lot more DVDs here than bodies in the mausoleum.

When I examined some on the bottom shelf, I found that, like those above, they were arranged from left to right and shelved by date. The earliest was labeled 1962.

He must have filmed those early victims in 8 mm, later using a video camera. As technology advanced, he transferred his archives to videotape and later to DVD. His experience in the movie industry and his wealth gave him the knowledge and the means to upgrade the filmed record of the abominations that he committed. Somewhere in the house, he must have a well-equipped little studio where he could edit his films and transfer them to more sophisticated formats as those were invented.

I didn't count the DVDs. I couldn't bear to. I'm sure there were more than 150.

I wondered where those other bodies were. I hoped never to find them.

I wanted to set the cabinet on fire. I figured that I knew what was on those discs: each woman alive and afraid, then what he did to her to amuse himself, and finally how he killed her, maybe with Victoria watching as she said he sometimes allowed her. I didn't think anyone should watch those women in their terror, as they were humiliated and degraded. Not even cops or prosecutors, or juries.

They were gone, and maybe it didn't matter, but it wasn't right. These demented home movies reduced each woman's life to the ordeal in which she was least herself, in which she was broken. And they would all have been broken emotionally and mentally, for Cloyce had so much experience in the tactics and techniques of terror that he would keep at each of them until he succeeded. He had all the time in the world to strip from his victim everything that was essential and momentous about her, and leave her diminished to the point that death would be a relief. All the time in the world.

The DVDs were evidence. Until they would not be needed in order for justice to be done, I could not destroy them.

As I accepted the fact of that, I knew what it meant: To ensure that there would be no need for the filmed evidence, I would have to deliver ultimate justice to everyone in Roseland except the boy, to the women as well as to the men. Seven deaths were warranted.

Subconsciously, I must have known what would be required of me the moment that I'd seen the preserved corpses in the subcellar of the mausoleum. But now I could no longer repress the awareness that my role here was to be a scourge, that I could not merely free the boy and leave with him. I could not restrict my killing to self-defense or to the defense of the child.

My legs felt weak. I sat in a nearby chair.

As usual, the house was hushed. No sound arose to distract me from my grim train of thought.

To spare Cloyce's victims further indignities to their memory, I must be a scourge. To prevent others from perhaps being infected by Cloyce's depravity by watching him at work, I must be a scourge. To prevent the time-management technology from falling into the hands of authorities who, if not already corrupt, would be corrupted by it, I must be a scourge.

Scourges aren't heroes.

I had never imagined myself a hero, but never had I imagined that I would be **this.**

Scourges assume authority they don't possess. I assumed the right was mine to spare the memory of the dead women from stain, and I assumed I had the authority to decide that time-management technology inevitably would be used for evil purposes if I didn't wreck it and destroy those who knew about it.

Scourges transgress against social and sacred order. Prince Hamlet wasn't the hero of **Hamlet.** His mission was to be a minister of Truth and perhaps also a scourge. But he couldn't entirely believe in the first half of that mission, while in the end he embraced the role of scourge.

Scourges always must be scourged themselves.

Hamlet did not survive **Hamlet.** Moses, having scourged three thousand people, never lived to see the promised land.

A killer like Cloyce was a murderer, killing for wrong reasons but compelled to do so.

A scourge went into darker territory than that. A scourge was not **compelled** to kill by mental imbalance or emotional confusion or selfish desire. A scourge made a carefully reasoned decision to kill in numbers that exceeded what was absolutely necessary to ensure self-preservation and the defense of the innocent. Even if he killed for a right reason, he was in rebellion against social order and commanding authority.

Who scourges will be scourged. In fulfilling this dark role in Roseland, I would bring about my own death.

Yet I knew that I would not retreat from my decision.

I sat there under the glassy-eyed animal heads, reluctant to get up and go on with it.

I got up and went on. The last of Constantine Cloyce's private quarters was the bedroom with ensuite bath.

Thirty-nine

ALTHOUGH THE BEDROOM LOOKED ordinary, it might have been where he tortured and killed them over the years. I couldn't know unless I watched some of the DVDs, but I would never play them.

His bed was stripped of linens. I suppose those sheets were in the laundry that I had not permitted Victoria Mors to finish.

Opposite the bed, in high contrast to the antique furniture, a large plasma-screen TV hung on the wall. I could imagine what he most liked to watch at night as he waited for sleep to overtake him.

Then I realized that before he did anything to a new captive woman, he might preview for her what she could expect by playing a couple of his favorite DVDs.

The day in Pico Mundo when I lost Stormy will forever be the worst day of my life, although since then each place I go seems in one way or another to be darker than the place before it.

I shivered and could not stop shivering.

On a counter in the spacious bathroom stood several antique apothecary jars with glass stoppers so well made that they seated as tightly as rubber plugs. The jars contained white powders of subtly different consistencies.

I have never considered escaping the weight of my gift through the buoyancy of drugs. I see enough strange things without teasing hallucinations from my mind. And I have witnessed others demonstrate by their addictions that chemically induced euphoria is subject to something quite like the law of gravity: What goes up must eventually come crashing down.

Although I would not be able to tell by smell or by taste which of the powders was cocaine, which heroin or something else, I didn't doubt they were drugs. For one thing, on a silver tray beside the jars was a short silver straw of the kind with which the more stylish users of coke inhaled it. Also on the tray were a deep-bowled spoon, a half-melted candle, and hypodermic syringes in sealed packages.

Cloyce was such an imposing figure, always with the posture and the carriage of an aristocrat who expected to be noticed and admired, so square-shouldered and muscular, so sharp-eyed and keenly alert, that I wouldn't have imagined that he might be a heavy user of drugs. But if by some simple act he could, at will, use Tesla's machine to roll back the years and be as young again as he wished, then perhaps he could also reverse the long-term debilitating effects of heroin and such.

If they could periodically undo all consequences of destructive drug use, maybe all seven of them were junkies. Self-imprisoned in Roseland, determined to escape death but with ever less experience of life to fill their time, they would have every reason—and no reason not—to pop pills, snort coke, or shoot whatever into their veins. Ever less given to travel, the trips they made were courtesy of narcotics, stimulants, and hallucinogens.

In the medicine cabinet were numerous bottles of prescription drugs. None of them appeared to be for the treatment of any disease or medical condition. They were for recreational purposes.

The chill of which I couldn't rid myself grew colder, until I felt as if I must have bits of ice in my blood.

Considering that these people were without moral inhibitions, that they expected to live for centuries, that they had divorced themselves from all human sympathies, that they believed there would be no consequences for anything they did, considering that their potential for brutality was not that of mere men and women but that of the heartless gods whom primitive men had first imagined, they would be unspeakably **vicious** and relentless in pursuit of their darkest desires.

To all that, add the effect of drugs, and their cruelty would make the pitiless predations of vampires seem genteel. By comparison, the people of Roseland were surely greater monsters than the freaks that Kenny called porkers.

What I had imagined the DVDs contained would be a fraction as horrendous as what actually had been recorded on them.

And suddenly I knew that Victoria had lied to me when she said that, although the others assisted Cloyce in acquiring women for his pleasure, they did not share his interest in torture and murder. If they didn't participate in Cloyce's bloody revelries, it was because they had horrific desires of their own to fulfill.

I had thought the secrets of Roseland were at last known to me, but now I understood that there were more and worse to be uncovered. I wouldn't search for them. I didn't need to know. I couldn't **stand** to know. Witnessing things demonic too intimately for too long would be to invite madness and worse into my heart.

Stepping out of the bathroom, I thought that I was finished here, but I found myself drawn across the bedroom toward a corner desk on which stood a computer. Intuition cast a line, hooking me and reeling me toward a sheaf of papers lying on the desk.

They were facedown, and when I turned them over, I saw that they were printouts of news stories that Cloyce had gotten off the Internet. Not recent news. They concerned the young fry cook who had brought down the killers committing mass murder at a mall in Pico Mundo, California, more than eighteen months earlier. Forty-one were wounded. Nineteen died. The police said that if the young fry cook hadn't acted, hundreds would have been killed. The so-called hero did not think himself a hero and wouldn't talk to the media. The only picture of him in the press reports was his high-school yearbook photo in which he looked foolish and clueless.

Cloyce had thought he needed to know me.

Knowing me, he suspected Victoria's disappearance must be my handiwork.

Now that I was known and being sought as surely as they were seeking Victoria, freeing the boy and escaping from Roseland would be just this side of impossible.

A hand clasped my shoulder, and I thought I felt my hair turn white. But it wasn't Cloyce. It was Mr. Hitchcock. He gave me the OK sign, as if to assure me everything would be all right.

I said, "Well, I hope so."

He gave me two thumbs up and considerately faded away.

Forty

STANDING AROUND THE CORNER IN the west wing, I listened to the searchers as they finished with the rooms off the long south hallway. They operated in pairs, and neither pair strayed far from the other.

If not afraid, they were at least damn worried. They assumed that Victoria might be dead. If she'd been killed, her ticket to physical immortality had been invalidated. And if she could be killed within the fortress walls of Roseland, so could the rest of them.

As they gathered at the end of the south wing, I heard them agree to go together to the ground floor by way of the back service stairs and then work forward from the kitchen. When the thumping of descending footsteps faded, I stepped into the south wing and hurried toward the boy's room.

The house was huge, and their caution would ensure they made slow progress, but before long they would find Victoria Mors bound and gagged behind the boilers in the furnace room. And then they would know that I was in the house, in spite of the evidence to the contrary. Victoria and the chef would join in the hunt. Henry Lolam, stuck in the gatehouse as long as the freaks were roaming the estate, would be the only one who wouldn't have the pleasure of putting a bullet in me.

At the boy's room, I entered without knocking.

If he had been in one of his trances, eyes rolled back in his head, his father and the others had startled him out of it when they searched his room. He sat in his armchair, surrounded by the books through which he tried to live a life otherwise constrained.

He looked small and miserable. Evidently, I hadn't convinced him that I could be counted upon to return.

Sitting on the ottoman in front of his chair, I said, "Timothy. That's your name. Timothy Cloyce."

"They're looking for you," he said.

"Not yet. They're looking for Victoria, but when they find her, then they'll start looking for me."

"Sondra," he said.

"What?"

"Her name back then was Sondra. I don't remember her last name. I don't think I ever heard it."

"You knew her?"

"Her and Glenda—who calls herself Valerie Tameed these days. They were his mistresses. They enjoyed threesomes—you know, going at each other in the same bed."

His understanding of sexual matters unsettled me, though I knew he wasn't the nine-year-old boy that he appeared to be. According to the plaque in the mausoleum, he had been born in September 1916. He was now ninety-five years old. He had the knowledge of a well-read man of those years, though none of the experience.

As on my previous visit, I was again struck by his ginger-brown eyes, by a quality that might have been loneliness so profound as to be despair, suggesting an interior landscape that was cheerless and dismal though perhaps not yet desolate. I had never met another pair of eyes that by their stare alone could fill me with such sadness.

Considering how long he had lived like this, it was a triumph for him not to have gone mad. Perhaps it was whatever part of his mind remained that of a child, with a child's wonder and stubborn hope, that kept him going.

Removing the towel from the pillowcase sack, unwrapping the hacksaw, I hesitated to ask about Madra, but I reminded myself that Timothy was not a fragile child—or at least not only a child.

"Your father shot your mother. Why?"

"She was supposed to stay with me on the Malibu estate, where he spent half his time. The other half, he was here. It was supposed to be **his** getaway, strictly for him and his buddies. My mother was sweet . . . and too submissive. Maybe she suspected he kept women, but she let him have his retreat. She never came here . . . until he took her favorite horse from the stables in the Malibu estate and brought it to Roseland."

I said, "A great black stallion. A Friesian."

"Its name was Black Magic, but they called it only Magic. He bought Magic for her. When it became her favorite horse, he decided it was his favorite, too. He was always giving her things and then taking them away."

Holding Timothy's right hand, I pushed back the sleeve of his sweater, and exposed the GPS transponder.

"She drove all the way up to Roseland unannounced, to get her horse back. She brought me because she thought he might refuse her, but not both of us."

I placed his arm on the arm of the chair and explained how he needed to grip the upholstery to keep the monitoring bracelet from sliding around under the hacksaw.

"It was a long trip in those days, four hours in a Model T, an amazing adventure, especially for a woman alone with a young boy. I still remember it, how thrilling it was."

The bracelet was just loose enough that I was able to press a corner of the towel between it and Timothy's wrist. When the hacksaw cut through the last of the steel, the barrier of cloth would prevent it from drawing his blood.

He said, "She wasn't surprised to find Paulie Sempiterno at the gatehouse. He was my father's body-guard for a long time. Paulie warned my father by phone before sending the two of us up to the main house."

Undoubtedly I had at least fifteen minutes, probably twenty or more, before Cloyce and his crew would locate Victoria Mors—once Sondra.

"Mother couldn't believe the grandness of Roseland. She knew he meant to make a first-rate retreat, but she didn't know it was this spectacular. He had kept the plans from her. He was domineering. And as I said, she was submissive . . . to a point."

After testing the tension on the blade, I adjusted the wing nut.

"Sondra and Glenda were living in the guest wing. My father told Mother that it was the servants' wing, and they dutifully played the part of maids for the short while she would be at Roseland. Of course it was neither the guest wing nor the servants' wing. It was really the whores' wing."

I might never grow accustomed to things like that coming from an apparent nine-year-old. I got up from the ottoman and leaned toward the boy to begin the job of freeing him.

"Mother saw the grooms and the trainer who came in daily to care for the horses but didn't live on the grounds. Yet she wondered how just two maids, a chef, and a few security men could care for such a large place. And where were the gardeners for all those lawns and flowers?"

The bracelet had three parallel rows of links, like the band of a wristwatch. If the rows had been aligned, I could have sawn through the weaker recessed connection between them. The center row, however, was offset from those bracketing it. I would need to cut through somewhat more than a quarter-inch thickness.

"Father told her that it was the gardeners' day off, the whole crew on the same day, though it was Tuesday. He said a large team of housekeepers came in three days a week, but that Sondra and Glenda were the only full-time maids."

Bearing down on the hacksaw to let the teeth get a bite of steel, not so hard as to snap the blade, I made a long easy stroke.

"I don't know what all he told Mother, but I think she must have known they were lies."

I sawed only with forward strokes at first, until a score line could be cut deep enough to hold the blade as it slid thereafter in both directions.

"That afternoon, he agreed to let her have Magic. But she insisted on traveling with the horse when it was taken back to Malibu, and it was too late to arrange transport. We stayed for dinner and the night."

The necessity to make a single score line and then to keep the blade within it required me to focus, and when I did not so much as glance at Timothy, his voice inspired images in my mind, so that I felt as if I were watching unfold the tale he told.

That fateful night, he was provided with blankets

and pillows for a sofa in the parlor of his father's west-wing quarters. His parents retired to the bedroom in the same suite.

Although tired, Timothy was also excited about being in a new place—and uneasy for reasons he couldn't quite explain. He slept only lightly and was awakened during the night when his father, wearing slippers and a bathrobe, passed through the parlor to the door and went out into the hall.

A fan of mystery shows on the radio, the boy suspected some plot must be afoot, and he determined that he would fill the role of detective. He got off the sofa, hurried to the door, quietly opened it, and slipped into the hallway.

With excitement but also with stealth, he followed his father down through the house, keeping at such a distance that he twice almost lost track of his quarry, and then he **did** lose him. Timothy wandered the mazelike mansion, making his way mostly by the full moon that pressed its ghost light through the big windows.

After a while, he came without knowing it to the guest wing on the ground floor, where hallway lights were aglow. He heard people in one of the rooms, a woman's soft laughter and another woman whimpering.

Listening at the door, occasionally catching a muffled word along with urgent cries and groans, both male and female, that might have been sounds either of pleasure or of pain, young Timothy grew convinced that something terribly strange and of enormous importance was taking place in there.

The radio-serial heroes whom he admired were clever, bold, and intrepid. They never feared for themselves and never retreated. And because they always seized the moment, they always triumphed.

He dared to ease open the door.

Beyond lay a shadowy sitting room brightened only by what light came through the open door to the adjoining bedroom.

As by a magnet drawn, the boy found himself moving across the outer room, toward the glow of two bedside lamps with pleated-silk shades that cast a peach-colored light.

Near the threshold of the inner room, he was halted by the sight of his father in there, on the bed with Sondra and Glenda. He was too young, in that more innocent era, to know quite what he was seeing, but he might have understood if the scene had not been made more mysterious by the bondage game that featured Sondra in a dog collar, bound to bedposts with black silken cords.

Equally as weird as all that was the presence of Chiang Pu-yi, who was known these days as Jam Diu. Timothy had seen him in Cloyce's company several times over the previous couple of years.

Later he would learn that Chiang Pu-yi was a very wealthy man with interests in Hong Kong and England. Chiang and Constantine had met in London, where both spent some days with Aleister Crowley, the practitioner of magic and the cult leader who called himself the Beast from Revelations. Each found in the other a reflection of himself, a will to power that would not be thwarted.

That night in 1925, Chiang Pu-yi sat on a chair, on the farther side of the bed from the open door, watching the threesome. He was dressed oddly. Timothy could not remember what Chiang wore because he was most struck by the fact that the man, who was much older than Constantine, looked like himself but many years younger than he had been the last time the boy encountered him.

Bewildered, Timothy stood in the thinner shadows just before the threshold for no longer than a minute, simultaneously repelled and attracted, fear growing by the moment, though fear of what, he did not know.

And then it seemed to him that Chiang's stare had shifted from the people on the bed to Timothy. When Chiang smiled, the boy was certain he had been seen, and he fled at once.

By the time he got back to the second-floor bedroom where his mother lay sleeping, the eerie allure of the scene in the guest wing had given way to terror. Although Sondra had not seemed to be afraid, the boy thought maybe they had been killing her.

He had some difficulty waking his mother, which he would later learn was because his father had slipped her a sedative after dinner. These hours later, it still had some effect. But he did wake her and convey to her, in his childish way, much of what he had seen.

Realizing that her clouded thinking must be the consequence of a drug, Madra determined that they must leave quickly. If her husband could do such a thing to her—and be part of what the boy had seen—there might be no offense that he was incapable of committing. In the years since their wedding, she had glimpsed a disturbing fierceness in him, which he tried to conceal. Without delay, she grabbed only the boy's coat and hurried with him downstairs.

When they left the house by the front door and did not find her Model T in the driveway, Madra didn't know where to look for it, as there was no obvious garage. And then she realized that even if she found the car, the key might not be with it.

She knew where the stables were, however, and where to find her beloved Friesian, Magic. And the stallion didn't require a key.

Although young Timothy was by now shaking and weak with fear and though his mother was struggling to clarify her thoughts, they were aware enough to know that Constantine should have by that time come looking for them. Later, the boy would learn that Chiang Pu-yi had been stoned and, though having seen the young snoop, had not for a while realized the implications; his mind had instead wandered into a sick fantasy about what role the nine-year-old might want to play in this debauchery.

Through the night to the stables, under the full moon, mother and son had fled on foot. An accomplished rider with or without a saddle, Madra took no time with tack but stood upon a mounting block, swung astride the horse, and pulled her boy up in front of her, instructing him to cling to the mane. She clung to it with her right hand, her left arm around her son, and they set off for the front gate at a canter, not risking a gallop that might unseat the boy, staying well clear of the main house.

The gatehouse wasn't manned at night, when no visitors or stable hands needed to be screened for admittance. Madra meant to open the gates herself, ride into town, and perhaps call someone she knew and trusted—or even the authorities—to report that her husband drugged her and that he was engaged in contemptible activities to which their young child had been exposed.

When my hacksaw blade broke, I was snapped out of the mind movie that the boy's words painted for me.

As I fished a spare blade from the packet that I had brought with the saw, Timothy said, "He was standing naked in the driveway, as pale as a ghost in the moonlight. We saw him with his rifle just a moment too late. I never saw him kill my mother that time, because he shot and killed me first."

Forty-one

PREVIOUSLY I MENTIONED MY HIGH-school yearbook photo in which I looked foolish and clueless. With Timothy's revelation, I felt my features settling into that too-familiar expression.

Earlier in the day, in the boy's suite, when Mrs. Tameed didn't know that I was hiding in the next room, she reminded him that he was different from the rest of them, and she called him "dead boy." I had thought those words were a threat. I didn't realize she meant them literally.

"His first round shot me off the horse, killed me instantly. The second took down Magic but didn't kill him. I'm told my mother rode the horse to its knees as he lined up his third shot, with which he killed her. Then he walked to the stallion and finished it. He shot her twice again, too, though she was dead."

I didn't dare allow myself to be distracted by any revelation, no matter how stunning, even if it struck me as an impossible claim. The searchers would soon be descending to the basement, if they were not there already, just a few minutes away from discovering Victoria Mors.

It now occurred to me, in light of the bondage games she played with Cloyce, that Victoria might perversely have enjoyed it when I punched her, bound her, and ultimately gagged her.

I **know** that she enormously enjoyed repeatedly spitting in my face.

Removing the broken blade from the hacksaw, I watched my hands trembling as I said, "Dead. I don't understand. You can't be dead. You're here alive."

That bell-clear, choirboy voice was characterized again by a solemnity too grave for a child. "Did you go to the mausoleum, as I told you to?"

"Yes. Down into the cellar . . . the subcellar."

Even in the warm light of the lamp, his face was ashen and his lips were pale. "So you have seen."

"Yes."

"Do you know about Nikola Tesla?"

"Yeah. Built under the estate, into the property wall . . . some machine that . . . manages time."

"The buildings and the grounds," Timothy said, "are kept in a state of—well, you could call it suspended animation, though it isn't that."

"Stasis," I offered.

"But the current that sustains the estate doesn't keep the people young. When they grow older than they wish to be, they have to use another part of the machine in the top of—"

"—the guest tower," I said as I fitted the new blade to the pins of the hacksaw. "I haven't seen it. That was just a guess."

My tremors made the work harder than it should have been, and I wondered at the reason for them. Nothing Timothy had told me was worse than the things that I had previously discovered in Roseland.

He said, "They call that part of the machine the chronosphere. If you think of the past as the depths of time and the present as the surface, then the thing moves through time like a bathysphere moves in the ocean. At least it does in one direction."

I adjusted the tension on the new blade. My hands shook worse than ever, as if I had succumbed to the confusion of time in Roseland and had aged to the point where I was afflicted with Parkinson's disease.

"When they ride it back in time," the boy continued, "the years fall away from them. Their bodies grow young and fit because bodies are material things. And though the effects of age on their brains are repaired as well, their personalities and knowledge and memories are unaffected because the mind is incorporeal."

"So why don't they age when they return to the present?"

"Because they don't return through time. They return **outside** of time. The chronosphere isn't just a time machine that travels back and then forward, but it also moves to the side, through the membrane that separates time and what lies outside of time. I don't pretend to understand it. I don't think any of them do. Only Tesla knew, and he might be the only one capable of understanding. And Einstein."

From the back of my mind, a half-formed dark idea beckoned to me like a phantom haunting the far end of a room. I tried to close a mental door on it, fearful of engaging it because I sensed that if I gave this idea consideration, I would inevitably act upon it, and by doing so would destroy myself and everything that mattered to me. Now I knew the reason for my tremors.

The ageless boy said, "They just ride the machine back and then return. It isn't advisable to get out of it in some other time."

"But it's possible to do so?"

"You can set the controls so the chronosphere will park in some other year. You can get out to explore any point in the past. But it isn't done."

"Why not?"

"The ramifications of time touring are beyond knowing. Better not to take risks. It seems clear, from what Nikola Tesla discovered, that you can't change anything about the past because it's set. What you do there can't change your future. What has happened will happen. Any change you make back there is undone by . . . call it fate. But the unknown risks are still considered too great."

I overcame my tremors and slid the new blade into

the score line on the bracelet. "But your father used the machine in just that way."

"He didn't intend to kill me, only my mother. Once the shooting was done, he had one moment of remorse."

Sawing at the bracelet, I said, "He rode the chronosphere back to some point before he killed you. He parked there."

"Shortly after it happened, he went back in time. He was waiting in the stable when my mother arrived with me. He took a handgun with him and shot her to death in front of me."

Earlier, speaking of the moment that his mother had been shot while riding Magic, the boy had said, **I never saw him kill my mother that time.**

That time.

"He didn't shoot Magic, only her. But when he brought me back with him to present-time Roseland, the stallion was still dead on the front lawn. And so was my mother. And so was I."

I raised the hacksaw from the bracelet.

Each time I looked directly into the boy's bottomless eyes, I was profoundly disquieted to see such a deeply wounded soul gazing out at me from the prison of his ageless body. Nevertheless, I was compelled to look, so he might see in my eyes that I understood his terrible anguish, without my having to speak of it.

"'What has happened will happen,'" I said, repeating his words to me. "'Call it fate.'"

By taking his son out of the settled history of the past, by taking him **outside** of time and then back to the present, Constantine Cloyce had created a paradox. I knew all about time paradoxes from movies and books, but none the equal of this one. If you thought too much about it, your mind would tie itself into a Gordian knot that could be neither untied nor cut.

Timothy said, "They put my mother's body in the subcellar of the mausoleum, so he could look at her whenever he wanted, for reasons only his twisted mind can fathom. Sempiterno and Lolam—whose names then were Carlo Luca and James Durnan—worked through the night with Chiang to get the horse off the lawn and into a grave in the meadow."

Setting to work with the hacksaw again, I said, "And your body? I mean . . . the body of that other Timothy?"

"The bullet had passed through. There was no way to know with what weapon I . . . he had been shot. So they jammed the corpse into the footspace in front of the passenger's seat in my mother's car. Glenda drove it very far south along the Coast Highway and parked it in a lay-by that was a lonely place back in those days. Sondra followed in another vehicle. They smeared my mother's blood on the driver's seat and floorboards, and left her car there with the doors wide open."

"An attempted kidnapping gone wrong?"

"That's what the cops were meant to assume."

"The bad guys took your mother but then she died on them before a ransom could be demanded."

"Something like that."

"And the cops bought it?"

"My father was widely respected. Besides, certain authorities could be bought then, just like certain of them can be bought now. He knew who, and how to do the buying."

"It must have been a big story."

"Not as big as you think. Remember, he owned lots of newspapers. He reined in his editors. And he had enough dirt on his competitors to rein them in, too. He had no political enemies, as William Hearst did, and when he withdrew into Roseland in apparent grief and became to all appearances a depressed recluse, they let him alone."

"Your ashes . . . the other Tim's ashes are in an urn in the wall of the mausoleum."

"Yes."

"Whose ashes are in her urn?"

"No one's. Officially, her body was never found. Her interment was strictly symbolic. Of course there aren't ashes in my father's urn, either."

The blade sawed through the last of the link, and the monitoring bracelet slipped off his wrist.

"For years, I was kept under lock and key, or literally on a leash, until technology developed that allowed them to monitor me like this."

I dropped the saw and got to my feet.

As he rose from the armchair, Timothy said, "I'm

dead. Yet I'm alive. The thread of my life was cut off that night, yet here I am. My mind has grown complex, mature, but physically I never change. I've lived as an adolescent and as an adult only through books, only by reading about life beyond nine. I'm a boy forever, and already I've been a boy longer than I can bear."

Forty-two

I'D PRETTY MUCH HAD ENOUGH. Enough death. Enough crazy. Enough surprises of the kind that didn't come with a party hat. Enough weirdness. Enough of Roseland. If they ever turned this place into a bed-and-breakfast, they weren't going to get an endorsement from me.

I led Timothy cautiously into the south hall on the second floor. The house was so quiet that I might have thought I'd gone deaf if my intestines hadn't been grumbling about my indulgence in Shilshom's quiche and cheesecake.

According to Timothy, Nikola Tesla's uncannily silent machinery not only managed time but, harnessing the thermodynamic consequences that arose from that management, also produced all of the power that the estate needed. It was in essence a perpetual-motion machine, a perfect example of green energy. Well, except for the humanoid pigs hell-bent on killing anything that crossed their path.

Also according to Timothy, several years usually passed between those occasions when the fantastical machinery for some reason pulled moments of the future into the present, though sometimes it happened more frequently. I was just lucky enough to arrive at the height of the season, which was way more exciting than being in Vermont when the trees put on their autumn colors.

Until the visitors from Kenny Mountbatten's hideous future were no longer phasing in and out of this current moment in Roseland's history, until the steel shutters went up, the only way out of the main house was the way that I had sneaked into it.

After Constantine Cloyce and his crew found Victoria behind the boilers in the furnace room, the lot of them would come charging up from the basement in unrighteous indignation, looking for a fry cook to kill. We had to be in position to get past them and out through the copper-clad tunnel to the mausoleum.

I didn't like the open sweep of the main stairs. I didn't like the complete exposure of the spiral bronze stairs in the library. I didn't like either set of service stairs because they were the ones most likely to be used by a spitting-mad Victoria Mors and her kinky coconspirators.

The only thing I liked was being beamed wherever we wanted to go, as in **Star Trek,** but such a convenient mode of travel hadn't been invented yet. With pistol in hand, I led the boy to the farther end of the south hallway, past the entrance to the library mezzanine, and along the west wing to the front service stairs.

I may not be able to chew gum and play basketball at the same time or even play basketball without gum, but I can think fast on my feet. I have to, because I never plan ahead. There's no point to planning ahead when any damn crazy thing can happen around me at any moment. Since I tend to make it up as I go along, I have got to be quick about making decisions when the crunch comes.

Unlike me, Timothy had a plan. He'd given his situation a lot of thought. He wanted to be taken to the chronosphere, to travel not to the night his mother was murdered, but instead to a time in 1915 that was certain to be before he had been conceived in her womb. He hoped that, entering time before he had existed, he would **cease** to exist.

Over the years, in his most despondent moments, he considered suicide but opted against it because he didn't believe his father would let him go that easily. If Constantine had ever loved his son, he had not loved him for many decades. But the elder Cloyce was ever passionate about his wealth, his possessions, his **toys,** and he would not tolerate having anything of his taken from him. By Constantine's way of thinking, the boy was his property, and he would surely try to undo the suicide by going back in time to just before the event, and bring to the present a

Timothy who had not yet self-destructed. Then they would keep the boy in even more restricted circumstances, and his existence would be more intolerable than ever.

I was sure he was right about that. But I wasn't sure he could know what would happen if he traveled back to a time before he had been conceived. The paradox he now represented might be a fraction as complicated as the one he would create with his plan.

Besides, even if his destiny had been to die at nine, back in 1925, and even if the prospect of living as a perpetual child was intolerable to him, I was disturbed about helping him to commit, via the chronosphere, what might be at best a passive suicide. I wanted hope for him, and hope lay in freedom, not in surrender.

Thinking on my feet as we descended the front service stairs, I decided that before we went to the third floor of the guest tower, we would go to the second. Annamaria might be as enigmatic as any character Alice met on the other side of the looking glass, but I knew she would be wiser about Timothy than I would be, considering the pathetic Odd Thomas Standard of Wisdom that she had to exceed.

When we reached the ground floor without being shot or spat upon, I chose to continue down to the basement, though the search team might still be on that level. The point of reconnoitering is to discover what lies ahead, and the danger of reconnoitering is being discovered **by** what lies ahead before you discover it.

Going down, I glanced back a couple of times, to be sure the boy was staying close, which he was. The second time, he smiled at me to acknowledge my concern, the first smile of his I'd seen. He might be ninety-five and counting, but he was boy enough and vulnerable enough to break your heart with that smile.

Right then, I knew that I would fail him.

His trusting smile was significant in the way that, during some buddy-cop movies, it is reliably significant when in Act 2 the lesser star tells the bigger star that he is going to ask the lesser female lead to marry him. No more than three scenes later, he will be as dead as dead gets, and the bigger star will have the motivation he needs to walk safely through a hailstorm of bullets, slaughter twenty gangsters, and become teary-eyed without anyone thinking that he's a sissy.

The vast majority of movies aren't concerned about imitating life, because life avoids the clichés that make for big box office. But sometimes life imitates movies, usually to devastating effect and without the compensation of popcorn.

At the bottom of the stairwell, the door stood wide open to the basement corridor. I hesitated on the last step, listening.

Nobody here but us chickens. I never have fully

understood that saying. Chickens can't talk, and even if they could talk, to whom would they say such a thing?

The air contained a faint ozone scent, as it had for the past few hours. I could smell nothing else—and could hear nothing at all.

I motioned for Timothy to stay where he was while I eased through the open door.

On the farther side of the hallway, doors stood wide or half open, as if the searchers had been in too much of a hurry to bother closing up behind themselves.

To the right, the length of the corridor was deserted all the way to the wine cellar.

Immediately to my left, the door to the construction shack that linked the house of the present to the undeveloped land of 1921 stood mostly open, and I could see the draftsman tables, the desks, the old wooden filing cabinets.

If the searchers were still working the basement, they would have been making noise. The deep silence suggested they had found Victoria, freed her, and returned upstairs to hunt down and smack down one ignorant clocker who didn't know his place in the scheme of things.

I glanced back at Timothy, still in the stairwell, and motioned for him to join me. I wanted him at my side, so that I could grab him and move him with me quickly if suddenly we needed to get out of sight in a room either to the left or right.

Long corridors are dangerous places. If well-armed people are looking for you, you're exposed to gunfire from one end to the other, in a space that, for the shooter, has all the benefits of an indoor target range.

The best thing you can do is to cover the territory in a timely manner, though it's not easy to move fast **and** be silent. The tendency is to adopt the Sylvester-the-Cat-stalking-Tweety-Bird exaggerated, high-speed tiptoe, which makes you look ridiculous and, anyway, never works that well for Sylvester.

I instructed Timothy to strive for quiet by cleverly raising one finger to my lips, and then side by side we walked quickly from the west end of the hallway toward the wine cellar at the farther end. The laundry was the next-to-last room on the right, and as we passed it, I saw that the door was open, though I had left it closed, which meant the searchers had been here and gone.

The door to the furnace room stood open as well, but before we quite got to it, Jam Diu stepped out of there, in front of us, his shotgun leveled at me.

My pistol was aimed at the concrete floor, so that my best hope of wounding him was with a calculated ricochet that not even Annie Oakley would have expected to pull off.

"Drop it," Jam Diu demanded as we came to a halt.

There was no doubt that he could squeeze the trigger of the 12-gauge and chop us with buckshot before I could bring up the Beretta and fire. But if I dropped the weapon, we were finished anyway. They would return Timothy to his prison, and the nicest thing Constantine Cloyce would do to me was carve me up like he did those women and put my body in the subcellar of the mausoleum, even though I wasn't his preferred gender.

"I said drop it," Jam Diu reminded me, as though he thought I had the shortest attention span in the world.

"Well," I said.

Frowning, he said, "Is that my Beretta?"

Conversation was better than blasting at each other. You never know when even a most disagreeable conversation might take a positive turn.

"Yes, sir. Yes, it is. It's your Beretta."

"You stole my Beretta."

"No, sir. I'm no thief. I borrowed it."

With rough affection, he said, "That is a wonderful pistol. I adore that pistol."

"Well, to be honest, I don't even like guns. But the way things have been going, I thought I might need one sooner than later. Like now."

"You broke into my rooms," he said, clearly offended that I had so little respect for his privacy.

"No, sir. I used a key."

"Constantine is a flaming idiot."

"That was Mr. Sempiterno's opinion earlier today."

"Why would Constantine bring you and that . . . that woman here?"

I shared with him one of my main theories: "Subconsciously he may be weary of all this and want someone to bring it to an end."

"Don't Freud me, fry cook. Freud is a load of horseshit."

"Well, there's also the fact Annamaria is uncannily persuasive."

"I don't find the bitch in the least persuasive."

"With all due respect, sir, you've not spoken to her. Give her a chance, and you'll see."

"Put down the pistol nice and easy."

Now that he recognized the gun as his, he didn't want me just to drop it. Apparently, even extremely wealthy immortals have a strong attachment to their stuff.

"Well," I said.

Timothy said, "Chiang, just let us go to the chronosphere. Let me go back where I belong."

I thought "let us go to the chronosphere" sounded like it should have been an old David Bowie song. Even in moments of peril, my mind takes curious detours.

The gardener had dropped his benign Zen persona along with his pretense of being a gardener. Hatred pulled his round face long, and in his eyes reflections of the overhead lights seemed to flicker like serpent tongues.

"If I had my way, boy, I'd slit you open and let you die trying to stuff your intestines back in yourself. And then I'd bring you back from ten minutes ago and do it all over again."

"Well," I said, because this didn't seem to be one of those disagreeable conversations that was likely to take a positive turn.

Perhaps realizing that the years of his imprisonment might be only the prelude to the horrors that an inventive man like this could visit upon him, Timothy sidled closer to me.

"One last chance to put the gun down, fry cook. Otherwise I blow you away and maybe bring **both** of you back for more."

"Killing me once will be enough, sir. I don't want to put you to any trouble."

Because I couldn't think of anything else to do, I bent my knees slightly and began to lower the adored Beretta to the floor, doing it slow and easy, as he had suggested, in fact so slow and so easy that I might live to see another birthday before I finally released the weapon.

I was hoping that some brilliant maneuver would occur to me and that I would astonish him as Jackie Chan astonished his foes in those martial-arts movies. But I'm no Jackie Chan, and as it turned out, the porkers pulled my bacon from the fire.

Twenty feet behind Jam Diu, the wine-cellar door flew open, and one of the freaks raged into the corridor. It wasn't a hunchback with a misshapen head and too-long arms, but was instead one of those that might be called a normal specimen of their kind. In the hoggish head: a leering mouth of rending teeth, the fleshy nostrils in the dripping snout, the yellow eyes like the fevered glare of something crawling through the moss-hung darkness of a swamp dream.

The beast had evidently discovered the guardian-angel door in the mausoleum wall, which I had been unable to close. It had found its way through cellar, subcellar, and tunnel to this moment of reckoning.

Jam Diu swung toward the door when it crashed open, but the swine thing was quicker than it appeared to be. It seized his right arm and snapped it like a dry stick. As Jam Diu, prince of time and a god among mere men, screamed, the buckshot tore harmlessly into the ceiling.

While this was happening, I shouted to Timothy to run, but he was already on the move. I chased after him, thankful that I hadn't put down the Beretta, although in these close quarters and against these beasts, a 9-mm pistol promised to be about as effective as fighting a T. rex with a set of lawn darts.

Two-thirds of the way to the west service stairs, down which we had come in more halcyon times, three minutes earlier, I glanced back and saw Jam Diu coming apart in ways I refuse to remember. Behind the first freak, a second entered the corridor, and behind the second came a third.

Forty-three

AFTER RACING UP TWO FLIGHTS OF the front service stairs, Timothy apparently thought, as I did, that going to the second floor would be a mistake. He flung open the stairwell door and hurried into the foyer, in the center of which he halted, looking around, unsure what to do next.

With three freaks in the house plus five heavily armed members of the self-improvement club called the Outsiders, all of them on the hunt, we were not likely to find a quiet corner where we could have tea and discuss literature undisturbed. And the sooner we went to the top floor, the sooner we would have nowhere left to go.

The freaks weren't brainiacs, weren't likely to spend a lot of time in a huddle strategizing their next move. They weren't stupid, either, and weren't entirely impulsive, but I didn't think they would linger in the basement when so much more meat could be found upstairs.

Although I didn't hear grunting and snorting and three-hundred-pound footfalls on the front service stairs, I figured they were coming. I pulled Timothy out of the foyer and into the main drawing room.

The giant goatish Pan still stood on the plinth under the central chandelier, and I knew whose side he'd be on in any battle between me and a wild boar with pretensions. We stayed to the shadowy perimeter of the room and stopped at the sofa behind which earlier I had hidden. Alert. Listening. We would probably smell them coming before we heard them.

After searching the basement, Cloyce and his crew had stationed Jam Diu there in case I got around behind them. But I doubted the freaks were well enough disciplined for one of them to be willing to remain below while the others were upstairs having all the fun. If we could stay alive for a few minutes, and if all of the freaks came upstairs, we could slip down again and leave as we originally intended, although I wasn't keen on having to plod through the remains of Mr. Diu.

I suddenly realized that we had been fearfully close to the invading freaks in the basement corridor but hadn't smelled them.

"They didn't stink," I whispered. "You always know they're nearby because of their stink."

"It's only the deformed ones that stink," Timothy said.

That was unfair. If they didn't stink, maybe they

could be quiet, too, when they wanted to be. I wasn't prepared for odorless, stealthy freaks that might abruptly loom out of nowhere.

In some distant part of the house, a shotgun discharged. The first cry was as much a bellow of rage as it was a squeal of pain, unquestionably issuing from a swine's throat.

But the second cry, fast on the heels of the first, was the most wretched human scream imaginable, the like of which I hoped never to hear again. It went on for half a minute or longer, an excruciating expression of terror and agony, so chilling that it brought to mind that horrific painting by Goya titled **Saturn Devouring His Children**, which is even more bloodcurdling than its title suggests.

Although none of the residents of Roseland was Timothy's friend, not even his father, the tormented screaming affected him so deeply that he began to shudder and to sob quietly.

Because a scream shares the character of the person's usual voice, I was certain that we had just heard the end of Chef Shilshom.

The limits imposed by reality on all of us were now apparent even to those here who believed that they lived with no limits, no rules, no fear.

I could not pity them, because true pity is joined with a desire to help. I had no intention of putting myself and Timothy at risk for any of them.

But I was unexpectedly moved by the despairing recognition of the inescapable void, which was a note that twisted through the long, tortured death cry. The worst and best of humanity stand in the same cold shadow, and even a deserved death can send a shiver of sympathy through me from skin to marrow.

In the wake of the scream, the silence in the house pooled deep.

If we were contending only with the Outsiders, we might try to hide somewhere exceedingly clever for a few minutes, until it seemed that all the freaks must have ascended in the house, and then return to the basement. But the swine things would probably smell us out everywhere except in the airtight walk-in refrigerator off the kitchen.

Besides the possibility of being trapped inside the walk-in, I didn't want to hide in a refrigerator for the same reason I wouldn't have hidden in the communal cookpot in a village of cannibals.

To Timothy, I whispered, "Freaks inside the house, there's no longer any reason not to go outside, more places to run. Where are the controls for the security shutters?"

"I d-don't know."

"Any guess at all?"

"No," he said. "N-n-none."

He reached for me. I took his hand. It was small and cold and damp with sweat.

In the ninety-five years of his singular existence, he had read thousands of books, which together comprised most of his experience. Thousands of lives in thousands of books, lived vicariously, plus so many years of grim familiarity with the many horrors of Roseland, yet he not only kept his sanity but also, in some part of his mind and heart, he remained a little boy, having held tightly to a kernel of innocence. Under the most oppressive and depressing circumstances, he had preserved at least a measure of the purity with which he was born.

I could not have done as much in his position, and I dreaded failing him, which I had been certain I would since that trusting smile he had given me on the service stairs.

The continuing silence seemed both to invite us to get moving and to warn us against rash action.

Diagonally across the vast room, near the southeast corner, the hidden service door in the paneling opened, and Mrs. Tameed entered like an experienced cop clearing a threshold: staying low, pistol in a two-hand grip, sweeping the muzzle left to right.

Although we were at the farther end of the room and in shadow, she saw us, and I could almost feel her fury before she spoke.

"You scum-sucking sonofabitch," she hissed, perhaps so chastened by the current peril that she felt obliged to clean up her language at least to some extent. "You let them into the house."

As I'd done with Timothy in the basement, I held a finger to my lips to convey my belief in the desirability of silence, because no matter how much we might despise each other, trading insults right now might bring upon us the fate of Jam Diu and Shilshom.

She took a shot at me.

Forty-four

JUST BECAUSE MRS. TAMEED WAS TO wickedness what Albert Einstein was to modern physics, just because she had never met a vice that she didn't embrace, just because she wallowed in depravity, just because she was insane, didn't mean that she shouldn't have the common sense to recognize what behavior was called for in the current situation. Ranting at me and shooting at me would draw the freaks to us.

Most insane people with a taste for homicide are cunning if not wise. They are as concerned with their survival as they are with finding a virgin to decapitate or a child to strangle. Mrs. Tameed's noisy antics were foolish. I was of a mind to tell her as much.

She shot at Timothy and me again. At a distance of sixty feet, especially in a cluttered and shadowy environment, you have to be a good marksman to plug your target. She missed.

I couldn't hit her from sixty feet, especially because guns are always a last resort with me, even if I am often given no choice but to use them.

Her third shot buzzed wasplike past my right ear, an inch from a bad sting.

Turning my back on the Amazon, expecting her to put a lucky shot through my spine, I pulled Timothy with me toward the second service door that was nearly hidden in the paneling, which I had used before when I'd gone to the library. As we approached it, the door started to open, and I drew the boy at once toward the hinge side, so that we were concealed behind it as it swung wide.

Although I couldn't immediately see who had entered, a low growl identified the newcomer as one of the yellow-eyed pack. When it took two steps into the room, its immense muscular back was toward us.

The door began ever so slowly to ease shut, further exposing the boy and me. Because it was a door intended not to disrupt the lines of the paneling, it had no knob or lever that I could easily grasp to prevent it from arcing away from us. When you wanted to open it, you pushed on it to disengage a touch latch, and you pulled it open with a finger groove concealed under a strip of molding.

The freak stopped where it was and stared across the drawing room at Mrs. Tameed, whom I could still see in the shadowy distance. Muttering to itself, the beast brandished its hatchet at her.

Mrs. Tameed fired two more rounds. She seemed

to be aiming at me rather than at the brute that should have been of more concern to her.

The slugs cracked into the wood paneling. I supposed that no sooner had the wounds in the wall opened than the Methuselah current began rewinding the damage.

The freak issued a noisy challenge, half bleat and half roar.

Mrs. Tameed began shouting at it, calling it a stupid pig, though she tossed the F word in both before and after **stupid**. She shouted at it to look behind itself and encouraged it to "Get the bastard, get him, gut him."

I never imagined that the freaks could understand English, and I guess they couldn't, because this one just shrieked at her again and raised its hatchet high.

The wide-set eyes on its long skull provided it with excellent peripheral vision. If Timothy or I made the slightest move, the creature might become aware of us.

In that case, I would need a lot of luck to take it down before it could fully turn and swing the hatchet at me. Its arms were long enough to reach me if it lunged just one step.

Slowly, so the movement might not draw its attention, hoping to shoot it before it sensed us, I raised the Beretta.

The service door that had been drifting shut was suddenly thrust open. A second freak entered behind the first. This one didn't entirely clear the door, which rested against its flank.

The new arrival was so close that I could have touched it without completely extending my arm. I had no hope of killing both of them before one of them could kill us.

If the excitement of the recent slaughter hadn't caused the creatures to mutter continuously and to growl low in their throats, they would have heard me trying—and failing—not to breathe.

Mrs. Tameed fired another round, perhaps this time at one of the freaks.

The brute in the lead threw his hatchet at her with such force and accuracy that it spun across the drawing room and embedded its blade in her chest.

Mrs. Tameed's claim to immortality and the absolute license of a god had been declared invalid. Her death came so suddenly that she didn't have a chance to cry out in protest.

As the woman dropped, the hatchet-throwing freak loped toward her, shrieking in triumph as it crossed the drawing room. There was something apelike about it, too, perhaps because it moved rather like a man but was not a man, though also because its emotions were always at the surface and instantly expressed in action, as were those of the lower primates. And it had an apelike capacity for violence so extreme that each of its killings was also an atrocity that made Constantine Cloyce's murders seem like the work of a prim and proper villain in an Agatha Christie mystery.

Watching the thing caper toward the body of Mrs. Tameed, I was reminded of that unspeakably awful news story a few years back, the one about the innocent woman who was attacked by her friend's large and enraged pet chimpanzee. It bit off her fingers, plucked out her eyes, and tore off her face all in a frenzied half minute.

The second freak remained within arm's reach of us, the door against it and half concealing it. Although shadows swaddled the boy and me, light from the service hallway behind the beast revealed the side of its head, a hideous profile. This was the face of something **designed** to strike fear in the hearts of all who saw it, **designed** to terrorize and kill. By the mutilation and desecration of its victims, it left survivors with the demoralizing thought that human beings were nothing but meat, just another animal in a world where there was no natural law, where the only virtues were strength, power, cruelty, and ferocity.

Pressed against me, Timothy shuddered uncontrollably. I held fast to him with one hand, worried that the proximity of the freak would at some point make him reckless with fear, and that he would bolt.

Maybe he really did want to be taken back into the past and no longer be a perpetual boy, to have his life ended on the night that his father shot him. But no matter the depth of his despondency, he couldn't want to fall into the hands of one of the freaks, look into those yellow eyes as the talons tore him open and the teeth bit into his face.

To die that way would be perhaps to die twice, the first death being that of the soul, of the sense that there was anything unique and sacred about humanity, the second death being merely physical.

The creature at the door hissed and gnashed its teeth as it watched its companion make its way through the groups of furniture, knocking a lamp off a table, overturning a chair.

At the farther end of the drawing room, the triumphant beast set upon the body of Mrs. Tameed. Shrieking in glee, it rended her as a furious child might rend a doll. The killing itself was not satisfying enough and must be followed by one outrage after another.

We were in Poe territory again, this time "The Murders in the Rue Morgue," where the ape in the night, straight razor in hand, does not find murder alone sufficiently rewarding and must visit some indignity on the bodies of its victims.

The brutal sounds of dismemberment caused Timothy to shake more violently than ever. If he began to sob again, as he had done when listening to Shilshom's protracted death scream, he would reveal our presence and assure that we would go the way of Mrs. Tameed.

Warily, I prepared to empty half of the seventeen-round magazine into the freak at point-blank range. I was all but certain that the thing would survive long enough to lash out punishingly at us in its death throes.

Abruptly abandoning its position at the door, the demonic creature loped across the drawing room, holding high a claw hammer. It was unable to resist the urge to express its hatred and contempt by joining its comrade in the profane mutilation of the dead woman's remains.

From out of the foyer, hurrying with a combat shotgun at the ready, Paulie Sempiterno moved toward the two beasts. He glimpsed Timothy and me, and judging by the hitch in his step when he saw us, I suspected that he would as soon cut us down as kill the freaks. But he knew what he needed to save his ammunition for, and he continued past Pan toward the blood-crazed pair.

The boy and I quickly slipped out of the drawing room, into the narrow service hall. The door eased shut and the latch clicked behind us.

I could have sworn this narrow hallway led only directly ahead, past a powder room and a supply closet, to a secondary entrance to the library. But we had stepped into a junction with a short length of hallway ahead and a longer one to our right.

That particular confusion overcame me again, the feeling that a unique geometry had been applied to the construction of Roseland, that what I saw before me was not all that lay there.

If Tesla's glittering machinery could harness time and put it to the purposes of which I already had become aware, there might be other effects that I couldn't imagine, effects so abstruse as to be almost mystical and far beyond my understanding even if I was to experience them.

As Sempiterno opened fire with his shotgun in the drawing room and the wounded freaks began to scream, I said, "Tim, where does this hall lead, here to our right?"

"I don't know every place in the house."

"But you've lived here all these years."

"Nobody knows every place in the house."

"Nobody? Your father must know. He built it."

"He put up the money for it. He and Jam Diu."

"So he must know."

"He doesn't understand the house. Even sometimes on ordinary days, it seems . . . not what it ought to be. But during a full tide like this, it always gets stranger."

Full tide. Waves of future time washing into this moment of the past.

I wished Roseland were only haunted. I could cope with haunted.

Previously the series of frosted dome lights overhead had properly revealed the passageway to the library. But now that hall was poorly illuminated, as was this previously unnoticed branch. In the longer hall, I saw two doors on the left side, none on the right, and one at the end.

Timothy said, "Jam Diu says it **can't** be fully understood, not even by Tesla."

In the drawing room, the freaks had fallen silent, as had the shotgun. If Sempiterno had killed them, he would quickly reload and come after us.

"I'm scared," Timothy said.

"Me too."

Neither the powder room nor the supply room in the short hall, nor the library at the end of it, nor anywhere we could go from the library, seemed to offer us any safety.

I wanted to get to the back service stairs, in the kitchen. They would take us down to the wine cellar.

Letting go of the boy, gripping the Beretta with both hands, I said, "Come on, this way. What do we have to lose?"

Forty-five

THE FIRST DOOR OPENED INWARD TO a shaft filled with golden radiance. The dimensions of it were difficult to ascertain because the walls were lined with mirrors that deceived the eye with the cunning of a mirror maze in a funhouse.

Shining ranks of spiral forms, similar to the paper decorations people sometimes hang from the ceiling in parties that have an Asian theme, turned at various speeds, although they were not paper. Like drill bits with wide spurs, they bore down through the shaft. No ceiling was apparent; the turning drill bits appeared out of a blur perhaps twenty feet above. They vanished into another blur twenty feet below. If one moment they seemed to be augering down into the earth, the next moment they appeared to be boring **upward**.

As elsewhere, the machinery operated in perfect silence. What might have been the cutting edges of the spurs glistened like molten gold, and what might have been the flutes between the spurs appeared to be as liquid and silver as mercury.

The sight was dizzying, the spiral forms receding to infinity in the mirrors. I felt a kind of hypnotic attraction to those coils, and I closed the door before I might step in a half trance across the threshold and go spinning down into the blur below.

I glanced back toward the junction of hallways, where we had entered from the drawing room. We hadn't yet been followed.

I urged the boy ahead, wanting to keep my body between him and the shotgun if Sempiterno should burst in upon us.

When I touched the knob of the second door, it was freezing. My hand nearly stuck to the brass.

The place beyond lay in such deep darkness that it didn't seem to be either a shaft or a room. Before me lay a void, utterly black, as though it were a view of the nothingness beyond the end of the universe.

The hallway light was dim, but it should have penetrated a few inches into this strange space. The demarcation of light and purest darkness was as straight as a ruled line along the inner edge of the threshold.

Having seen this once before, in distant Pico Mundo, I put my fingertips to what I hoped might be a solid mass, a barrier, but my fingers disappeared into the blackness and then my hand all the way to the wrist. I could see nothing of my fingers, and my arm ended as abruptly as an amputee's stump.

In the first of these memoirs, I wrote of such a room that I found in the house of a nasty piece of work whom I called Fungus Man. That room had been ordinary on one occasion, like this the next, and then ordinary again.

I won't recount again what that room in Pico Mundo produced, but I wanted none of it here. I withdrew my hand, closed the door, and looked at the boy, who seemed amazed that I still possessed the hand that I'd put at risk.

"Have you seen this before?" I asked.

"No."

Sempiterno should have come after us by now. Maybe he had killed the freaks at the expense of his own life. If so, I didn't intend to send flowers to the funeral.

When I opened the door at the end of the long hallway, which should have led us toward the back of the house, I found ahead of me the library, which should have been toward the front.

Bewildered by this discovery, the boy and I crossed the threshold before I saw Paulie Sempiterno. He was standing with his back to us, surveying the book-lined room, as if he'd just come through the same door ten seconds ahead of us.

Hearing us, he began to turn, the shotgun swinging around.

In this war of men and monsters, there was no reason to think he would side with humanity. He brought women to Roseland so that Cloyce could play with them. Perhaps he played with them, too. Perhaps in some corner of the estate, I would discover a collection of his that would make me wish I were blind. In that glimpse of the future, when I'd seen a blackened tree hung with the skeletons of children, was that a work of Sempiterno's on which he'd engage in years to come?

I squeezed off shots as fast as the semiauto would fire, and punched him down to his knees with the copper-jacketed hollow-point rounds. The shotgun clattered out of his hands. He fell hard onto his side, spasmed into the fetal position, and froze there, leaving this world in the position in which he had waited for months to enter it.

No satisfaction comes with killing, regardless of how deserving of death your adversary might be. The killing-machine heroes in books and movies, who toss off bon mots as they cut down villains by the score, seem to me to be disturbingly close in character to the freaks of Roseland, saved only by the fact that they are good-looking and can rely on writers to cloak them in charm that reliably distracts the audience's attention from the fullest meaning of all the blood.

As Sempiterno fell and curled in the womb of Death, I looked at the boy to be sure he was all right. Our eyes met for a moment. Maybe in my stare, he saw far more years than my face revealed, as I saw in his.

Then I turned away from him and stepped to the

service door by which we had entered the library. The long, dimly lighted hallway along which we had come was not there. Instead, it was the shorter hall leading directly to the drawing room, well lighted now and leading to no junction with another corridor.

No matter how many freaks might be prowling the grounds of Roseland, we needed to get out of here quickly, before perhaps the house itself became as much of a threat as the yellow-eyed pack.

Forty-six

EVERY CORNER WAS A DANGER, EVERY doorway a threat, the silence pregnant with peril. Maybe three freaks were dead, maybe only two. Maybe three had gotten into the house, maybe six or twelve, or for all I knew, twenty-four. Jam Diu, Mrs. Tameed, and Sempiterno were no longer of this world, and probably also Chef Shilshom. Henry Lolam was trapped in the gatehouse. That left Victoria and Constantine, the pair whose eternal love—as she called it—had matured into a love of murder.

My intuition, usually more reliable than my reason, told me that wherever Timothy and I were going between now and the end of all this would make the Valley of the Shadow of Death seem like a vacation spot. There was killing to be done, of the kill-or-be-killed kind, and I didn't think the freaks would do me the favor of taking out all three remaining Roselanders.

We made our way through the house, from the

library toward the kitchen, keeping to main rooms and hallways, avoiding service halls because I no longer trusted them to lead where they seemed to lead.

I wanted to return to the mausoleum and from there go overland to the guest tower. Since Timothy had told me about the chronosphere, a dangerous idea had pressed itself insistently upon me. At first it had been a half-understood phantom at the back of my mind, but it had come forward in my thoughts until it was fully fleshed and demanding a dialogue.

If I took the course of action I was considering, nothing fine could come of it. I would destroy myself and lose forever that one thing that had given me hope since the worst day of my life in Pico Mundo. But you can't stand an idea up against a wall and execute it. Neither can you wrap it up in a tissue of your better judgment and tuck it in a box of forgetfulness. An idea can be the most dangerous of all things, especially if it is an idea that promises you the most particular and exquisite happiness for which you've long yearned.

By the time Timothy and I arrived in the kitchen, I was steeled for the sight of Shilshom torn asunder, his innards festooning the appliances and his head perched upon the cutting board beside the sink. But the kitchen was not an abattoir. His death cry must have originated from elsewhere in the house.

When I opened the door at the head of the back service stairs, I heard heavy footfalls ascending, the snorting and grumbling of more than one freak. A trollish shadow twisted across the landing wall, a step or two ahead of the creature that cast it.

We had no time to flee the kitchen. I stepped to the walk-in pantry, pushed Timothy ahead of me, and followed him, pulling the door shut and holding fast to the knob.

An instant before we entered from the kitchen, Victoria Mors, unbound and ungagged and unhinged, entered from the chef's office, closing that door, as surprised to see us as we were startled by her. As I raised my Beretta, she seized the boy by his sweater, drew him against her, and pressed the muzzle of her pistol to his neck.

Although my Beretta was aimed at her head from a distance of just six feet, I didn't dare shoot because it looked as if the trigger of her weapon was halfway through its double action. In the moment of her death spasm, she might reflexively complete the pull and kill Timothy even as I killed her.

On the other hand, if I lowered my pistol, she might try to pop me, even though the shots would tell the freaks where to find us. Stalemate.

Timothy's eyes were wide with fear, his pale lips pressed tight as though he had determined both to be brave and to survive. But I worried he might arrive at the conclusion that Victoria could do something for him that was akin to what he hoped to achieve with the chronosphere: with one shot end his unnaturally long and depressing childhood, thereby ensuring for him the death, the peace, that was his destiny in 1925.

Snorting, grumbling with suspicion, making inquisitive noises, like the fabled three bears finding their porridge bowls empty after Goldilocks raided their cottage, the freaks arrived in the kitchen. At least two. Maybe three.

In the hand with which she gripped Timothy, Victoria held a key on a stretchy pink plastic coil. **"Take this,"** she whispered. She was still such an elfin beauty, her pale-blue eyes sparkling as if with the reflections of fairies only she could see, that she seemed to be offering not merely an ordinary key but instead a magic talisman that could give us the power to find a hidden treasure and summon dragons. **"The keyhole in the steel plate."**

She let go of the boy for just one second, to toss the key to me, and she clutched him again before he could think to escape.

To catch the key, I had to let go of the doorknob. If one of the freaks tried to inspect the pantry, I wouldn't be able to hold the door shut for long, anyway.

"A quarter turn to the right, back to vertical, and withdraw it," she whispered.

The pantry door had no lock. The keyhole she meant was in a small steel plate in the wall beside the door.

To do what she wanted, I would have to look away from her. I asked, "Why?"

In the kitchen, cabinet doors were wrenched open, slammed shut. Something clattered to the floor.

Victoria's whisper grew fierce. **"Damn you! Hurry, before they kill us all!"**

Maybe the brutes in the kitchen would find the cheesecake, the almond croissants, a cookie jar if there was one, and be distracted. Or maybe they didn't like sweets.

Victoria clearly wanted to spit on me again, but her fury was inspired by terror and by my hesitation. I saw no deception in her wrenched face.

I turned away from her long enough to insert the key and do as she had instructed. The moment I withdrew the key, the floor moved beneath my feet.

Startled, I swung the Beretta toward her face.

After a moment of disorientation, I realized that under the pantry must lie a shaft. The floor descended smoothly and silently within it.

After pocketing the key, I took a two-hand grip on the pistol.

As more of the walls appeared, the pantry became a higher space. The shelves laden with canned and packaged food remained above us, growing farther away by the moment.

The deeper we descended, the less well the ever more distant overhead light revealed us to one another. Irrationally but perhaps understandably, given my mood, I expected that we would drop into such depths that the lamp above would be as dim as a star and we would be nearly invisible to one another, in a deep darkness with two guns, one of us having no limits and no rules.

When we had gone down perhaps twenty feet, an opening began to appear in the wall to my right, behind Victoria and the boy. Seconds later, we came to a stop, and the opening proved to be a seven-foot-high, six-foot-wide copper-clad passageway like the one connecting the mausoleum to the house. Evenly spaced fluorescent tubes striped the tunnel with bands of shadow and light. Embedded in the walls were glass tubes through which pulsed those golden flares that seemed to be receding and approaching at the same time.

Almost thirty feet overhead, at the top of the shaft, a pantry door opened. A freak peered in, looked down. It shrieked at us but didn't want to make the long jump.

Victoria pulled Timothy with her, into the tunnel. When I followed, the pantry floor began to rise through the shaft, lifted by what appeared to be a hydraulic ram, although without the hiss and hum common to such machinery. It ascended past the ceiling of the tunnel, moved out of sight in the shaft, and the shrieking of the freak far above was now muffled.

Forty-seven

THE FREAKS IN THE KITCHEN NOW knew that the pantry was a kind of elevator to a subterranean realm, but they didn't have a key to operate it. We seemed to be safe from them.

Standing in the copper-clad corridor, Victoria Mors and I were, however, not safe from each other, and Timothy wasn't safe from her.

Pressing the muzzle of her pistol to the boy's throat with such force that the front sight gouged his flesh, she told me how effing much she hated my effing guts, how effing much she wished I were effing dead with my effing brains blown out of my effing skull.

For a woman who had lived well over a century, she had a sadly limited vocabulary.

In potentially deadly confrontations where I see no easy exit, I tend to think less than talk. I have found that if I say whatever comes into my mind, without calculation, all filters removed, I often talk my way to a solution that I don't see coming until it arrives. It's not that I'm opening a spillway to some huge dam of subconscious wisdom. Believe me, no such dam exists.

Maybe it's just that before anything came the word, and words are the roots of everything that our senses perceive. Nothing can be imagined, nothing can be visualized in our minds, until we have a word for it. Therefore, when I give myself to the free flow of any words that trip off my tongue without prede-termination, I am tapping into the primal creative power at the heart of the cosmos.

Or maybe I'm just a bullshit artist.

When Victoria told me how intensely she hated me, I kept the Beretta aimed at her face, but heard myself say, "I don't hate you. Maybe I detest you. Maybe I abhor you. Maybe I loathe you, but I don't hate you."

She called me an effing liar and said, "Hate makes the world go around. Envy and lust and hate."

"I stopped hating anyone when I realized hating can't restore to me anything that's lost."

"Envy and lust and hate," she insisted. "Lust for sex, power, control, **revenge**."

"Well, I'm just a simple clocker with a simple phi-losophy." I suddenly remembered something she'd said in the furnace room, between the times that she spat in my face. " 'You bear the whips and scorns, but we don't and never will.' "

"True unless you've ruined everything," she said,

twisting the muzzle of the pistol back and forth in the boy's neck, so that the front sight broke the skin.

Timothy whimpered in protest, and the thinnest thread of blood unraveled along his neck.

"Shakespeare," I said. " 'For who would bear the whips and scorns of time.' **Hamlet.**"

"You don't know anything. Shakespeare, my ass. Constantine. My Constantine."

I reminded her of something else she'd said: " 'Your thoughts are enslaved to a fool, but ours will never be.' I think that's from **Henry IV, Part 1**. It goes . . . 'But thought's the slave of life, and life time's fool.' "

She seemed to think her look of contempt would draw my blood as the front sight of the pistol had drawn the boy's. "What are you trying to do, you little piss-ant? Play with my head? An ignorant clocker like you?"

"You told me the women he killed were just animals, 'walking shadows, poor players. Their lives signified nothing.' "

"Just as yours signifies nothing. Constantine's truth stings you, doesn't it. **Doesn't it?**"

"**Macbeth,**" I said. " 'Life's but a walking shadow, a poor player that struts and frets his hour upon the stage and then is heard no more.' "

Constantine, the leader of her cult and the poet of her dark heart, was not a poet but instead a plagiarist, cribbing from the best. The sparkle in her pale-blue eyes became a sharper glint. If his poetry was stolen, and not just stolen but also twisted from its original meaning for a wicked purpose, then the wisdom of his philosophy, of his insane gospel of earthly immortality, might also be secondhand and false, a prospect that she dared not contemplate at this late hour in the history of Roseland. She hated me more fervently for this revelation.

I recited the rest of that quotation for her, thrust it at her: " 'It is a tale told by an idiot, full of sound and fury, signifying nothing.' "

To please my friend Ozzie Boone and to please myself, I have read Shakespeare's plays, many more than once, and I have memorized some lines. But I'm no dedicated scholar with a photographic memory. The quotations came to me because I gave myself to the free flow of words much as a spirit medium with a pencil and paper might find herself writing voluminous messages that didn't arise in her own mind. I was no less surprised than Victoria was to hear these things spilling from me.

"You said the foot would be on my neck within the hour," I reminded her. "You said 'the inaudible and noiseless foot.' That's from **All's Well That Ends Well**. 'The inaudible and noiseless foot of time.' "

She told me to shut my effing mouth.

Instead, from me poured another Shakespearean reference to time that she had **not** quoted to me in the furnace room: " 'And so, from hour to hour, we ripe and ripe, and then, from hour to hour, we rot and rot.' "

Judging by her stricken look, I could see that

something rather like those lines had been presented to her by Constantine Cloyce as his own creation, a poetic doctrine of his cult.

She said, "No. That's not it at all. Not at all. It goes . . . 'And so, from hour to hour, we ripe and ripe, and then, from hour to hour, **they** rot and rot.' **They** rot, you rot, you ignorant clockers rot and rot, not us."

Unshed tears stood in her eyes, although they didn't move me. I thought those salty waters must be as poisonous as a viper's venom.

"You vicious little shit. You've ruined everything," she said with such bitterness that I knew she meant I'd ruined more than their depraved life at Roseland, that I had as well sowed at least a seed of doubt about whatever philosophy and mythos Constantine Cloyce had conjured up to justify their life of no limits, no rules, no fear. And I'd sawn a thin score line in the cord of "eternal love" that she had claimed bonded her to the master of Roseland.

She looked as if she might take her chances, kill the boy and then hope to shoot me before I shot her, just for the thrill of spite.

By doing so, she would be acting on her dearest principles. Envy and lust and hate. Sex, power, control, revenge.

I heard myself declare, "I haven't ruined everything. Not yet. We can still put everything right, if you're willing."

Although I wasn't sure where I meant those words

to take me, I knew I didn't dare glance at Timothy again. Victoria would interpret any look that passed from me to him as an assurance that I was still his protector and her enemy.

"Nothing can be put right," she said. "They're **dead.** You let the freaks into the house, and they killed everyone."

"I didn't let them in," I said, which wasn't exactly a lie. I certainly hadn't **intended** to let them inside. "Anyway, not everyone is dead. You're still alive. Henry Lolam in the gatehouse. And Constantine, for all I know. You and Roseland can go on . . . if I get what I want."

"Let me tell you what **I** want." She said she wanted to see me effing dead, effing beheaded, my effing reproductive organs cut off and stuffed in my effing mouth.

Although I wasn't looking directly at the glass tubes in which flares of light seemed to travel in op-posite directions at the same time, the display be-hind the woman was playing more games with my head than I was playing with hers. I felt as if the tunnel might be in fact a long boxcar, racing under-ground, rocking back and forth ever so slightly, as a train tends to do. She was more familiar with this effect and probably unaffected by it. I grew increas-ingly queasy. If queasiness developed into full-blown nausea, the stalemate might end the instant she saw that I was disoriented.

Suddenly, in response to her F-word storm, I found

myself playing a bad boy, pretending that my previous persona had been as phony as the name Victoria
Mors. "You're a hot-looking piece, but you're a stupid
bitch. Of course we want the same thing. Everybody
wants the same thing. You said it yourself."

"Don't screw with me."

"Someday you'll beg me to screw with you," Bad
Odd said. "Next time I tie you up, bitch, it'll be on
a bed. Now shake the stupid out of that pretty head
and let me shove some smart in your empty skull. If
we don't work together, **none** of us is going to survive."

She was suspicious, but I could see that Bad Odd
made more sense to her than the Odd she had known
until this moment.

I said, "I need to know some stuff, Vicky. How
long will this full tide last, before we're rid of the
freaks?"

She glared at me for a moment, but then said, "As
little as another hour, at most two or three."

"How often do the full tides come?"

"We never know. A year, three years, five. It starts
with eddies in the night a couple of days before. The
ozone. That cry."

"The loon," I said.

She shuddered. "It's no loon."

"The freaks, the porkers—they've never gotten
into the house before?"

"No. They've never carried axes and hatchets before, either. Just clubs. They're getting smarter."

The lights raced to and fro in the tubes, and a sourness rose in the back of my throat.

I swallowed hard, hoping she didn't notice, and said, "Where does this tunnel go?"

Reverting to type, she told me that she wasn't my effing tour guide. She moved her left arm up to encircle Timothy's neck, and she shifted the muzzle of the pistol to his right temple.

Bad Odd didn't respond well to backtalk. I took a step toward her, so that the muzzle of the Beretta was about two feet from her face. "Listen, you stupid slut, I'd just as soon blow your brains out. If you think I care about the boy, you don't understand the situation. The only person I care about is me. If I'm the only one who walks out of here, I'm happy with that. But it doesn't have to be that way. **Where does this tunnel go?**"

She studied me for a moment, and then relented. "It runs east for a ways, then branches northeast and south."

"Northeast to what?"

"The machine rooms under the stables."

"And south?"

"To the guest tower."

"That's what I wanted to hear. So the two other security guards you said were on vacation. They don't exist, do they?"

"Maybe they do."

"Yeah, and maybe Santa Claus does, too. So here's the way it's got to be, Vicky. Annamaria and I are staying in Roseland. I like the lifestyle. I can get used to being rich. And the idea of being young forever. I killed Sempiterno. I'll take his place. We'll beef up the defenses here. We'll be ready for the freaks, whether it's a year from now or ten years."

"This isn't going to happen," she said.

"Like hell it isn't. If there's only three of you now, you'll need backup on the next full tide."

My stomach seemed to turn like an eel twining lazily about itself, and I concentrated intently on Victoria's face.

She said, "Constantine won't let you stay."

"You forget that Constantine **invited** us. Besides, we have a gift for him that he really wants."

"What gift?"

"Annamaria's baby."

The horrific implications of my statement didn't faze her. Her eyes looked as without depth as those of a doll, one of those dolls that, in movies, comes alive and reveals a keen interest in cutlery. "That's not Constantine. That's more Paulie's kind of thing."

My dark mood darkened as I wondered what, other than machinery, might wait to be discovered in the machine rooms under the stables. I did not intend to find out.

I said, "Remember, Paulie's dead. As for Constantine . . . tastes change, become more sophisticated. If that's not **your** thing, you and I can invent some new game. You look like you'd be a lot of fun when you let your hair down."

"You said you detested, abhorred, and loathed me."

"No. I said **maybe** I did. But don't you see? Don't you agree that the greatest thrill of all might be giving yourself to what you detest, abhor, and loathe? The freedom of not caring."

Bad Odd was beginning to scare me.

Victoria's tongue tasted her lips. "Living here, being freed from time's oppression does something to you."

"What something?"

"It's like a fever in the blood, not an illness, an exhilarating liberation. We call it dispossession fever."

"Dispossession of what?"

"We are dispossessed of all impossibilities, of everything that seemed once beyond doing. Every desire can be fulfilled as easily as it was conceived. And every desire eventually gives way to one more deliciously outrageous. The possibilities before us are infinite."

Together we had found our way to that crossroads of self-love and self-loathing that is the modern madness most in vogue. She assumed that the very fact I recognized this place in the mind and heart must mean that I was as enthralled by it as she was, that I was ready to live a life that would be a deathwork.

Sometimes not to take a risk is to embrace failure. I took the risk of holstering my Beretta.

She held Timothy against her, arm around his neck, muzzle of the gun against his temple.

In his eyes, I thought I saw both fear and relief, and the latter saddened me.

Victoria released him. She lowered her weapon, muzzle toward the floor.

"When I spat on your mouth," she said, favoring me with that elfin smile, "you must have liked the taste of it."

I drew my pistol and shot her point-blank twice in the chest before she could raise her gun arm.

Forty-eight

EXCEPT FOR THE WOUNDS, THE BLOOD, Victoria on the passageway floor was an elfin loveliness, shorn now of the spirit that didn't measure up to the beauty of her material form.

I said to the boy, "Don't look at her."

"I've seen worse."

"Just the same," I said, "don't look. Go on up the tunnel a little ways. I'll join you in a minute."

He did as I asked.

My nausea had abated. The cause of it hadn't been the pulsing lights in the walls. The cause had been the recognition of what I would do to her if, by deception, I could win her trust.

I owed this woman nothing other than what I'd given her, and in spite of how young she appeared to be, her death was not untimely. Yet death is always first and foremost death even when it might also be something else, like justice.

In spite of what she was and what she had done,

once very long ago she'd been someone else who had not yet cast aside all innocence. In respect of the better girl who had once been, I wished that I had a blanket to drape over her rather than leave her exposed in the indignity of death.

My sports coat would cover only her head and torso, which would somehow seem a mockery.

Her 9-mm pistol lay on the floor. Because I was so rapidly going through my supply of ammunition, I picked up the weapon. I ejected the magazine—and discovered it was empty. The chamber didn't contain a round, either.

Having exhausted her ammunition before we even encountered each other, she'd not been an immediate threat either to me or to Timothy.

I snapped the magazine back into her pistol and put the gun on the floor beside her.

Nothing could have been different. What happened was the only thing that could have happened. Nevertheless, that moment was far from a high point in my life.

I turned my back to her and replenished the ammunition in the magazine of my Beretta.

When I joined Timothy farther along the passageway, I said, "Are you all right?"

"No. Last time I was all right, my mother was still alive."

I put a hand on his shoulder. "You said no one can go from the present to the past and have any effect on what happened to make the present what it is."

"They tell me that Tesla said so, and it turns out to be true."

"Your father brought you back from 1925, from minutes before he accidentally shot you, but your dead body was still on the lawn with your mother's and the horse."

"Yeah. My life ended when he shot me."

"But here you are, a paradox. Alive . . . though never changing."

"Because I have no life—no destiny—to grow into."

I settled on one knee, to be at his height. "If we brought your mother back from before he shot her, she would be like you."

"Like me. Never changing physically. Haunted by the future. Never able to leave Roseland." He glanced toward Victoria's body. "Except by being killed again."

This was news to me. "You can't leave Roseland?"

"They say . . . they think I'd cease to exist if I did. I'm out of time, out of **my** time, here in a century where I don't belong. Maybe I'm sustained only by the energy field, Tesla's field, that encircles Roseland."

If that turned out to be true, I had saved him only to sentence him to death, one way or another.

The freaks had taken out Jam Diu and Mrs. Tameed and perhaps even Constantine Cloyce, sparing me from dispatching as many people as I had thought I would be called upon to kill, perhaps even sparing me from being the scourge that I dreaded being. And if I shut down the estate and put an end to the last of the Outsiders, which might be Henry Lolam, I had perhaps saved the lives of all the women and children upon whom this demented cult would have preyed in the decades to come. That was a good day's work, especially for a fry cook who was out of a job.

But this perpetual child, grown wise from books and seasoned by his suffering, was such a survivor that I was distressed by the thought that I could help him only by putting an end to him. After all that he had endured here, after the terrible things he had seen and heard, he still held fast to his innocence, at least in the sense that he was blameless, guileless, harmless, uncorrupted. He deserved better than a second death.

If his fate had been mine to craft, I would have given him life, hope, and happiness. I am, however, without such godlike power. I am only an itinerant janitor these days, going where I have to go, cleaning up one kind of mess or another, and then moving on to the next toxic spill.

When he revealed that he would cease to exist as soon as he walked outside the gates of the estate, I didn't know what to say to him. I could only put my arms around him, hug him, hold him tight. I guess that must have been the right thing to do, because he hugged me, too, and for a moment we took strength from each other, deep in Roseland's maze, while freaks stalked through other passageways and also through the sunlit world above, feeding on human flesh with the enthusiasm of the Minotaur prowling the labyrinth under ancient Crete.

As we set out to find the branching tunnels of which Victoria Mors had spoken, I said, "There's someone I want you to meet."

He shook his head. "I just want to be sent back. To be one Timothy again, not two, just one and finished in 1925, like I was meant to be."

"Maybe that's best," I admitted. "But often what we want **isn't** what's best. There's this friend of mine in the guest tower. She's a nice lady. I want to see what she thinks before we decide what to do."

"Who is she?"

"I sure would give just about anything to be able to answer that one, Tim."

Where the copper-clad passageway forked, far beneath the manicured acres of Roseland, we turned right, toward the guest tower.

I'd been so distracted by Timothy's revelation that he would cease to exist beyond the walls of the estate, I only now registered the importance of something else that he had said. I quoted him: " 'Haunted by the future.' "

"In the past, I'm dead. And having died there, I don't belong to the present. Yet I'm alive. My mind is both in and outside of time. So maybe that's why . . . I see things that might come to pass."

"The future?"

"I guess it is."

"Earlier, I came into your room. You were sitting in the big chair. Eyes rolled back in your head. Were you in a trance?"

"I can enter it when I want. But sometimes it comes over me when I don't want it."

"You said something about their faces melting off their skulls, they turned to soot, blew away. . . . You mean that's something you saw happening someday?"

"Blasts of bright white light," he said, "turn everything to soot and dust."

"The schoolgirls in uniforms and kneesocks. Their clothes and hair on fire, flames flying out of their mouths. You mean . . . war."

"I see different things at different times. I don't know which just might happen and which **will** happen."

After a hesitation, I asked, "Do you see some good things, some might-happens that we'd want to live in?"

"Not many."

"If the future isn't set . . . why do the freaks keep showing up here over the years? Why doesn't some other, alternate future bleed into Roseland now and then?"

"Maybe because in **most** of the possible futures, like eighty or ninety percent of them, the freaks are created and the whole world is wrecked by war."

"But that's not inevitable?"

"No. We've seen some things change from full tide to full tide."

"Like what?"

"Like there didn't used to be those giant bats."

"That's a change for the worse," I said.

"Yeah. But if there can be a change for the worse, there can be a change for the better."

We walked the rest of the way in silence.

The passageway ended at a spiral stainless-steel staircase that was tightly wound. I led the way up perhaps fifty feet. At the top, I knew by the copper dome forty feet overhead that we were on the third floor of the guest tower.

The entire large chamber—even the floor—had been clad in bright copper. Patterns of what appeared to be silver discs were inlaid in the copper, each bearing the symbol for infinity.

The chronosphere was the most spectacular but not the most astonishing thing in the room. I felt at once a strange quality to the light. Neither too dim nor too bright, bathing us in the warm golden radiance reminiscent of candleglow but without the flicker, it lent the room a welcoming ambiance that made even this bizarre space seem familiar, although it was like nothing I had ever experienced before. I needed the better part of a minute to realize that the light was strange because it had no source. No lamps, no sconces, no overhead fixtures. End to end, top to bottom, the room was evenly illuminated, no spot darker or brighter than any other. It seemed that the light must be as integral to the space as the air, and beyond saying that, I am at a loss to better describe the effect.

I remembered that in his Colorado laboratory, in 1899, Nikola Tesla had lighted two hundred lamps at a distance of twenty-five miles, without wires. He transmitted electricity through the air. Always a font of new ideas, he had quickly moved on to other tasks, and today the technology behind that feat is lost.

The difference between the Colorado experiment and this tower chamber was the lack of light bulbs. The entire room seemed to serve as a bulb, though it was not a vacuum and lacked a filament. Timothy and I could breathe, and we were not affected by an electric current. No shock. No faintest tingle. The fine hairs on the backs of my hands did not bristle with static.

Timothy and I cast no shadows. Neither did the chronosphere or anything else. Being universal, the source and the brightness of the light defeated shadows.

The chronosphere will be no less difficult to describe.

The outermost part of it was a giant gimbal mounting, every arm of which was curved and plated in silver. This measured approximately eighteen feet wide and twenty-seven feet from base to crown, leaving a four-to-five-foot walkaround.

Centered in this first and larger gimbal mounting was another, this one plated in gold. And within the second mounting was the wheel of a gyroscope, except that instead of a wheel it was a golden egg about eight feet end to end and six feet in diameter at its widest point. I suppose the egg didn't make the exotic construction exactly a gyroscope, but something without a name, at least without one in my vocabulary.

In ways that defeated the eye, the gracefully curved arms of the inner mounting were attached to the outer in some fashion that allowed them to turn smoothly, silently, describing lazy-eight arcs in the air. Those arcs seemed to intersect and therefore to conflict with one another, but the continuously moving arms of the mounting never collided. At the center of this smaller mounting was the egg, at the moment rotating on an axis that kept its narrowest end at the top.

The magically turning arms of the elaborate inner gimbal didn't cast shadows. But along their edges, the air—or the light itself—rippled faintly.

Pointing to the egg, Timothy said, "That's the capsule. That's what moves in time—and out of it. It can carry one or two people. You can send me back alone, and if it's not set on PARK, it'll return here empty."

I had a lot of questions, but this wasn't the time for them. I spotted a copper door in the copper wall, and taking Timothy by the hand, I led him around the chronosphere to the exit.

Beyond lay the curve of stairs that would take us down to the second floor, where Annamaria waited.

I didn't have a key to this upper chamber. I took a pair of dollar bills from my wallet, wadded them, and stuffed them into the receiving hole in the striker plate on the door frame, so that the latch bolt could not engage and we could return when we wished. Millions of years of the past were mine for just two dollars.

Forty-nine

THE DOOR OPENED AS I PREPARED TO knock on it, and Annamaria stood in the middle of the room, facing us, as if a moment earlier some public-address system had announced, **"Odd Thomas has entered the building."**

To her left stood the golden retriever, Raphael. To her right, my ghost dog, Boo.

Draperies covered the windows, and the Tiffany lamps were dark. The only light came from three glass vessels like squat long-necked vases, one clear and two the color of brandy, in each of which a burning wick floated on a pool of oil.

Annamaria held out her right hand, and Timothy at once went to her, as if he knew her. When he took her offered hand, she bent to kiss his forehead.

In Magic Beach, the day I met her, Annamaria had preferred oil rather than electric lamps. She said that sunshine grows plants, the plants express essential oils, and years later those oils fire the lamps—giving back "the light of other days," which she found more appealing than electric light.

No oil lamps were provided with my guest suite. Perhaps she had asked for these. Maybe Constantine Cloyce himself had brought them to her.

She led Timothy to the sofa, and they sat in the middle of it. Raphael leaped aboard, curled up, and put his head in the boy's lap. Boo cuddled beside Annamaria.

One of the lamps stood on the coffee table. Directly above it, a few watery circles of light and shadow quivered on the ceiling, reflections of the glass vessel.

She held the boy's right hand in both of hers. They smiled at each other.

On the small dining table stood another oil lamp, likewise projecting tremulous suggestions of its form on the ceiling.

Also on that table, in the large shallow blue dish floated one huge waxy-petaled flower where before there had been three.

"Who do you see when you look at me?" Annamaria asked the boy.

He said, "My mother."

"But I'm not your mother, am I?"

"No," Timothy said. "Not my mother. Or maybe you could be."

"Could I be?"

"That would be nice," he said, for the first time sounding more like a child than like an old man in a child's body.

With one hand, she gently smoothed the hair back from his brow and pressed her palm to his forehead as if to determine if he might have a fever.

Something important was happening here, but I didn't have a clue what it might be.

The third oil lamp, the clear-glass one, stood on the counter in the kitchenette. Impurities in the wick caused the flame to flutter and to elongate until it slithered for a moment into the long, narrow neck of the vessel before raveling back to the pool of oil on which it fed.

Taking Timothy's hand in both of hers once more, Annamaria said, "How have you kept yourself as yourself all these years?"

"Books," the boy said. "Thousands of books."

"They must have been the right books."

"Some were, some weren't. You figure out which are which."

"How do you figure it out?"

"At first by how you feel."

"And later?"

"By reading what's there on the page and also what's not."

"Between the lines," she said.

"Under the lines," he said.

I had so little purpose in this encounter that I felt

not like a fifth wheel on a cart but rather like a fifth wheel on a tricycle.

I was suddenly distracted from their conversation by a ruckus outside, a clang and clatter that drew me to one of the windows. I pulled aside the drapery and pressed my forehead to the glass, the better to see down.

One story below, agitated freaks swarmed around the base of the guest tower, both the hideous kind and the more hideous. I heard them grunting and snorting, and then came the loud clang again as one of them swung an axe hard against the iron bars that protected a ground-floor window directly below the one at which I stood.

Even if they were to chop away at the masonry in which the iron was anchored and were to pry loose those bars, the windows were too small for them to squeeze through. These beasts were primitive, emotionally volatile, mentally unstable, one deep-fried pork rind short of a full bag, but they were not so stupid or so rabidly mad that they would continue futilely attacking the windows when the front door awaited them.

That door was ironbound, not entirely ironclad. Edged with iron, banded with iron, it nevertheless offered swaths of oak at which to chop. And though it was exceedingly thick and though the hardware was forged to withstand a siege by dumb brutes that, at best, might try battering it down, it hadn't been installed to withstand an assault by freaks armed with axes and hammers.

Victoria Mors had said the freaks were never armed like this before, that they had carried nothing but simple clubs until this full tide. She'd said they were getting smarter.

One of them saw me at the second-floor window and began to shriek at me and shake one fisted hand. His rage infected the others, and they all faced me, howling for blood and brandishing both fists and weapons.

I thought of Enceladus and the Titans, crushed under the stones that they had piled high in order to reach the heavens and make war with the gods. But I was not one of the gods, and the second floor of the tower wasn't as far away as the heavens.

Turning from the window, I interrupted Annamaria and Timothy in their half-scrutable conversation. "The freaks are here. As soon as they decide to come at the door, we'll have ten minutes at most."

"Then we'll worry about it eight minutes after that," Annamaria said, as if the mob outside was nothing more than an Avon lady eager to show us a new line of personal-care products.

"No, no, no. You don't know what the freaks are," I told her. "We haven't had time to talk about them."

"And we don't have time now," she said. "What I have to discuss with Tim takes precedence."

The boy and the dogs seemed to agree with her. They all smiled at me, amused by my nervous excitement about the arrival of a few overwrought pigs with a reverse luau on their minds.

"We have to go up to the third floor," I said. "The only way out of here is the way Tim and I came in."

"You go ahead now, young man. We'll follow just as soon as we're done here."

I knew better than to press her further on the issue. She would respond to each of my urgent arguments either with a few words of quiet reassurance or with an enigmatic line I would not understand for maybe three years, if ever.

"Okay," I said, "all right, fine, okay, I'll go up to the third floor and just wait for you, for the freaks, for a ghost horse, for a marching band, whoever wants to come, anyone, everyone, I'll just go wait."

"Good," Annamaria said, and returned to her conversation with Timothy.

I left her suite, closing the door behind me, and I ran down the stairs rather than up. In the vestibule between the outer door and the door to my suite, I could hear the freaks milling around out there, making a variety of piggish noises and some that were human enough to give me the creeps big-time. They seemed to be pumping up one another, like members of a team psyching themselves for the next big play.

In my suite, from the highest shelf in the bedroom closet, I retrieved the plastic-wrapped brick of money that had been given to me by the elderly actor Hutch Hutchison before I'd left Magic Beach just a few days earlier. If I shut down Roseland forever and fled, Annamaria and I would need this bankroll.

During my weeks in Magic Beach, I had worked for Mr. Hutchison, and we had become friends. I didn't want his money, but he insisted with such grace and kindness that refusing it one more time would have been the basest kind of insult.

When Mr. Hutchison had been nine years old, a lot of banks had failed in the Great Depression. Consequently, he didn't entirely trust such institutions. He concealed bricks of cash in his freezer, wrapped tightly in pieces of white-plastic trash bags and sealed with plumbing tape.

Each package was labeled with code words. If the label read BEEF TONGUE, the brick contained twenty-dollar bills. SWEETBREADS identified a fifty-fifty split between twenties and hundreds. When Hutch gave me one such package in a pink hostess-gift bag with little yellow birds flying all over it, he wouldn't tell me how much money it contained, and thus far I hadn't looked.

I'd forgotten the code word on the label of this brick. When I retrieved it from the closet, I saw that it said PORK RIND. At the center of the universe is someone who has a sense of humor.

Clutching Mr. Hutchison's gift, I left my suite and locked the door behind me.

The freaks had not yet begun to chop at the front door.

I hurried up the winding stairs, past Annamaria's

suite, to the third-floor door, where I'd stuffed two dollars in the receiving hole for the latch bolt.

When I entered the high chamber, Constantine Cloyce stepped out from behind the door and slammed the butt of his pistol-grip shotgun in my face.

Fifty

I WAS IN AUSCHWITZ AGAIN, TERRIFIED of dying twice. I was not digging fast enough to please the guard. He kicked me once, twice, a third time. The steel toe of his boot ripped my left cheek. Out of me poured not blood but instead powdery gray ashes, and as the ashes flowed, I felt my face beginning to collapse inward, as if I were not a real man but merely the inflatable figure of a man, a hollow man stuffed with straw that had turned to ash and soot without my being aware. And in the ground where I was digging with inadequate speed there appeared a chair on which sat T. S. Eliot, the poet, who read to me two lines from a book of his verse: "This is the way the world ends. Not with a bang but a whimper."

I woke on the copper floor of the high room, for a moment not sure how I had gotten there. But then I remembered Wolflaw. . . . No, Cloyce. Constantine Cloyce. His eyes the gray of brushed steel, his matinee-idol chin thrust forward, his jaws clenched, his small, full-lipped mouth twisted in a sneer of contempt as he drove the butt of the shotgun into me.

My face hurt. I tasted blood. My vision was blurry. When I blinked rapidly, I couldn't see any better, but each blink caused my head to throb painfully.

I could hear him singing softly. At first I couldn't identify the song, but then I realized it was an American standard, Cole Porter's "Let's Misbehave."

Hesitant to move for fear I would draw his attention before I could see well enough to defend myself, I remained facedown, head turned to my right, for perhaps a minute until my vision cleared.

On the floor, about two feet from me, was the brick of money wrapped in plastic. Whatever my pathetic treasure might amount to, it wouldn't buy my life from a murderer who was a billionaire.

Beyond the package of cash rose the chronosphere. I couldn't see Cloyce's feet moving anywhere in that glimmering construction, only the inner gimbal mounting as it silently carved lazy eights in the air, the arms of it moving impossibly but ceaselessly. And in the golden light that arose equally in every cubic inch of the chamber, my enemy cast no telltale shadow.

I was lying with my right arm trapped under me. When I moved the fingers of that hand, I could feel the swell of leather that was the belt-slider holster.

Slowly, taking care not to move otherwise, I wormed my hand to the Beretta—and found that it had been taken from me.

On the floor between me and the brick of money lay a tooth. I searched my mouth with my tongue and found not one hole but two. The way the blood thickened in my throat and the taste of it were beginning to sicken me.

Judging by his voice, he was behind me, several steps removed.

Lacking a weapon, my best hope seemed to be to get up fast and rush away from him, around the chronosphere, try to keep it between him and me until I got to either the copper door or the stainless-steel stairs.

I thrust up, but dizziness and pain stalled me when I got as far as my hands and knees. Cloyce kicked my left arm out from under me, and I fell facedown again.

Now he was softly singing a different Cole Porter number: "I Get a Kick Out of You."

His choice of songs alerted me to what was coming next, but I was powerless to escape it. He kicked me in the hip, in my left side, again in my side, and I felt a rib crack.

He jammed one boot on my back, put his weight on me, and the cracked rib seemed to catch fire and burn through my flesh.

I now understood my dream:

What the Nazis hoped to do to the Jews they

killed, to the Gypsies and the Catholics they killed, was to kill them twice. It is what all tyrants hope to do, those armed with the mighty power of the state, like Hitler, and those with lesser power, like Cloyce. Mere physical destruction does not satisfy them. They use fear to wither your spirit, continuous propaganda and cruel mockery to confuse you, torture and forced labor to break more than just your body. They want to reduce you, if they can, to the condition of a frightened animal who has lost any faith that might have sustained him, who accepts his humiliation as deserved, who descends into such depression that he forsakes all belief that justice is attainable, that truth exists, or meaning. After they first kill your soul, they are then satisfied to kill your body, and if in fact they have succeeded, you cooperate meekly in your own physical—second—death. They are all in the army of the damned, and if they have a stronger faith in the righteousness of evil than their victims have in the reality and power of good, they cannot lose.

The only responses we can have to their viciousness are the courage to fight back or the cowardice to acquiesce. Well, one other option might be the pretense of acquiescence.

As the broken rib burned in my side and as waves of pain swelled through my battered face, I begged him not to hurt me any more, not to kill me. I pleaded, beseeched, implored, and groveled with my face pressed to the floor. The tears were easy to produce because the pain squeezed them from me, but he could mistake them for tears of terror and self-pity if he wished.

He grabbed me by the back of my sports-jacket collar. Commanding me to get up, he hauled me to my feet. He slammed me against the wall so hard that the pain in my chest seemed to drive a spike all the way into my skull to puncture awareness and let darkness flood my mind once more. I barely held on to consciousness, but the black wave passed.

Now Cloyce was singing "Anything Goes." Not singing it so much as muttering it, snarling the words, his face right in mine. He was a tall man, muscular, strong. Having surprised the fight out of me with the shotgun butt, he was going to enjoy beating me to death with his fists. His breath smelled of something sour and vile. He grabbed a fistful of my hair and a handful of my crotch, and between words of the song, he suggested I should submit to him sexually as all the terrified women had done before he killed them.

My right hand fumbled its way into that pocket of my sports jacket, though there was nothing in there but a few spare rounds of ammunition and the pantry key on the stretchy pink plastic coil.

Suddenly Tesla loomed beside us, his gaunt face wild with rage. He reached for Cloyce but reached through him, **passed** through him as he had passed through me.

Perhaps thinking that I had hoped to be saved,

Cloyce said, "It can't help you. It's not him. Just an aspect of him. Spun off in an experiment, bouncing around in time because it doesn't belong anywhere."

Twisting my hair, twisting a handful of my crotch, Cloyce began laughing at me, highly amused by the tears that streamed down my face and by the helplessness they seemed to represent.

Pinching the bow of the key between thumb and forefinger, with all my strength I drove the serrated blade of it into the soft tissue behind his chin, as deep as it could go, perhaps into the underside of his tongue, and then twisted it violently.

As a gush of warm blood spilled over my hand, Cloyce reeled backward, clutching at his throat, keening in pain, probably sure that I had shoved a knife into him.

Before he might comprehend that he would survive the wound, I staggered away from him, snatched the shotgun off the floor, turned, pumped a round into the chamber, and delivered to him his second death.

Fifty-one

JUDGING BY THE SILENCE, THE FREAKS hadn't begun chopping at the front door yet, but surely by now they had begun to examine it and fiddle with the doorknob. The axes would start to flash soon.

My jaw ached from ear to ear, the broken-off roots of two teeth throbbed, and the right side of my face was swelling, threatening to reduce that eye to a slit. I kept swallowing fresh blood that welled up in my mouth, and I was also bleeding a little from my nose. None of the elements that constituted my crotch felt good, either, but I could walk without whimpering.

Psychic magnetism works best when I'm trying to locate a person, wandering around with the face and name of my quarry in mind. But occasionally it functions as well when I'm searching for an object while conjuring a mental image of it.

I couldn't picture the master switch of which Tesla had spoken, because I didn't know what it looked like. I assumed, however, that anyone as obsessed with detail and order as Nikola Tesla would label the damn thing MASTER SWITCH in capital letters. I pictured those two words in my mind's eye, hoping that what I wanted was in this high room, which seemed to be the Grand Central Station of the time-management machinery.

For a minute I circled the chronosphere, but then I was compelled to move into it, through the larger fixed gimbal mounting, toward the arms of the inner mounting that scissored multiple lazy eights simultaneously from the air. Even closer, I was not able to see how they moved in such elaborate arcs yet continued to support the rotating egg—the passenger capsule—which was always floating at the center.

Later, I would read as much about gyroscopes as my fry-cook brain could tolerate. I didn't absorb a lot, just enough to wonder if this had been an electrostatic gyro, in which the rotor—or in this case the egg—was supported by an electric or magnetic field. But if I understand correctly, the rotor of an electrostatic gyro has to be in a high vacuum, and the egg was not in a vacuum.

As I drew near to the swooping golden arms of the inner gimbal, they seemed to make an approach to the egg impossible. I would surely be battered to death if I tried to dart among them to the prize.

But then, as if sensing my approach, the great gold-plated arcs slid into new rhythms and patterns. As they wove among one another, describing lazy eights in the air, they still seemed to occupy some of the same places at the same times without catastrophe, but now an open path lay between me and the egg.

Trusting that those golden jawbones would not abruptly snap me in two, I moved toward the passenger capsule without fear or shadow. When I was within a few feet of the egg, its rotation slowed, slowed, stopped. The capsule seemed to float unsupported in the air, a foot off the floor, the top of it about two feet above my head.

A five-foot-high segment of the egg swung upward, an access hatch invisibly hinged at the top. Within the capsule waited two leather cockpit chairs with a console between them.

When I stepped inside, turned, and sat in one of the chairs, the hatch closed, presenting me with what appeared to be a simple control panel.

At the top of the panel, a fourteen-window clock presented the current year in the first four windows; the month, day, hour, minute, and second were displayed in two windows each. Black numbers, painted on drums, rolled down like cherries and lemons in an old low-tech slot machine. As far as I could tell, the time was precisely correct.

Under the first clock, a second remained blank. Fourteen knobs, one below each window, allowed me to turn the drums until I dialed up the desired date to which I wanted to travel.

The other controls consisted of just five labeled

push keys as big as those on a toy for little children. The first, on the left, advised LOCK DATE.

Beside that one was a key marked TRAVEL ONLY. Below it, a third key offered PARK. Between those two keys, painted on the console, was the word OR. I assumed that if the Roselanders wanted to take forty years off their appearance, they punched TRAVEL ONLY. If they wanted to get out of the capsule in spite of the risks known and unknown, they punched PARK instead of the key above it.

Aligned with the first two keys was another labeled LAUNCH. Beside that one, the fifth and final key promised RETURN.

Time travel for dummies.

While wandering around the chronosphere before approaching the egg, I had taken the Gypsy Mummy fortune-teller's card from my wallet without realizing what I was doing. I stared at it in my hand: YOU ARE DESTINED TO BE TOGETHER FOREVER.

If I went back in time to the day before the act of terrorism that took her life, I could park the capsule, slip quietly out of the Roseland of that period—where I was not yet known—and make my way to Pico Mundo.

I could warn Stormy that she was going to be shot dead the following day. Although my story would have fantastic elements, she would believe me for two reasons: First, she knew well that my life has always been **riddled** with the bizarre and the absurd, and she'd been involved in many such moments with me; second, we never lied to each other, and we never doubted each other.

YOU ARE DESTINED TO BE TOGETHER FOREVER.

But because nothing I could do in the past would change the present from which I traveled, I would return to a world in which Stormy remained dead. Yet the Stormy I brought with me would be **her,** not some kind of clone or soulless automaton, but Stormy Llewellyn complete. Like Timothy, she would be a living paradox.

I would be able to hear her voice again, her laughter. Her hand in mine once more. Her lovely, loving eyes. Her face, such a face. Her kiss.

She would never age. But if I found a way to take Roseland for my own, I would have this machine, and therefore I would never age, either. We could fulfill the destiny that Gypsy Mummy had promised us. We could live here together forever.

The pain of my injuries was unrelenting, and I found myself in tears again, though not because of that pain. They might even have been tears of joy.

My psychic magnetism might not have brought me to the master switch I sought, but it had brought me to what I wanted, what I so needed, to what my heart demanded.

I entered my destination date in the second clock. I pressed LOCK DATE.

I made my selection between TRAVEL ONLY and PARK.

I hesitated, considering the risks, which were incalculable, and the implications, which were many and some devastating. I considered how much I might come to regret my choice, and I urgently reminded myself that people should never be treated like toys. I warned myself that the human heart is a great deceiver, deceitful above all things. Still I wept.

And then I pushed LAUNCH.

If the capsule began to rotate at high speed again, I had no awareness of spinning. I had no sensation either of moving up or down, or side to side, or back and forth. I **did** feel some motion but one I had never experienced before: a turning inward, as if I were a slack watch spring being wound tight again. That isn't an accurate description of the feeling, although it's the only one I am capable of giving.

During this, as I moved backward in time, my pain relented. I could feel my ribs knit again and the blood recede from my mouth. My tongue found all my teeth where they belonged, and the swelling in my face quickly declined until my eye was no longer pinched to a slit.

I knew instantly when the capsule slipped sideways, out of time. My heart no longer beat, and I drew no air into my lungs. Neither the ebb and flow of breath nor the rush of blood was required to sustain life in this timeless realm.

I wished the capsule had windows, that I might see what lay around me, but no sooner had this thought occurred to me than I realized how wrong and dangerous it was. Whatever might lie outside of time, it would astonish and amaze. It would inspire a sense of wonder beyond conception. But the awe aroused by the sight might be of an intensity so exhilarating **and** so terrifying, so profound, that no living person was ever meant to see it—or could remain sane and go on living after having seen it.

The shift back into time set my heart beating again, and once more the bellows of my lungs labored automatically.

I hadn't needed to press the RETURN button to come back to the present, because I had never pressed PARK. I had not gone back to a time when Stormy Llewellyn was still alive, but only back one day, not to grow that much younger, but to reverse the damage that Constantine Cloyce had inflicted on me, just as the Roselanders had used the machine to reverse the aging process.

Stormy believed that this life is boot camp, preparing us for a life of service and great adventure that comes between this world and our third and final one, which some call Heaven. Although she was Catholic, her theology was certainly not orthodox. But if she might indeed be engaged now in some grand exploit, my love for her, even as deep and enduring as it was, did not give me the right to disturb the time line of her life and thereby possibly diminish, in ways I could not fathom, the joy she might take from that adventure in which she currently found herself.

When it seemed that the egg had come to a rest, out of curiosity I attempted to set the destination calendar to a future year. But as I expected, it wouldn't allow me to do so.

Because we have free will, our tomorrows are never determined until we make them day by day. I couldn't travel into the future because one didn't exist, only many **possible** ones. The past is as locked in stone as a Jurassic fossil, but by our daily actions, we continuously change the future.

As the hatch lifted, before I could get up, I was startled by the appearance of someone in the seat beside me. Tesla. His hawkish face, his proud nose, his eyes as penetrating as radiation.

"Sir," I said, in such awe of him that no other words occurred to me.

"A great and terrible mistake, all of this," he declared, and then he went into a rant, though a solemn and dignified one. "But J. P. Morgan, Westinghouse, all the financiers, they underfund your research, nevertheless make **fortunes** from it, then penny-pinch the budget on your **next** project! There are no **visionaries** among them!"

"Sir," I said.

In the high room, past the swooping arms of the inner gimbal mounting, Annamaria appeared with Timothy.

"No visionaries whatsoever! They seek nothing more than profit, not knowledge, not wonder, **not the secrets of God**! Cloyce and Chiang presented themselves as visionaries, and they had all the money in the world. But they were thugs, liars, **mental midgets!**"

"Sir," I said.

From behind Annamaria and the boy, a booming arose as blows were struck at the copper-clad door. The freaks must have gotten into the tower. They were trying to chop down the door of our final redoubt.

"Mental midgets," Tesla repeated, "nothing but superstitious fools. **Perverts!** They were perverts, **fiends!** We must pull the master switch."

"Sir, the pigs are coming."

He tried to open the lid of the console between our seats. His hand passed **through** it. "**Great Caesar's ghost!** I am a carbon-copy Tesla, rolled through the platen of time's typewriter! Spun off in one of the first experiments with the chronosphere, ricocheting through the years, belonging nowhere, effective nowhere, **useless!**"

I opened the console box and found what looked like one of those sports-car gearshifts that offers a full-hand grip instead of a knob. It was labeled MASTER SWITCH.

"Pull it!" Tesla urged. "Put an end to this and me."

Before I pulled it, I said, "I would have liked to know you, Mr. Tesla."

"Likewise. From what I've seen of you here and there, you're a righteous lad with the pluck and the brains to do great things."

"Not really, sir. I just make it up as I go along."

He shrugged. "Who doesn't?"

When I pulled back hard on the master switch, Tesla vanished. Beyond the capsule, the inner gimbal mounting, previously in silent and unceasing motion, came to a halt with a great grinding noise.

The freaks broke down the door.

Fifty-two

I SCRAMBLED OUT OF THE EGG AND joined Annamaria and Tim under the great golden rib cage of the dead machine.

The boy had snatched up my Beretta from the floor where Cloyce had discarded it after taking it from me. Following my encounter with Victoria in the tunnel, I had replenished the magazine.

Four freaks were in the room, however, and seventeen rounds might not be sufficient. I didn't think they would be sporting enough to allow me time to reload.

I had expected the full tide to end instantly upon throwing the master switch. I didn't know why the freaks failed to vanish like Tesla, and at that moment it didn't seem to matter worth a damn that I had an excellent pancake recipe.

Annamaria and Tim and I stood with our backs to one another, so that we could watch the four beasts as they warily circled the chronosphere, beyond the first gimbal mounting. They grumbled and snarled and didn't seem to trust the machine. They snorted, grimaced, and shook their heads as though they smelled something disagreeable, and they blew gouts of mucus from their fleshy snouts into their hands and wiped their hands on their flanks, as if they wanted to disgust us as much as they wanted to terrify us.

Beads of sweat stippled my brow.

"If they rush us all at once," I said, "you two drop low, so I can turn in a circle and fire over your heads."

"They won't rush us," Annamaria assured me. "This unpleasantness is almost over."

"They might rush us," I disagreed.

"You worry too much, odd one."

"Ma'am, I don't mean this to sound harsh, but you don't worry enough."

"What does worry accomplish except to breed more worry?"

We might have gotten into our first argument then, although a genteel one, but the largest of the four freaks changed the subject when it spoke in a low rough voice that caused spiders of dread to skitter up my spine: "Woman with baby."

Until this moment, there had been no indication that these monsters had the capacity for language, let alone that they could speak English.

"Give me baby," the thing said.

The speaker had a larger head than the others,

with a brow less sloped. Maybe it was the only one of them that could talk.

"Give me baby," it repeated.

I was sweating worse by the moment. I was sweating like, well, a pig.

"You may not make demands of me," Annamaria told the talking freak. "You have no power here."

"We kill," it said. "We eat baby."

"Be gone from here," she said. "Know your place and be there."

The four of them began to move slowly toward us, as shadowless as we were, pale skin and tufts of gray wiry hair, but nevertheless four figures of darkness, as if their shadows had slithered within them to nest and then had multiplied into legions to fill them with blackest hate. Three had axes, and one carried a hammer.

Taking a two-hand grip on the Beretta, I aimed at one of the three who hadn't yet spoken.

The chatty one said, "I was born to eat baby, your baby, **that** baby."

"This is not your time," she said calmly, "nor will there be any time for you to kill me or to touch this baby. Go now. Go to your misery."

Maybe it was just me, just the state of my mind at that moment, which wasn't good, but it seemed that something more was going on here than I quite understood. I often had that feeling when in the company of my mysterious companion, but never more so than at that moment.

"Go to your misery," she repeated.

They rushed us—as I **knew** they would—but in the rushing, they rippled, as if approaching us through thermals of heat rising from the floor, and vanished.

"It's getting really hot in here," Tim said.

I had attributed the heat to the pressure of the confrontation, but it proved not to be a subjective reaction to stress. The room was rapidly growing hotter.

Remembering what Timothy had told me earlier, that the time-management machinery was secondarily the power plant for Roseland, harnessing the thermodynamic consequences of its primary purpose, I suddenly wondered if Tesla might have been wise enough to provide a master switch that not only turned off the machine but also destroyed it with its own stored heat.

"We better get out of here," I said. "This place is gonna blow."

"Worry only breeds more worry," Annamaria reminded me.

"Yeah, yeah, yeah, yeah," I said, and I hustled them around the chronosphere, keeping them away from Cloyce's body, snatched up the plastic-wrapped bundle of money, and followed them across the broken-down door into the stairwell.

Freaks on the landings faded away as we approached them, and freaks in the yard brandished weapons at us and howled and might have assaulted us if they, too, hadn't shimmered away on the receding tide of displaced time.

Raphael and Boo suddenly sprinted past us, ears flat to their heads and tails tucked.

As we hurried along the path through the eucalyptus grove, I heard something collapsing high in the tower, a colossal noise that rang like a carillon of tuneless bells. When I glanced back, every pane shattered and golden dust blew out of every window. The walls shook, and stones began to rain down through the trees.

When we escaped the eucalyptuses and reached the long slope of lawn that led up to the main house, we found the dogs frozen with their hackles raised. They were focused on the long green fairway that was the Enceladus lawn leading off to the south, away from the house, but it was not the distant statue of the Titan that caused Raphael and Boo to bare their teeth.

Something moved in the cloaking shadows beneath the live oaks that bordered the west side of that lawn. At first it was only an immense paleness, a heaving shapeless mass that surged insistently through the grove, snapping a few lower limbs where they impeded its progress, shuddering the trees. From it came the eerie, silvery cry, sewn through with sorrow and longing, that had awakened me each morning during our visit to Roseland, the cry that never had been that of a loon. Such a poignant sound issuing from a creature so large was more chilling than it had been when it came from an unknown source in the night. This thing, if it could be better seen, might have been the size of an elephant, although it was nothing that had ever walked the Earth before. For a moment it loomed at the edge of the woods, a sickly white behemoth, its thick cankered folds of flesh revealing extreme malformation, enough like a swine to be related to the freaks, but even more bizarre than the most badly deformed of those smaller beasts. Given a few minutes, perhaps it would have surged fully into the sunlight, or maybe it would have continued to shelter in the shadows in the same way that the worst monsters of our nightmares never quite reveal themselves. The things in dreams are often aspects of ourselves that we cannot face directly, and perhaps this land leviathan, aware of its horrific nature, could not bear to fully expose itself to itself, and needed shadows the way that any guilty soul needs its justifications.

As the time-management machinery self-destructed, the full tide receded from the shores of our time. The creature in the woods faded away into the future where the sky lowered yellow and was shot through with rivers of soot.

Across the vast lawns, the topography changed as underground rooms and passageways collapsed upon themselves. The steel shutters flew up at all the doors and windows of the main house as we hurried toward it. Windows burst and glittered down upon the terraces.

The original carriage house, separate from the

main residence, was remodeled in 1926, as it became clear how rapidly the automobile would come to rule the highways. The keys to the various estate vehicles hung on a Peg-Board.

I chose a Cadillac Escalade. Boo leaped through the closed tailgate, and after I opened it, Raphael followed him.

To Annamaria, I said, "What happens to Tim when we're past the walls of the estate?"

The boy clung to her as she said, "Nothing happens. He lives and thrives."

"But he said—"

"What was is not anymore, young man. And now we shall see what will be."

Now was not the time to have one of our baffling conversations. I slid behind the wheel, and she got into the backseat with the boy.

As we drove past the house, it began to implode and to collapse into its foundations, into whatever secret rooms might lie beneath it, and thick plumes of smoke rose from some deep fire.

Perhaps following the final effects of the disintegrating machinery, no more would remain of Roseland than could be found of the House of Usher after it sank into its fetid marsh.

As we drove past the portico at the front of the house, Mr. Hitchcock was standing beside the driveway. He waved at me, and I waved back. I almost stopped to tell him that I was ready for him now, but I really wasn't quite yet.

He smiled broadly at the sight of Roseland in ruins. Cloyce must have been as nasty a studio chief as he was a nasty human being.

The gatehouse had fallen into a hole of its own, most likely taking Henry Lolam with it.

I was about to get out of the Escalade to throw open the gates, when the perimeter walls began to collapse and seemed also to melt in upon themselves. The gates tore loose of the molten stone and crashed to the ground. I drove over them and away, as fast as I dared, eager to be gone but equally eager not to draw the attention of any police I might pass.

Before I'd traveled fifty yards, Madra raced past me on the magnificent stallion, white nightgown flowing over the horse's black flanks. She glanced back once, and I saw her smile before she and the Friesian galloped out of this world into the next.

Ancient oaks flanked the two-lane road. Through the gaps in the great black limbs, rain abruptly fell in torrents from the clouds that had been gathering all day. For a moment, fear gripped me again as the world blurred away beyond the windshield, but when I turned on the wipers, the world was still there.

I drove down through the hills to the Coast Highway and turned south. The gray sea folded up into the gray sky at the horizon, which was obscured by mist, and silver rain slanted through the day, as the tires sizzled across the puddled pavement.

Fifty-three

WE ABANDONED THE ESCALADE IN A supermarket parking lot, and we rented a three-bedroom cottage by the month in a quiet town along the coast. Yellow bougainvillea draped half the roof, and the front porch faced the sea.

Of other renters, the owner would have required identification, but Annamaria's smile, her touch, and cold cash charmed us into our new home.

Roseland started as a big story but quickly became less of one as Homeland Security seemed to exercise authority that was definitely unconstitutional. Rumors on the Internet pegged the place as a den of terrorists bent on some nefarious plot. The military personnel and scientists that were camped out on the grounds and probing through the ruins lent credence to that theory.

During the first month in our new haven, I slept in my room, and Tim stayed with Annamaria, afraid to sleep alone. He was not the same person as he had been. He was still the boy who had read thousands of books and been formed by them, but he never spoke of Roseland, as if he had no memory of it. He spoke sometimes of his mother, of how he missed her, but he seemed to think she had died in a fall from a horse, and of his father he knew nothing.

I didn't ask Annamaria how this change in Tim had been effected because I was afraid that she would tell me, at length, and that I would not understand a word she said. As time goes by, I find that I am increasingly satisfied not to chase mysteries that my sixth sense does not absolutely require me to chase.

Tim was excited to discover that his hair was growing. He said that it had never grown before, though he admitted that was a strange assertion. We made a celebration of his first trip to a barber by following it with a session at an arcade, and ice cream.

After that, he slept alone in his room.

Here by the sea, I wrote these memoirs in what psychologists call a flow state. The words spilled from me as though I were taking dictation.

The dogs do the usual doggy things. Because Raphael can see Boo as clearly as I can, he has a playmate, but my ghost dog has all the advantages in their games.

I dream no more of Auschwitz and do not fear dying twice.

I dream of Stormy, of the years we had together,

which were years rich in experience, and of how it might be when at last we are together again, though that is a thing that can only be seen in dreams.

My journey isn't yet at an end. Sooner than later, I will be called to the road again. I learn by going where I have to go.

Annamaria says I'll know when we must move on because I will wake in the night to hear the ringing of the pendant bell that I wear around my neck.

She is now in her eighth month, but she's grown no larger. When I worry that she should have pre-natal care, she tells me that she has been pregnant a long time and will be pregnant longer still, whatever that means.

Two nights ago, at dinner, in the center of the table, one of those large, waxy-petaled flowers floated in a shallow green bowl. She said she plucked it from a tree in the neighborhood, but though I've gone on a few long walks in search of it, I've not yet found that tree.

I asked her to show me the trick with the flower. As it turns out, she showed it to Tim back in Rose-land. But she says it is not merely a trick, and the time for her to show it to me will come when I know the real name for it. Go figure.

Our friend Blossom, from Magic Beach, who calls herself the Happy Monster, phoned to say she will join us in another week. She was gravely disfigured as a child, when her drunken father set her on fire. Why so often childen, and why so often their parents? I guess it's just the nature of this long, long war. Anyway, I can't wait to see Blossom, for she is beautiful in her disfigurement.

Yesterday, shortly after Tim took his morning shower, he was overcome by the feeling that he was still dirty. He showered again, and then a third time. After that I found him washing his hands incessantly at the kitchen sink, and weeping.

He did not know why he felt this way, but I knew it was the years at Roseland that he had not yet forgotten as thoroughly as he needed to forget them.

Even Annamaria could not soothe him, so I took him to the front porch, just us guys, with a Mr. Goodbar for each of us. As we watched the shorebirds kiting in the sky, I told him about the best part of a Mr. Goodbar.

The best part of a Mr. Goodbar is not the wrapper, is it? No, and the best part of a Coke is not the can. On those nights when you lie awake, either man or boy, wondering about yourself, peeling away one layer of oddness after another, you should remember and always be grateful that the woefully imperfect person that you are, with all your contradictions and unworthy desires, is not the best of you, any more than the wrapper is the best part of a Mr. Goodbar.

Tim said he didn't understand me any more than I understand Annamaria, but he felt better. That's all that matters, really: that we can make each other feel better.

For a while I did **not** feel at all good about how

I had turned away Mr. Hitchcock in that glen in Roseland. I worried that he wouldn't return to seek my help.

This morning, however, as I sat on the front porch drinking coffee, he strolled by on the beach in a three-piece suit and black wingtips. He waved at me and kept walking, but I suspect that any day now, when I come out for coffee on the porch, he'll be there.

It's a little daunting to consider what the director of **Psycho** might wish to convey to me. But then he was also the director of **North by Northwest** and other films that were as funny as they were suspenseful. And he made some great love stories. I'm a sucker for love stories, as you probably know by now.

And so I wait for the bell to ring in the night. I dream of Stormy, I walk in search of Annamaria's mysterious tree, I go down to the sea to swim in the shallows with Tim, and I wait for the bell to ring.

YOU ARE DESTINED TO BE TOGETHER FOREVER.

About the Author

DEAN KOONTZ, the author of many #1 **New York Times** bestsellers, lives in Southern California with his wife, Gerda, their golden retriever, Anna, and the enduring spirit of their golden, Trixie.

www.deankoontz.com

Correspondence for the author should be addressed to:

Dean Koontz
P.O. Box 9529
Newport Beach, California 92658

Odd Thomas's journey continues in . . .

Deeply Odd

by #1 **New York Times** bestselling author

DEAN KOONTZ

———

Sign up for Dean Koontz's e-newsletter
at DeanKoontz.com and be the first
to know when it's available.

LIKE WHAT YOU'VE READ?

If you enjoyed this large print edition of
ODD APOCALYPSE,
here are a few of Dean Koontz's latest
bestsellers also available in large print.

BROTHER ODD
(paperback)
978-0-7393-7851-9
($27.00/$32.00)

ODD THOMAS
(paperback)
978-0-7393-7850-2
($27.00/$32.00C)

77 SHADOW STREET
(paperback)
978-0-7393-7847-2
($28.00/$30.00C)

**WHAT THE NIGHT
KNOWS**
(paperback)
978-0-7393-7797-0
($28.00/$33.00C)

Large print books are available wherever books
are sold and at many local libraries.

All prices are subject to change. Check with your
local retailer for current pricing and availability.
For more information on these and other large print titles,
visit www.randomhouse.com/largeprint.